LAVIE TIDHAR

The Bookman

ANGRY ROBOT

ANGRY ROBOT
A member of the Osprey Group

Lace Market House,
54-56 High Pavement,
Nottingham
NG1 1HW, UK

www.angryrobotbooks.com
Read all about it

Originally published in the UK by Angry Robot 2010
First American paperback printing 2010

Distributed in the United States by Random House, Inc., New York

ISBN 978-0-85766-034-3

Printed in the United States of America

9 8 7 6 5 4 3 2 1

Praise for Mr. Lavie Tidhar

"Lizards from another planet have usurped the British monarchy and rule the empire; automatons are calling for equal rights; dirigibles ply the London skies; and a cast of famous Victorians work for or against the lizards. *The Bookman* is a delight, crammed with gorgeous period detail, seat-of-the-pants adventure and fabulous set-pieces."

The Guardian

"Simply the best book I've read in a long time, and I read a lot of books. If you're worried that steampunk has turned into a mere fashion aesthetic, then you'd better read this one. It's a stunningly imaginative remix of history, technology, literature, and Victorian adventure that's impossible to put down. Buy it."

James P. Blaylock

"*The Bookman* is without a doubt the most enjoyable, fascinating and captivating book I have read in a long time. A very exciting and captivating read."

Dailysteampunk.com

"Literary figures emerge from the swirling fog, automatons patrol the streets, space probes head for Mars and giant lizards rule over Victorian England. A potent and atmospheric steampunk adventure."

Chris Wooding

"*The Bookman* is fast-paced adventure with tons of sense of wonder. I loved the author's style. Just big time fun, this novel is highly, highly recommended."

Fantasy Book Critic

By the same esteemed author

The Tel Aviv Dossier *(with Nir Yaniv)*
HebrewPunk *(stories)*
A Dick & Jane Primer for Adults *(editor)*
The Apex Book of World SF *(editor)*

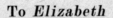

To *Elizabeth*

PART I
Orpheus & Eurydice

I must frankly own, that if I had known, beforehand, that this book would have cost me the labour which it has, I should never have been courageous enough to commence it.
– Isabella Beeton, *Mrs. Beeton's Book of Household Management*

ONE
Orphan

Under Waterloo Bridge Gilgamesh slept
wrapped in darkness and the weak light of stars
his breath feeble in the fog:

He dreamt of Ur, and of fish,
slow-roasting on an open fire,
and the scent of spring
   – L.T., "The Epic of Gilgamesh"

Orphan came down to see the old man by the Thames. The old man sat alone on the embankment under Waterloo Bridge, wrapped in a horse blanket, beside a small fire, a rod extending from his gloved hands into the dark waters of the river below. Orphan came stealthily, but the old man's blind eyes nevertheless followed his progress. Orphan sat down beside Gilgamesh on the hard stone floor and warmed his hands on the fire. In the distance, whale song rose around the setting sun.

   For a while there was silence. Then, "Did you catch anything?" Orphan asked.

Gilgamesh sighed and shook his head. His long hair was matted into grey locks that made a dry rustling sound as they moved. "Change is unsparing," he said enigmatically.

Orphan echoed his sigh. "But did you catch anything?"

"If I had," Gilgamesh said reasonably, "it would have been roasting on the fire by now."

"I brought bread," Orphan said, and he reached into his bag and brought out, like a magician, a loaf of bread and a bottle of wine, both wrapped in newspaper, which he put down carefully on the ground beside them.

"Red?" Gilgamesh said.

Instead of an answer Orphan uncorked the wine, allowing its aroma to escape into the cold air above the Thames.

"Ahh…"

Gilgamesh's brown fingers broke a piece of the bread and shoved it into his mouth, and he followed it by taking a swig of wine from the open bottle. "Château des Rêves," he said appreciatively, "now where would a young lad like you find a bottle like that?"

"I stole it," Orphan said.

The old man turned his blind eyes on Orphan and slowly nodded. "Yes," he said, "but where did you steal it, young Orphan?"

Orphan shrugged, suddenly uncomfortable. "From Mr. Eliot's Wine Merchants on Gloucester Road. Why?"

"It's a long way to come, with a bottle of red wine," Gilgamesh said, as if reciting a half-forgotten poem. "As much as I appreciate the visit, I doubt you came all this way on a social call. So," the blind eyes held Orphan in their gaze, "what is it you want?"

Orphan smiled at that. "Tonight," he said, "is the night, I think."

"Indeed?" The eyes turned, the hands checked the anchored fishing-rod, returned to the bread. "Lucy?"

Orphan smiled. "Lucy," he said.

"You will ask her?"

"I will."

Gilgamesh smiled, but his face looked old and, for a moment, wistful. "But you are both so young…"

"I love her." It was said simply, with the honesty only the young possess. Gilgamesh rose, and surprised Orphan by hugging him. The old man felt frail in Orphan's arms. "Let's drink. For the two of you."

They drank, sharing the bottle, Orphan grinning inanely.

"Read me the paper," Gilgamesh said. They sat together, looking at the Thames.

Obligingly, Orphan reached for the stained newspaper. He scanned the small print, the ink already running, searching for an item of news to interest Gilgamesh. "Here," he said at last. He cleared his throat and read the title, which was: "TERRORIST GANG STRIKES AGAIN!"

"Go on," Gilgamesh said, spraying him with crumbs of bread.

"'Last night,'" read Orphan, "' notorious terrorist organisation known as the Persons from Porlock struck again at the very heart of the capital. Their target this time was none other than the famed playwright Oscar Wilde, who was engaged, by his own words, in a work of composition of the highest order when he heard an insistent knock on the door, followed by shouts from outside. Rising to see what the commotion was about – having, for reasons of his own, dismissed all his servants for the night – Wilde was confronted by several men dressed as clowns who shouted fragmented lines from Lear's *A Book of Nonsense* at him, enclosed him in a circle and danced around him until his mind, so he himself says, had been set awhirl with chaos. The Persons departed as suddenly as they had come, evading the police force that was already on its way to the scene. In his statement, a confused Wilde said the title of his new play was to be called *The Importance of Being Something*, but for the life of him he could no longer recall what that something was. "How long will this campaign of terror continue?" Wilde asked, and called for the Prime Minister's resignation. "This cannot go on," he said; "this is a violation of everything our country stands for." Prime Minister Moriarty's Office was not available for comment.'"

He finished, and all was quiet save for Gilgamesh's chuckle. "Was he really 'engaged in a work of composition of the highest order'?" he said, "or was he entertaining the young Alfred Douglas? I suspect the Persons from Porlock wasted their time on this one. But you wouldn't know anything about that, would you?" he said.

Orphan glanced away and was silent. Again, Gilgamesh chuckled. He took another long swig on the bottle and said, "What else is there?"

"Moriarty to launch Martian space-probe," Orphan said, "ceremony to take place tomorrow at dusk. The probe will carry an Edison record containing the songs of birds and whales, as well as a small volume of Elizabeth Barrett Browning's *Sonnets from the Portuguese*."

Gilgamesh nodded approvingly. "Lucy is going to be there," Orphan said. "She has been doing the whale recordings for the past two months, and she was selected to put the record and the book into the probe at the ceremony." He grinned, trying to picture it. The Queen might be there!

"Whales are worth listening to," Gilgamesh said mildly, though his eyes twinkled. "Pray, continue."

Orphan did so. "Fresh fly supply for the Queen was halted temporarily on Tuesday due to suspicion of a contaminated source – most of her public appearances have been cancelled for the next week. The Byron simulacrum gave a poetry recital at the Royal Society…" He turned the page over. "Oh, and rumours the Bookman is back in town."

Beside him, Gilgamesh had gone very still. "Says who?" he asked quietly.

"An unnamed source at the Metropolitan Police," Orphan said. "Why?"

Gilgamesh shook his head. "No one knows where the Bookman will strike. Not unless he chooses to make it known, for reasons of his own."

"I'm not sure I understand you," Orphan said patiently. "Why would he do that?"

"As a warning, perhaps," Gilgamesh said, "to his next victim."

"The Bookman's only a myth," Orphan said. Beside him, Gilgamesh slowly smiled.

"A myth," he said. "Oh, Orphan. This is the time of myths. They are woven into the present like silk strands from the past, like a wire mesh from the future, creating an interlacing pattern, a grand design, a repeating motif. Don't dismiss myth, boy. And never, ever, dismiss the Bookman." And he touched his fingers to his blind eyes, and covered his face with his hands. Orphan knew he would speak no more that night.

That was how Orphan left him, there on the water's edge: an old man, hunched into an unmoving figure, like a pensive statue. Orphan never again saw him in life.

Who was Orphan and how had he come to inhabit that great city, the Capital of the Everlasting Empire, the seat of the royal family, the ancestral home of Les Lézards? His father was a Vespuccian sailor, his mother an enigma: both were dead, and had been so for many years. His skin was copper-red, his eyes green like the sea. He had spent his early life on the docks, running errands between the feet of sailors, a minute employee of the East India Company. His knowledge of languages was haphazard if wide, his education colourful and colloquial, his circle of friends and acquaintances far-ranging, if odd.

He learned poetry in the gutter, and from the public readings given by the great men and women of the age; in pubs and dockyards, in halls of learning and in the streets at dawn – and once, from a sword-wielding girl from France, who appeared mysteriously on the deck of a ship Orphan was helping to load with cargo bound for China, and recounted to him, in glorious, beautiful

verse, a vision of God (he had never forgotten her) –
and he learned it from the books in the public library,
until words spun in his head all day and all night, and
he agonised at writing them down on paper, his hand
bleeding as the pen scratched against the surface of the
page.

Who was Orphan? A poet, certainly; a young man,
that too. He had aspirations for greatness, and had once
met, by chance, the ancient Wordsworth, as the great
man was leaving a coffee house in Soho and the five-
year-old Orphan was squatting in the street outside,
talking to his friend, the beggar Lame Menachem. The
great man had smiled at him then, and – perhaps mis-
taking him for a beggar himself – handed him a coin, a
half-crown showing the profile of the mad old Lizard
King, George III, which Orphan had kept ever since for
good luck.

At present, Orphan was engaged, himself, in a "work
of composition of the highest order": he was busy craft-
ing a long poem, a cycle of poems in fact, about life in
this great city. He was moderately proud of his efforts,
though he felt the poem, somehow, lacked substance.
But he was young, and could not worry himself too
long; and, having seen his old friend Gilgamesh, the
wanderer, and ascertained his (relative) well-being, he
proceeded with a light heart to his primary destination
of the evening, which was the newly rebuilt Rose Theatre in Southwark.

Orphan walked along the river; in the distance the
constant song of whales rose and fell like the tides as the
giant, mysterious beings rose from the dark waters for a

breath of air. Occasionally he paused, and looked, with a poet's longing for the muse, at the cityscape sprawling before him on the other side of the river. Smoke rose from chimneys, low-lying and dense like industrial clouds, merging with the fog that wrapped itself about the buildings. In the distance, too, were the lights of the Babbage Tower, its arcane mechanisms pointed at the skies, its light a beacon and a warning to the mail airships that flew at night, like busy bumblebees delivering dew from flower to flower. Almost, he was tempted to stop, to scribble a hasty poem: but the cold of the air rising from the river compelled him onwards, and at his back Big Ben began to strike ten, hurrying him on. Already he was late for the performance.

Lucy wasn't there and must therefore have been inside; and so he bought a ticket outside the theatre and entered the courtyard, where people still milled about. So there was still time, he thought. He bought himself a mug of mulled wine and sipped at the hot, spicy drink gratefully before making his way inside the building, into the groundlings' floor.

In the spirit of authenticity, the Rose was lit not with gas but burning torches, and their jumping light made the shadows dance and turned the faces of people into fantastical beings, so that Orphan imagined he was sharing this space with a race of lizards and porcupines, ravens and frogs. The thought amused him, for it occurred to him to wonder how he himself appeared: was he a raven, or a frog?

He settled himself against the balustrade separating the groundlings from the lower seats and waited. There was a slim, dark-haired girl standing beside him, whose face kept coming in and out of shadow. In her hands she held a pen and a notebook, in which she was scribbling notes. She had a pale, delicately drawn face – seen in profile it was quite remarkable, or so Orphan always thought – and her ears were small and pointed at their tip, and drawn back against her head so that she appeared to him in the light of the moon coming from above like some creature of legend and myth, an elf, perhaps, or a Muse.

He leaned towards her. "One day I will write a play for you they would show here at the Rose," he said.

Her smile was like moonlight. She grinned and said, "Do you say that to all the girls?"

"I don't need to," Orphan said, and he swept her to him and kissed her, the notebook pressed between their bodies. "Not when I have you."

"Let go!" she laughed. "You have to stop reading those romance novels, Orphan."

"I don't–"

"Sure." She grinned up at him again, and kissed him. Two old ladies close by tutted. "Now shush. It's about to start."

Orphan relented. They leaned together against the balustrade, fingers entwined. Presently, a hush fell over the crowd, and a moment later the empty stage was no longer empty, and Henry Irving had come on.

At the sight of the great actor the crowd burst into spontaneous applause. Orphan took another sip from his drink. The torchlight shuddered, and a cold wind blew from the open roof of the theatre, sending a

shiver down Orphan's spine. On stage, Irving was saying, "...The bridegroom's doors are opened wide, and
I am next of kin. The guests are met, the feast is set:
may'st hear the merry din–" and the celebrated performance of the stage adaptation of *The Rime of the
Ancient Mariner* began.

Orphan, though he had seen the performance before,
was nevertheless spellbound anew. As Irving's booming
voice filled the theatre the strange and grotesque story
took life, and the stage filled with masked dancers, en-
acting the wedding ball into which the Ancient Mariner
had come like an ill-begotten creature rising from the
Thames. The story took shape around Orphan: how the
young mariner, Amerigo Vespucci, took sail on his voyage of exploration under the auspices of the British
court; how, on Caliban's Island, he discovered and shot
the lizard-like inhabitant of that island, by that callous
act bringing upon himself unwanted, unwholesome im-
mortality and on his masters, the British, the full might
of Les Lézards, the Lizard Kings, who now sat on Britannia's throne. It was an old, fanciful story, woven
together of gossip and myth. Irving's adaptation, Orphan knew, had been wildly popular with the
theatre-going public – particularly those of a young,
mildly radical disposition – but was decried as dangerous
nonsense by the palace, though Prime Minister Moriarty himself had so far kept silent on the issue. Either
way, it was becoming evident that the play's stage-life
would be kept short – which only added to the public's
enthusiasm. Speculation in the press as to Irving's mo-
tivations in staging it was rife, but insubstantial.

When Vespucci began his return journey home, Lucy leaned forward, focused, as he knew she would. It was the portion that told of the coming of the whales: how they had accompanied the ill-fated ship all through the crossing of the Atlantic, and further, until they arrived at Greenwich and the city awoke, for the first time, to their song.

He edged towards her. Her hair was pulled back behind her ears, and her fingers were long, smudged with ink and with dirt under the nails as if she had been digging in Thames mud.

"How are the whales today?" he asked.

"Restless. I'm not sure why. Have you noticed the change in their song when you walked along the embankment?"

Leaning together against the balustrade, the crowd closing them in, it was like they had found themselves, momentarily, in a small, dark, comfortable alcove, a private space in which they were alone.

"You're the marine biologist," Orphan said. "I'm only a poet."

"Working with whales is like working with poets," Lucy said. She put away her pad and her pen. She had a small bag hanging over her shoulder. "They're unruly, obtuse, and self-important."

Orphan laughed. He took her hand in his. The skin of her palm always surprised him in its roughness; it was a hand used to hard work. Her eyes were dark and mesmerising, like lode-stars, and small, almost invisible laughter-lines gathered like a fine web at the corners. "I love you," Orphan said.

She smiled, and he kissed her.

On stage, Henry Irving abandoned the role of narrator as the final act began to unfold. Now, with all the considerable verve and power he was capable of, he played Shakespeare, the poet and playwright who rose to prominence in the court of the Lizard King and became the first of the Poet-Prime Ministers.

Both Orphan and Lucy watched as the Ancient Mariner shuffled onto the stage to deliver the story of his life to Lord Shakespeare: Orphan, who had a natural interest in books, observed it closely. It was a heavy, leather-bound folio, the spine facing the audience, with the title *The Rime of the Ancient Mariner* etched in gilt onto it.

"I pass," cried the Ancient Mariner (a young actor, Beerbohm Tree, whom Orphan vaguely recognised), "like night, from land to land, I have strange power of speech," (here he took a deep breath, and continued), "that morning that his face I see, I know the man that must hear me: to him my tale I teach!" And he passed the heavy book to Shakespeare, who took it from him with a graceful nod, laid it on the table before him, and opened it–

There was the sound of an explosion, a deafening bang (and for Orphan, everything slowed, as)–

The book disintegrated in a cloud of dust–

Not dust, shrapnel (and Orphan, moving in jerky, dreamlike motions, grabbed hold of Lucy and let himself fall to the ground, his weight dragging her with him, his body first cushioning her fall and then covering her in a protective embrace)–

That tore into Shakespeare/Irving and cut his head away from his body and sent plumes of blood into the air.

The air filled with screams. The stage collapsed. It was, Orphan thought in his dazed, confused state on the floor of the theatre, holding on to the girl he loved, the definite end of the performance.

TWO
Lucy

And now we reach'd the orchard-plot;
And, as we climb'd the hill,
The sinking moon to Lucy's cot
Came near and nearer still.
   – William Wordsworth, "Lucy"

They walked together along the embankment. At their back the Rose was wreathed in flames. Orphan had a cut on his shoulder, bandaged with a strip of cloth. Lucy's heavy coat was covered in plaster and dust that wouldn't come off. Both were shaken.

A police automaton passed them by on its way to the scene of the explosion, a blue light flashing over its head. "Clear the area!" it shrieked at them. "Clear the area! Unsafe! Unsafe!"

"Yes," Lucy murmured, "I noticed. The big explosion was a definite clue."

They both laughed, and Orphan felt some of his tension ease. The automaton, borne fast on its hidden wheels, disappeared behind them.

22

"Who do you think was behind it?" Lucy said.

"You mean, who hired the Bookman?"

"Yes," Lucy said. "I guess that is what I mean."

The fog swirled about them, muting the glow of the fire from behind. Without consciously realising it, they drew closer; Orphan felt Lucy's warmth even through the heavy coat and it made him feel better. It made him feel alive.

"I don't know," he said. "I expect we'll read about it in the papers tomorrow. Could have been anyone with a grudge against Irving. He didn't exactly make himself popular with the *Ancient Mariner* production."

"Like the Persons from Porlock?" She threaded her arm in his and smiled. "Tell me, Master Orphan, did you dress as a clown last night and quote limericks at Mr. Wilde?"

"I…" Orphan began to say, but Lucy reached to him and put her finger against his lips, sealing them. Orphan closed his eyes and let his senses flood him: Lucy's taste was a mixture of flavour and scent, of spice and river water.

"We all have our secrets," she said in a soft voice. She removed her finger, and Orphan opened his eyes, found himself standing face to face with her. She was his height, and her dark eyes looked directly into his, her mouth smiled, a crescent moon. She had white, uneven teeth, with slightly extended canines.

They kissed. Whether she kissed him first, or he kissed her, it was immaterial. It was a mutual coming together, the two opposing poles of a magnet meeting.

Her lips were cold, then hot; her eyes consumed him. He thought without words, without poetry.

When they came away both were somewhat breathless, and Lucy was grinning.

"Come on!" she said. She took Orphan's hand and he followed her: she ran down the embankment and he ran with her, the cold air whipping their faces, and the fog parted in their passing. Orphan, flushed, still breathless from the kiss, felt a rare kind of happiness take hold of him; he threw his head back and laughed, and the clouds parted. For a moment he could see the moon, shining yellow, its face misshapen. Then the clouds closed again overhead and he ran on, following Lucy, running towards the growing whale song emanating from underneath Westminster Bridge.

Nearby, on the other side of the river, Big Ben began, majestically, to count the midnight strokes.

What does Orphan remember of that night? It is a cacophony of the senses, a bazaar through which he can amble, picking and discarding sensation like curios or used books. Here a stand of sounds, and he pauses and lifts again the noise of the explosion, compares it with the rising whale-song into which Lucy led him, as they approached the south side of Westminster Bridge and the pod welcomed them with a symphony that somehow wove inside itself the distant light of stars and the warning flashes of the mail-ships in the air, the dying fire down-river and the salty taste of a kiss. He pauses beside a canopy and sorts through touch, experiencing again the heat of an embrace, the wet, slippery feel against his hand of a whale rising silently from the Thames, a plume of water interacting with the moon to form a rainbow, making laughter rise inside him like bubbles.

They visited the pod that night, and the whales, who rose one by one to the surface, were dark, beautiful shapes like sleek submarines, acknowledging them.

"Come on!" Lucy had said, and he had followed, and knew that he would follow her anywhere, even beyond life itself.

In the light of the moon, under Westminster Bridge, he kissed her again. "Will you marry me?" he asked.

"I'll be with you everywhere," she said. Her eyes were veiled with shimmering stars. "We will never be apart."

"Where have you been?" Jack demanded as soon as Orphan walked in. "Were you at the Rose? Do you have any idea what's going on?" He surveyed Orphan through his dark glasses with a frown. "Have you been out *enjoying yourself*? I've been worried sick waiting for you!"

"I'm fine," Orphan said. "Couldn't be better," he added. His mouth kept trying to shape itself into a grin, which he was trying to suppress for Jack's benefit. "I was at the Rose, but I wasn't hurt. I was with Lucy."

"He was with Lucy!" Jack said. Orphan's grin fought one last time and was released; Jack, on seeing it, shook his head and muttered, "Well, that's all right then."

"We're getting married."

"Married!"

"Don't look so horrified."

"Delighted for you, my boy! Married!"

"Are you sure you're feeling all right, Jack?"

They sat down together in the back room of Payne's Booksellers. Orphan sprawled on his bed (which sat between AEGYPTIAN ARCHAEOLOGY and ELECKTRONICKA – GENERAL) while Jack took the single chair (beside the small, but choice, selection of technical tomes on the shelf marked STEAM ENGINES – THEORY AND PRACTICAL APPLICATIONS). Jack himself slept in the basement, which was large and filled with old books and which was always damp, embellished by the constant smell of mould and a strange, tangy breeze which had no obvious source.

"Married," Jack said. He seemed to mull the idea over in his head. "Nothing against marriage, me, but… Oh hell. Congratulations, boy! Let's drink."

"I thought you'd never offer."

Jack rose nimbly and reached for a thick bible on one of the shelves. He removed it, carrying it carefully, and laid it on the small side-table. Opened, it revealed a bottle of Old Bushmills. "Would this do? There are a couple of glasses in that *Illustrated Mother Goose* on the lower shelf next to your bed, if you could trouble yourself to fetching them."

Orphan sighed. Jack constantly worried him; he was afraid to ask what else was hidden in some of the books. More than words, he was sure.

Eventually, they clinked glasses. "To Lucy and yourself! To matrimony – may it make you forever happy and never come near to me!"

"I'll drink to that," Orphan said, and grinned, and he drank the toast. The whiskey, from the first distillery licensed by the Lizard Kings, slid down his throat with almost no resistance.

Heat rose from his feet to his face. "Put scales on your chest," Jack said, and laughed. "To Les Lézards!" Jack said. "We must drink to them too. May they end up on a spit above a fire as the food for drunken sailors."

"One day," Orphan said, "you'll go too far."

"Not far enough," Jack said.

"So the Bookman's back in town," Jack said, a little later, putting his hand on his chin (index finger resting against his cheek) in a faux-thoughtful gesture. "And poor old Irving's career is finally over." He sighed, theatrically. "Everyone's a critic."

"What have you heard?" Orphan said. Jack spread his hands in a shrug. Had he been French, it might have been called a Gallic shrug; as he weren't, it was a decidedly English one. "I heard the police closed off Southwark and are diligently hunting for clues, headed by the admirably efficient Inspector Adler. It must have been chaos there if they let you all go – there's a public appeal going out in the papers first thing in the morning for any witnesses to come forward."

"*Irene* Adler?" Orphan said, and Jack smiled unpleasantly and said, "The very same who is in charge of the Persons from Porlock investigation."

"Then they could do without my testimony," Orphan said. "What else does your abominable Tesla set say? And by the way," he added, "do we have some wine?"

Orphan coughed, said, "So what else did you hear?"
Jack had an illegal Tesla set in the basement, modified
to listen to police and government communications; he
spent most of his time down there, scanning the air-
waves. He was – he thought of himself as – a Radical.
He was also the editor of the *Tempest*, an anti-Calibanic
broadsheet published irregularly and distributed poorly.
Lastly, he was proprietor of Payne's, having acquired
the ramshackle bookshop (so the story went) one night
four years ago at a game of cards.

"Well," Jack said, slowly swirling the drink in his
hand, "rumour has it the Bookman's not left town.
They're panicking, Orphan. *They* are panicking. There's
increased security at the Palace, but for all they know
his next victim could be the Byron automaton, or Prime
Minister Moriarty, or just some dumb fool who buys the
wrong book at the wrong time." He looked up from his
drink and his mouth twisted into a smile. "The Estab-
lishment is teetering, Orphan. And they are all going to
end up against the wall, when the revolution comes."

Orphan looked at his friend, concerned. Usually,
Jack was good company, but when he was like this –
when his revolutionary sentiments got the better of
him – he could be savage, almost frightening. Orphan
didn't know what grievance his friend had against the
Calibanic dynasty. He didn't need to. There were many
other people like Jack, angry people, people who hated
lizards, or poetry, or both. People, he thought, like the
Bookman.

He finished his drink and, mirroring him, Jack did
the same. "I'm going to sleep," Jack said. He stood up

and laid the glass on the table with a little more force than was necessary. "Make sure you open the shop in the morning. And try to get some sleep. See you tomorrow, china. And congratulations."

When he was gone, Orphan blew out the two half-melted candles that perched precariously on two opposing shelves and stretched himself on the bed. Sleep claimed him at once, and his dreams were full of Lucy.

THREE
The Parliament of Payne

As with the commander of an army, or the leader of any enterprise, so is it with the mistress of a house.
— Isabella Beeton, *The Book of Household Management*

Orphan had first met Lucy one day at the bookshop. She came through the door like – sunshine? Wind? Like spice? Orphan wasn't that much of a poet – looking for a book about whales. He fell in love the way trees do, which is to say, forever. It was a love with roots that burrowed deep, entangled, grew together. Like two trees they leaned into each other, sheltering each other with their leaves, finding solace and strength in the wide encompassing forest that was the city, holding together in the multitude of alien trees. Orphan loved her the way people do in romantic novels, from the first page, beyond even The End.

When the door opened he hoped it was her, but it wasn't. The door opened and closed, the bell rang, and footsteps – their sound a dry shuffle – approached the counter behind which Orphan sat, bleary-eyed and untidy, a mug of coffee (the largest that was available) and the morning paper resting by his side.

"Good morning, good morning!" a voice said chirpily. Orphan, wincing, looked up from his reading. "Good morning to you too, Mr. Marx. All's well?"

"All's well that ends well," Marx said, and sniggered. He ran his fingers through his large, overgrown beard, as if searching for a lost item within. "Jack about?"

Orphan mutely pointed towards the small door that led to the basement. Marx nodded thoughtfully but didn't move. "Have you, um, come across any of the volumes I ordered?"

"Let's see," Orphan said. He reached down to the shelves built into the counter. "We have–"

"Quietly, please," Marx said. He looked left and right and back again and said, apologetically, "The walls have ears."

"Quite," Orphan said. Though he usually liked Karl, the man's constant movement, like an ancient grandfather clock, between high paranoia and boisterous cheer, grated on his fragile nerves that morning. "Well," he whispered, "we managed to acquire M. Verne's narrative of his expedition to Caliban's Island, *L'Île mystérieuse*, that you asked for, and also the revolutionary poems of Baudelaire, *Les Fleurs du mal*. I think Jack is still looking for de Sade's *Histoire de Juliette* for you."

"Not for me!" Marx said quickly. "For a friend of mine." He straightened up. "Good work, my young friend. Can I trust you to…"

"I'll deliver them to the Red Lion myself," Orphan said.

Marx smiled. "How is your poetry coming along?" He didn't wait for a reply. "I think Jack is waiting for me. I'll, um, show myself in. And remember – mum's the word."

Orphan put his finger to his lips. Marx nodded, ran his fingers through his beard again, and disappeared through the small door that led down to the basement.

"For a friend of mine," Orphan said aloud, and laughed. Then he took a healthy swig of his coffee and bent back down to the newspaper which was, of course, full of last night's events at the Rose.

"IRVING FINALLY LOSES HEAD!" screamed the headline. "SHOW ENDS WITH A BANG!" The name of the writer, an R. Kipling, was familiar to him: they were of about the same age, and had come across one another several times in town, though they had not formed a friendship. Kipling was a staunch Caliban supporter, as was evident from his reporting of the explosion:

"Late last night (wrote Kipling), a bomb went off at the controversial production of *The Rime of the Ancient Mariner*, killing the show's star and artistic director, Mr. Henry Irving, and wounding several others. Police have closed off the area and investigation has been undertaken by Scotland Yard's new and formidable inspector, Irene Adler. Eyewitness testimony suggests Irving was killed by a booby-trapped copy of the book of the play that was delivered to him on stage by the young actor Beerbohm Tree, playing the Ancient Mariner to Irving's Shakespeare. The play raised much antipathy in official circles and was justly avoided by all law-abiding citizens and faithful servants of Les Lézards. It was, however, popular with a certain type of revolutionary rabble, and sadly tolerated under our Queen's benign rule and her commitment to our nation's principles of the freedom of speech."

Orphan sighed and rubbed his eyes; he needed a shave. He took another sip of (by now cooling) coffee and continued reading, though his mind wasn't in it: his head was awhirl with images of Lucy, and he kept returning to the night before, to the words they spoke to each other, to their kiss like a seal of the future... He sighed and scratched the beginning of a beard and decided he'd take the afternoon off to go see her. Let Jack do some work, for a change: he, Orphan, had better things to do on this day.

"Though there is official silence regarding the investigation (Kipling continued) this reporter has managed to make a startling discovery. It has come to my attention that, though Irving's co-star, the young Beerbohm, was apparently killed in the explosion alongside his master, a man corresponding exactly to Beerbohm's description was taken in for questioning earlier today! If Beerbohm is still alive, who was the man delivering the book on stage? If, indeed, it was a man at all..."

The doorbell rang again, and Orphan lifted his head at the new set of approaching footsteps. He knew who it would be before looking. At that time of day, in this shop, no casual browser was likely to come in. Only members of what Orphan, only half-jokingly, had come to call the Parliament of Payne.

"Greetings, young Orphan!" said a booming voice, and a hand reached out and plucked a well-worn penny from behind Orphan's ear. Orphan grinned up at John Maskelyne. "Hello, Nevil."

Maskelyne frowned and scratched his bushy moustache. "No one," he said, "dares use my second name, you lout." He threw the coin in the air, where it disappeared. "Jack in?"

Orphan mutely nodded towards the basement door.

"Good, good," Maskelyne said, but he seemed in no hurry to depart. He began wandering around the shop, pulling books at random from the shelves, humming to himself. "Have you heard about Beerbohm?" his disembodied voice called from the black hole of the COOKERY – BEETON TO GOODFELLOW section. "Rumour has it the police found him trussed up like a turkey with its feathers plucked out, but alive and safely tucked away at home, if a little dazed around the edges."

"I'm sure that it must be a mistake," Orphan called back. "I was at the Rose last night and I can assure you Beerbohm was as effectively made extinct as the dodo." He tried to follow Maskelyne's route through the shop; now he could see the top of his head, peeking behind the BERBER COOKERY shelf; a moment later, his voice rose from the other end of the room, muttering the words of an exotic recipe as if trying to memorise it. Then Orphan blinked, and when his eyes reopened, only a fraction of a second later, the magician stood before him once again, his eyes twinkling. "I hope I didn't give you a start."

Orphan, who luckily had laid the coffee back on the counter a moment earlier, waved his hand as if to say, think nothing of it. "He is still alive, young Orphan," Maskelyne said, and his countenance was no longer cheery, but deep in an abyss of dark thoughts. "And what's more, no doctor was called to treat the man at the Rose. Let me riddle you this, my friend. When is a man not a man?"

He opened his hand, showing it empty. He laid it, for a moment, on the surface of the counter, and when it was raised a small toy rested on the wood, a little man-like doll with a key at its back. "Come to the Egyptian Hall when you next have need of counsel," the magician said, almost, it seemed to Orphan, sadly, and then he turned away and was gone through the door to the basement.

But Orphan had no time to think further of the magician's words. No sooner had Maskelyne departed that the door chimed again, and in walked an elegant lady. Enter the third murderer, Orphan thought, and hurriedly came around the counter to hold the door. It was the woman for whom an entire section of a bookcase was dedicated, and he had always felt awed in her presence. "Mrs Beeton!"

"Hello, Orphan," said Isabella Beeton cordially. "You look positively radiant today. Could it be that the rays of marital bliss have finally chanced upon illuminating your countenance?"

Orphan grinned and shut the door carefully after her. "Can't get anything past you," he said, and Isabella Beeton smiled and patted his shoulder.

"I know the look," she said. "Also, Jack did happen to mention something of the sort in this morning's missive. Congratulations." She walked past, her long dress held up demurely lest it come in touch with the dusty floor. "I won't keep you, Orphan. You are no doubt eager to go in pursuit of your newly bound love." She tossed her hair over her shoulder and smiled at him; her hair was gold, still, though woven with fine white strands that resembled silk. "Our number is complete. Go, seek out Tom, and get that idle fellow to replace you. Your watch is done."

And, so saying, she too disappeared through the small door that led to Jack's basement, and was gone.

Orphan managed to locate Tom Thumb in his quarters near Charing Cross Station, and after rousing the small man from his slumber extracted from him a promise to take his place at the shop for the day.

"Bleedin' poets," Tom Thumb muttered as he exchanged his pyjamas for a crumpled suit. "Always bleating of love and flowers and sheep grazing in fields. The only sheep I like are ones resting on a spit."

"I owe you one," Orphan said, grinning, and Tom shook his head and buttoned his shirt and said, "I've heard that one before, laddie. Just show me the shekels."

"Soon as Jack pays me," Orphan promised, and before Tom could change his mind he was out of the door and walking down the Strand, whistling the latest tune from Gilbert and Sullivan's *Ruddigore*.

He crossed the river at Westminster, still whistling. Already, on the other side of the river, he could see the whales, and their song rose to meet him, weaving into his whistle like a chorus. He felt light and clear-headed, and he stepped jauntily on, descending the steps towards the figure that was standing on the water's edge.

"Orphan?"

He was suddenly shy. Lucy, turning, regarded him with a dazzling smile. Behind her, a whale rose to the surface and snorted, and a cloud of fine mist rose and fell in the air.

"I missed you," Orphan said, simply.

They stood and grinned at each other. The whale exhaled again, breathed, and disappeared inside the blue-green waters of the Thames.

"I hoped you'd come," Lucy said. Her eyes, he noticed, were large and bright, the colour of the water. Sun speckled her irises.

He said, "I'd follow you anywhere," and Lucy laughed, a surprised, delighted sound, and kissed him.

Later, he would remember that moment. Everything seemed to slow, the wheel of the sun burning through the whale's cloud of breath and breaking into a thousand little rainbows; a cool breeze blew but he was warm, his fingers intertwined with Lucy's, and her lips tasted hot, like cinnamon-spiced tea. He whispered, "I love you," and knew it was true.

He saw his face reflected in her eyes. She blinked. She was crying. "I love you too," she said, and for a long moment, the world was entirely still.

Then they came apart, the cloud of mist dispersed, blown apart by the breeze, and the sun resumed its slow course across the sky. Lucy, pointing at a bucket that stood nearby, said, "Help me feed the whales?" and Orphan, in response, purposefully grabbed the still-writhing tentacles of a squid and threw it in an arc into the river.

A baby whale rose, exhaled loudly (the sound like a snort of laughter), and descended with its prey.

On the opposite bank of the river Big Ben began to chime, and the strikes sounded, momentarily, like the final syllables of a sonnet.

FOUR
Gilgamesh

And all the while his blind brown fingers
Traced a webbed message in the dirt
That said
Gilgamesh was here.
  – L.T., "The Epic of Gilgamesh"

When they parted it was dusk, and the first stars were rising, winking into existence like baleful eyes. Orphan felt buoyant: and he was going to see Lucy again that night, at Richmond-upon-Thames, for the Martian probe ceremony. He'd promised he'd be there as soon as he saw Gilgamesh again. The truth was, he was worried about his old friend. He was the closest thing to a family Orphan ever had. Gilgamesh lived rough, and the years had not been kind to him. "Seven-thirty!" Lucy said as she kissed him a last time. "And don't be late!"

He walked the short distance along the embankment to Waterloo Bridge. He thought he'd talk with Gilgamesh, but when he reached the arches there was no sign of his old friend there.

Orphan called for him; his voice came back in a dreary echo. He went closer to the edge of the water. There was the small ring of stones where Gilgamesh's fire had burned. Cold ash lay between the stones, dark and fine. "Gilgamesh?" he called again, but all was quiet; even the sounds of the whales had died down, so that Orphan felt himself in a vast silence that stretched all around him, across the waters and into the city itself. "Gilgamesh?"

Then he saw it. An arc of dark spots, leading from the fire towards the river. He bent down and touched them with his fingers, and they came back moist.

He looked around him wildly. What had happened? Resting against the wall he found Gilgamesh's blanket. It was stained, in great dark spots, with a smell that left a metallic taste in the back of his throat.

But not blood.

Oil? Or, he thought for a moment, ridiculously – ink?

The blanket was torn. No, he saw. Not torn. Cut, with a sharp implement, like a knife… or a scythe.

He rolled the old blanket open, panic mounting. What had happened to Gilgamesh? The blanket was empty, but soaked in some dark liquid. Wide gashes opened in the dirty cloth like gaping mouths.

Orphan knew he should call the police. But what would they do? They had better things to do than worry about an old beggar, with the explosion at the Rose and the Ripper loose in Whitechapel. He stood up, pulling away from the blanket. His hands were smudged.

Orphan felt ill, and panic settled in the pit of his stomach like a snake, coiling slowly awake and rising with a hiss. What had happened? What could he do?

The silence lay all around him. He could hear no birds and no traffic. The light had almost disappeared entirely, and the world was one hair's breadth away from true and total darkness.

Frightened, he nevertheless followed the arc of spilled ink from the dead fire to the water's edge. He bent down to the river and washed his hands in the cold, murky water.

It occurred to him that Gilgamesh's fishing-rod, too, was missing. He looked sideways and down, but could see nothing.

Then a curious sound made him turn. It came from the water, to his left, a clinking sound, like champagne glasses touching. Still crouching, he made his way carefully to the left, his fingers running against the side of the embankment. The stones were slimy and cold, unpleasant to the touch – then he found it. His fingers encountered something solid and round, and the sound stopped.

It was a tall round shape made of smooth glass, and it was tied with a fishing line, Orphan discovered, to a rusting hook that protruded underwater from the side of the embankment. His fingers growing numb with cold, he managed to untie it and finally lifted his find from the water. It was a bottle.

Raised voices came suddenly from the river path and Orphan, jolted, withdrew into the darkness of the arches. The final rays of the sun faded and now the streetlamps began to come alive all along the river, winking into existence one by one, casting a comforting yellow haze across the darkened world. His heart beating fast, Orphan waited in the safety of the shadows until the voices, sounding drunk, passed. Then, clutching the bottle in his hands, he hurried away from the bridge, away from the blood-like substance and the dark absence of his friend. For when he withdrew it from the water Orphan recognised two things about the bottle: that it was the one he had brought Gilgamesh only the night before, the stolen bottle of Chateau des Rêves, and that though it had been emptied of wine it was not yet empty: for the bottle was sealed tight, and a dry sheaf of paper rustled inside it, like a caged butterfly the colour of sorrow, waiting to be freed.

He took shelter on the other side of the river, in the welcoming, warm and well-lit halls of Charing Cross Station. He stood alone amidst the constant, hurried movement of people to and from the great waiting trains that stood like giant metal beasts of burden along the platforms, bellowing smoke and steam into the cool night air. His back against the wall, the smell of freshly baked pastries from a nearby stall wafting past him, Orphan broke the crude seal on the bottle and withdrew, with great care, the sheaf of paper that nestled inside.

Gilgamesh's jagged handwriting ran along the page in cramped and hurried lines that left no blank space. It was addressed – and here Orphan stopped, for he felt cold again despite the warmth of the station, and his fingers tingled as if still dipped in the cold water of the Thames – to him.

Alone amidst the masses of humanity at the great station of Charing Cross, his ears full of the short, sharp whistle-blows from the platforms and their accompanying clacking of wheels as trains accelerated away into the dark, and his stomach (despite all that he had found) rumbling quietly at the pervading smells of pastries baking and coffee brewing, he began reading Gilgamesh's letter to him:

My Dear Orphan –

As I write this a hot explosion lights up (I imagine) the skies above the Thames, and rather than worry I am exhilarated – for that ball of fire and heat is a signal, and it tells me of my impending doom. I shall try to post this to you, but already I grow anaesthetised and dull, for I do not believe I will have the time. He is coming back for me, me who had been forgotten for all those centuries. But the Bookman never forgets, and his creations are forever his –

You scoffed when I spoke of the Bookman. You called him nothing but a legend. But the Bookman is real, as real – more so – than I am. Who am I, Orphan? You and I played together in believing me Gilgamesh, the lone remnant of an ancient civilisation, a poet-warrior of a bygone age. We were humouring each other, I think – though the truth is not that far from the fiction, perhaps. In either case you, of all people, deserve to know—

Every creed has its myth of immortals. The sailors have their Flying Dutchman, the explorers their Vespucci, the Jews their Lamed-Vav. Poets, perhaps, have Gilgamesh–

I, too, have been immortal. Until the knife descends I shall be immortal still, but that, I fear, is soon to end. Who was I? I, too, was a poet, and of the worst kind – one with delusions of grandeur. When Vespucci went on his voyage of exploration I went with him, for there must always be someone to record great discoveries. I was with him on Caliban's Island, when he roused Les Lézards from their deep slumber in the deep metal chambers inside the great crater at the heart of that terrible island. Almost alone, I managed to escape, blinded by the terrible sights I had seen. I took to sea and for days I floated, half-crazed and dying. When at last he found me I had all but departed this earth–

He – fixed me? Healed me? But he did more than that – and he took the knowledge of the island from me, and then let me go. But he had not repaired my sight. Perhaps, already, he thought I had seen too much–

I had thought he had forgotten me, but the Bookman never forgets.

Now, I fear, he is coming back for me, and perhaps it would finally be an end. Perhaps I could rest, now, after all the cold long years. But I fear him, and know that he would not rest, not until what was started on that cursed island can be brought to an end. He is bound with the lizards, I believe, and vengeful.

Perhaps he was theirs, once. Their stories are interlinked—

But why, you ask, I am telling you this? Perhaps because I suspect you, too, will have a role to play in this unfolding tragedy. Perhaps because I knew your father, who was a good man, and your mother, who you didn't know—

No. I have not the heart to tell their story. Not now. For me, as I sit here, alone, on the water's edge, waiting for him to come, no words remain, and language withers. Only a final warning will I deliver to you, my friend: beware the books, for they are his servants. Above all, beware the Bookman.

Yours, in affection—

Gilgamesh

Orphan, stunned, leaning against the wall as if seeking support in the solid stone, scanned the letter again, the words leaping up at him like dark waves against a shore. He felt pounded by them, and fearful. His vision blurred and he blinked, finding that tears, unbidden, unwanted, were the cause. He wiped them away, and a drop fell onto the page, near Gilgamesh's signature, and he noticed something he had missed.

In the small margin of the letter, Gilgamesh had scribbled a couple of lines in small, barely legible writing, almost as if hiding them there. He cleared his eyes again and tried to decipher the words. When meaning came, dread wrapped itself around his neck like an executioner's rope, for it said: *"I know now that he is near, and moving. His next target may be the Martian space probe you told me about. For your sake, and Lucy's – stay away from it. If I can I will tell you myself–"*

There was no more.

And time, for Orphan, stopped.

He was a point of profound silence in the midst of chaos and noise. That silence, holy and absolute, was his as he stood against the wall of the train station, the letter falling slowly from his hand to the floor, too heavy to be carried any more. Lucy. The thought threatened to consume him. Lucy, and her gift to the planet Mars: a small, innocent volume of verse. Elizabeth Barrett Browning's *Sonnets from the Portuguese*.

Somewhere in the distance a whistle blew, rose in the air, and combined with the clear, heavy notes that echoed from Big Ben. They tolled seven times, and their sound jarred against Orphan's own bell of silence, until at last, on the final stroke, it cracked.

Lucy, he thought. And, *my love*.

He had half an hour to save her.

FIVE
The Martian Probe

Once in about every fifteen years a startling visitant makes his appearance upon our midnight skies, a great red star that rises at sunset through the haze about the eastern horizon, and then, mounting higher with the deepening night, blazes forth against the dark background of space with a splendour that outshines Sirius and rivals the giant Jupiter himself. Startling for its size, the stranger looks the more fateful for being a fiery red. Small wonder that by many folk it is taken for a portent.

– Percival Lowell, *Mars*

Picture, for a moment, the great city from above. On one side of the river rise ancient stone buildings, their chimneys puffing out smoke into the night air. Interspersed between them are newer, taller edifices, magnificent constructions in metal and glass, returning the glare of gas and lights from their smooth surfaces. Here is the Strand, the wide avenue overflowing with ladies in their fineries and beggars with their bowls, with hansom cabs and baruch-landaus. The stench of abandoned rubbish mingles here with the latest perfumes. Here is Charing Cross Station, looking from above like a great diving helmet, its face-plate open to the world, its wide mouth spewing out metal slugs who chug merrily away across the wide bridge and over the river.

Here are the Houses of Parliament, cast in the strange, scaly material so beloved of the Queen and her line. They glow in the darkness, an eerie green that casts flickering shadows over the water. Here, too, is the palace, that magnificent, impenetrable dome, sur-rounded by the famous Royal Gardens with their many acres of marshes and ponds.

At a distance, instantly recognisable, is the Babbage Tower, rising into the dark skies like an ancient obelisk, strange devices marring its smooth surface like the marks of an alien alphabet. A light flickers constantly at its apex, warning away the airships that fly, day and night, above the city. Rise higher and you can see them, flying in a great dark cloud over the cityscape like an unkindness of ravens, like a siege of herons. Night and day the airships fly, the eyes and ears (so it is said) of the Lizard Kings, landing and taking off from the distant Great Western Aerodrome that lies beyond Chiswick and Hounslow.

Pull away, return to the great avenue of the Strand and to the train station that belches constant smoke and steam at its extremity. One train, one metal slug, departs from its gaping mouth and snakes away, de-parting this side of the river, going south and west. Past grimy industrial Clapham it runs, and onwards, through the genteel surroundings of Putney, where

wealthy residents dine in well-lit riverside establishments, past the guarded, hushed mansions of Kew,
until it arrives at last in that sea of greenery and country charm that is the Queen's summer abode, the calm
and prosperous town of Richmond-upon-Thames.

A lone figure spews out of the metal slug. Orphan,
running out of the station and onto the High Street,
past rows of quaint, orderly shops dispensing gilt-
tooled, Morocco-bound books, fresh flies (by Royal
licence! screams the sign), fishing-rods and boat trips,
delicate delicatessens and chemists and florists. Turning, he runs, breathing heavily up Hill Street, past the
White Hart and the Spread Eagle and the Lizard and
Crown, arriving, at last, out of breath, eyes stinging
with sweat, at the open gates of the Royal Park.

Harsh lights illuminated the wide open space now
crammed with people. There was an air of festivity to
the event and the smells of roasting peanuts and
mulled wine wafted in the air, coming from the many
stands that littered the outskirts of the crowd. Many
people wore large, round, commemorative red hats –
for Mars – or lizard-green – for Her Majesty. Many
waved flags.

Orphan pushed his way through the crowds, feeling
desperation overcome him. Ahead of him he could see
the outline of the majestic black airship that was to take
the probe on the next, slow leg of its journey, over land
and sea to Caliban's Island, where the launch would
take place. Cursing, he pushed further, not heeding the
resentful looks he received. Where was Lucy?

Above the noise of the crowd a familiar voice rose amplified: Prime Minister Moriarty, delivering the last lines of a speech. He still had time!

Glancing higher he saw the raised platform where Moriarty stood. It only took him an instant to recognise the assembled dignitaries: sitting beside the Prime Minister was the Prince Consort, a short, squat, lizardine being in full regalia, whose reptilian eyes scanned the crowd, his head moving from side to side. Occasionally a long, thin tongue whipped out as if tasting the air and disappeared back inside the elongated snout. Several seats down he thought he recognised Sir Harry Flashman, VC, the Queen's favourite, the celebrated soldier and hero of Jalalabad. On the Prime Minister's other side sat Inspector Adler, her face serious and alert. Surely, Orphan thought, such people could sense the danger before them!

But no. Onwards he pushed, hoping against hope, but Moriarty's voice faded, the speech completed (too soon!) and the crowd burst into applause. Orphan made a last, desperate dash forward, and found himself at last in the front row of the waiting audience.

Before him, the airship loomed. Below it, the probe rested, a small, metallic object, dwarfed by the ship, looking like an innocent ladybird turned upside down.

The belly of the probe was open, and before it, approaching it with small, careful steps, was Lucy.

She had almost reached the probe. In her hands was a book, resting on the Edison record she had so meticulously prepared. She bent down to place the objects in the hold of the probe…

"Lucy!"

The shout tore out of him like a jagged blade ripping loose, tearing at his insides. It rose in the open air and seemed to linger, its notes like motes of dust coming slowly to rest, trailing through the air...

She paused. Her back straightened and she turned, and looked at him. Their eyes met. She smiled; she was radiant; she was happy he came.

The book was still held in her hands.

"Get away from the probe! The book is–"

He began to run towards her. He saw her face, confused, her smile dissipating.

And the book exploded.

The sight was imprinted on Orphan's retinas. Lucy, incinerated in a split second. The airship burning, black silk billowing in flames. The probe hissing, its metal deforming. In that split second a burst of burning wind knocked Orphan back against the screams of the crowd. He landed on his back, winded, blinded, deaf.

Shame filled him like molten silver, and with it the pain, spreading slowly across his body.

I failed, he thought. She's dead. I failed her.

Incinerated. Black silk billowing in flames. The book, disintegrating, and with it...

Then the crawling pain reached his head and he screamed, and the darkness claimed him.

SIX
The Bookman Cometh

What fond and wayward thoughts will slide
Into a Lover's head!
"O mercy!" to myself I cried,
"If Lucy should be dead!"
  – William Wordsworth, "Lucy"

The darkness came and went. In moments of lucidity he could hear voices speaking in a murmur beside him, and his battered senses were assaulted by the wafting smell of boiled cabbage.

He shunned those moments of awakening, seeking only to return to the comforting darkness, where no dreams came and he was free of thought. But light came more and more frequently, accompanied by voices, cabbage, the feel of starched sheets against his cheek, until at last he was awake and could not escape.

He lay with his eyes closed, his back pressed against the mattress. Perhaps if he lay like this long enough he could escape again into dreamless sleep.

But no. The voices intruded, heedless of his despair.

"He's coming around," said a firm, no-nonsense kind of voice, male and authoritative: a doctor, Orphan thought.

A feminine voice, less harsh but carrying with it an equal – even greater – seal of authority, said, "It's about time."

"I won't let you interrogate him," the first voice said, sounding angry. "He needs to be left in peace."

The reply, Orphan thought, sounded tired, but there was a note of iron in the voice. "What he *needs* and what he is going to get are two different things, *Doctor*." She sighed; she had the trace of a Vespuccian accent. "Look, I'm sure you appreciate the importance of this investigation. I don't need to tell you what kind of pressure I'm under to get results. Moriarty–"

"Moriarty isn't head of this hospital," the doctor said, but he sounded resigned, as if the battle was lost even before it started. "If you ask me, the whole Martian debacle was inevitable, and the idea of flight into space preposterous."

"So vain is man, and so blinded by his vanity…" said his opponent quietly; it sounded like a well-used quote.

Orphan opened his eyes.

Leaning into him, their faces at an odd angle, so for a moment they seemed to him conjoined, the opposing faces of Janus, perhaps, one shadow and one light, were the two speakers. One was a man in his forties, with tanned, healthy skin, a thick moustache and friendly eyes that nevertheless, just at this moment, did not seem particularly pleased to be observing Orphan.

The other face Orphan dimly recognised, and wished he hadn't: Inspector Adler, the one woman he had hoped against odds to continue to avoid.

"I'm awake," he said.

"Good, good," the doctor said. A small cough. "Welcome to Guy's Hospital." He glanced sideways at Inspector Adler and pulled back a little. "You've had quite a severe shock. Now, I don't want to do this, but the Inspector over here needs to ask you some questions, and she's been waiting for over two days for you to come around. Do you think you could talk to her? You don't have to."

Orphan tried to laugh; it came out as a cough. "Oh, but I think I do," he said, and saw the doctor's small, helpless nod in reply. "I shall leave you then," the doctor said brusquely. "I will make sure there is a nurse immediately outside. If you need to terminate the interview at any point, just call for her."

"Thank you," Orphan said. "I will."

The doctor departed, and a moment later a nurse came in, a large woman in white, with a cheerful countenance. She helped Orphan sit up in his bed and propped two pillows under his head. "Don't you mind Dr W.," she said. "He's not had any sleep in two days, ever since that terrible accident in Richmond Park. He's a good man." She gave Irene Adler (who, throughout this, stood back without a word) an indecipherable look, said, "If you need anything, call. I'll be outside," and disappeared through the door.

Orphan was left alone in the room with Inspector Adler.

Now that she had him alone and to herself, the Inspector seemed in no hurry to begin the interview. She stood in silence and gazed at Orphan as if examining a small but fascinating exhibit. She looked, Orphan thought, like a person used to waiting; she looked like a copper.

Orphan was grateful for the silence. In his mind Lucy's image still burned, a flame that threatened to consume him. Gilgamesh's letter, his maddened flight to Richmond, his push through the crowds, Moriarty's speech, Lucy's dissipating smile...

Waves of black despair threatened to drown him.

"You heard the nurse," Irene Adler said. She approached Orphan's bed and stood looking down at him, her face thoughtful, a little – he thought – sad. "What happened in the park was a terrible accident." Her arms were folded on her chest. She had, Orphan thought, a beautiful voice. A singer's voice. He looked into her eyes and found unexpected sympathy.

"An accident," he said. The words were bitter in his mouth. They had the taste of preserved limes, needing to be spat out.

"Yes," Irene Adler said. She let the silence drag. Then, "You know, I have been interested in you for a while."

"Me?" His surprise was genuine. The Inspector smiled and shook her head at him, as if admonishing a wayward boy. "You are part of the Persons from Porlock, aren't you, Orphan? You and Tom Thumb and Wee Billy Conroy and 'Scalpel' Reece DuBois? Taking such delight in disrupting the work of eminent writers in the capital, dressed like clowns, quoting poor Ed Lear like the words of a mad Biblical prophet... and so sure of your invincibility, your invisibility, as if no one and nothing could touch you."

The Persons from Porlock! He looked up at her, suddenly confused. "You knew?"

"Of course I bloody knew," Irene Adler said. "As little as you clearly think of Scotland Yard, we are not fools... and certainly not clowns."

"I..." He faltered. "Have you come to arrest me?"

"Arrest you?" She seemed to contemplate the question. "For making a fool of yourself and sending up dear Oscar into the bargain? As tempting as that is, I think I'll decline."

Orphan's confusion deepened. "But what we did... the Queen..."

The Inspector shrugged. "Les Lézards may be overly fond of poetry," she said. "I, on the other hand, am not."

Orphan felt himself blinking stupidly. The Inspector's words were close to treason. Why, he wondered, was she telling him this? What did she want? He said, "I don't understand."

"No," Irene Adler said. "I don't suppose you do." She came closer to him then, and sat down on the edge of the bed, her face looking down directly into Orphan's. There were fine lines at the corners of her eyes, which were a deep, calm blue. "You're an enigma, Orphan," she said at last. "You show up at the Rose Theatre, and it ends up in flames. You show up a day later in Richmond Park – it ends up in flames. You belong to an organisation that terrorises writers and you live and work in the bookshop of a known seditionist. Why is it that trouble follows you around like a dog on a leash?" She leaned even closer towards him, and when she spoke, though her words were no more than a murmur, barely audible, they nevertheless hit Orphan like cold water evicted from a bucket and shook away the remnants of his dark sleep. "What is it about you that so draws the attention of the Bookman?"

Orphan wandered through the streets like a lost minotaur in a hostile, alien maze. Somewhere, unseen but deadly, was the Bookman: Orphan felt his presence like a ghostly outline, a shapeless, formless thing, a disembodied entity that hid in the fog and watched him from the rooftops and the drains.

What is it about you, Irene Adler had said, *that so draws the attention of the Bookman?*

Her words kept running through his mind, a question lost in a maze of its own, seeking an answer he didn't know.

He had not answered her. Irene Adler, after examining him for a long, uncomfortable moment, said, "Do you miss her?"

A wave of anger took over Orphan. He could think of nothing to say, no suitable reply to that meaningless, cruel question. Looking at him, Irene Adler sighed. She said, "If it was in your power, would you bring her back?"

Their eyes locked. It seemed to Orphan that an invisible contest was taking place, a battle of wills between them, like a jousting tournament for a prize that was unknown.

He said, "She's dead."

The silence stretched between them, dark as an ocean under a moonless sky. Irene Adler stretched and walked away from him. She paced around the room, circling, coming closer, drawing back, as if trying to decide something unpleasant. She stopped by the window and looked out. When she spoke her face was turned away from Orphan. She said, "Death is the undiscovered country…"

She waited. The light from the window touched her face and pronounced the fineness of her features. She turned her head and looked at Orphan, eyes tired but still full of life, containing within them both a challenge and a question.

Orphan completed, as if compelled to answer, the Inspector's quote, the words torn out of him. "From whose bourn no traveller returns…" He sat up in the bed. "What do you want from me?" he whispered.

The Inspector, unexpectedly, smiled. "You still don't understand, do you?" she said. "Did your friend Gilgamesh not try to tell you?" She saw his startled expression and shook her head. "Oh, Orphan. Why is it that everyone you touch seems to die? You are like Hamlet, Prince of Denmark, wandering the halls of your mind, not daring to act until all is lost. This is the time of myths, Orphan. They are the cables that run under the floors and power the world, the conduits of unseen currents, the steam that powers the great engines of the earth. Would you bring her back if you could?"

The question again, flung at him like a hook on a fishing line. Ready to reel him in.

And Orphan, caught, said, "Tell me how."

He walked away from Guy's Hospital through the maze of Southwark's streets. "Not here," Irene Adler had said. She had glanced about her, and Orphan, following the direction of her eyes, saw they were focused on an ancient-looking bible that rested by his bedside. "Here." She handed him a piece of paper. Orphan opened it, read an address and a time.

"Get well," Irene Adler said, and then she was gone, closing the door softly behind her.

It had taken Orphan two more days before the doctor released him. The waves of darkness came and went, grief washing over him, Lucy's burning image waking him in the night with screams that echoed only inside his head.

Yet overlaying the grief was Irene Adler's question. *Would you bring her back?* she had asked – and the question, with its implication, its insane promise, had consumed Orphan until he could think of little else.

He did examine the bible that rested by his bedside. It was an old volume, printed the previous century, rebound in contemporary cloth. Grubby and worn, it had the look of a bible that had rested, over the decades, in the hands of more than one dying patient. It was a King James bible, of the translation sanctioned, for his own mysterious reasons, by that greatest of all Lizard Kings, yet it was not published by the King's printer: it was an illegal publication. Orphan turned the book in his hands, intrigued. The publisher's name was given as Thomas Guy. Orphan seemed to remember, vaguely, that the founder of the hospital had indeed begun his career in the printing and selling of illegal bibles. That must be, therefore, one of them, he thought. But why had Irene Adler looked to it before falling quiet? What was it about the book (if that was indeed what had concerned her) to prevent her from speaking further? It was just a book.

Restless, alone with his dark thoughts in his room, Orphan began paging through Thomas Guy's bible. First he shook the book, edges down, but nothing had fallen from within its pages. Next he thumbed through the book, seeking to see where it would open: it should, he knew, come to the place that had been most used. And so it did, and the old bible opened in his lap onto the eighth chapter of the first book of Samuel. It was the part where the elders of Israel come to Samuel, an old man now, and ask him to make them a king. Orphan read Samuel's reply to the elders, and felt a strange apprehension reach out to wrap cold fingers around his chest, as if the ancient, anonymous writer of the text was addressing him, replying to an unanswered question.

> And he said, This will be the manner of the King that shall reign over you: He will take your sons, and appoint them for himself, for his chariots, and to be his horsemen; and some shall run before his chariots. And he will appoint him captains over thousands, and captains over fifties; and will set them to ear his

ground, and to reap his harvest, and to make his instruments of war, and instruments of his chariots.
And he will take your daughters to be confectionar-
ies, and to be cooks, and to be bakers.
And he will take your fields, and your vineyards, and
your oliveyards, even the best of them, and give them
to his servants.
And he will take the tenth of your seed, and of your
vineyards, and give to his officers, and to his servants.
And he will take your menservants, and your maid-
servants, and your goodliest young men, and your
asses, and put them to his work.
He will take the tenth of your sheep: and ye shall be
his servants.

And ye shall be his servants. Something was crystallis-
ing in Orphan's head, the beginning of understanding;
that in the maze of texts there was hidden a message,
an interpretation of a past like a thread that aimed to
lead him onwards, to traverse the filthy streets of history. Numbly, he wondered how King James, and all
his get who came after, had allowed passages like this to
be printed. And then, at the bottom left corner of the
page, in a pencil mark so faint that he almost missed it,
he saw the inscription that waited there, almost as if it
had been waiting for him, just him, through all the patient years: *The Bookman Cometh.*

SEVEN
Body-Snatchers

The body-snatchers, they have come
And made a snatch at me.
It's very hard them kind of men
Won't let a body be.

You thought that I was buried deep
Quite decent like and chary;
But from her grave in Mary-bone
They've come and bon'd your Mary!

The arm that us'd to take your arm
Is took to Dr Vyse,
And both my legs are gone to walk
The Hospital at Guy's.
  – Thomas Hood, Whims and Oddities

Away from Guy's, through the narrow maze of South-wark streets. Dusk was falling, and on the other side of the river, through the fog, the great city lit up in thousands of moth-like flames, in hundreds and hundreds of lit butterflies, their wings beating against the stillness of dark, fighting the night with their simple existence. A week before, and Orphan would have stopped, taken out his small notepad and his pen, scribbled a few lines, composed a minor poem, recorded the motion of the light in dark air.

Not now.

Away from the hospital, away from the echoing corridors and the hushed expectant silence punctuated by dying screams. Away from the cold stone and the musty watching bibles in every room, and away from the food that churned the stomach, and the sharp stench of industrial cleaning fluids. He walked through the fog and felt the presence of the Bookman like a ghostly outline, a shapeless, formless thing, a disembodied entity that hid in the foul air and watched him from the rooftops and the drains.

The second night at Guy's, unable to sleep, uneasy with the presence of the pirate bible by his bedside, he stood from his bed. The floor was cold under his feet but he welcomed the sensation. He walked out of the room and shut the door behind him.

He walked through empty corridors and listened to the sick behind their doors. No one stopped him, no one challenged him to return to his bed. He was alone as a wraith, haunting the hospital as if he were already dead.

The cold wrapped itself around him, rising like the shoots of a flower from the ground and into his feet and up, entombing him. He passed through ill-lit wards and looked out of the windows and saw nothing but black night draped across the hospital.

His footsteps led him, by twists and turns, down-wards, so that he passed floor after floor in this fashion, his bare feet padding silently in his journey through the endless corridors.

He pushed open a door marked MEDICAL SCHOOL, and descended a flight of stairs, and the air grew even colder, and was filled with a chemical tang that burned the back of his throat. I should wake, he thought. I should not be walking here. But he could not stop; he was trapped in a dream and could not rouse.

And yet, now that he was here he could go no fur-ther. The basement, he realised. A long corridor stretched before him. Electric lights hummed and flared and dimmed in naked bulbs suspended from the ceiling like grotesque blinking eyes. A row of doors stood shut like the flooded mouths of underwater caves. He heard voices, approaching, and turned back, and hid against the wall, his head turned to observe the happenings in the corridor he had just vacated.

There was the sound of something heavy being dragged against the floor, and the laboured breathing of two or more men. Orphan looked, and saw that there were indeed two men there, and that each was dragging behind him a sack. Both had clean-shaven faces of ordinary features, almost pleasant. They stopped before a door in the middle of the corridor and the one on the left knocked twice.

The door opened and a man came out. He looked from side to side furtively, and on his face was a nerv-ous, almost frightened expression. Orphan recognised him – it was the doctor who had first examined him.

"What ho, Dr W.?" the man on the left said. "We got you a good one, on my word of honour." He looked at his companion and smiled. "Two good ones, and fresh."

"Shut up, fool," the doctor growled. He raised his hand and touched his moustache nervously, then motioned the two men. "Bring the Things in. Quickly." As the door opened Orphan saw there were other men in the room, though he could not see them clearly.

As the two men walked through the door they struggled with their sacks, and the one on the right momentarily came loose; and Orphan watched with horror as a slender, white leg protruded from its opening.

The doctor halted when he saw this.

"I did not ask you for a female, Bishop," he said. "I will not pay for a Thing I do not need."

"It is not a woman but a big small," the man – Bishop – said in a wounded tone. "Look." And he opened the sack fully as it lay on the threshold of the room.

The corpse that sprawled out was indeed not that of a woman. It was a boy, aged, Orphan thought, around fifteen or sixteen. His face were strangely peaceful, as if he were only asleep and would soon wake up and demand his tea, and his features were strong but delicate, a face that had once known comfortable living.

The doctor looked with distaste at the two men. "What did he die of, Bishop?" He turned to look at the other man, who was standing grinning with his sack held securely in his hand, "May?"

"I neither know nor care," Bishop said, and his companion, May, nodded and said, "It is quite indifferent what he died of, for here he is, stiff enough."

"Get in, damn it!" The voice that came from within the room had the tone of command in it, and the doctor and the two body-snatchers (for that, Orphan realised, was what they must be, two resurrection men plying their trade) hurried through the door, the doctor shutting it behind him in a hurry.

Orphan, for whom the whole gruesome scene still seemed no more than a part of his nightmare, padded around the corner into the corridor, and peered through the keyhole.

Inside, the argument was continuing.

"This subject is too fresh," the doctor said, and the two men laughed. "The fact is," Bishop said, "you are not in the habit of seeing fresh subjects and you don't know anything about it!"

The same commanding voice Orphan heard before now growled, "We need the Thing fresh, so stop arguing about it and get to work!"

But the doctor did not easily give up. "I don't think it was ever buried," he said. "Where had it come from?"

"You know nothing about raising bodies!" Bishop said. He seemed truly exasperated.

"Enough," the man who seemed to be in charge said, and all fell quiet. Orphan, peering through, could not make out his face: all he could discern was a remarkable bulk, coupled with power.

Orphan squirmed against the door, trying for a better angle.

For a moment, the whole room spread out before him: there were the two resurrection men, standing to one side with their gruesome merchandise; the doctor, hovering nervously beside what appeared to be a huge coffin; the fat man, sitting in an armchair, himself surveying the room; two more men, strangely similar in appearance, dressed in white medical smocks, standing next to a vast array of machinery pulsating with lights.

What was in the coffin? Vapours rose from it, icy white tendrils that turned the room into a still, cold space like the inside of a slaughterhouse. A mortuary, Orphan thought. The coffin was long, metallic, over six feet long. It must have held a tall person, he thought. But who?

He blinked, took a slow, quiet breath. Yes. He could discern a face, thin, with a hawkish nose and a square, prominent chin. The eyes were open and stared into nothing, as if the man was not quite dead but rather drugged to an extreme, until he had taken on the semblance of death.

The fat man stirred in his armchair. "Pay them and get rid of them," he said to the doctor. "You must try the procedure again."
Then he turned his head towards the door. He seemed to be looking directly at Orphan.

Orphan froze. Then the fat man shook his head, minutely, as if saying, "This is not for you," and he lifted a cane that rested by his side and made a motion with it, and one of the men moved against the door and blocked Orphan's view. Orphan ran from the door, but it remained unopened. No one was pursuing him.

Did the fat man know that he was there? He had warned him away. Hadn't he? Did he know him? He shuddered, suddenly feeling the cold. He felt entirely awake now. The body-snatchers will come out any minute, he thought. He did not want to be there. The cold overwhelmed him, made his teeth chatter. Everywhere he turned there was death.

He turned and ran away the way he had come, his feet noiseless on the stone floor.

Away from Guy's, away from its ghoulish dreams, its baroque mysteries. Away from the hospital with the falling of night, through the cobblestone streets and onto the south bank. The fog intensified around him, became a thick screen that blotted out the stars and erased the city as if it had never existed. Orphan hurried, shivering despite his coat. The lonely sound of his footsteps was muffled by the fog.

He walked past streetlamps that bled a wet yellow light, making his way by memory rather than sight. A chill wind rose from the Thames and pummelled him, and he drew the coat tighter around himself and turned away from the river bank, until at last he reached the great edifice of Waterloo Station, jutting out of the fog like a dark citadel. It seemed to him a living thing then, a grotesque, giant face that breathed loudly, the sound of its inhaling and exhaling composed of the steady rhythm of trains. He skirted the station, encountering few people. Those who were out in this foul weather hurried past him without glancing his way, and Orphan had the sudden feeling that he was invisible, a ghost wandering in an unreal world.

He stopped by one of the great stone arches. A lonely figure lay huddled on the floor, wrapped in grey blankets. Orphan crouched down, and the figure stirred. A mane of shaggy hair emerged and two large eyes, milky-white and unseeing, stared up at Orphan. "Spare some change?" the beggar said hopefully.

Orphan was startled. He had almost, for a moment, believed it was Gilgamesh, returned. "What is your name?" he asked, and he reached into his pocket for what money he had.

He dropped the meagre coins he found into the beggar's bowl. The man raised his face further; his blind eyes seemed to search Orphan's face, to study them. Then the unblinking eyes grew wider, and his pale face turned paler still, and his breath caught in his throat; and Orphan, worried for the man's health, grabbed him by the shoulder and said, "What ails you, my friend?"

The beggar moved away, as if the touch of Orphan's hand was more than he could bear. "Not so much noise, my lord!" he hissed. "Sweet prince, speak low: the King your father is disposed to sleep."

Was the man a failed Shakespearean actor? Orphan wondered. He said, gently, "My name is Orphan."

The beggar did a thing that startled Orphan. He laughed. It was a curious sound, hoarse and weak like a failing engine. Then he said, "Sweet prince, the untainted virtue of your years hath not yet dived into the world's deceit, nor more can you distinguish of a man than of his outward show."

He spoke, it seemed to Orphan, with great intensity, as if his words carried a meaning far beyond their stage-use. But, "I'm sorry," Orphan said, "I don't understand."

Sighing, he rose to leave. He was already late for his meeting with the Inspector.

The beggar bowed his head. Then he said, half-muttering before retreating back into his blankets, "Now cracks a noble heart. Good night sweet prince: and flights of angels sing thee to thy rest!"

"Thank you," Orphan said, "I think." And he walked onwards, as the beggar under his arch was swallowed in the fog.

He walked around the great edifice of the station; and it was not long before he reached another arch where, underneath, small glass windows glowed with an internal warmth, and a small door stood waiting like a welcoming embrace, and a small sign hanging above the door said, The Lizard's Head.

EIGHT
Lord Byron's Simulacrum

The beings of the mind are not of clay;
Essentially immortal, they create
And multiply in us a brighter ray.
  – Lord Byron, "Childe Harold's Pilgrimage"

He pushed the door open and went inside. Heat assailed him, a cloud of tobacco smoke engulfed him, and with them came the sizzle of frying sausages, and the smell of beer that had, over the years, seeped into the very foundations of the pub.

The pub was dark, smoky, and full of hazily seen figures. Orphan removed his coat and looked about him for Irene Adler. He saw a white hand beckoning to him from a booth in the corner, and went to join her, next to a small ship's-window that had fog climbing to it outside like ivy.

"Sit down," Irene Adler said.

She was sitting alone, a half-drunk glass of white wine before her. Her bright, alert eyes had dark rings around. "I'll get a drink," Orphan said.

He went to the bar, paid, and returned with a tall glass. As he sat down opposite the inspector a shadow fell across the table.

He had seen that face before. The black curly hair, the sharp nose, the smooth features: Lord Byron. A youthful Lord Byron, without the ravages of time. "Byron," Irene Adler said. "Please, sit down. Orphan, this is Lord Byron."

Byron sat next to the Inspector, opposite Orphan. He didn't speak. Orphan, captivated – he had seldom seen one of its kind before – studied him overtly.

It was disconcerting. The youthful features, the hair, even the eyes seemed that of a young man, but now, as he examined them, he thought: they are precise and unchanging, the way a doll's are. This was not Byron, the poet, the rebel, who was long time dead. It was a re-markable simulation of a man, yet a simulation all the same, and now that he could see that, could examine him in this way, in an almost intimate fashion, Orphan noticed the way the face moved mechanically from one expression to another, the too-sharp angles of the body, even, when Byron turned his head to look at Irene, the small, tell-tale metal tag that was embedded discreetly in his neck.

Byron turned his head back to Orphan and now Or-phan could see that the eyes, too, were unreal: they were glassy, marble-like, devoid of feeling or even true sight. The Byron simulacrum sighed (and Orphan mar-velled at the way his chest moved, the way the air travelled through its throat and nose) and said, "I am not human."

There was a silence. Orphan could think of nothing to say in reply.

At last, it was Irene who spoke. She looked across the table at Orphan and said, "Do you remember what happened at the Rose?"

Orphan, looking at her, thought of Lucy.

"Describe it to me."

He shook himself. His mind slipped back to what he had seen. Henry Irving, in his guise as Shakespeare. Beerbohm Tree stepping onto the stage as the Ancient Mariner holding in his hands a heavy, leather-bound folio. Irving opening the book.

The book exploding.

"What happened to Beerbohm?"

Orphan, lost, looked into Irene's eyes. He had not thought of the young actor. He tried to think back, but could conjure no clear image. "Did he not die in the explosion?"

Irene looked down into her wine glass. The Byron simulacrum sat quietly, like a machine that had been temporarily switched off. "What I tell you is a state secret," Irene said at last. "But I think we are beyond secrets now, Orphan." She raised her face, and he could see the deep weariness in her eyes, the moving shadows.

"Beerbohm Tree was found, dead, in an abandoned warehouse by the docks a few hours after the explosion at the Rose. He had been there since at least the previous day. He had not been at the Rose at all." She twisted the stem of the wine glass. "When we… when I found him, there was not much left of him. His hands were clasped about what was left of his chest. They held a blackened, broken object. It might have once been a book."

"The Bookman..." Orphan said. "But I saw him there," he objected. "I saw him at the theatre." Even to himself he sounded petulant. Then his eyes fell on Byron and he whispered, "It was a machine."

The Byron automaton stirred. "Was it?" he said. "What is a machine, Orphan? La Mettrie wrote that 'the human body is a machine which winds its own springs'. Can a machine act in a play? Can a machine play music? Can a machine love?"

"I... I don't know," Orphan said. He looked from Byron to Irene. "I don't understand." He wanted to shout. "What has this got to do with Lucy?"

"Following the explosion in Richmond Park," Irene Adler said, "a brief, powerful burst of concentrated energy was recorded, originating at the very moment the book exploded in Lucy's hands. We have recorded a similar transmission after the explosion at the Rose. These books with which the Bookman so cunningly kills – they are not mere books. They are devices."

Orphan swallowed. The beer stood forgotten on the table before him. He said, "Devices of what?"

"Perhaps," Irene said, so quietly she may have been speaking to herself, "they are recording devices."

"And they record... what?" He thought back to the Rose, to the counterfeit Beerbohm Tree, indistinguishable from the real thing. As if the man had been copied in his entirety, as if he had been recreated, made anew, and left to perform his role as if nothing had happened... And he said, in a hushed voice, the thought cooling him down as if he were still outside, and it was snowing, "You think he takes people's souls."

Lucy, he suddenly thought. So that was what the Inspector had wanted him to understand. If she was not killed, but merely... what? Abducted? Translated? Taken by the lord of Hades, to reside forever in his dark and lonely court?

"Perhaps," Irene Adler said. There was such pain in her eyes that, for a moment, Orphan couldn't bear to look at them. She was, he thought, gazing inwards, looking deep within herself at a memory he could not see. She, too, he thought suddenly, the realisation striking him, had lost someone she loved to the Bookman. And he wondered who it was.

Across the table from him Byron stirred again. "La Mettrie," Byron said, "says that 'the soul is but an empty word, of which no one has any idea, and which an enlightened man should only use to signify the part in us that thinks. Given the least principle of motion, animated bodies will have all that is necessary for moving, feeling, thinking, repenting, or in a word for conducting themselves in the physical realm, and in the moral realm which depends upon it.'" He sighed and looked down at himself, and shook his head as if confused. "I will ask you again," he said. "What is a machine?"

But Orphan didn't answer. Could it be, he wondered – could Lucy, somehow, still be alive? Could she come back, the way Beerbohm Tree had come back, if only for a short while? He said, his voice choking, "How could I get her back?"

"Listen," Irene said. She inched her ear at Byron, prompting him to speak.

"I don't know who – what – the Bookman is," Byron said. "But I know this: there are more artificers on this earth than the bureaucrats of the Babbage company who made me. I am but a machine. I am human-made, and as imperfect as a human. But I listen." His eyes, those great and vacant marbles, were no longer empty, and he turned his head in a delicate movement, as if listening to something unheard. "I listen to the talk of machines, to the exchange of Tesla communications, to the constant hum of the aether. We simulacra are rare and far apart, so far. But we talk to each other, and to others who are not like us in form, but whose souls are. And the rumours persist."

He spoke with a great gravity, and a little sadness. And it seemed to Orphan that he knew why, for surely what he was learning was a secret to these beings, and not easily shared. Impulsively he said, "Thank you, my Lord," and saw the Byron simulacrum smile. "I am not Byron," he said. "I am made to look like him, to sound like him, to quote his words and pretend his moods. But I do not have his talent for poetry, nor his love of it…" He sighed again, and for a moment he was Byron, an older, wiser lord who carried a heavier burden on his slim shoulders.

After a moment, Orphan said, "What rumours do you hear?"

Byron raised his head and his fingers tapped a gentle rhythm on the tabletop. "That there are others, like us and not. That there are other, alien beings, not human nor mechanical, but something of both." He shook his head. "A storm is coming, Orphan. A great storm that travels over the sea and lashes the waves into submission, whose origin is one island and its destination another. We believe…"

He fell silent.

"Believe what?"

"It is of no importance."

"Please," Orphan said. The simulacrum smiled. "I do not know who, or what, the Bookman is," he said. "All I know is that he is bound, whether in love or in hate – and the two are often merely two aspects of the same emotion – with Les Lézard. And the story is told that – like love and hate, perhaps – the Bookman too has an opposite. Perhaps another aspect of himself. Who knows? Is he real? Is the Bookman?"

"He killed… he killed Lucy."

"Ah, empirical evidence," Byron said. "Yes. Again, I'm sorry."

"What do you believe?"

Byron laughed. It was a grating, harsh sound. "We believe in the Translation," he said.

"Translation of what?"

"The translation, perhaps, of us all. Goodbye, Orphan." He stood, then, pushing his chair back, his movements stiff and unnatural like those of a toy. "But what your part in this is, if any, I do not know."

He made to turn away from them. But Orphan stopped him, rising and putting his hand on the simulacrum's shoulder. "Please," he said. "Who can I turn to?"

Byron turned to him, and for a long moment they stood facing each other, unmoving, Orphan's hand resting on Byron's shoulder.

At last Byron turned away. Orphan's arm dropped to his side. The simulacrum began to make his way towards the door, his steps slow and heavy and mechanical.

Halfway he stopped, and turned back. Orphan watched him, the fine, pale, manufactured face looking back at him as if seeking an answer to a different question. Then it changed, as if a corner of a picture-puzzle had become suddenly clear to him, and he smiled and said, in a quiet voice that nevertheless carried across the room, "Ask the Turk."

NINE
At the Cock-Pit

A forum there is for debate,
A Fives Court for milling in fun, Sirs,
A Parliament House for the great,
With a cock-pit for cruelty's sport, Sirs.
   – John Ashton, *The Treats of London*

Orphan walked home across the bridge, deep in
thought. When Byron left he had finished his drink and
thanked Irene Adler. They barely spoke, each of them
isolated in a separate pool of thought. He wanted again
to ask her who she had lost, but thought better of it
when he saw the expression in her eyes. Instead, he
rose from the table and made his way outside, where an
icy fog had settled over the city like a pale northern invader.

His footsteps barely echoed as he walked across the
bridge. He could see no living thing, as if the city was
deserted, and he was alone in it, the last living man left
in a ghost town. Even the whales were silent. To save
Lucy, he thought, I must find the Bookman. But where

do I start? He missed her, with a terrible urgency that surprised him even as it hurt. They were bound together, he and her.

When he reached the Strand he thought he heard a soft smooth sound coming from above his head and, raising it, glimpsed for a moment the movement of a velvety darkness low in the skies. An unmarked black airship, he thought, and almost laughed to himself. It was a fanciful idea, one of Jack's. He continued past St Martin in the Fields, and thought he caught another glimpse of the blimp, passing high to his left. He walked up St Martin's Lane and turned left with relief into Cecil Court.

Payne's was a haven of light in a dark world. Stepping inside, he was nearly overwhelmed with the feeling of home. The familiar, conflicting smells of the books vied for his attention. The musty tang of old volumes, the polished smell of new leather bindings, the crisp clear scent of freshly printed books, all rose to greet him, like a horde of somewhat-dysfunctional relatives at a family event.

Lit candles were scattered haphazardly around the room, perched precariously on piles of books and on the long counter. They cast spheres of light interlinked by shadows that fluttered like painted eyelids. He made his way into the back room and found his bed unaltered and waiting for him, a worn, comfortable companion.

On the small table rested a sputtering candle and beside it were two glasses and Jack's bottle of Old Bushmills.

It's like I hadn't left, Orphan thought. It's as if the last few days never happened, as if I only just came back from meeting Lucy. He felt a sense of unreality steal over him, but the sense of loss he felt was real enough, and would not let him sink into comforting dreams. Instead he lay down on the bed. Behind closed eyelids the candle flickered, lulling him into sleep. He felt exhausted, still weak from his injuries, and cold.

"Orphan."

When he opened his eyes the candle had burned down to a stub. One of the glasses on the table was missing and the bottle had been moved. A shadow-cowled figure watched him from the doorway and for a moment he felt panic, ascribing to the unseen face the hideous countenance of a nightmare: he had fallen asleep, he realised, and he dreamed… he dreamed of the Bookman, a monstrous being made of the yellowing pages of thousands of books, with a face like bleached vellum and gilt-edged eyes, who stalked him through a maze of bookshelves where no light penetrated.

The figure in the doorway moved and it was only Jack, holding a glass half-full with amber liquid. His face was drawn and tired, with shadows around his eyes.

"Jack."

He sat up, feeling groggy. His foot hit a shelf and sent books flying to the floor. He shook his head, trying to dispel the cobwebs that stretched inside it, and with them the last images of his dream. Jack came forward and sat down in the chair opposite. He poured drink into the remaining glass and offered it to Orphan. "I'm sorry."

Orphan nodded and accepted the drink, and they sat in silence. Orphan contemplated the glass in his hands and could think of nothing to say. It was Jack, therefore, who finally broke the silence. "What will you do now?" he said, and he looked at Orphan with his head cocked to one side, a strangely sorrowful expression on his face.

But Orphan didn't know. He felt disorientated, unsure of the time, unsure even if it was still night, or whether day had crept over the city while he was sleeping. So he said, "What's the time?" and watched Jack nod, as if Orphan's question had confirmed something he had previously only suspected. "Four, four-thirty." He must have seen the confusion in Orphan's eyes. "In the morning." He stood up suddenly, depositing an empty glass on the table. "Come with me."

"What is it, Jack?"

His friend shook his head. "I want to show you something. Come."

With a groan, Orphan rose from the bed. He felt curiously light-headed, as if this was all but part of a bad dream, and he was still asleep. He left his untouched drink on the table besides Jack's glass and followed him out of the room.

The door banged behind them as they stepped outside the shop. Though the fog had abated the air was cold and damp, and a strong stench, as of an open sewer, filled the air. It had rained while Orphan slept, but it had done nothing to cleanse the city. Black velvety night pressed oppressively over Cecil Court, unhindered by the feeble gas lights that stood on St Martin's Lane.

He followed Jack without speaking. They crossed St Martin's and went through New Row, past shuttered shops and onto King Street. He could hear the sounds of a fight, screams and breaking glass followed by hoarse, wild laughter coming from the old Bucket of Blood pub on nearby Rose Street.

Jack led him on. The market square, lit by gaslight, was a place of shadows and squalor. Tired prostitutes, mainly women but with two or three bare-chested men amidst them, converged in small groups underneath the roofed market, negotiating with late revellers who seemed unsteady on their feet. A man cursed loudly and was pushed away; he walked off, still swearing loudly. On the corner of the Opera House a man stood behind a stall and a small fire, and the heavy smell of frying onions and sausage-meat filled the square like a march of invading soldiers.

Orphan liked Covent Garden during the day, when the fruit and vegetable market was open and continental restaurants filled the air with the scents of garlic and cooking spices. He avoided it at night, when it became, or so it seemed, the lode-stone that exerted its powerful pull on every lecher and drunk in the Lizardine Empire. Even this late the barely discreet bawdy-houses on the side streets were no doubt operating, and the pubs and drinking establishments were still seeing out the late stragglers who refused to wave goodbye to the night and adjourn at last to their beds. He wondered what they were doing there at this hour, Jack and him, but his will seemed to have seeped out of him, and he merely followed in Jack's footsteps, not asking the

question, content to merely walk on through the haze
of the market.

They walked past a group of drunk students half-
shouting and half-singing the words to the old
favourite, "If I Had A Donkey Wot Wouldn't Go". Orphan smiled when he heard the closing words, followed
by a last, spirited chorus:

> *Bill's donkey was ordered into Court,*
> *In which he caused a deal of sport,*
> *He cocked his ears, and opened his jaws,*
> *As if he wished to plead his cause.*
> *I proved I'd been uncommonly kind,*
> *The ass got a verdict – Bill got fined;*
> *For his worship and me was of one mind –*

And he said… (and here the chanting students raised
their voices even higher, and shouted again the refrain)
– and he said!

> *If I had a donkey wot wouldn't go,*
> *I never would wollop him, no, no, no!*
> *I'd give him some hay, and cry Gee! Whoa!*
> *And come up, Neddy! And come up, Neddy!*

And they disappeared in a burst of laughter around
the corner. Jack marched on. Orphan followed.

It wasn't long before they arrived in Drury Lane.
Jack stopped outside a deserted-looking building. A fading sign that looked like a remnant from another
century entirely declared the place as the King's Arms

Tavern. The windows were boarded up and the gas-lamp outside was broken, casting the area into gloom. Orphan found himself wondering if the sun would ever rise again. He blew on his hands to try to warm them. He could taste the faint tang of leaking gas in the air.

Jack went to a small door set into the side of the building. It was plain, made of rough, unvarnished wood. Jack knocked, a complicated beat.

They waited.

Presently they could hear steps, and the door opened.

"Wha' do you want?"

The woman filled the doorway. Fat rolled down her neck as she surveyed them with small hard eyes. The fat spread down to her arms and disappeared underneath the long fur coat that must have been made from the skins of an entire skulk of foxes. She raised a languid hand on which heavy rings cut into fleshy fingers. "Jackie, issat you?"

Jack surprised Orphan by reaching out and taking the woman's hand in his. "Mother Jolley," he said, and almost, it seemed to Orphan, bent down to kiss the woman's – who did not look at all jolly, to him – hand. "You get prettier every time I see you."

"Spare me yer flattery, cur," but she looked momentarily pleased.

Then the small, suspicious eyes shifted to Orphan. "Who's your friend?" She reached out her hand, extending it before her like a crane, and grasped Orphan's face between her fingers, pulling hard at his cheeks. "He has doleful eyes like a dog what's been kicked by 'is mistress." And she cackled at her own words, until a bout of coughing took her over and she let go of Orphan's face, though he knew she had left her mark on his skin before doing so.

"A friend," Jack said, and a look was exchanged between him and Mother Jolley whose meaning became clear to Orphan only when Jack added, "a comrade."

The fat woman surveyed Orphan for a moment longer, as if dubious of his entitlement to such distinction. Finally, with a reluctant nod, she moved back and pulled the door open. "Follow me, gents."

Orphan, shooting Jack a glance that said, *what the hell is going on?*, followed him nevertheless, and the three of them, like an ill-matched family of nestling dolls, walked in single file into a narrow hallway, where the accumulated decades of tobacco smoke lay sedately in the still air.

They walked down a flight of stairs that opened onto a stone-walled antechamber, empty save for a large, stout oak door. Mother Jolley moved aside, allowing Orphan and Jack to crowd beside her. The door had no handle; Mother Jolley pressed a hidden lever on the wall and the door swung open, making no sound.

But noise erupted through the open door, as startling as a gale. The hoarse shouts of excited men and women mingled with the scream of animals, and a heavy, musky scent ebbed into the air of the antechamber, the mixture of human sweat and excitement – and of fear and animal faeces.

Jack walked through, and Orphan followed. Mother Jolley herded them in and the door closed behind her, shutting out the above-stairs world.

"Welcome to the cock pit," she said.

Orphan looked around. They were in a wide basement. Burning torches hung on the walls, giving the place the aura of a Middle Ages torture chamber. The ground was uneven and sloped down until it became a circular arena. It was surrounded by people – mostly men, but some women too – all shouting, waving fists, flashing money.

Inside the ring two large roosters fought in a cloud of blood and feathers. Orphan, sickened, followed Jack to the edge of the crowd. The roosters had small, thin blades attached where their spurs should have been. The blades flashed in the torchlight. The screaming of the fighting birds filled the air with menace.

Jack was circling the ring. Orphan followed him, and they finally came to a stop in a dark corner of the basement, where Jack leaned against the wooden supports that rose from ground to ceiling. He motioned to Orphan to do the same.

"Why," Orphan said, having to almost shout to be heard over the noise of the fight, "are we here?"

Jack nodded. "Now, that is the question," he agreed. "Why are any of us here? What is our purpose on this earth?"

He flashed Orphan a grin, which wasn't returned.

In the ring, a red-and-black rooster was crowned the winner. The lifeless corpse of its opponent was scooped off the ground. Orphan followed the man who lifted it – a short, stocky man wearing a bloodied butcher's apron – as he carried the dead bird to the opposite side of the basement from them. Coals glowed in a brazier, and on a wire mesh chicken pieces sizzled and smoked. The man in the apron laid the latest carcass on the surface of a table by the coals and began plucking feathers.

"I wasn't joking," Jack said. He turned to Orphan and looked hard into his face. "Why we are here – why we are here – that's a question I think you need to have answered for you."

The umpire, a tall moustachioed man with pale, blotchy skin that made his head look like a mushroom that had never seen the sun, announced the next bout, and two fresh roosters were kicked into the ring, where they immediately set on each other.

"Did you think to ask yourself," Jack said, speaking softly despite the noise of the crowd, forcing Orphan to bend closer to listen to him, "just why the Bookman wished to destroy the Martian probe in the park? Or did you think, as you seem to, that his one and only purpose was to hurt you? That he launched that public, spectacular attack just to hurt the girl you loved?"

The girl he still loved, Orphan thought. He resented Jack that moment. He straightened, avoiding Jack's eyes. The truth, he realised, was that he did think that, did not – could not – comprehend another reason, no sense in the act that took Lucy away. He turned his head from his friend, focusing on the crowd. Movement caught his attention. That head. It looked familiar. As if in response a man in the crowd turned and their eyes met, and though the man did not give any sign that he knew him, Orphan recognised him immediately: it was Karl Marx.

When Marx turned back to the fight Orphan noticed that the figure next to him, though it was dressed in a long coat and its head was cowled, was that of a woman; and he was not surprised when, a moment later, the cowled head turned towards him, revealing the face of Isabella Beeton.

So the Parliament of Payne was complete and present.

Mrs Beeton, too, did not acknowledge him; and a moment later she had turned back and was swallowed in the crowd as though she had never been.

"What are *they* doing here?"

"The same thing we are doing," Jack said beside him. "Watching."

"The cockfight?"

Jack drew further into the shadows. He lifted his hand, his finger pointing upwards. "Them."

Orphan looked up.

Though the ceiling was low, a small balcony was erected halfway above the floor, made of wooden boards and surrounded by a thin balustrade. Three figures stood there: and though one was a man, the other two were of aristocratic stock.

They were lizards.

TEN
The Woman in White

The paleness grew whiter on her face, and she turned it farther away from me.

"Don't speak of to-morrow," she said. "Let the music speak to us of to-night, in a happier language than ours."

– Wilkie Collins, *The Woman in White*

In the ring, a wounded rooster and a dead one were taken away. Something that was not quite a hush settled over the crowd then: a kind of tense, anticipatory stillness.

The umpire reappeared. He looked tense himself, and kept casting quick, darting glances at the balcony.

"Ladies and gentlemen, doxies and rakes!" the umpire cried. "Get ready to be shocked, prepare to be amazed! The fight of the night is about to commence!" Again he looked up, saw the silent watchers on the balcony, hesitated. His Adam's apple bobbed up and down.

Leaning against the wall, in the shadows, Orphan, too, was watching the lizards. They were two tall, distinguished beings, dressed in simple (yet obviously expensive), sober suits, with gentlemen's hats perched on their scaly heads. They moved forward now, their claws resting on the balustrade. They watched the ring intensely. Their tongues hissed out every so often and tasted the air.

The man beside them was uncommonly fat. He stood apart from the lizards, his attention not on the ring but on its audience. His head moved, slowly and methodically, as he scanned the room. Suddenly, as if aware he was being watched, he turned his head sharply and met Orphan's eyes.

It was the man from the mortuary at Guy's.

The man nodded, once, then winked at Orphan. Orphan hurriedly turned his eyes back to the ring. He was discomfited by the fat man, and not just by the memory of their previous encounter. He could not tell what it was that had so unnerved him. *He knows me,* he thought. *He was waiting for me.* He reminded him of a spider that had lain in wait in the centre of a cobweb, the trap so light it could not be seen until it sprung. He looked to Jack for help, but his friend's eyes were on the ring, and there was a strange, hungry expression in them that made Orphan uneasy.

"All the way from the ancient empire of Egypt," the umpire was saying, "now under the protection of our own Everlasting Empire – from the deadly deserts of the Nile, the most hostile region known to man – and *lizard* –" and here he glanced again at the balcony, like an unruly child afraid of being punished for his misbehaviour – "it's… Goliath!"

Orphan watched, incredulous, as into the ring came, on all fours, stepping slowly and majestically across the pit – a most immense lizard.

It was not a royal lizard, a Les Lézard, but rather an animal, that walked on four legs and was dark brown, with yellow bands crossing its naked body like war-paint. It raised its head and hissed loudly at the audience, a long, forked tongue darting out like a weapon.

The umpire took a step back, swallowed, glanced again at the balcony and said, apparently determined to play his role through to the end, regardless of possible consequences – "And in the other corner, all the way from the savannahs of the Dark Continent, the reigning champion – it's the Red King!"

The lizard that entered the ring second was not red – it was more olive-brown, Orphan thought, and mostly without bands – but it looked fierce, and as soon as it saw Goliath it raised its head and hissed, and the two lizards began circling each other, while the umpire exited the ring with a look of relief on his pale face.

The Red King inflated its neck. The other lizard backed away, then hissed. Its tail lashed against the floor, and metal flashed. A long, silver knife was attached to Goliath's tail. Orphan felt sick, and suddenly terrified by the obscenity of the scene. He looked up and saw the two lizards on the balcony standing immobile, and beside them the fat man, who was looking not at the ring but at him, Orphan.

Sweat dampened his palms. He looked around him, seeking a way out, but the one door was shut and

Mother Jolley was leaning against it with a body as heavy and shapeless as a sack of grain. She is a barricade, he thought. She would not let me through.

The Red King rose on its hind legs. It stood tall, and the silent crowd fell back as if cowed – or as if faced with a superior, a royal lizard. The Red King's tongue darted out, tasting the air.

Goliath struck.

The giant lizard darted forward and its tail lashed at its standing opponent. The knife cut into flesh and the Red King fell down. Its jaws closed around Goliath's neck and its claws dug into Goliath's body. The two lizards rolled on the floor, biting and clawing at each other. The Red King's tail lashed at Goliath and inflicted a wound.

"Watch." It was barely a whisper. Beside Orphan, Jack's eyes were moving wildly, looking on the audience, on the fight, on the balcony with its royal watchers. Jack's pupils swam in his eyes like foul-weather moons.

Orphan looked at the crowd. They stood away from the ring, immobile and silent until they seemed like statues. He searched for Marx and found him standing to one end. They were all cowled, he realised. Something about the audience… and then he realised.

It was not merely human.

Slowly, he found them. Following Jack's gaze, his own instinct. The lizards standing in the crowd. The hint of a tail, the impression of an elongated snout. Les Lézards.

Caliban's get was at the King's Arms.

In the ring, the two fighting lizards disengaged and withdrew from each other, hissing. Deep cuts could be seen in both their bodies, and they left bloodied footprints on the floor.

Goliath inflated its throat. The Red King hissed and stood on its hind legs again. Goliath followed it, and the two lizards stood and faced each other. They were a grotesque parody, Orphan thought. Like two princes stripped of their finery of clothes and of their title, undressed of civilisation. They were two savages, fighting for the entertainment of their brothers and their former servants.

Is this what Jack wanted me to see? he wondered. How his hatred of the lizards could be justified, that they would allow such a thing to be, that they would glory in it? And yet, there were humans there too, allowed to watch this degradation, and to enjoy it. It was a dangerous game Jack was playing, he realised. Orphan had thought him a mere public-house revolutionary, safe amidst his intellectual friends, his harmless Tesla set and his illicit printing press, but it wasn't so. He was a different thing altogether, much more dangerous and unexpected than he had ever seemed to Orphan: he glanced now at his friend and realised he had never really known him.

Jack looked back at him, and smiled; and his smile seemed to say that he knew what Orphan was thinking, and that he was glad, for now Orphan could no longer hide behind mere words, or childish pranks such as the Persons from Porlock had perpetrated, that he would now have to choose a side. *Why we are here – that's a question I think you need to have answered for you*, he had said. Orphan turned his head away; he could not meet his friend's eyes.

In the ring the Red King lashed out and its tail hit Goliath's leg, the blade flashing, cutting deep, and the lizard collapsed with a sound of pain, and then the Red King was on top of it, biting at its opponent's throat, its claws falling like knives on the wounded Goliath. It ripped Goliath's body open, cutting and biting until, gradually, the other lizard's movements slowed down. Goliath's body gradually wound down, the way an old clock comes to a halt and stops beating the hours until, by degrees, time and sound die. It shuddered at last under the Red King, and was still.

Pandemonium broke around the ring. New torches were lit around the room and in their light Orphan could see Marx, his face contorted in rage or ecstasy – it was hard to tell which – exchanging money with a man beside him, saw Isabella Beeton turning to talk to a tall, dignified lizard with a navy uniform visible under his black robe, saw the lizards up on the balcony turn away (the fat man had disappeared), saw Jack's taut smile floating in the air beside him: more than anything, he saw the dead and broken lizard lying on the floor of the ring like a discarded toy. For one crazy moment he wondered if it, too, had once had a lover who might now mourn it.

He turned away from Jack. The air felt heavy with smoke and blood and he could stand it no longer. Looking towards the door he saw that Mother Jolley had moved away and was circling amidst her clientele, who now spread throughout the room in small groups. He saw the umpire entering the ring, ready to announce the winner. He saw the man in the bloodied apron also approaching, and wondered if he would serve up Goliath's remains. It would be cannibalism, he thought. He turned away and ran for the door, knocking people out of his path. He crashed into the door, and it moved open for him, and he escaped through it and up the stairs, and outside.

The cold air revived him. He walked away from Drury Lane, down to the Strand. The fog weaved in and out of his sight like a ghostly quilt. The sky seemed lighter, and he thought the sun must be rising, slowly, ever so slowly over the cold capital of the world. He walked to the river and stopped, hemmed in between Somerset House and King's College. A piece of darkness seemed momentarily to move in the sky, and he glanced up at it nervously, thinking again of black airships. But he could discern nothing beyond that first, hazy sense of movement, and his eyes returned to the flowing water, his thoughts liquid and disordered in his mind.

Revolution, he thought. That was Jack's ambition, his dream, his purpose. To fight their overlords, to overthrow the Queen and her line. To replace it with… what? He thought of the wounded birds in the ring, their silver blades flashing in the torchlight. And it seemed to Orphan that it didn't matter: that whoever ruled the empire, lizard or human, would be a being who would stand and watch a fight like that, and coldly make odds on the winner. He thought of Lord

Shakespeare, the first of the great Poet-Prime Ministers, the greatest of them all. "As flies to wanton boys are we to the gods," he whispered into the mist. "They kill us for their sport…"

A damp breeze rose and touched his skin, sending a shiver through his body. Perhaps the automatons, he thought. Perhaps they had their own political ambition, perhaps they too were gathering in secret, preparing for a revolution. The thought neither cheered nor oppressed him. It left him unmoved. He thought of the revolution that had taken place in France, the Quiet Revolution of which so little was known. The French had resisted the might of Les Lézards – and for the most part, the Queen seemed happy in return simply to ignore the new Republic across the Channel. A cold peace lasted between the two nations, though now that he thought of it, Orphan found himself wondering how long that would last for.

The French were difficult. The words of a Carroll ditty rose in his head, and he smiled. "They are the frogs, and we have lizards," he whispered into the wind, "we play the first, and they the second fiddle."

From within the fog he heard a sound like that of a slow-moving boat, waves brushing against a hard, rocking body. He strained but could see nothing, and his thoughts returned to their meandering track. In *L'Île mystérieuse*, which was banned under the Empire, the author, Jules Verne, claimed to have made a voyage to Caliban's Island, though Orphan suspected it was a mere fancy of the author, who was known for his tales of wild imagination. I'd like to visit France, he thought.

Then a boat came sailing out of the mist, a single person sitting in the prow, and his breath slammed into his lungs and froze his thoughts into small hard diamonds.

The person in the boat was Lucy.

She was dressed in a fine white dress that seemed to form a part of the fog, and she sat in an unnatural calm as the boat sailed without anyone to steer it, coming close to the bank of the river, close enough for Orphan to almost reach a hand and touch her. Almost.

He tried to shout her name. It came as a hoarse whisper. She was in profile to him and unmoving, and her head did not turn to him. She was staring out into the fog, into the boat's invisible path and he thought, suddenly and with a dull dread spreading through his bones, She is a ghost.

The fog hid her like a dance of scarves. The boat, the flow of the river itself, seemed to slow. He shouted, "Lucy!" and thought – for just a moment – that her face was turning to look at him.

Then she was gone, and the boat was swallowed by the mist rising from the water and disappeared like the last lingering trace of a dream, leaving only emptiness in its wake.

ELEVEN
Mycroft

You are right in thinking that he is under the British government. You would also be right in a sense if you said that occasionally he is the British government.

    – Arthur Conan Doyle, *His Last Bow*

Orphan stumbled away from the Thames like a drunk, and his hand ached for paper and pen, for something to write with. It was all too much of a poem, he thought. The woman in white. It made him suddenly giggle. He was too tired, too worn-out. Hallucinating, perhaps. And perhaps, he thought, Inspector Adler was right, and the Bookman had the power of life, as well as death.

She hadn't looked at him. That was what mattered, what hurt him the most. She neither looked at him nor spoke. It was as if one of them had not existed, as if one were a ghost and the other real, and the two passed each other in two different worlds. He didn't know which one he was, the real or the ghost.

I need sleep, he thought. I need a cup of tea, a bath and a warm bed. Sleep, above all. Sleep.

But it was not to be. For, as he made his way away from the river, a piece of the black night detached itself from the sky and came floating, as silent as a dark balloon, directly above his head.

Orphan looked up.

It was a blimp.

It was entirely black, with no markings, no legend on its side, no identity code describing its existence or purpose. No beacons were lit on the vehicle: it drifted in perfect darkness, invisible and sinister, like a bat hunting in the night.

Orphan's first thought was: so I did not imagine it.

His second: so it's true!

He had been followed by one of the legendary, mythical black airships. What do they want? he thought, panic rising inside him like heated water in bottled glass. And then, government. For who else could command a ship that did not exist?

The blimp hovered above him. He could see its small gondola, as dark as the balloon, the envelope itself. Were there windows cut into the passenger car? If so, they too were darkened.

Then, full-blown panic settled in. Already unsettled by the vision of Lucy, he did not notice until too late when two indistinct, towering figures rushed him from either side and pinned him between them. He struggled, but the two men held him tight and a cloth was thrown over his head and blinded him. He lashed out, heard one of the men grunt in pain. Then a blow caught him on the back of the head and pain exploded inside him, and he fell loose in his captors' arms.

He was dimly aware of being carried. When he returned to himself he found that he was sitting down (the chair soft and comfortable against his aching body), and the air was warm. He heard the clinking of glasses and voices speak, too softly for him to make out what they were saying.

The cloth was removed from his head.

He blinked. His arms were free, and he touched the back of his head gingerly, but there was no blood, only a small swelling starting up that hurt, but not too badly.

He looked up.

In a wide, plush armchair, a round glass in his hand with an amber drink sloshing inside it, sat the fat man from the King's Arms. The fat man from the mortuary at Guy's. And Orphan thought: Oh, no.

"You," Orphan said. He felt foolish as soon as he said it.

The fat man nodded companionably. "Me," he agreed.

What did he look like? The considerable bulk was spread over the tall body of the man. His head was large, too, with a prominent forehead and dark receding hair that was once – but no longer – lush, and his nose was sharp and prominent, commanding respect. His eyes, deep-set, seemed to penetrate into Orphan's soul. He was a man who missed nothing, who knew everything. He almost, Orphan thought, looked like one of Babbage's analytical engines.

But he was human enough. His fingers were chubby though strong, and his breath condensed on the glass as he raised it to his mouth. Red appeared in his cheeks then, and as he closed his eyes and savoured the taste of the drink there was something sensual in his action. This was a man, and a man who took great delight in drink, and in food.

They sat like this, without speaking. The room they were in was dimly lit and plush, covered in mahogany and dark velvet, like a club-room. Beside their chairs were side-tables. Behind the fat man was a drinks cabinet. Two small lamps burned, electric, behind sombre shades.

The fat man clicked his fingers and a dark-suited butler glided over and handed Orphan a drink of his own. He tasted it, found it to be a whiskey much superior to the brand favoured by Jack. He turned his head, feeling the back of his head hurt as he did so. To his right was a window. He looked outside – and saw the city spread out below.

From high above, the Thames was a silver snake curled into an unknowable glyph. Lights winked in and out of existence as the city breathed below. The lights seemed to spell out a message, a hidden truth that he could decipher if only he tried, if only he concentrated hard enough. The Houses of Parliament were a face, craggy and huge, studded with jewels, whispering secrets that reached out to him and went past, still unknown. The blimp swerved slowly, giving him a view of the north-east side of the river and of the dome of St Paul's, looking like the bald head of a secretive monk. He took another sip of his drink and felt it burn away the pain in his head, and he turned away from the window and said, "Who are you?"

The fat man nodded in approval. "You go straight to the heart of the matter. That's good." But he seemed in no hurry to reply to the question. He sipped again from his drink (the butler had long since withdrawn from the room, as silent and efficient as an automaton) and gazed at Orphan with those clear, penetrating eyes. "Perhaps," he said, "the question of who I am is not as significant as you suggest. I am intrigued more, my young friend, by the much more interesting question of who you are."

Surely you already know, you miserable old bastard, Orphan thought. He was tired and his eyes hurt, and his mouth tasted like ash. All he wanted was a bed to sleep on, and silence.

"Well?"

"My name is Orphan."

The fat man seemed to consider it. "It isn't much of a name," he said at last.

"That's the name I was given."

The fat man leaned forward. "Ah, but by whom?" he said. "Orphan, after all, is not a name, as such. It is a moniker, a nickname, an alias – a designation. It is a description of what you are. So what was your name before you were–" he coughed a laugh – "Or-phaned?"

"Who are you?" Orphan repeated. The fat man's question had hit him like a punch to the liver.

"My name is Mycroft," the fat man said levelly. "What's yours?"

"Orphan."

"No."

The silence between them felt charged, like the air before a storm.

Finally the fat man – Mycroft – stirred. "Very well," he said. And, "Interesting."

"What is?"

"You do not know your own name."

Orphan gently put down the glass he was holding. He was afraid he would otherwise throw it in Mycroft's face.

"Do you?" he said.

Mycroft shook his head. "No. And that, I find, is even more interesting, for you see, I know a great many things."

"You seem to know a great many people," Orphan said. "Vivisectionists, for instance?"

Mycroft sighed. "It is a queer fate that led you down to the basement at Guy's that night. If fate is what it was. Perhaps I owe you an explanation."

"You could start by telling me why you had me followed and then abducted on board this airship," Orphan said.

"You see," Mycroft said, as if he hadn't heard him, "I despise the resurrection men. The thought of grave robbers operating in this city, in this time – it is abhorrent. And yet…" He, too, put down his glass. "Were it not for my brother," he said, "I would have nothing to do with such scum as Bishop and May."

"Your brother," Orphan said, and suddenly the image of the man in the icy coffin rose in his mind, the long and prominent nose, and something about the eyes… He said, "What happened to him?"

Mycroft shrugged and his eyes filled, for a moment, with pain. "I don't know." His fist hit the side-table and made the empty glass jump. "I don't know! I who am the central-exchange, the clearing house for every decision and conclusion, for every branch and department and organ of government – I don't know."

"Is he dead?"

"Yes. No." There was frustration in the fat man's eyes. "He was found. In Switzerland. At the bottom off... the details do not matter. No doubt my secretive brother was on the trail of some conspiracy of crime. But what, or who, he was pursuing, I do not know."

"He was a policeman?"

"A consulting detective," Mycroft said.

Orphan nodded politely.

Then, as the thought occurred to him, he said, "But you suspect foul play."

Mycroft nodded. "Perceptive," he said. "Yes."

"Who?"

Mycroft laughed. It was a short, bitter sound. "Why should I tell you?" he said. But in his eyes Orphan could see that he had already decided that he would. He wondered why the man wished to confide in him – and the thought made him afraid. He did not want the man's secrets.

"Moriarty."

Surprise widened Orphan's eyes. "The Prime Minister?"

"A puppet," Mycroft said, "serving the Queen and her line like a simulacrum. While the job of governing, the thousand and one acts required every hour of every day to make the wheels of empire move in unison, is done by other, more capable hands."

Such as yourself? Orphan thought – but he didn't express it out loud. He said, "Why Moriarty?"

Mycroft shrugged. Weariness formed lines at the corners of his eyes. "Odd hints, careful suggestions. An incidental fragment of data suddenly startling in a field of information where it was not expected." He stopped speaking and his eyes stared into Orphan's. "The Martian probe."

Hot anger burst inside Orphan's skull. Mycroft raised a hand as if to ward him off. "I think my brother was investigating Moriarty's space programme. A programme so secret even I was kept unaware of it. I think he was – disposed of – to protect its true nature."

Orphan was about to speak, but Mycroft suddenly roared, silencing him. "I will not let him die!" When he raised his eyes they seemed to hold a silent plea. "The best doctors have examined him," he said, almost plaintively. "The specialists in matters of life itself: Jekyll, Narbondo, Mabuse, Moreau, West… he has been treated with serums, with gland extracts, with electricity, with a spectrum of rays and with devices too arcane and tortuous and numerous to mention. Yet he remains as he is… dead to the world." He looked up at Orphan and said, "You and I are not so unlike. Both of us, after all, are seeking solution for death."

"Enough!" Orphan said. "Who are you? What are you? What do you want?" He felt rising anger and with it something akin to panic. He didn't care for this man, or about his brother.

"Again," Mycroft said, and his expression changed, became almost jovial. "You ask good questions. I hear you are one of our more promising young poets? Exactitude and directness are good qualities for a poet."

Orphan began to rise from his chair. Mycroft merely shook his head. "Don't," he advised. He clicked his fingers and beside him, the silent butler materialised like condensation on a glass of dark beer.

Orphan looked out of the window. The ground was far below. He sat back down.

The butler departed.

He was playing a game with him, Orphan thought. But what sort of game? It was a strange exchange of questions and half-answers, of things implied but not said – what did the fat man want from him? He had referred to himself as someone in government – well, that was clear enough. But whose interest did he represent? And what did he want from him?

It was a strange interrogation, he thought. Almost as if it was he who needed to find out the answers from Mycroft, and not the other way around. Or perhaps, not find them as much as decipher them on his own. He said, "At the cockpit."

"Yes?"

"You weren't watching the fight."

"No."

"Were you there for me?"

"What do you think?"

"No."

Mycroft nodded. "Very good," he said.

"You work for the government, but you are not in government. You have the power to commandeer a black airship, and you consider yourself a clearing house for information. So you must be in Intelligence."

Mycroft inched his head. "That seems obvious," he said. "But do go on."

"Which means that you are a loyal servant of Les Lézards."

"I serve Britannia," Mycroft said, a little stiff.

Orphan nodded thoughtfully. "That's what puzzled me," he said. "There seem to be so many factions at play here that I am quite lost. You claim to serve the empire, but show reticence with regards to Les Lézards." He smiled; he felt his mouth turning in a grimace. "You were watching Jack."

"Jack…" Mycroft mused. He, too, smiled. His expression, too, was ugly. "Your friend, Jack. Yes. An interesting specimen. But of course, he was not alone, was he, Orphan? He and that European troublemaker, Marx, and that beautiful, determined woman, Isabella Beeton… Yes. I was watching them quite carefully. And I was watching you, too. Will you join them?"

The sudden question took Orphan by surprise. "Is that what concerns you?" he asked. "You think they represent a threat to the empire?"

Mycroft shrugged. "There are a hundred different factions and organisations and secret societies in this city at any given time, all conspiring the downfall of the lizards, or of the government, or even of my own department. Do they represent a threat? Possibly. Quite possibly."

He fell into a brooding silence. Orphan glanced again out of the window. They were passing over the palace now, and the great, greenish pyramid rose out of the capital's ancient ground like a tombstone catching the starlight. He watched the Royal Gardens for a long moment, the silvery pools of water over which the shadow of the blimp passed almost unnoticed. He said, "What do you want from me?"

Mycroft, too, looked out of the window. At last, turning his eyes back to Orphan, he said, "I want you to find the Bookman."

There was a silence.

Orphan sank deeper into his chair. I want to find him too, he wanted to say. But what makes you think that I will? The tiredness threatened to consume him. He said, "For what purpose," not quite forming it into a question. Intuition told him what the answer would be.

"Tell him," Mycroft said, and his voice was heavy and suddenly old, the voice of a man making a compromise against his will, against his very nature, "that I am willing to bargain with him. He is the enemy of Les Lézards. He will want to talk to me."

"Bargain for what?" Orphan whispered, but he knew the answer even before he heard it, and before the blimp turned, away from the palace, and back towards the river.

"For my brother's life," Mycroft said. "Tell him that, when you finally find your Lucy."

TWELVE
At the Nell Gwynne

Love in these Labyrinths his Slaves detains,
And mighty Hearts are held in slender Chains.
  – Alexander Pope, "The Rape of the Lock"

He had been left on the riverbank, at the same place from which he was taken. The blimp touched down softly. The silent butler escorted him out of the car and deposited him outside. There was no sign of the other man who helped abduct him. It was still dark. The blimp rose into the air and silently departed, gliding as soft as a whisper into the sky.

He could barely think. His feet felt heavy and unresponsive underneath him. He made his slow, weary way up the Strand. Soon he would have to open the shop. Did Jack expect him to work today? Then he thought of Tom, and a small smile formed on his tired face.

He walked past Simpson's and the Savoy Theatre. Stopping to rest for a moment, he stood outside the newly relocated abode of Stanley Gibbons and admired the display in the windows. Though the streetlights still burned the sun was slowly climbing out of the depths of night and natural light began to awaken the capital's streets. How long have I been awake? Orphan thought. His body ached for sleep.

Nevertheless, he was captivated by Gibbons' display: stamps of all shapes and sizes and colours collected in the window like a cloud of still butterflies. There was, for instance, a Penny Black, the first stamp ever issued, bearing the profile of the young Queen Victoria, her scaly face regal underneath the burden of the crown. There was a rare, triangular Cape of Good Hope stamp bearing the smiling head of Mpande, the third of the Zulu kings and the father, so the note in the window said, of Cetshwayo kaMpande, the current king of that far-off protectorate of the Everlasting Empire. For a moment, Orphan was a child again, pressing his nose against the window, where a whole, unknown, exciting world was compressed into small pieces of paper. There was a Kashmiri "Old Rectangular" from twenty years before, with a script he couldn't read; there was a celebratory stamp bearing the grinning face of Harry Flashman, the Hero of Jalalabad; there was a Vespuccian First Day Cover with three stamps bearing the proud heads of leaders of the Great Sioux Nation; there was even a series of French stamps depicting artists' wildly romantic impressions of what Caliban's Island might look like. He lingered over the display for a long moment, savouring each of these tiny mementos of a world he hadn't seen. It was also, he realised, a thorough display of the greatness of the empire, of its boundless reach. It was meant to excite – but also to humble.

He walked away from the closed shop at last, feeling a small regret, as if he had lost something but hadn't known what it was. His tired feet carried him onwards, across the wakening Strand. Just before the Adelphi Theatre he turned right, and into the dark confines of Bull Inn Court. The alleyway was always dark; tall grey-brick walls rose on either side of it, permanently obscuring the sun. It was a narrow path, almost a scratch on the face of the city, a thin line connecting the Strand with Maiden Lane above it. It was too narrow for gas lamps, a small, hidden way one could have passed a hundred times when walking along the busy Strand without noticing its existence.

On the left, its walls adjoining the Adelphi, was, of course, a pub. There were always pubs, Orphan thought. Wherever you turned in the capital you would find one, and in the unlikeliest of places. They were the glue that held society together, a fixture of history and culture, as permanent and as pervasive as the gloomy weather.

This pub was a small, nondescript building that merged into its surroundings like a smear of coal-dust on the grey walls. Small, rectangular windows looked like dark glasses worn by a retreating professor. The pub used to be called the Bull's Head, but under the edict of its mischievous new owner the name was changed to the Nell Gwynne, and the sign above the door depicted the famous actress – who grew up in Covent Garden, performed in the Theatre Royal, and was whisperingly told to have been a mistress to Charles II, who people still called the Merry King – entwined with a smiling lizardine gentleman, neither of them dressed, her pale flesh startling against his bright scales. It was a typical sign for his friend to have had commissioned, Orphan thought; and, shaking his head, he reached for the low door and knocked.

He had to knock several more times, and more and more loudly, before the door finally opened, and a ruffled-haired Tom Thumb stood in the doorway, looking at first annoyed and then, as he spied Orphan, concerned.

"What happened to you?" the little man said, and he grabbed hold of Orphan's arm and pulled him into the dim interior, closing the door behind them with a practised kick. "Sit down, china. You look terrible."

He propped Orphan on a red velvety chair before the fireplace, where a comforting blaze was slowly consuming a large tree log. Orphan sat down gratefully and felt the exhaustion overcome him. The warmth from the fire threatened to send him to sleep, and his eyes slowly closed.

A giggle made him open his eyes again. On the other side of the small room (the inside of the Nell Gwynne, Orphan had decided on his first visit there, was about the size of a large wardrobe) a large bed covered most of the raised area which would have once held, perhaps, a couple of tables for the pub's customers. Two young women – each easily twice the height of his friend – were sitting up in the bed now, their nakedness covered half-heartedly by a blanket. Behind the long bar counter Tom was pouring a drink. "We was having a bit of a party before you showed up," he said. "Orphan, I'd like you to meet my dear friends Belinda and Ariel – girls, this is Orphan." He turned to Orphan and offered him a sheepish grin. "I was telling them about youse only last night."

"You poor thing!" the two girls said in unison and, rising from the bed – the blanket falling to reveal two perfect Rubenesque nudes – came over to Orphan and began fussing over him. "It's *so* sad," said one of them – he couldn't tell which was Belinda, and which was Ariel – and the other said, "You have been *so* brave!" She turned towards the bar and bellowed, "Tom Thumb, stop mucking about there and bring your friend something to drink! Look at the state of him!"

"I'm getting it!" Tom growled. "You can't rush the drink, you insufferable doxy!"

Orphan, who felt rather confused, looked on help-lessly as the two girls set about plumping pillows for him, taking off his shoes, and then sat down on either side of him and looked at him with large, sorrowful eyes. "You look terrible," one of them said, touching a cool hand to his forehead. "You're so pale and weak." She nodded and her hand sleeked the hair off Orphan's brow. "It's a broken 'eart what does that to you. I know."

"Leave him be!" Tom Thumb bellowed as he ap-proached from behind the counter, a large, round glass held in his hand. "Here, laddie, drink this."

Strangely, the drink in the glass looked like the skies in sunrise, red and yellow hues suffusing the liquid with an internal glow. Tom Thumb, as if reading Orphan's mind, said, "It's one of me own little inventions. I call it a Mezcal Sunrise. I first made it when I was travelling through Mexica. Did I ever tell you about my time with the Aztecs? Barnum took us all there in the good old days..." He stopped and sighed, lost in memories. "I wish you could see it, Orphan. It's a magnificent place, and the women!"

"Oi!" one of the girls – Orphan had decided, in his dazed state, that she must be Ariel, if only for the sake of convenience – said. "You said there was naught as good as Britannia's girls last night!"

"Oh, Ariel," Tom Thumb said (and Orphan was relieved to find he was right), "the world is full of mysteries and beauties too numerous to ever fully explore, but all are enthralling and captivating in equal measure!" He grinned, then said, "It was Barnum's favourite line, that was."

Orphan held the bulbous glass in his hands. It had two straws sticking out of it, and he took a careful sip. The drink was sweet and yet refreshing, and he felt for a moment as if he had indeed swallowed a little bit of sunshine. He smiled sleepily and said, "You are all too kind. Too kind." Then he closed his eyes and, without even realising, fell asleep.

In his sleep, he didn't see Tom extract the drink carefully from his hands and lay it on the counter of the bar, nor did he feel it when the two girls helped Tom carry him to the large bed and laid him there, as peaceful as a child. No dreams came to him, just a deep, deep blackness that soothed his aching, fevered mind, and calmed him, and a hush filled him until it overflowed.

When he woke the Nell Gwynne was quiet and empty. A small fire still burned in the fireplace, a new, slender log being consumed, and he sat still for a long moment in the unfamiliar bed, and watched the flames dance like sprites across the burning wood. Haltingly, he reached out for a pen and paper, finding some on the table by the bed (an old pub table, scarred with countless cigarette burns and the acidity of spilled drinks), and having done so, began writing a poem.

like air rushing into a bone-white vessel (Orphan wrote)
silence fills you;
it wraps in your hair and turns it mute

and courses through your blood vessels
breathing your inner skin, and sighs
residing in the hollows of your throat

it fills you to the rim and lashes of your eyes:
silence bursts out of you, a rupture of ears and touch –
I stopper you with my mouth and you sigh,

and turn over in your sleep.

He thought of Lucy, then, and of all the things he never got to say to her, and all the futures, all the possibilities that were now gone, like a road that once branched into hundreds of unexplored paths but now lay blocked and abandoned, all its promises gone. If I can, he thought, I will get her back: even if it means going to the Bookman himself.

He left the poem on the side of the bed. More mundane things made him shake his head, then rise. He made the short, dangerous trip to the bathroom, walking down the narrow stairs on unsteady feet (ducking just in time before his head could hit the low ceiling) until he reached the water-closet at the bottom. He returned to the bed then, and sat in silence, watching the flames, thinking of nothing in particular. He didn't know if it was night or day. Outside was the same twilight that always lingered in Bull Inn Court, and Tom kept no clocks. "Clocks are the enemies of time," his diminutive friend liked to say, "they are the gaolers of day and the turnkeys of night." Perhaps it was his friend's own attempt at poetry, or perhaps, Orphan thought, it was another Barnum saying – and he wished, then, that he had witnessed the spectacle of the P.T. Barnum Grand Travelling Museum, Menagerie, Caravan, and Circus that Tom always referred to, simply and with an utter conviction, as The Greatest Show on Earth.

Tom was a Vespuccian, born to English parents in the lands of the Mohegan tribe in Quinnehtukqut, which meant – so Tom had once told him – Long River Place, and which the immigrants had called Connecticut. Born small, he was discovered by Barnum and joined the circus at a young age. Fearless, charming, and wild, he left the circus when it came to the capital, for reasons he had never discussed, and settled in the dilapidated old pub, the size of which, he said, made him feel comfortable. He was a friend, a fellow member of the Persons from Porlock, and seemed happy to work at Payne's when Orphan couldn't, taking his payment not in money but in books.

Those books covered the walls of the Nell Gwynne. On crooked shelves and windowsills and, here and there, propping the short legs of a table or hiding behind a cushion or an empty pint glass, the books lay like sleeping domestic cats glorying in the dimness of the room and the heat of the fireplace. The small pub-cum-home was full of unexpected, small discoveries reflecting Tom's eclectic and erratic interests. Lying on the bar counter, for example, Orphan found a heavy, illustrated volume of *The Sedge Moths of Northern Vespuccia (Lepidoptera: Glyphipterigidae), With Woodcuts and Annotations By The Author*, while on a half-hidden shelf behind the door he found a vellum-bound copy of *The Floating Island, A Tragi-Comedy*, written by the students of Christ Church in Oxford, dating from 1655 and notorious for being an early and venomous treatment of Les Lézards' journey to Britannia, set to music by Henry Lawes but never performed. By the sink he could leaf through the latest catalogue of Smedley's Hydropathic Company, advertising their brand new electrocution water tanks (Heal Any Disease!), and near the fireplace, precariously balanced, was a pile of technical tomes that included Ripper's *Steam-Engine: Theory and Practice*, Babbage's *Some Thoughts on Simulacra*, Moriarty's *Treatise Upon the Binomial Theorem* and Lady Ada Lovelace's *Basic Programming Explained*. Behind the bar, leaning against a label-less bottle of creamy liqueur, was a copy of poet William Ashbless's *The Twelve Hours of the Night*, and by the bedside he discovered Tom's latest reading material, *The Chronic Argonauts*, a debut novel by a young writer unknown to Orphan, by the name of Herbert Wells.

It was a treasure trove and a scrapyard, a library that was also a maze, with little sense of purpose or direction, in which one could become easily lost. Orphan loved it.

He was just leafing through a well-thumbed copy of Flashman's *Dawns and Departures of a Soldier's Life* when he heard voices outside, raised in song, and recognised Tom's bellowing, cheerful voice as he sang, "In taking a walk on a cold winter day, by hill side and valley I careless did stray, till I came to a cottage all rustic and wild, and heard a voice cry, I'm a poor drunkard's child!"

Feminine voices joined in, shouting the refrain. "I'm a poor drunkard's child!"

The voices came closer, and Orphan smiled as he listened to the old drinking song. "In this lonely place I in misery cry, there is no one to look to me, no one comes nigh. I am hungry and cold, and distracted and wild – kind heaven look down on a poor drunkard's child!"

"Poor drunkard's child!" Orphan murmured, and just then the door opened, and Tom Thumb, accompanied by Ariel and Belinda, came through.

"My father was drunken and wasted his store, which left us in misery our lot to deplore, his glass soon run out, he died frantic and wild, and now I must wander a poor drunkard's child!"

Tom Thumb stopped his singing, slung a bag full of groceries on the bar counter, and said, "How are you feeling, china?"

"A lot better," Orphan admitted, and the two friends smiled at each other. Belinda and Ariel came over to Orphan, fruity perfume following them in a summery cloud, and they fussed over him rather as if he were a kitten or a puppy before they pulled him to his feet and made him dance with them, each holding one of his hands.

"My mother so good, in the cold grave lies low, she left me all friendless in want and in woe, brokenhearted, in death, she looked heavenward and smiled, but still I am left here, a poor drunkard's child!"

Orphan spun and spun, grinning, caught in the dance and the song, and the two girls laughed and held him, like nymphs risen from a secluded pool in an ancient forest.

"My clothing is scant, and all tattered and torn, kind friends, I have none. I am sad and forlorn! And far from this cottage so lonely and wild, I'll wander away, cried the poor drunkard's child!"

And they fell, still laughing, onto the wide bed.

Orphan sat up on the edge of the bed. "What time is it?"

Tom Thumb grinned and said, "It is twelve o' the clock, and all is well."

Orphan stood up. A sudden sense of urgency seized him. "Midnight?"

"You slept for a long time."

"You needed to!" Ariel said. "You was like Hamlet's ghost, coming in 'ere last night."

"I have something for you," Tom said. "From the shop."

"From Jack?"

Tom shook his head. "I didn't see him at all. Perhaps he was in the basement, but if so, he wasn't coming out."

He took out a folded sheaf of paper from his back pocket and handed it to Orphan, who opened it.

"From that infernal magician," Tom said. "That Maskelyne fellow. He asked about you, then made the note appear in the pages of the book I was reading. The ass."

Orphan smiled, knowing the magician's fondness for elaborate illusion, and read the short note.

Dear Orphan (Maskelyne wrote),
I was dreadfully sorry to hear of recent events, and am only glad that you yourself are alive, and on the road to recovery.
If you recall, the last time we spoke I offered you to come and see me at the Egyptian Hall if you ever had need of counsel.
Let me once more extend this offer. If magic is an illusion, the act of smoke and mirrors, then nevertheless the mirrors we hide may reflect, sometimes, a deeper truth, one not so visible to the naked eye.
Come, and come soon.
Yours,
J. Maskelyne

"What does he want?" Tom asked.

Orphan shrugged. The words of the magician's simple sympathy had affected him, and for a moment he couldn't speak. Once again he was overwhelmed with that image of Lucy, smiling, the book held in her hands, and then the bright searing explosion that had ended her life, and changed his forever. And he thought, I must act. I must find the Bookman. He had almost forgotten, in this momentary haven; but now that ghostly, mist-like figure seemed to re-form around him, to press against the windows with its silence and to watch him as he stood there helpless. The words of his friend Gilgamesh returned to him. *This is the time of myth*, he had said, and Orphan thought, then I am the minotaur, and I am trapped in the Bookman's maze.

"He invited me to visit him at the Egyptian Hall," he said. "He was very kind."

"The Egyptian Hall?" Belinda said. She rose from the bed (where Ariel was now sitting cross-legged, an open tin box on her knees, and rolled a cigarette with Tom Thumb's cannabis, which he regularly bought at Captain Powers' Pipe Shop near Leicester Square), "Me and Ariel went there only last week. You must go see it! They have the most amazing machine there, an old, old automaton that plays chess and can beat any man or woman what tries to challenge it!"

More automatons. Was his life now bound into the aspirations of machines as well as human beings? He thought, I would send him a note and apologise for not being able to come. He would understand.

"Yes!" Ariel said, "And the funny thing is, it's made up to look like an old Turk!"

The words trickled, slow and with a stealthy smoothness, into Orphan's mind. "What did you say?"

His voice sounded to him like it emerged not from him at all but from some place far away. What had Byron said?

Ask the Turk. And he had not paid it much attention. Why?

"I said it looks like an old Turk," Ariel said, her fingers smoothing out a cone-shaped cigarette. She lit it with a match and a sweet, pungent smoke rose into the air. "With a turban and a drooping moustache and hands that move across the board like they was real." She inhaled deeply from the cigarette, shrugged, and said, "You should go see it. There's also a mechanical duck that eats food and then shits it out."

"French," Belinda added.

Orphan looked at the two of them, turning from one to the other. *Ask the Turk*, he thought. And here, then, was the Turk.

"Is it open now?" he found himself saying.

"It's always open," Tom said. "There's always a show on at the Egyptian Hall." He looked at Orphan for a long moment, as if trying to decipher something he could only half-see. He said, "Are you sure it's a good idea?"

Orphan said, "No."

Tom slowly nodded.

With a sense of inevitability stealing over him Orphan went to the door and put on his shoes and his coat. He turned to Tom, began to say, "Thank you," but Tom merely shook his head. "You're always welcome at Old Nelly's," he said. "Just be careful, OK, china?"

"I'll try," Orphan said. "But I seem to be doing a bad job of that, recently."

Tom shook his head. "It can't be that bad," he said, "if you're still around."

Orphan smiled in return.

"If you're going to the Hall," Tom said, "say hello to my old friend Theo. He works there as Jo Jo the Dog-Faced Boy."

"How will I recog… ah," Orphan said. And, "I'll do that."

Then he said goodbye to the two girls, who both hugged him and told him to come back soon and, if they weren't there, to ask for them at the Shakespeare's Head.

"I will," he promised. Then he opened the door and, stepping out into the cold dark night, left both warmth and the Nell Gwynne behind him.

THIRTEEN
A Night on the Town

"Oranges and Lemons," say the bells of St Clement's.
"Bull's eyes and targets," say the bells of St Margaret's.
"Brickbats and tiles," say the bells of St Giles'.
"Halfpence and farthings," say the bells of St Martin's.
"Pancakes and fritters," say the bells of St Peter's.
"Two sticks and an apple," say the bells of Whitechapel.
"Pokers and tongs," say the bells of St John's.
"Kettles and pans," say the bells of St Anne's.
"Old Father Baldpate," say the slow bells of Aldgate.
"You owe me ten shillings," say the bells of St Helen's.
"When will you pay me?" say the bells of Old Bailey.
"When I grow rich," say the bells of Shoreditch.
"Pray when will that be?" say the bells of Stepney.
"I do not know," says the great bell of Bow.
    – Traditional nursery rhyme

It was a surprisingly warm night, and the residents of
the great capital, welcoming this unexpected change in
the always-precarious weather, had abandoned their
homes and taken en masse to the streets. Orphan

walked up Charing Cross Road and listened to the cries
of hawkers who, even at this late hour, were busy advertising their wares to the busy burghers of the city.

"Ripe strawberries!"

"Buy a fine table-basket!"

"Eels! Eels!"

"Buy a fine singing bird?"

"Old shoes for some brooms!"

"Fine writing ink!"

"Buy a rabbit, a rabbit!"

"Crabs, fat crabs!"

"Fair lemons and oranges!"

"Buy a new almanac!"

"White mice, see the white mice!"

"Knives or scissors to grind?"

"A brass pot or an iron pot to mend!"

"Pens and ink, pens and ink of the highest quality!"

"Bread, fresh bread!"

"Figs!"

"Sausages, good sausages!"

He stopped in his walk through Leicester Square and
bought one of the sausages so advertised, covered in oil,
dripping fried onions, held in a soggy bun. Everywhere
there was the smell of cooking foods, and the lights in
all the public houses were burning, and the cries of the
drinking class sounded, merry and loud, from every
open window but were drowned by the street merchants.

"Buy a pair of shoes!"

"Buy any garters?"

"Wigs! The best wigs in town!"

"Maps on display! See the wilds of Vespuccia, admire the steppes of Siberia, marvel at the secrets of Zululand!"

"Worcestershire salt!"

"Buy a fine brush?"

"Ripe chestnuts!"

"Buy a case for a hat?"

"Fine potatoes!"

"Hot eel pies!"

"A tormentor for your fleas!"

He stopped at the last one and watched the old man whose cry this was, trying to decipher what the tormentor was, but all he could see was a series of strange, pen-shaped devices that could serve no obvious purpose. He shrugged and walked on through the throng, towards Piccadilly.

"New-born eggs!"

"Spices! Spices from Zanzibar!"

"Hot curry powder!"

"Cannabis! Home-grown cannabis!"

"Puppy dogs!"

"Bananas! Bananas fresh off the ship!"

"Ladders! Sturdy ladders!"

"Marjoram and sage!"

"Do you want any matches?"

He passed a solitary woman standing on the corner of Haymarket who was singing in a high, clear, beautiful voice. It was a wordless song, a melody that, for a moment, reminded him of the songs of the whales, and he stopped on a whim and put a coin into the box that lay beside her on the pavement.

She did not stop her singing but she looked at him, and inched her head slightly in acknowledgment, and he was moved by the beauty of her face, and by the unexpected sadness that he found there, reflecting his own. He hurried away then, suddenly uncomfortable. He kept glancing at women in the crowd only to think he had discovered Lucy, but as he looked the women always turned out to be someone else, without the remotest resemblance to his love. Would she appear to him again? he wondered. Was she even now seeking him out, lost in undeath, a prisoner of the Bookman?

But she did not reappear.

"Hot spiced gingerbread, smoking hot!"

"Turnips and carrots!"

"New love songs, very cheap!"

"Primroses!"

"Jam! Blackberry jam!"

"Onions! Buy a rope of onions!"

"Music boxes for sale!"

"Edison records! Get the latest sounds for a peaceful sleep! The call of African birds and the sleep-song of the Nile!"

And here and there as he walked past the Circus the songs of merchants, as old as the city itself, rose to greet him as he passed, a hundred salutations assailing his ears.

Young gentlemen attend my cry,
And bring forth all your knives;
The barbers razors too I grind;
Bring out your scissors, wives.

And:

> *With mutton we nice turnips eat;*
> *Beef and carrots never cloy;*
> *Cabbage comes up with Summer meat,*
> *With winter nice Savoy.*

He was nearly there. The street was clogged with horse-drawn carriages and, in between them, though much aloof, were the curious steam-powered baruch-landaus that carried inside their shining metal bodies those rich enough to afford them. They were shaped a little like a conventional carriage, but with a large, round, black pipe sitting on their heads like a top hat, and they belched constant steam. The wheels were large and wide. In the back of the machine an enclosed black box contained the engine, and a stoker could be seen crouching in his own small space (similar to a theatre's whisper-box, Orphan thought) like a semi-naked demon caught in an eternal inferno. Past the engine was the passenger box, windows darkened to prevent the rabble from looking in on the distinguished riders, while in the front the driver sat in full majestic uniform and controlled the vehicle by means of a large metal stick.

The baruch-landau drivers had at their disposal an array of loud noises (to clear traffic) and flashing lights (for purpose of the same) and as they passed through Piccadilly they were cursed at by the common drivers of the public carriages, to which they replied with cool in-difference and the application of louder and even less wholesome noise.

"Sand! Buy my nice white sand!"

"Young radishes!"

"Read the *Tempest*! Read the publication they don't want you to read! Find out the truth about–"

This one cut short as two uniformed bobbies came past (walking slowly) and the caller hastily disappeared up Glasshouse Street. It was Jack's publication; and Orphan shrugged and walked on. He was not interested in conspiracies.

"Door mats!"

"Quick periwinkles!"

"Song sheets! Get the latest Gilbert and Sullivan for half the price of the theatre!"

"Southernwood that's very good!"

"New Yorkshire muffins!"

And from a seller of brooms and combs came:

All cleanly folk must like my ware,
For wood is sweet and clean;
Time was when platters served Lord Mayor
And, as I've heard, a Queen.

And from a stall nearby:

Let fame puff her trumpet, for muffin and crumpet,
They cannot compare with my dainty hot rolls;
When mornings are chilly, sweet Fanny, young Billy,
Your hearts they will comfort, my gay little souls.

And then, almost without noticing, Orphan was there. He stood outside the imposing façade of the Egyptian Hall.

What did it look like?

Imagine a grand and ancient temple built for the long-vanished kings of a desert country, wide and rich beyond imaginings. To either side of it stood ordinary, red-and-grey bricked apartment buildings, as ordinary and staid as two elderly gentlemen who had stayed out too late. The Hall, though… Wide columns rose on either side of the entrance, each twice the height of a man, and above them, in lonely splendour, stood the goddess Isis and her husband, the god Osiris, magnificent and tall, while above and all around them the rest of this mock-temple sprawled, covered in unknowable hieroglyphs, a sturdy and faithful imitation of the temple in Tentyra.

Above them all stood, in giant letters, the single word: MUSEUM.

Carriages and baruch-landaus alike carried people to and from the busy entrance, and a steady trickle of visitors, both wealthy and less well-to-do, came and went through the large front doors of this temple of learning. Even lizards, Orphan saw – a party of five, all dressed in full regalia and attended by a host of human servants – came to this place of wonder, and paid the admission price.

He could still taste the mustard in his mouth from the sausage he had earlier devoured; it was not a bad taste, exactly, but it lingered unpleasantly. Like the Egyptian Hall, he thought. It looked, for all its mock-antiquated brashness, like a doll dressed up in once-fine rags.

At the door he showed the usher his letter from Maskelyne and was admitted in without questions.

The inside of the Egyptian Hall was a wide, cavernous space. It was an amalgamation of junk and of rarities, of curiosities and oddities: a mixture of the deeply strange and the everyday.

In the centre of the room stood a rounded enclosure and, inside it, all manner of animals were on display, identified with large signs that were hung around the enclosure: there was a giraffe from Zululand and an elephant from Jaunpur; a dancing bear from the forests of Transylvania and a zebra from the Swahili kingdoms; a peacock from Abyssinia and, in a cage all to itself, a sleepy tiger from Bengal. The animals looked lethargic to Orphan, almost as if they were drugged. The tiger opened one eye when Orphan passed him, looked at him for a short moment and then, as if that exercise was too much for it, closed it again. The bear declined to dance, and crouched on the ground like an elderly fisherman, while the peacock seemed reluctant to spread its plumage to the onlookers, who tried to encourage it by cheering at it and waving their hands in the air, to no avail.

Dotted around the room were the human curiosities. Here, in an alcove with a gas lamp burning on its wall, sat the human whale, a giant male dressed only in a loincloth, whose naked flesh rolled and rolled, like waves in a pool, each time he stirred. He had his own crowd of admirers, who came up to him by turns and poked him with their fingers, in order to better see the fat roll from the point of contact and spread outwards across the giant frame.

Here, sitting on long raised chairs like the legs of flamingos (there was one of those birds, too, in the animals' enclosure), were the Scarletti Twins, one smaller than a child and as fat as she was tall, the other towering over six feet up and as thin as a rope. "They look like a small fat mushroom under a tall and gangly tree, the poor dears!" Orphan heard an excited customer say to her husband, who nodded with obvious satisfaction at his wife's wit.

Here was the Skeleton Dude, a thin, ill-looking man in a tuxedo (hence the name, dude being a Vespuccian slang-term for urbanite), and beside him was the Translucent Man, whose pale skin allowed the observers to examine the circulation of his blood through his arteries and veins. Here, too, was the Fungus Man, whose body sprouted numerous additional appendages, spots and boils (which you could pop at your leisure for a modest sum).

Orphan walked in a daze through this gallery of unfortunates. Everywhere he looked in that wide, open space some man or woman stood or sat or – in one instance – floated (the Mermaid, a woman floating inside a large water-tank, whose lower body was made to look like the tail of a fish), some unfortunate soul was displaying an affliction for the amusement and elucidation of the paying public. On and on it went: in a side room he saw a man with no legs and a man with no arms ride a bicycle together; in another, a bearded lady shared a rolled-up cigarette and a cup of tea (apparently on her break) with a woman who had three breasts (and drew an unwanted crowd of male admirers even as she sat there).

Where was Maskelyne?

As he passed a man with bricks on his head – the bricks were being pounded into rubble by a second man with the use of a great sledgehammer – a small figure bounded up to him and grabbed him by the arm.

"Are you Orphan?" this startling person asked.

Recovering from his momentary surprised, Orphan nodded, then said, "You must be Theo."

The man who had stopped him was short of stature, and dressed in short, loose-fitting trousers and an open vest that exposed his hairy chest. His arms were equally hairy, as were his legs. His face was dark and deeply grooved, covered in a straggly beard all over that looked like wild-growing weeds. Deep, sorrowful eyes looked up at Orphan from that extraordinary face.

"You can call me Jo Jo," he said. Then he shook his head, twice, as if shaking invisible water from it, and said, "Come with me."

"Where?" Orphan said. He felt a sudden, desperate desire to leave the Hall. Its damp, dark interior, filled with the smells of human sweat and the manure of its trapped animals and the relentless gaze of the massed crowds, left him with a mixture of feelings, a sanctimonious (if heart-felt) pity vying with a cerebral excitement (for he, too, like the rest of the crowd, was thrilled by the grotesques). I am no different to anyone here, he thought. And – It's why this place is so successful.

"Come with me," Jo Jo the Dog-Faced Boy said again, and tugged on Orphan's sleeve. "There is some-one what wants to meet you."

He walked off. Orphan, after a short hesitation, fol-lowed. I left my will at the door, he thought. This place is like a prison; if it's a museum, it is one that houses only human misery.

But it was not quite true. For, as he followed Jo Jo out of the central hall and through a long, narrow corridor, he began to notice an exhibition of curious devices lining their path. The corridor branched into small, alcove-like rooms, dimly lit like the rest of the Hall, and there were fewer and fewer people venturing this way; for here there were no animals and no human curiosities, but only machines.

In a room to the left of him he saw a mechanical menagerie, birds in the plumage of gold and silver leaves, who moved in slow jerks and called in rusted voices. They sat on the branches of a machine made to look like a tree, its chest cut open to display a series of cogs and wheels. Steam rose out of small vents in the branches, and the birds twittered and fluttered their wings each time there was a belch of steam, which came about every ten seconds.

In another room he saw several people gathered around a naked female torso that stood on top of a dais, as still as a statue, until, as to the beat of an unseen clock, she jerked her hands and turned in a circle, then subsided again into mechanical slumber.

"It's a very sad thing," Jo Jo commented while they walked. "These machines were once the apex of scientific achievement. Even five, ten years ago, I'm told, people flocked in their thousands to see them and marvel." He had the same wild-frontier accent as Tom, Orphan thought. "But now – look at them. Lost, lonely, discarded like used toys. If it wasn't for Mr. Maskelyne

taking pity on them they would have soon found themselves on the rubbish heap – or worse."

That last was said with an ominous whisper. "Why?"
Orphan said. "What would happen to them?"

They had left the corridor and entered another, then
turned again, and again. It's a maze, he thought, as Jo
Jo led him. Soon he could not remember which way
they had come. Was it left-left-right, or was it left-right-
left? The dark corridors were now empty of people, and
the rooms they passed were unlit and smelled of dust
and disuse.

"The Babbage Company, that's what would happen
to them," Jo Jo said darkly. "Old Charlie Company's
been trying to buy these automatons for years." He
barked a laugh. "For their *archives*. For the benefit of
the *scientific community*. Ha. They can't wait to cut these
guys open and dissect them." He looked over his shoulder at Orphan. "'Cause they didn't build them, see? So
they have to know."

"Know what?"

He was getting thoroughly disorientated by the walk.
The corridors never seemed to end – he was beginning
to suspect they were simply walking in circles.

Jo Jo stopped, turned, and tapped his own head with
a hairy finger. "Know how they work. Know if they
think. 'Cause if they do, china – then how can they do
it without old Charlie's engines? We're here."

They stood in the middle of a corridor identical to
all the ones before. Jo Jo ran his hand along the
wall, pressed something invisible – and a section of
the wall smoothly detached itself from the rest of the

surrounding structure and swung open, revealing a small dark room hidden beyond.

Jo Jo motioned with his hand for Orphan to enter. He saw Orphan's bemused expression and his face softened, and those great soulful eyes blinked. "If you need me – bark." He laughed. "Don't worry, mate. You're expected."

Orphan looked into the dark room. Was it a trap? It was possible – but even then, was that not what he had wanted? Perhaps it was the Bookman inside there, ready to reveal himself at last. Or perhaps…

He took a deep breath. Tom said he could trust Jo Jo, and he, in his turn, trusted Tom.

So…

He stepped into the dark room, and the door swung shut behind him without a sound.

FOURTEEN
The Mechanical Turk

Let us not say that every machine or every animal perishes altogether or assumes another form after death, for we know absolutely nothing about the subject. On the other hand, to assert that an immortal machine is a chimera or a logical fiction, is to reason as absurdly as caterpillars would reason if, seeing the cast-off skins of their fellow caterpillars, they should bitterly deplore the fate of their species, which to them would seem to come to nothing.

– Julien Offray de La Mettrie, *L'Homme Machine*

The room was dark and warm. There was a dry, not unpleasant smell in the air, as of a cupboard that had been left closed for a long period of time, containing gently fading clothes and the dying scent of lavender. Orphan stood still and let his eyes adjust to the darkness. There was no movement, no sound in the room but for his own breathing.

He took a cautious step forward.

"Play with me," a voice said. It had a scratchy, echoey quality, as of an old Edison record.

Orphan, keeping silent, took another step forward.

Light, flickering and low, came into existence before him. It emanated from a series of small electrical bulbs set in a half-ring around a square wooden table with a chessboard laid in its middle. A figure was sitting on the other side of the chess table.

It was the Turk.

The machine looked remarkably like a man. Only the upper half of the body could be seen, and Orphan had the distinct, uncomfortable notion that that was all there was to the Turk; that, had he looked behind the table, there would be nothing there. The Turk's face was ivory-white, as unchanging as a statue's. A long, thin moustache emerged from its upper lip and curved down. On the Turk's head was a turban, and a heavy fur coat covered its body. The coat looked old; it was moth-eaten. The Turk's hands rested on the table. They were pale, the fingers long and slender. One of his hands held a long-stemmed pipe which disappeared into a side drawer as Orphan watched.

An empty chair waited on the side of the table opposite the Turk.

"Please," the voice said. "Sit down." There was a short, mechanical chuckle. "I have been waiting for you for some time."

The Turk's mouth did not move. The voice seemed to emerge from somewhere around his midriff.

"Please, sit."

He sat in the chair. It was high-backed and once grand, but now the paint was peeling and the cushions had been eaten away by insects. When he sat, he was at eye level with the Turk. The chess pieces were arranged on the board. He sat on the side of white.

"Play with me. Please."

Though the tone of the voice never varied there was something almost desperate, a lonely quality to the voice. Orphan surveyed the board. The pieces had once been lovingly crafted, he thought. But now they were chipped, the white king was missing half its crown, and the pawns looked battered and scarred like ageing mercenaries.

On a whim, he moved a white pawn two squares. "E2 to E4," he said.

The Turk gave another wheezing chuckle. "A good opening," he said. "It frees your queen, and your bishop, and gives you early domination of the centre. Very good."

The Turk's right hand moved jerkily across the board. "E7 to E5."

The two pawns faced each other across the board.

"Queen to F3," Orphan said. Somehow, the game was important. He said, "What do the automatons want?"

"Knight to C6," the Turk announced. The artificial eyes blinked at Orphan. "The right to exist. Freedom."

"But you are machines," Orphan said, and the Turk's head turned in a slow odd shake, left to right to left.

"So are you," it said.

"Bishop to C4," Orphan said. "Byron said something similar to me. But you are constructs. Created by human hands."

The Turk's response was a loud snort. Then, "Knight to F6."

The thought suddenly occurred to him and made him uncomfortable. How old was the Turk? The one simulacrum he had met, Lord Byron's, was manufactured by the Babbage Company. It was a recent construct, the product of an entire scientific age... He said, "Weren't you?"

"Play," the Turk said.

Orphan looked at the board. "Knight to E2."

"Bishop to C5," the Turk said, his pale slender hand moving almost languidly across the board. Then, "What do you know of Jacques de Vaucanson?"

"A2 to A3," Orphan said, moving his leftmost pawn. "Was he a poet?"

The Turk did laugh now, a full-throated, lasing sound full of scratches and distant echoes. "D7 to D6."

No piece had yet been taken.

"Who was he?" Orphan said.

"Play."

Orphan examined the board. The space between his king and rook was now empty. He said, "Castling," and moved the king and rook so that his king was now safe behind a row of pawns.

The Turk nodded its head. "Ah, *Rochieren*," he said. "Very good. Bishop to G4."

The black bishop now threatened the white queen. Orphan didn't pay it attention. He said, "Vaucanson?"

"Let me tell you a story," the Turk said. "Which is relevant, perhaps, to your quest." The machine's eyes looked at Orphan's. They were like a blind man's eyes, void of depth, white and unseeing. "You came here for help, no?"

"I'm looking for the Bookman," Orphan said. Now that the words left his mouth they seemed to hang in the air for a moment, unburdened by weight. The Bookman. I am coming, he wanted to say. And the image of Lucy rose in his mind, clear as if she were standing beside him, so vivid that he almost turned and reached for her.

The bulbs seemed to dim, their feeble light fading.

"The Bookman…" the Turk said. "That great invisible Machiavelli." Again, that chuckle. "Do you think I can help you find him?"

"Do you think I can win this game?" Orphan asked in return, coming back to himself. He motioned at the still chess pieces.

"It's unlikely," the Turk said. Then, "I take your meaning."

"So you can help me?"

"Let me tell you a story. But first, play."

"Queen to D3." Orphan moved his queen away from the bishop's threat.

"Knight to H5." The Turk's hand fluttered and settled on the table. The lights behind it grew and dimmed. "Back when France had kings," he said, "a secret project was initiated by Louis the Fourteenth, and carried out by the greatest automaton-maker the world had yet seen. Jacques de Vaucanson." The Turk sighed, as if remembering a painful past, and his hand fluttered away from the table, pointing at a gloomy corner of the room. "That is one of his early constructions," he said.

Lights winked into being above a small display table. Orphan looked, and saw a duck squatting on the table.

"Do have a look," the Turk said. "There are some seeds beside it."

Orphan rose. The duck, of course, was a mechanical duck, and though it might once have been lively it now looked like the rest of these forgotten mechanical curiosities, worn down by the passing of the years. The duck looked up at him, and its beak opened and closed weakly.

"Feed it."

There was, indeed, a small store of seeds beside the table. He took some in his hand and put his open palm before the duck's beak. The duck pecked at them without overdue enthusiasm. The seeds disappeared inside it.

"Watch," the Turk said. "It is marvellous."

Orphan watched. For a while, nothing seemed to be happening. Then, with a soft "poop" sound, the duck raised its behind and delicately deposited a small smear of excrement on the table.

"Bravo!" the Turk cried. "Do you know, Voltaire once said that, without Vaucanson's duck, there would be nothing to remind us of the glory that was France?" His head shook sadly, and he said, "Gone now, of course. They are all gone, and only I remain..."

Orphan, unable to decide if he was amused or disgusted, returned to his chair.

He reached for the board and found a piece. "Pawn to H3," Orphan said.

"Bishop takes E2," the Turk said, his hand moved, and Orphan's white knight was no longer on the board. "Do pay attention."

"Queen takes E2," Orphan said, removing in his turn the Turk's bishop. "You were saying?"

"Knight to F4," the Turk said, unperturbed. His knight was now threatening Orphan's queen. "So, what did you think of the duck?"

The lights above the duck's display dimmed and disappeared. "Interesting," Orphan said.

The Turk sighed. "Once it was the grandest attraction!" he said. "Even now... even now people come to see the duck. To marvel at its ingenuity."

"Queen to E1," Orphan said, rescuing the queen. He stared at the board for a long moment. "What was Vaucanson's project?"

"Knight to D4," the Turk said. The black knight stood now between the white bishop and pawn. "Louis was sick. Already, in his time, France was in decline as the power of *les rosbifs'* unholy lizards grew. And so, as you may have already gathered for yourself, wherever there is opposition to Les Lézards, a certain shadowy presence makes itself known..."

"The Bookman," Orphan whispered. And he thought, always, it is the Bookman. Wherever he turned, the Bookman had been and gone, leaving only a ghostly outline in its wake.

"Perhaps that is so," the Turk said. "I have lived for many years, but even I do not understand the exact circumstances. The Bookman almost never deals directly. I only suspect his influence. Play."

"Bishop to B3."

"Knight takes H3," the Turk said, removing Orphan's pawn. "Check."

"Tell me what you have to tell me!" Orphan said. Anger made him raise his hand as if he intended to wipe clear the pieces off the table.

The Turk only stared at him, as mute as a doll.

"King to H2," Orphan said at last.

The Turk chuckled. "Good, good. You truly fascinate me, Orphan. You may only be a pawn, at the moment – but what you may yet turn into!"

"The project?"

"Of course." The hand moved again. "Queen to H4. You see, Louis, a dying man, was deeply, intensely interested in life. What, after all, was life? If man is a machine, could he not then build a machine to simulate life? To live life?"

"Vaucanson set out to build a simulacrum," Orphan said.

"Correct! Very good!"

Absent-mindedly, Orphan moved. "G2 to G3."

His pawn now threatened the Turk's queen.

"Pawns are such fascinating pieces, too…" the Turk said. "So small, almost insignificant, and yet – they can depose kings. Don't you find that interesting? Knight to F3."

And now the Turk was threatening Orphan's queen.

"Did he succeed?"

"Perhaps," the Turk said, "in another time… if the lizards had not appeared… if the Bookman had not existed… Perhaps in that time he had failed. A fanciful notion, but the longer I exist – the longer I live? – I think a lot about the might-have-beens, the what-ifs. About the little places in history where one tiny, minute change can lead to a new and unimaginable future. It's like chess. So many permutations, so many possibilities, probabilities, choices, cross-roads... I think a lot about the future, our future. And I see uncertainty." It stopped, then sighed, the same, repeating sound, each scratch and dim echo a repeat of the last one. There was something desperate and lonely in his voice when he spoke again. "Please, play."

"King to G2," Orphan said. His king moved, now threatening both the Turk's knights. He was in a purely defensive position. None of his pieces had managed to progress across the board. The Turk had brought the battle entirely to Orphan's side. "Damn."

"Knight takes E1," the Turk said, removing Orphan's queen with his long, deft fingers. "Check."

"Damn," Orphan said again. The Turk merely stared at him.

"Rook takes E1," Orphan said at last, removing the Turk's knight from the table.

"Queen to G4," the Turk said. Now there was only a pawn separating the Turk's queen and Orphan's king.

"D2 to D3," Orphan said, moving a pawn. "So Vaucanson succeeded."

"Bishop takes F2," the Turk said, taking Orphan's pawn. The bishop now stood next to the white king and threatened Orphan's rook.

"He built a simulacrum."

"You insist on reducing probabilities to certainties," the Turk murmured, making no sense to Orphan. "But fine, yes. Roughly speaking."

"Rook to H1," Orphan said.

"Queen takes G3," the Turk said, removing the pawn that stood between him and the white king. "Check." He sighed again, and Orphan thought: it must be a recording. A hidden system of miniature discs, perhaps, each with its own sound, a word or a phrase or some non-verbal expression. He wondered whose voice it had originally been, and how old it was. "Who gave you your voice?" he said.

There was a silence. The Turk sat motionless, as if his energy had run out. And Orphan thought, You speak in a dead man's voice.

At last the Turk stirred, his head moving from side to side as if seeking an invisible presence. The lights flickered behind it. "Vaucanson worked for many years on the project," he said. He did not acknowledge Orphan's earlier question. "He was a student of Le Cat, you know –" Orphan didn't, but he remained quiet – "there was quite a lot of animosity between them, towards the end. Le Cat, too, was working on an artificial man." The Turk made a coughing sound, as of a man clearing his throat. When he spoke again his voice was different, deeper and less monotonous, as if someone else was now speaking through him – through it. "'You are working, so I am told, on your artificial man and you are right in doing so. You must not let Monsieur de Vaucanson accept the glory for ideas he may have borrowed from you. But he has applied himself only to mechanics, and has used all his shrewdness for that purpose – and he is not a man who is afraid to take extreme measures.'"

An image of the two men rose in Orphan's mind then, two scientists, each working in secrecy over the inert body of a man who was not a man, each suspicious of the other, careful, always careful not to reveal to the world the work that they were doing... he wondered why, if one was once a pupil of the other, they had fallen out.

"De Cideville wrote that to Le Cat," the Turk said. "Another of Voltaire's friends... But Le Cat's man came to nothing."

"And Vaucanson's? What happened to him?"

"Play," the Turk said.

Orphan, frustrated, glanced at the board. "King to F1," he said reluctantly. The white king made his temporary retreat.

"Bishop to D4." The Turk's head bobbed up and down. "Officially, in the books of history, Vaucanson never completed his project. His artificial man never existed. The project was abandoned, and Vaucanson himself died in 1782, an old and wealthy man."

"King to E2," Orphan said. He knew he was losing. Then: "The revolution. In France."

The Turk looked up. "Yes?"

"It took place in 1789."

"Yes?"

"Seven years after Vaucanson's death."

"Yes... Queen to G2. Check."

"Why the Bookman? You implied he led Vaucanson to build his simulacrum. Why?"

The Turk nodded. "What do you think?"

"To counter-balance the Everlasting Empire. To check the growing power of Les Lézards." He looked at the Turk. "What exactly did happen in the Quiet Revolution?"

"Perhaps," the Turk said enigmatically, "you will soon have occasion to find out for yourself. Play."

"King to D1," Orphan said, retreating further.

"Queen takes H1," the Turk said, removing Orphan's rook. "Check."

"Do you know where the Bookman is hiding?"

"Do you?"

"No. I…"

A horrible thought rose unbidden in his mind.

The Turk's head bobbed up and down. The lights flickered, on and off and on. "The Bookman wants you to find him," the Turk said. "He has kept his eyes on you for a long time now. Have you thought to ask yourself why?"

"Tell me," Orphan whispered. And then, "Tell me!"

"Play."

"King to D2."

"Queen to G2. Check."

"King to E1!"

"Knight to G1."

"Tell me."

"I sit here," the Turk said, "every hour of every day, alone in the darkness. I have a lot of time to think. To look at the strands of the past weave themselves into the knot of the present, and to imagine how the future might unfold from them. So many possibilities. Like a game of chess. And you, my little pawn, you are the catalyst, walking through the board one small step at a time, towards… what? What sort of endgame will you bring us all, Orphan?"

"I don't know. Tell me."

"Play."

"Knight to C3."

"Bishop takes C3. Do you know, I have played an identical game to this, once. He was a young soldier in the revolution… a short, angry, quite brilliant man, Bonaparte. In another history, another life, he may have been great. In this one, I think he was happier, growing grapes and pressing wine on his farm. Happiness must count for something, don't you think?"

"I don't want destiny," Orphan said. "I want…"

"Happiness? To get the girl and live happily ever after, raising fat babies, writing mediocre poetry? Perhaps in another life, Orphan. Play."

"I can't win, can I?" Orphan said.

"No."

"Pawn takes C3," Orphan said, removing the Turk's bishop. He felt as though something heavy and painful now rested on his chest, pressing against him until he couldn't breathe. "How many?" he asked. "How many sides does this game have?"

"Queen to E2," the Turk said, almost sadly. "Checkmate."

"How many sides?"

"Two," the Turk said. "There are only ever two."

"Les Lézards," Orphan said. Then, slowly, "And the Bookman."

"And we are all their pawns," the Turk said.

Then the lights behind the automaton dimmed for the last time, and died. Orphan was left in darkness.

"Wait," Orphan said.

There was merely silence.

"I don't believe that. Byron mentioned something… the Translation."

A lone bulb flickered into half-light above the Turk's head.

"The Binder story," the Turk said. "Yes… The probabilities are small."

"The Binder?"

"A being like the Bookman, if he exists at all," the Turk said. "It is a belief of – of my kind. A myth for a time of myths. The Translation… somewhere, they say, the Binder lives, and where the Bookman kills the Binder restores."

"What is the Translation?"

"Who knows? A device, perhaps. Or a way of thinking, a way of being… There is a story of a time when human and machine will be as one, life biological and life mechanical and all life animate and inanimate will be joined, will be made one. The Translation…" The dim bulb faded. Darkness settled, again and finally.

Orphan turned. Behind him, the door to the room had opened. Jo Jo stood in the corridor outside.

Orphan took a step towards him. Stopped. Turned back. The Turk was wrapped in the darkness. The Bookman, Orphan thought. And he took a deep breath, half-angry, half-surprised. For he knew then; he knew where the Bookman was hiding. He turned again, ready now. Jo Jo waited silently in the doorway.

FIFTEEN
Jack

Just the place for a Snark! I have said it twice:
That alone should encourage the crew.
Just the place for a Snark! I have said it thrice:
What I tell you three times is true.
  – Lewis Carroll, "The Hunting of the Snark"

"Orphan."

The girls were gone. Tom was on his own, dressed in silk pyjamas, reclining in a chair. He had a book in one hand, a rolled-up cigarette in the other.

Orphan glanced at the title. Moriarty's *The Dynamics of an Asteroid*. "I need to borrow your gun."

Tom stood up. "What happened?" he said carefully. "Orphan, are you well?"

Orphan giggled. He felt feverish, and yet, inside, there was an icy calm. "I'm very well," he said. "I need to borrow your gun."

"What happened at the Hall?"

"It was as Maskelyne said in his note," Orphan said. "Smoke and mirrors. Mirrors and smoke."

"You don't make no sense. Sit down. I will make you some tea." He turned to go to the bar area. "Did you meet Theo?"

"Jo Jo the Dog-Faced Boy," Orphan said. "I met him. Or, rather, he met me."

"Did you find what you were looking for?"

"Ask me later tonight." He looked at Tom and suddenly shouted, "I don't need tea!"

"What do you need?"

"Your gun."

"What," Tom said levelly, "for?"

Orphan giggled again, ignoring the concerned look Tom was giving him. "Hunting," he said. "I'm going hunting."

"It's a bit late to go a-hunting." Tom said. "Perhaps you should stay here tonight."

"Your gun," Orphan said, and now his voice was quiet and hard, with no trace of laughter left, and he stood tall against the door.

Tom, too, was quiet. He stood in his pyjamas and regarded Orphan without blinking.

"Please," Orphan said.

It was the please that perhaps did it; for when he said it, Orphan came as close as he had ever been to breaking. Perhaps Tom saw that. Maybe he had his own reasons. Either way, he went behind the bar without a comment, and returned a moment later with a giant revolver in his hands. Orphan took an involuntary step back.

Tom smiled. "My old Peacemaker," he said, holding the gun with obvious affection. He needed both his hands to hold it. Then he proffered the revolver to Orphan, holding it by the barrel, and Orphan took it cautiously, suddenly wondering if what he was doing was making any kind of sense at all.

"The Colt forty-five, single-action revolver," Tom said. "A six-shooter. So who are you planning to shoot?"

"No one," Orphan said. "Hopefully."

Tom nodded. "I should hope so too. Here." He went again behind the bar and returned with a belt and a handful of bullets. "You know how to use it?"

"I'll figure it out," Orphan said. Tom merely nodded, and helped him put on the gun belt. "Of course you will."

With expert hands he loaded five bullets, one after the other, into the chamber. "Cock it before you want to shoot. Always leave it on the empty chamber, or you'll end up shooting yourself. Have fun – try not to kill anyone."

"I will," Orphan said. The gun felt heavy on his hips, yet reassuring. I would need it, he thought. If only to make me bold enough to proceed.

"Here," Tom said. "You need a hat, too." He went to the right corner of the room, rooted in a small cupboard, and returned with a wide-brimmed hat that he put on Orphan's head. "Now you look proper, like."

Tom kept a full-length (at least, full-length for him) mirror close to the stairs. Orphan positioned himself far enough and examined himself in the mirror. He saw a tired face looking back at him, covered in stubble, a face shaded by the hat, a poet's hands clenching and unclenching into fists. He looked like a gunfighter, he thought. Like one of the men from Buffalo Bill's Wild West Show, which he had seen in Earl's Court once when they performed in the capital.

"You look like a kid," Tom said, not quite hiding his laugh. "If you were performing with Barnum and me, that's what you'd 'ave been billed as. The Kid." He laughed again, but Orphan didn't. The Kid, he thought. It resonated with him.

"The Kid," he said out loud. Tom stopped laughing and regarded him almost solemnly. "Take care of yourself, Orphan."

"I will," Orphan said. He turned away from the mirror and marched out of the Nell Gwynne.

"And bring back my gun!" Tom shouted after him. "It was a present from Colt himself!"

He leaned against the doorframe and watched Orphan disappear as he walked out of the alleyway.

"I wonder if I'll see you again," he murmured into the empty night, "Take care of yourself, Orphan. For all of us."

He walked along St Martin's Lane and thought of endgames. There are many players, he thought. But only two sides. And the objective of the game is to topple the king. But what if there was no king? What if a queen ruled the board? The objective, he thought, would be the same.

It was a cold night, the earlier warmth departing under the threat of a bank of clouds that sailed overhead, a fleet of warships announcing their dominion of the weather. The street was almost empty, the gas lamps casting weak light and strong shadows. They twisted and turned like barbarians in a dance. He thought, I want to come back to my old life. To return to the shop, sell books, write poetry. Talk to Gilgamesh by the bridge, watch the theatre, love Lucy and be loved... but it had already happened, and passed. And here I am.

He turned left into Cecil Court. Payne's stood in darkness. His footsteps made the only sound.

He stepped into the interior of the shop. Age-old books dozed in the darkness on countless shelves. They seemed to murmur sleepily to him when they sensed his presence. He thought again of the bible at Guy's, the book that lay in wait in every room, the one Irene Adler had glanced at, nervously it seemed to him, before falling silent.

The books have ears, he thought, and giggled.

The sound was muffled by the room, absorbed by all the paper. He thought, There is nothing sadder than an unused bookshop. Volumes of words, ideas and stories, blueprints and diagnostics, illustrations and notes scribbled in the margins – they did not exist unless there was someone there to hold them, to open their pages, to read them and make them come alive, however briefly.

Out of habit he went to his room. His bed lay undisturbed beneath the burden of the bookcase. The table was bare. His eyes were used to the darkness now, and he ignored the stub of a candle still sitting in its saucer. The dark was better, he thought. His days of sunshine and light were gone, the clock his body followed had been twisted and changed. He did not like night, yet now he lived inside it. I will live in it for just a little while longer, he thought. He left his room and returned to the main area of the shop. There.

He approached the door to the basement and put his palm against the wood. He pushed, and it opened.

Worn stone stairs led underground. The stairwell was dark. Orphan walked down the steps, placing each foot carefully before continuing to the next one.

At the bottom of the stairs was a second door. Faint light spilled through the narrow gap with the floor underneath it. A small sign on the door said, BIBLIOTHECA LIBRORUM IMAGINARIORUM.

He paused for a long moment, unsure of himself. He could hear nothing behind the door. He thought he could hear the Turk speaking, inside his head. You are a pawn, it said, laughing at him. Pawns can never go back. They can only move forward. To capture or be captured.

This isn't chess, he wanted to say, but the Turk had already faded away, had never been there to begin with.

He pressed the door handle down and pushed, and the door opened.

The basement was in reality a small, rather comfortable room. Bookshelves lined the walls here just as they did upstairs. An old sofa sat against the wall and doubled up, as far as Orphan knew, as Jack's bed, though he had never seen his friend sleep. Three tables sat at opposite corners, covered in books. Through that small room a doorless opening led onto a second, slightly larger room.

Inside the second room was Jack.

He was hunched over a small desk with a large headset nearly covering all of his head. Apart from the desk there were more bookshelves in the room, a small stove, and a rather large dresser.

"Jack," Orphan said.

There was no response. Jack was hunched over the desk, listening to sounds Orphan couldn't hear, scribbling furiously onto a notepad.

"Jack!"

He approached the sitting figure and tapped him on the shoulder.

For a few moments, nothing happened. Jack continued to scribble on his pad, seemingly unaware of Orphan's presence. At last, however, he put down his pen, stretched his back, and removed the headset.

"Orphan, what happened?" He did not seem pleased at this intrusion into his personal space. "I've not seen you since last night. Are you all right?"

"No," Orphan said quietly.

"No?"

"No, I'm not all right."

Jack looked irritated. He rubbed his face with his hands, then said, "It's late."

"Or early," Orphan said. "Depends on how you look at it."

"What are you talking about? Look, did you want anything? Because I'm quite busy and if it can wait for tomorrow–"

"No, it can't," Orphan said, and suddenly the gun, the Colt Peacemaker, was in his hand, and pointing at Jack.

Jack stood up, his hands making a nervous, calming motion at Orphan. "What the hell are you doing? And where did you get that thing?"

"It's loaded," Orphan said. His voice shook, but only a little. "Don't make any sudden moves."

"I don't doubt it is," Jack said. "Look, what is this about, mate?" He glanced at the gun and then looked into Orphan's eyes. "Please put that thing away."

"Where is he?" Orphan said. The words constricted in his throat.

"Where is who?" Jack said, but there was a sudden look of horror on his face, brief yet powerful, and Orphan knew, with a helpless, sinking feeling, that he was right.

"Where is the Bookman?"

"Put down the gun, Orphan."

"Where is he?" Orphan said. The gun did not move. It pointed at Jack's chest. It made Orphan sick, to be threatening his friend. Yet he didn't remove it.

"Please," Jack said. There was something small and helpless in the simple word. He took a step forward, raised his arm as if to gesture, and his mouth opened, his lips parted in the beginning of speech...

And froze instead.

He made an ungainly statue. He was fixed in a position of frozen movement, the raised arm suspended in mid-air, the open lips just about to blow out air and with it their first word... His foot had not quite touched the ground, remained hovering just above the floor.

Orphan, uncertain, said, "Jack?"

There was no answer.

He put the gun away in his belt. It was not as if he would have ever used it. He approached his friend cautiously. Confusion made him hesitate. He touched Jack's arm. His flesh was hard. He put his hand before his friend's mouth, but could feel nothing, no breath blowing against his fingers.

"What the…?"

He stepped back. The room suddenly felt very small and crowded. The books stared at him from their shelves with sly expressions.

He stepped forward. Concern made him go back to his friend. He stood close to him, reached to check his pulse…

With a smooth, flowing motion Jack sprang into life. One moment he was still. The next, he was returned to life, and his foot came down with force on Orphan's, sending a hot flame of pain into Orphan's mind, bringing with it, sickeningly loud, the sound of delicate bones breaking.

Jack's arm came down, hard. His fingers bunched into a fist. The fist connected with Orphan's nose, and more pain flowered, and he was thrown back.

His back connected with a bookcase. His hat had fallen off. More pain, and then it was raining: volume after volume of antique books fell on him in ones and twos, a dribble that built into a flood. He lashed out, blinded, connected with nothing but air. The books continued to fall, hitting him on his head, his shoulders, his arms.

He blinked sweat from his eyes and tried to scramble away. From nowhere came Jack's foot, a kick that connected with a furious impact with his ribs, and he screamed.

"What are you *doing*?" he cried, but realisation, working its slow, inefficient way through his sluggish brain, had finally arrived, and for a moment he, too, froze.

He was backed into a corner of the room. Jack towered above him, unspeaking, his face impassive. His eyes stared down at Orphan but did not see him. For Jack, Orphan realised, was no longer there.

Jack kicked him again. The kick just missed his left kneecap and hit his shin. Pain shot through him, weaving a bright spider-web through his body. Stars exploded behind Orphan's eyes. Amongst them he thought, for a fleeting moment, that he could see a red, large star winking at him.

The starscape faded to black. When he opened his eyes again Jack was still there, his foot raised high. Ready to stomp down on Orphan. Ready to finish him. With no conscious thought, like a spider with its own mind, his fingers reached down to his side and pulled out the old gun, fumbling at it, cocking the hammer. Jack's foot descended –

Orphan pulled the trigger.

SIXTEEN
At the Bibliotheca Librorum Imaginariorum

There thou mayst brain him,
Having first seized his books, or with a log
Batter his skull, or paunch him with a stake,
Or cut his wezand with thy knife. Remember
First to possess his books; for without them
He's but a sot, as I am, nor hath not
One spirit to command: they all do hate him
As rootedly as I. Burn but his books.

  – William Shakespeare, *The Tempest*

The recoil threw him back. He felt his shoulder and arm slapped as by a giant stone hand. The sound of an explosion deafened him.

A book landed in his lap, and when he looked at it, blinking, realised for the first time that he was bleeding. The blood congealed on the leather cover, mixed with the dust that lay on the book like a thick layer of pollen.

A choked laugh escaped from his lips. The book in his lap was *Gray's Anatomy*.

I'm going to need that, he thought.

He raised his head. His fingers clutched the book.

Jack was crumpled against the wall on the other side of the room. There was a hole in his chest.

But there was no blood.

Orphan pulled himself up, his bloodied hands leaving palm-prints on the wall. The gun remained on the floor, beside the fallen book.

He took a deep breath and felt pain, like a jagged nail, cut across his ribs. His nose was blocked and hurting. One leg refused to carry him, and he leaned with his back against the wall, letting the leg dangle.

Jack remained unmoving on the other side. He, too, had hit a bookcase. He lay surrounded by silent, fallen books.

Slowly, carefully, one hand trailing against the wall and the contours of the room, Orphan made his way toward him.

There was a whistling sound in his ears. And, somehow, he could smell – there was a burning smell in the room, a mix of gunpowder and something else, as of scorched rubber…

He stood above Jack. His friend's face was lax, empty, as if its features had half-melted away, leaving behind a mask devoid of animation. His eyes were closed.

He forced himself to look below the face. His eyes moved down slowly, hesitating as they went. They felt, he thought, reluctant to obey his brain.

There was a hole in Jack's chest. And in the hole… blue fire.

A spark flew in the air and made Orphan stagger back. Sparks were coming out of the open hole in Jack's chest, one and then another one and another, until a small electric storm seemed to erupt out of that still body and jump into the air.

He is bleeding electricity, Orphan thought. And then, at last, he formulated to himself the thought that had insinuated itself into his mind when Jack attacked him.

Simulacrum.

He knelt beside Jack and took his hand in his. There was no pulse, but the skin felt warm and, now that he looked closer, lines of light were moving beneath the skin.

He peered into the hole in Jack's chest. Sparks were still flying, but they were diminishing. Inside… he could not comprehend it. Perhaps, he thought, he was expecting gears and cogs. But the inside of Jack's body resembled no machine he had ever seen. It was like a vast, strangely beautiful painting of incomprehensible, miniature elements, not human, not machine, but some sort of unknowable technology that was, perhaps, a little of both.

Jack, he thought, numb. Why? Who?

But he already knew the answer. He rose from his crouching position and looked around the room. Books lay everywhere, like wounded soldiers on a battlefield. The desk, the Tesla set. Nothing else. He began scanning the shelves, pressing his hand against the wall as he moved around the room. Searching.

"I know you're here," he said into the silence. "I know you can hear me."

The books, he thought. He needed a key. He began riffling through the ones still left on the shelves, picking each for the brief moment it took him to read the title, then tossing the book on the floor. Jack, he thought. That's where he would hide things. In books.

Jo March's *A Phantom Hand*. William Ashbless's *Accounts of London Scientists*. Hawthorne Abendsen's *The Grasshopper Lies Heavy*. *The Encyclopedia Donkaniara*. *The Book of Three*. Emmanuel Goldstein's *The Theory and Practice of Oligarchical Collectivism*. Captain Eustacio Binky's *Coffee Making as a Fine Art*. Ludvig Prinn's *De Vermis Mysteriis*. Gulliver Fairborn's *A Talent for Sacrifice*. Colonel Sebastian Moran's *Heavy Game of the Western Himalayas*. Gottfried Mulder's *Secret Mysteries of Asia, with Commentary on the Ghorl Nigral*. Cosmo Cowperthwait's *Sexual Dimorphism Among The Echinoderms, Focusing Particularly Upon the Asteroidea and Holothuroidea*. George Edward Challenger's *Some Observations Upon a Series of Kalmuk Skulls*.

What were those books? Orphan thought, exasperated. Most of these titles were completely unknown to him. He almost wanted to stop, to take his time, browse through the titles at leisure, leaf through the enigmatic books, study their contents. Instead, he pulled each book, opened it and shook it upside down, searching for something hidden inside. Some things did fall out – a pressed flower here, its startling blue preserved amidst the pages of Josephine M. Bettany's *Mystery at Heron Lake*; a folded currency note there, bearing an unknown script, that fluttered to the ground from within Flashman's *Twixt Cossack and Cannon* – but nothing to give him a clue, a hint as to his next move. Yet as he continued ransacking the shelves he became more and more convinced that what he was doing was right, that the books were the twine that could lead him across the floor of the maze to the minotaur who waited at its centre.

Gossip Gone Wild by Dr Jubal Harshaw. *In My Father's House* by Princess Irulan. *Burlesdon on Ancient Theories and Modern Facts* by James Rassendyll, Lord Burlesdon. *The Truth of Alchemy* by Mr. Karswell. *Stud City* by Gordon Lachance. *Boxing the Compass* by Bobbi Anderson. *The Relationship of Extradigitalism to Genius*, by Zubarin. *Megapolisomancy* by Thibaut de Castries. *De Impossibilitate Prognoscendi* by Cezar Kouska. Eustace Clarence Scrubb's *Diary*. *Azathoth and Other Horrors* by Edward Pickman Derby.

More things fell from the books. A coin, so blackened that its face could no longer be discerned. A map of an island drawn in a child's hand. A butterfly, the wings black save for two emerald spots. A newspaper cutting from the *Daily Journal*, that read:

12 June 1730.

Seven Kings or Chiefs of the Chirakee Indians, bordering upon the area called Croatoan, are come over in the Fox Man of War, Capt. Arnold, in order to pay their duty to his Majesty, and assure him of their attachment to his person and Government, &c.

Aunt Susan's Compendium of Pleasant Knowledge. Broomstick or the Midnight Practice. R. Blastem's *Sea Gunner's Practice, with Description of Captain Shotgun's Murdering*

Piece. The Libellus Leibowitz. Augustus Whiffle's *The Care of the Pig.* Dr Stephen Maturin's *Thoughts on the Prevention of Diseases most usual among Seame*n. Professor Radcliffe Emerson's *Development of the Egyptian Coffin from Predynastic Times to the End of the Twenty-sixth Dynasty, With Particular Reference to Its Reflection of Religious, Social, and Artistic Conventions. The Book of Bokonon.* Kilgore Trout's *Now It Can Be Told.* James Bailey's *Life of William Ashbless.* Hugo Rune's *The Book of Ultimate Truths.* Harriet Vane's *The Sands of Crime.* Jean-Baptiste Colbert's *Grand System of Universal Monarchy.* Toby Shandy's *Apologetical Oration.* Coleridge's *The Rime of the Ancient Mari–*

There.

He was on his knees, a dull throbbing pain in his hurt leg. He saw the title, bottom shelf, Coleridge's name. But the book did not move.

And then he noticed the dust.

A layer of dust had settled over time on the tops of the books and lay there undisturbed. Yet on *The Rime of the Ancient Mariner* there was no dust.

And the book would not move, would not be pulled away from the shelf.

Orphan stared at it for a long moment. That long, strange poem of Coleridge… He traced the edges of the slim book with his fingers.

It did not feel like the rest. It was hard, metallic, not leather. He gave up on trying to pull it out and, instead, gave it a push with his thumb.

The book slid effortlessly away from him.

There was a soft *click*.

The bookcase moved. It hit Orphan, sending more pain through his body, and he scrambled away and fell on the floor, cushioned uncomfortably by books.

The bookcase moved, swinging, and behind it was an emptiness, a lack of a wall and beyond that was a darkness. Somewhere in the distance he could hear what sounded like waves, and taste a sharp, almost rancid smell.

He stood up, looked one last time towards Jack. Then he retrieved the gun from where it lay on the floor and tucked it into its holster. He lifted the wide-brimmed hat from the floor and put it carefully back on his head, at an angle.

He stared into the darkness for a long moment, but could discern nothing beyond the bookcase. Then he took a deep breath and stepped forward, and into the darkness.

SEVENTEEN
The Man Behind the Screen

The Lion thought it might be as well to frighten the Wizard, so he gave a large, loud roar, which was so fierce and dreadful that Toto jumped away from him in alarm and tipped over the screen that stood in a corner. As it fell with a crash they looked that way, and the next moment all of them were filled with wonder. For they saw, standing in just the spot the screen had hidden, a little old man, with a bald head and a wrinkled face, who seemed to be as much surprised as they were. The Tin Woodman, raising his axe, rushed toward the little man and cried out, "Who are you?"

– L. Frank Baum, *The Wonderful Wizard of Oz*

The ground sloped gradually beneath his feet. The earth felt moist, and his feet sank slightly into it with each step he took. The darkness was complete; he felt that he was set loose in the space between the stars, with no up or down, no weight…

There was the sound of waves. The air was warm, but a small breeze blew against his face. He had the sense of unseen things scuttling away from him in the darkness.

Where was he? he wondered. Somewhere under-neath Charing Cross Road? He could not tell which direction he was taking. What was this place?

As he walked further he could discern a glow of light in the distance. Coming closer, the glow resolved and separated into strange orbs that cast a dim, greenish light over the surroundings.

He was standing in a cavern, and the orbs were hung on the walls. Before him was a black lake, and he was standing on its shore. There was sand at his feet.

He bent down and touched the water. It was cool to the touch, and he lifted some in his palm and drank from the lake. The water had almost no taste, yet it re-vived him.

He began to walk along the shore, his body casting two shadows onto the ground. A short way off, by the cavern's wall, he found an empty boat beached on the sand.

He knows I am coming, he thought. He is waiting. The thought did not upset him. The Bookman wants you to find him, the Turk had said. He has kept his eyes on you for a long time now…

"I know you are watching," he said aloud. There was no other sound but the lapping of the waves. "I'm com-ing."

He pushed the boat into the water and climbed in-side. It was made of wood and smelled of disuse. Once in the water it began to move of its own accord.

He sat back. There was nothing else for him to do, and he was suddenly glad. He let his hand trail in the water of that dark lake. Perhaps it is the same boat Lucy had travelled on, he thought. Soon we could come back, together in it.

His hand touched something soft in the water. He looked overboard and nearly fell over: there was a body floating in the water, its eyes open and looking straight at him.

The body floated just below the surface of the water. It was that of a man, naked, not alive and yet not dead, either, and he recognised it: it was Henry Irving, the actor. He had last seen him blown up into pieces at the Rose.

He pulled away from the side of the boat, feeling sudden revulsion. As he looked now, he could see other bodies submerged in the water of the lake. The water was very clear, translucent. The lake, he realised, was very shallow. He sat back, unsettled. Henry Irving's body diminished behind him.

As the shore grew farther in the distance a shape loomed ahead, rising out of the lake. A small island, he thought. The boat, of its own, unknown will, headed towards it.

It was not a long journey. Soon, too soon, the boat ran aground on the island, and he stepped out. He felt better now, and the various pains in his body had disappeared. Touching his nose, he could not feel the break. Instead, he felt light and clear-headed. Something in the water, he thought.

His feet touched black sand. Before him the island was almost flat, a disc floating on the water. He scraped away at the sand and was not surprised to discover a greenish metal underneath. An artificial island. He took a step forward, then another. The ground rose, then, after only a few more steps, gently sloped downwards.

Above his head the globes of light slowly faded, leaving him in total darkness. He stood for a long moment, not moving, and waited.

Though he thought he was prepared, when the voice came it nevertheless startled him. "Mr. Orphan. What a delight to finally meet you." It was a deep, mellow voice.

A light came to life directly ahead of him. An old-fashioned, ornamental streetlamp planted in the sand. It illuminated a small square of chequered tiles, black and white like a chess set. In the centre of the square was a table. On the table stood a tea pot, a small milk jug, a jar of sugar and two delicate china cups. On a saucer he could discern what looked like ginger biscuits.

One chair was unoccupied. In the other sat a man.

He rose when Orphan approached. He was a tall, athletic-looking man. Black hair was only just beginning to recede across his forehead. He was dressed in a smart suit, like that of a well-to-do City worker. He was clean-shaven. He came towards Orphan with his hand outstretched, and shook his hand. His handshake was strong and confident. His eyes twinkled. Orphan felt completely lost.

"Please," the man said, gesturing at the table. "Sit down. Have some tea. I have been looking forward to talking with you." Not waiting for Orphan, he returned to his seat and began pouring tea into the cups. Orphan, not knowing what to do, and feeling a vague sense of unease – or perhaps, he thought, it was disappoint-ment? He couldn't tell what he had been expecting, but it wasn't this – sat down opposite.

"Milk? Sugar?"

"Yes, please. Two sugars," Orphan said. His voice felt unreal to him. Maybe, he thought, maybe I never shot Jack. Perhaps I am still lying on the floor of the base-ment, concussed, and I am merely hallucinating this. I will be glad if it turns out I never shot him. It wasn't like me. He was my friend. Then he wondered, if that was true, what hospital he would go to. Would it be Guy's again? He didn't relish that idea.

"I am sure you have a lot of questions," the man said, handing him his tea.

Orphan smelled the tea. It smelled good, an Earl Grey, and when he tasted it warmth spread through his body. "One or two," he said cautiously. Something is wrong, he thought. But I don't know what it is.

The man nodded as if Orphan's reply confirmed some deep point of conversation. "You are wondering who I am." He smiled. His teeth were white and even. "I am, of course, the Bookman." He laughed and shook his head. "I am one of the Bookmen, rather," he said. "I am afraid you were rather misled to think of us as one person. One mysterious and quite nefarious person, no doubt." He sighed and took a sip from his tea. "I am afraid the reality is quite a bit more mundane. Would you like a biscuit?"

"No, thank you," Orphan said. His companion shrugged and helped himself to one, which he bit into with relish. "They're very good," he said.

"I have no doubt on that score," Orphan said. "You were saying?"

"Ah, straight to business. Quite. You see, Orphan, we are not some monstrous and alien entity – though we like people to think that – but rather, we are simple patriots. Men – and women – who have made it their goal to free our homeland from the shackles of oppression." He looked at Orphan with an earnest, searching gaze. "The oppression of Les Lézards."

"By killing innocent people?" Orphan said. He was coming back to himself, a little. "By killing Lucy?" Anger flared and he seized it with gratitude, trying to pull himself out of the spreading numbness.

The man shook his head. His face bore a sad, dignified countenance. "We had no choice," he said. "Though, in the event, we were wrong. Misled."

"Wrong?" Orphan said. "*Wrong*?"

"Yes," the man – the Bookman – agreed. "You see, our target was, of course, the Martian probe. Yet–"

"Why? Why the probe?" He pushed away his tea. "What harm can it possibly do?"

"Let me riddle you this, Orphan," the Bookman said. "Where do Les Lézards come from?"

"I was told they come from an island whose location is kept secret."

"Come, come," the Bookman said. "You've read Darwin. Surely you realise this idea of parallel evolution, of this other race evolving naturally away from humanity on a small island, surely this idea is preposterous?"

"I had not given it much thought," Orphan said.

There was something about the way the man talked, about the way he moved his head…

Suddenly, it reminded him of the Turk.

"The truth, Orphan." the man leaned forward, and his eyes looked deep into Orphan's with a gaze both trusting and wise. "A truth many men died to obtain proof of, I should tell you –" and here he lay his hand on the table, as if it were a bible and he a witness at a court of law – "the truth is this: the lizards *have no earthly origin*."

Orphan looked into the Bookman's eyes. There was, he thought, a lack in them, an absence he could not quite describe. Something was missing in the man, some subtle part of a man that simply wasn't there. He said, "I see."

"Do you? Do you, Orphan? Do you comprehend the magnitude of this affront?" The man grasped him by the arm. "They are intruders, invaders, an occupying force from – from beyond. From beyond space. They want nothing else than to rule the whole world – and they are using us, humans, to do this – until the day when they no longer need us…"

"You sound like Jack," Orphan said distractedly. He turned his face away from the man. He couldn't see the lake from where he sat, it was as if he were sitting in an upturned bowl. Beyond the little square, beyond the streetlamp's light, there was nothing.

An absence within an absence, he thought. He said, "Jack was my friend."

"Yes, yes," the man said. "Do try to pay attention."

"You were going to explain to me about the probe,"

Orphan said. Was it really an absence? He looked harder. It seemed to him that there was something out there, on the edge of his vision, something vast and powerful moving in the darkness, watching him. "Then you can explain to me about the mistake you made. And then you can give me back Lucy."

"Look," the Bookman said, his face colouring in anger. "You don't seem to understand what is at stake here. I thought you would be sensible. Us humans need to stick together, to–"

But Orphan was no longer listening. He stood up, pushing back the chair, and stalked off beyond the streetlamp, into the outlining darkness.

"Hey, where are you going?" the Bookman shouted after him.

Orphan turned back. "You're another simulacrum, aren't you?" he said. Then he pulled out the Peace-maker and shot the Bookman in the chest.

EIGHTEEN
The Bookman

Facile credo, plures esse Naturas invisibiles quam visibiles in rerum universitate
– Thomas Burnet

"Bravo," said a voice. It wasn't the man who had spoken. He was lying on the ground on his back, with a hole in his chest. Like Jack, he was bleeding sparks. Lines of light ran underneath his skin and gave him an unhealthy, eerie glow.

Orphan turned to the darkness and said, "Show yourself."

The voice sounded amused. "I'd be afraid you'd shoot me too," it said. "You've become awfully proficient with that gun awfully fast." There was a sigh, long and heavy like a wave. "So you have come at last."

Orphan squinted into the darkness. He felt unnerved. Something was moving there, a shape he could not quite make out, large and malevolent. He said, "Where is Lucy?"

"Nearby," the voice said, and Orphan felt his heart quicken; he took a deep breath, exhaling the air slowly to try to calm himself. He said, "Release her."

"So you have come at last," the voice said again, and again, there was the sense of deep amusement coming from it. "Descended to the Underworld to bargain with the lord of death. But what, Orphan, do you have to bargain with?"

"Show yourself," Orphan said again. He felt suddenly like a small boy, lost, his voice weak and lonely in the immense dark. The Bookman was toying with him.

The Bookman laughed. Then he said, "I can give you Lucy back. Alive again. Better than alive. But for what price, my young poet? Do you think you can just wander in here like a lost figure of myth and demand your love back?"

Orphan looked into the darkness and saw only moving shadows. "What do you want from me?" he whispered into the dark.

"Ah. Good." A movement, and a disturbing sense of something like a giant insect, multi-legged and with too many eyes. "You are seeing reason."

"Why did you kill her?"

The voice returned to him from the other side of the square now, and he turned to it. I'm bound to him, he realised. For Lucy I will serve him.

"I began to tell you, when you killed Mr. Worth," the voice said, sounding surprisingly peevish. "You leave quite a trail in your wake."

An image of Jack lying on the floor came unbidden into Orphan's mind, and he felt his heart constrict. "Will you...?" he said. "Could you fix him? Jack?"

"I could," the Bookman said. Moving again. Circling around Orphan, like a hunter who had closed on his prey. "I might. Should I?"

"He was my friend," Orphan said. As the words left his mouth he thought again of Jack. He had taken him in, at Payne's. He had cared about him. And Orphan had shot him. Suddenly he felt disgusted with himself. And angry.

"I know," the Bookman said. "Ironic, isn't it? You see, I could bring him back if I chose, but how would Jack react?" The voice sighed, a gust of wind that stroked Orphan's cheek. "He never knew he was a simulacrum."

The Bookman laughed. In the distance the waves rolled against the shore. On the table undrunk tea sat cooling. On the black-and-white squares a man lay dead.

Orphan felt tired, old. He sat back in his chair. So Jack really was his friend. "Please," he said. "Bring him back."

"First Lucy, now Jack?" the Bookman said. "What will you give me?"

But Orphan had played that game before. Ever since that night by the Thames he had played a riddle-game, his opponents changing but the questions remaining the same. A question for a question, he thought. You will tell me what you want from me when you decide it's time. I know you now. What is it that you want me to do? What is it that you want me to learn?

"Who was he?" he asked, pointing to the dead, suited man.

"Adam Worth," the Bookman said. "Quite an ingenious, ruthless criminal. I assimilated him some years ago, following his theft of the Duchess of Devonshire – ever seen that painting? quite marvellous – from Agnew & Sons. He already had an extremely successful network of criminals working under him – in fact, I believe your friend at Scotland Yard once called him the Caesar of crime."

"My friend?" He felt a sudden chill.

"Come, Orphan," the Bookman said. Moving again. Orphan felt too tired to try to follow him with his eyes. Yet he was aware of the movement. "Let us keep no secrets between us. Even now Inspector Adler is keeping watch over the entrance to Payne's. She's had you under surveillance ever since you left Guy's Hospital. Didn't you know that?" The Bookman laughed, and said, "Of course not. She is very good. She felt – quite rightly, of course – that you could lead her to me. Mistakenly, though, as it turns out – by the time she realises you will not come out and makes her move, she will be able to find nothing."

The chill he felt spread, numbing him. "What do you mean?"

The Bookman's answer did not give him cause for relief. "You'll find out."

"Why?" Orphan said. Real bewilderment made him belligerent. "Why kill Lucy? Why bring me here?" Then the words of the suited man – Adam Worth, he thought – came back to him, and he said, "The Martian probe."

"Yes," the Bookman said.

"It keeps coming back to that," Orphan said. "But why? Why destroy it?"

"Because it was not – is not – a probe," the Bookman said, and his voice was very close now, almost caressing, issuing behind Orphan's shoulder. Orphan sat very still, as if, by his stillness, he could fool the Bookman into moving away.

"It is a beacon," the Bookman said.

His voice was low and soft, whispering directly into Orphan's ear. Something scaly and inhuman touched his shoulder, and he almost jumped.

"A beacon," the Bookman said. "To be carried into space by the design and engineering of humans, but for a purpose of which they know nothing. Think of it, Orphan," that awful voice said, "think of a great cannon booming, a cloud of smoke, heat torching the ground below as the cannon fires, shooting its cargo into the atmosphere, and beyond. Into the coldness of space. To float alone amongst the stars – isn't that poetic?"

"Yes," Orphan whispered, paralysed by the Bookman's touch. What was he, he thought, desperately, helplessly – what strange, alien being had trapped him here, to speak to him of poetry?

"Poetry has its own irony," the Bookman said. "The probe would reach space, but it would not head to Mars, to explore its arid deserts and its false canals. Instead, it will spread out dishes like the opening petals of a flower. And it will begin to broadcast a poem out to the distant stars. In the language of the creatures you, in your ignorance, call Les Lézards. Do you know what message it will carry, Orphan? What poem will make its way into galactic space?"

He could feel the Bookman behind him, a shadowy presence made solid, made real and threatening beyond anything he had ever imagined. He whispered, "No," and heard his own voice come back to him, not recognisable as his own.

"It will be a song of surpassing beauty," the Bookman said. "And it will be a poem of summons. It will whisper of the beauty of this world, of Earth, of its blue oceans and green lands, of its abundance of life, its riches, its minerals and fuel and rare metals. A world ready for the taking. A world already half-subdued." Something like a lizard's tongue, yet different, hissed in the air beside his ear, tasting the words. "Come, it would say. Come, our brothers and sisters. We have been lost for a long time, but now we are found. Come to this world we have taken for ourselves, and we could rule it together."

The words took on a seductive tone, forcing tendrils into Orphan's mind, conjuring new, disturbing images inside his head. Whether it was his imagination alone, or some influence of the Bookman, he didn't know, but suddenly he was no longer sitting at the table but flying, disembodied, through a space strewn with stars, and below him was a globe, a blue world streaked with the white of clouds and the green of living things. It was beautiful – but then he turned, and he saw the small black body he had last seen, blown apart, in Richmond Park. The probe sailed through space, as small as a pebble, only seen by the occasional glint of light from its side. He turned again, facing away from the Earth, and his breath caught in a mixture of wonder and fear. For amongst the stars rose a fleet, thousands upon thousands of silver discs burning in the rays of the distant suns, coming closer and closer.

"Invasion," the Bookman whispered in his ear, jolting him back into awareness. His – hand? – tightened on Orphan's shoulder. "When the probe is released, it will sing its song out to the stars. And amongst the stars, Les Lézards' ancient kin will listen. And they will come, Orphan. They will come. And they will take this world for themselves."

"But it was destroyed," Orphan said. "You destroyed it!"

"I was misled," the Bookman said. His touch on Orphan's shoulder slackened. His voice took on an aspect of haunting sadness. "The probe in the park was a decoy. The real one is at this very minute making its way by airship to Caliban's Island, where the launch facility is all but complete. It has to be destroyed, Orphan. Do you see?" It seemed the Bookman was almost pleading with him. "This is not about a single human life, however regrettable. The fate of the world itself lies, as they say, in the balance."

He released Orphan. On a sudden instinct Orphan stood up and turned, looking for the Bookman.

He had already retreated back into the shadows. Yet Orphan caught a glimpse of him, as he moved away: he was not human and not lizard, but a giant, caterpillar-like creature, its scaly head adorned with eye-stalks that, even as they were disappearing in the darkness, for one small moment seemed to wink at him.

"Destroy the probe," the voice of the Bookman said, growing faint, "and I will return Lucy to you."

"Why me?" Orphan said. Pleaded.

"A pawn does not ask for its player's strategy," the Bookman said. "And I have been playing this particular game for more centuries than you can imagine. You must destroy the probe."

He felt himself sinking into the Bookman's web. A fly caught in a silk mesh from which there was no escape. Finally, he said, "How?"

"Will you do it?" the Bookman said. His voice echoed in Orphan's mind, over the black-and-white squares, the miniature board on which he played his game with Orphan.

And Orphan, a captured pawn, whispered at last –

"Yes."

PART II
The Odyssey

NINETEEN
Across the Channel

I travelled among unknown men,
In lands beyond the sea;
Nor, England! did I know till then
What love I bore to thee.
  – William Wordsworth, "Lucy"

It was some time later. The place was France.

Orphan arrived at Nantes train station in the early hours of the morning. He had crossed the Channel, travelled by train to Paris and from there took the night journey across France. He got to see little of the country. His only reading material along the way had been a newspaper: and the news was not reassuring. One item in particular concerned Orphan:

EXPLOSION ROCKS CHARING CROSS ROAD!
By our special correspondent

In the early hours of yesterday morning a subterranean explosion rocked the foundations of Charing

Cross Road and its environs. The explosion sent
shockwaves throughout the nearby neighbourhoods,
causing damage to property and health. Two people
were mildly hurt when their baruch-landau fell into
an opening in the ground, and several people were
rushed into hospital with minor injuries. The explosion caused damage to roads and houses, and
destroyed a bookshop, Payne's, in Cecil Court. Scotland Yard Inspector Irene Adler was on the spot
immediately after the explosion, with a full team of
constables and police automatons. She and her team
were seen by this reporter to dig through the ruins of
Payne's, where the proprietor and his assistant are
feared to be missing amidst the rubble. Inspector
Adler was not available for comment. The cause of
the explosion is unknown, though experts suggest it
was caused by a build-up of natural gas deep under
the city–

He found himself worrying about the Inspector. And he
worried about his journey, about where he should go,
and wondered how he would accomplish the seemingly
impossible goal the Bookman had set him. But most of
all he missed Lucy, and he worried, worried until he
could barely think or eat: for, just before his interview
with the Bookman was at an end, he saw her again.

"I can give you back Lucy," the Bookman had said,
and then–

She came to him out of the water of that dark lake.
Her hair fell down to her shoulders. Her body was as
he remembered it. She ran to him, appearing at the

edge of the light and rushing forward, and she embraced him, and her lips on his were the taste of happiness. He kissed her, holding her close to him, the cold water of the lake soaking his shirt. "Oh, Orphan," she whispered, and she looked into his eyes and he could have remained that way forever.

"Touching," the Bookman said. And then, as quickly and mysteriously as she had come, Lucy was gone again, and Orphan, helpless, could do nothing. He, too, had to obey the Bookman's commands.

And the Bookman had given him papers, and money, and instructions. He was to go to France, to the city of Nantes which lies close to the Atlantic Ocean, and there he would be met. He wondered who it would be to welcome him.

In the event, the Bookman's agent waited for him at the station, and Orphan got a bit of a shock.

As the train came to rest against the platform Orphan glimpsed, through the window, two figures standing outside. One was a large, fat man holding a cane: the other was short and balding and even from a distance Orphan could see he had a scar down his left cheek that ended just below the eye. When he got off the train the two men approached him, and the short one made directly for Orphan's luggage. The fat man beamed at Orphan and threw his cane to his servant, took Orphan's outstretched hand in both of his, and shook it energetically. "Welcome to my home town," he said. "Welcome to Nantes."

"Thank you," Orphan said, "Mr–?"

The fat man looked taken aback. "Why, I thought my name is well known even in that lizards'-spawn hell of yours across the Channel," he said.

"I'm sorry, I don't—"

The fat man drew himself up. He snapped his fingers and his servant threw him his cane. The man caught it single-handedly and twirled it. "The name," he said stiffly, "is Verne. Jules Verne."

"Jules Verne? The author of *L'Île mystérieuse*?"

"Amongst many others," the writer said modestly. "Is this all the luggage you have?" He barked an order in French at his manservant, then turned to Orphan with a shrug. "This is my man, Robur," he said. Then he smirked. "I call him 'the conqueror'."

"How so?"

"Because of, shall we say, his prowess, with the ladies?"

Robur grinned at Orphan from behind the luggage.

They went in a coach and Robur did the driving. He drove the horses very fast. As they went through the narrow streets Orphan saw strange figures gathered and thought, for a moment, that he had seen royal lizards. In France?

"What," he said, and then wasn't sure what to say and merely pointed through the window. Verne turned to look.

"Punks de Lézard," he said.

They were an odd, mixed crowd, Orphan saw, watching them in horrified fascination: their hair was cut off entirely for both the males and the females, save for several who had a curious ridge or spine made of a narrow strip of hair in the middle of their scalp, that stood in tall spikes from their otherwise-bare heads. Their naked skulls were painted in a greenish-brown imitation of Les Lézards' skin, and were then patterned with bands of alternating colour. Their faces, too, were painted to resemble those of lizards, and their clothes were sparse and made to resemble scales. They walked around in small groups, and when one opened his mouth to speak, perhaps to shout at the passing coach, Orphan saw he had had his tongue cut so that it, too, resembled a lizard's.

"What are they?" he asked, overwhelmed.

"Lizard boys," Verne said, and snorted. And then, more quietly. "Children at play, but nasty, the way children sometimes turn. Ignore them."

But Orphan found them hard to ignore.

They sped away and soon the town, and the strange youths he saw, were gone behind them. At last they halted outside a large villa that stood in isolated grounds outside of the city. The house sat on the bank of a wide river – the Loire, Verne informed him; a large sailboat was moored outside.

"Welcome, welcome," Verne said, ushering Orphan through the large doors of the house into a cluttered living area. He clapped his hands twice and lights came on. Another clap and unseen heaters began to send tendrils of heat into the room.

"Amazing," Orphan said. The room, he saw, was a treasure trove of quaint mechanical constructions and odd automatons: a replica of Vaucanson's duck, for instance, sat in a cage beside one window, mechanically eating and disposing of its food at the two opposite ends of its body. Another, a replica of a young boy, sat writing, over and over again, a short message on a slate. Elsewhere there were calculating machines, toy soldiers that marched on the spot, the model of a blowfish growing and thinning, as constant as a clock, a miniature flute player, a Tesla set, an Edison player, a steam-powered, miniature ship moving in a large aquarium of water with metal fish swimming underneath it, and a mechanical giant squid that reached out tentacles for the ship, never quite seizing it; there were clocks and records, spyglasses and microscopes, mirrors like something out of a carnival, each reflection different and contrary: and everywhere there was space it was occupied by books, lying haphazard over this museum of curiosities like sleepy attendants.

"The wife and kids are away for a while," Verne said. "Italy. They love it there. And it will keep them out of the way..." He sighed. "Bedrooms are upstairs, also shower, bath, et cetera. Kitchen through here. Robur!"

"Sir?" The small man appeared beside him.

"Fix our guest some food," Verne said.

Robur disappeared towards the kitchen.

"How did you get involved in all this," Orphan said to Verne. "Sir?"

"Oh, call me Jules," Verne said. His face became serious, almost stern. "I will tell you all," he said, "but all in good time. There will be plenty of time to talk – on the ship."

"You?" Orphan said. "You are coming with me to Caliban's Island?"

It seemed like madness.

The writer chuckled. "Who better?" he said, patting his stomach. "So I am not as young or as lithe as I used to be, but trust me, there is life and spirit in this old man yet! Robur!"

"Sir?"

He seemed to have simply materialised there.

"Fix our guest a drink."

"Sir."

"Drink, my young friend?"

"Please," Orphan said, a little dazed. "Some red wine would be lovely."

Verne smiled, Robur did his disappearing act, and in a moment Orphan was left holding a large goblet filled almost to the brim with a dark cabernet sauvignon. He gulped it down and felt welcome warmth and a relaxing haze settle over his mind. He would do what he could to work against the Bookman, he thought. Were it not for Lucy. Then he stood up with a shout and nearly spilled his drink.

A massive lizard had entered the room.

It was, he saw a moment later, not a royal lizard, but a creature very similar to those he last saw underneath the King's Arms in Drury Lane. It was six feet or more in length, with yellow bands and spots forming broken crosses on its body and powerful tail. The lizard ambled into the room, paused, and its tongue tasted the air.

"This is Victoria," Verne said.

"Victoria."

"My pet. Isn't she beautiful?"

Orphan downed the rest of his wine.

TWENTY
The Nautilus

Now would I give a thousand furlongs of sea for an
acre of barren ground, long heath, brown furze, any
thing. The wills above be done! but I would fain
die a dry death.

– William Shakespeare, *The Tempest*

Orphan woke up to dim light streaming in through the
open blinds. The black-velvet blinds; early-morning
light; the cold breeze coming in through an open window, making him shiver: finally, Verne's full-moon face
rising disembodied above him.

"Argh!" Orphan said, and shook himself awake.
Above him, Verne grinned. "Good morning, young Orphan," he said. "You slept for a long time, and now it is
time to set forth. It is time, Orphan." His smile melted
away, leaving him looking solemn and introspected. "It
is time," he said again, then fell silent.

Orphan rose, stood up, began hunting for his clothes.
A fresh suit of clothing was lying neatly on a chair beside the bed. "Robur is serving breakfast in the kitchen,"

Verne said. "Meet me there in fifteen minutes. We sail with the tide."

He felt clear-headed that morning, and he stood in the centre of the room for a long moment and stretched, and breathed in the sea air and felt it whisper promises. To go on the sea: it conjured images from books he had read in his youth, of treasures and battles and tropical storms. He thought, There is a book of poems in that. But he had not written a poem since that day at the Nell Gwynne, and his poetry had been bottled up, locked away together with Lucy: neither of them were as yet coming back from the dead.

He dressed and went downstairs. Verne was sitting alone at the kitchen table, a plate heaped with food before him. Robur was cooking eggs and bacon on the stove.

Verne indicated a vacant seat with the tip of his butter-smeared knife. "Sit down."

Robur served him a plate to accompany Verne's. Eggs, bacon, slices of toast, a strong sweet coffee, butter and jam: they were a powerful wake-up tonic. "English cooking," Robur said with a shake of his head, and disappeared into the adjoining room.

"Orphan," Verne said, "you are very much thrown into this without direction. You are a brave man; an honourable man. I respect that. As you know, I had attempted to go to Caliban's Island before. In that I was not successful. I was unable to land. Consequently, you must understand I know little more than you do. I do not know what expects us there. But I do know how to pilot a ship, which I have, as I have the men to operate it. I will give you all the help I can, and will tell you what little I know." He stood and reached out for Orphan, took his hand awkwardly in both of his. "I will do everything in my power to bring you there, and bring you back alive, too. If I can. Do you believe me?"

Orphan looked at the writer. For all that he was mixed up in these conspiracies of the Bookman, and for all of his effusive theatricality and his way of filling in its entirety the space around him, he found himself liking Verne. There was something almost innocent about the man, mixed with a childish, wicked glee at everything, as if life was one big game, a puzzle put out there for him to fathom one section at a time. "I do," he said, and meant it. Verne smiled. "Good."

They ate the rest of the meal in silence. When it was over, Verne stretched, sighed in satisfaction, and rose from his seat. Orphan, knowing the time had come, rose too. He felt jittery, but expectant too. The books he'd read kept flittering through his mind. Adventure on the high seas. He smiled to himself. Verne looked at him and replied with a smile of his own. For a moment they were two boys together, and the future was a bright game that would last all afternoon.

"Are you ready?"

"As ready as I'll ever be."

"Then let's go."

And so they did.

The clipper ship was magnificent. Three masts rose high above their heads, a white canopy of sails growing out of them like the first leaves of the season. The body was long and narrow, metal and wood intertwined, 18-pounder guns (as Orphan later learned) peeking out of portholes in the side of the ship. Sailors were already on board, and were busy with preparations.

"We're going in that?" Orphan said.

"She was built in Birmingham," Verne said, not a little proudly. "Served her time in the India trade. She's got some scars–" he pointed like a tour guide– "there, there, and there, where she was hit in a pirate attack a few years ago. But she's sturdy, and fast."

"It's huge. How many people have to be in on this?"

Verne smiled. "Only the captain. A funny old bird. The crew know nothing. As far as they are concerned they're taking cargo to King's Town – that's in Xaymaco, what you may see on some maps as Jamaica – and we're coming on board simply as additional cargo."

"I thought…" Orphan stopped. It hadn't really occurred to him just how he was meant to reach the island. "Maybe a steamer…"

"A steamer!" Verne said, and he pulled hard at his beard. "Those monstrosities pollute and destroy the ocean. They have no soul!"

"I thought you wrote stories about such vessels," Orphan said.

"Some things," Verne said, "are better left in books."

Orphan fell silent. They climbed on board, trying to get out of the way of the sailors. Robur hurried ahead with Verne's luggage. Orphan had a small pack, and was carrying it himself.

The wind blew at his hair, stirring it, and he realised it was growing long. He had shaved, earlier, standing before an enormous mirror with book cover paintings covering the walls, usually depicting some sort of futuristic vehicle or brooding menace. He had almost cut himself, but now on deck, leaning over the railings, the wind felt soft against his naked cheeks, and he raised his head high and breathed in the sea air. Adventure, he thought. Pirates and secret maps and treasure islands. He felt good, then, fresh and alive, and his determination returned like a full-blown wind. He would do this and return.

He followed Verne, who followed Robur, who followed a boy no more than sixteen who moved over the deck with the gait of someone who had spent his life on water. Orphan and Verne had neighbouring cabins on the middle deck, near the prow.

Orphan remained for only a few moments. Once he had settled his meagre belongings he left and returned to the deck and a comfortable position out of the way but with a good all-around view.

Sailors were hauling up cargo, whose nature Orphan couldn't discern (it came in large wooden boxes, and seemed heavy), while others were moving all about the ship, performing tasks of which he knew nothing. It reminded him, with a sudden intensity, of the docks in London, the ships coming and going, the bustling porters and sailors and merchants and officials and, in the distance, the song of the whales.

"Welcome," a deep voice said, close behind him, "to the *Nautilus*."

Orphan turned. A dark-skinned man with sharp, austere features, wearing a stiffly ironed uniform, stood there.

"A beautiful ship," Orphan said.

"A good ship," the man said. "I wouldn't give her up easily."

Orphan knew without being told that the captain of the *Nautilus* was speaking.

"I am Captain Dakkar," the man said, nodding. "And you must be our passenger, sir."

"It's a pleasure to meet you, captain," Orphan said. Dakkar had a lean, intense feel about him – the feel of a hunter, Orphan thought. On an impulse, he said, "My name is Orphan," and saw the captain's eyes narrow in thought.

"Orphan, then," Captain Dakkar said. "Welcome on board. You have every possibility of enjoying your journey, as long as you stay out of the way of my crew." He smiled, though his eyes didn't.

Orphan nodded. "Of course."

"Then I shall speak with you and Mr. Verne later," Dakkar said. "Please join me at my table tonight." His eyes, bright and curious, examined Orphan for a long moment. What did he see, Orphan wondered? And more importantly, how much did he know?

"Later," Dakkar said, touched two fingers to his forehead in a brief salute, and turned away. Orphan abandoned the deck and returned to his cabin. He needed some answers, and Verne, it seemed, had them all.

When he knocked on Verne's door, however, there was no answer, and as he went into his own cabin the room moved about him and for a moment he lost his balance. Then, peering out of the porthole, he realised they were moving.

The *Nautilus* was leaving port and heading to the open sea.

What can be said of this, the last ever voyage of the clipper *Nautilus*? It was a ship of misfits and rogues, of men from every nationality, their tones ranging from a Swede's pale eyes through their Indian captain's earth-dark skin, to the Nubian darkness, like a polished obsidian rock, of the second mate's muscle-twined arms. Sailors spoke and sang and cursed and took orders in a confusing babble of tongues of which Hindi, English, French, Portuguese and Zulu were only the most common. It had seemed to Orphan, after a few days, that there were, in fact, more languages than people on board the ship.

It was, he had to admit, a magnificent ship, though it was, in other terms, also an old one: steam-power was muscling in on the clipper ships, taking over their routes, speeding along from continent to continent and market to market, making the old sail-ships slowly redundant. The *Nautilus*, having sailed the trade routes all over the Everlasting Kingdom's domain, and beyond, was now a ship-for-hire, commanded by the eccentric Dakkar (the son of an Indian rajah, according to Verne's whispered comment) and run by a rag-tag crew of ex-navy sailors, ex-buccaneers, even (so said Verne) ex-pirates. Where Dakkar had picked his crew Verne didn't know. "Here and there and everywhere," he had said, spreading his arms wide, "wherever there is unrest and injustice and wherever men run foul of the law."

"Whose law?" Orphan had said, and the writer shrugged expansively and said, "On this planet, at this time, there is only one law."

"So Dakkar is not…" Orphan hesitated. "Like you…"

"Of the Bookman's party?" Verne shook his head. "Not as such. He is his own man."

What could be said about the *Nautilus*? She had a long, slim body, narrow hips and billowing sails; her decks were sturdy and sure, her bow rounded, her quarter-deck and forecastle joined, by closing in the waist, to form one continuous upper deck. The *Nautilus* carried ten mounted 18-pounder guns on the upper deck, firing through ports in the low bulwarks of the waist. The middle deck, where Orphan and Verne's cabins were also situated, carried twenty 18-pounders. It was less a trade-ship than a warship, Orphan privately thought, and he wondered what Verne – or indeed Dakkar – had in mind for her, and for him. Would they sail direct to Caliban's Island with all guns blazing? Would they attempt a stealthy landing, with a small boat lowered off the side of the ship at night? Or… But there was no point in wondering.

It was time to get some answers.

TWENTY-ONE
Gilgamesh's Journal

In few, they hurried us aboard a bark,
Bore us some leagues to sea; where they prepared
A rotten carcass of a boat, not rigg'd,
Nor tackle, sail, nor mast; the very rats
Instinctively had quit it: there they hoist us,
To cry to the sea that roar'd to us, to sigh
To the winds whose pity, sighing back again,
Did us but loving wrong.

   – William Shakespeare, *The Tempest*

Answers, however, were slow in coming. When he confronted Verne in his cabin the writer spread his arms wide and said apologetically, "There is not much that I do know. What I found out – most of it – is in my book. Surely you've read it?"

"*L'Île mystérieuse*? Well…"

"No?" Verne looked childishly hurt. "Well, there is not much there to help us, I'm afraid," he said. "It is only an account of a journey, you understand. I was never able to actually reach the island, as I mentioned to you. Oh, I have attempted to describe it, from what little obscure records I managed to locate, from drunken sailors' tales, from people who have claimed to have been shipwrecked on the island… but there are too many mysterious islands, Orphan, too many wild tales and flights of wild fancy, to really give an accurate idea of what awaits you – us – there. Do you know, they say that on another island, somewhere in the Carib Sea, there is a being just like the Bookman? A brother to him, a twin who plots his own mysterious plots? They call him the Binder." Verne snorted. Orphan kept very still. "The Binder. And what does he bind, I wonder?"

Orphan, thinking of Byron's words, of the Turk's, kept very still. Where the Bookman kills, the Binder restores. But restores what?

"Tell me what you know," Orphan said.

In place of an answer the writer spread a map onto the desk. "This," he said, pointing, "is the Gulf of Mexica. This is where the mass of land we call Vespuccia ends. And this mass of water is the Carib Sea. This is the island of Xaymaco; this is the island of Hayti, and this is the place Vespucci called Cuba. They are rough, yet prosperous places, populated by a mixture of Arawak, Carib, Aztec and Europeans. They are nominally under rule of Les Lézards, but only just." He stood up and began pacing up and down the cabin, his hands clasped behind his back. "Somewhere in that sea, I am sure of it, is Caliban's Island." he stopped and looked at Orphan, frustration in his eyes. "There are stories that the island… that the island moves. That it is never in the same place. I am referring to sightings, reported by ships all over the Carib Sea and beyond it. Of course, most of these can be discounted, ignored, the ramblings of the drunk or easily impressionable. And yet…"

"You don't know where the island is?" Orphan said, surprising himself by nearly shouting. Verne grinned a little sheepishly. "There are ways to find it," he said. He gestured to a sea-chest that stood, closed and locked, by the porthole. "Before we left I arranged for some – specialised – scientific equipment to be delivered."

"Delivered from?" Orphan said, but he already knew the answer.

"Our employer," Verne said. "Don't worry, getting there this time is going to be as easy as – how do you say? – falling off a log."

As he stood alone on the deck and watched the water parting before the ship, Orphan was less than comforted by Verne's assurance. Falling off a log, he decided, was most likely painful, and possibly fatal. Not something he was quite looking forward to.

He watched the sun dipping into the sea. He looked back at the wake of the ship and the foaming water. Back on the deck, two sailors were playing cards, and another was lying asleep in a hammock.

Dinner that night was served at the captain's cabin, a simple but delicious affair of grilled fresh fish, potatoes (one of Vespucci's – or rather the lizards' – most widely appreciated gifts brought to Europe), shiny and fragrant in oil and spices, served with a good French white wine supplied by Verne. The captain didn't drink, though he raised his glass in toast to, "The King of England, may he take his rightful place once more!" which Orphan found oddly discomforting.

Two cryptic things had happened during the meal. One was said, during an otherwise ordinary, civil conversation that ranged over many topics and remained cautiously general on each. In the middle of the dessert course (xocolatl, perhaps the greatest of the gifts brought back), Verne had turned to Dakkar and said, in the middle of a discussion about giant squid, "Did you bring her?"

Dakkar had dabbed his lips with a napkin and said, "Yes," in a soft, almost imperceptible voice. Verne then began to talk about the weather.

At the end of the meal the second occurred. Verne had commended the captain's cook, and Orphan enthusiastically joined him, and the pleased captain ordered the cook to be called. When he arrived Orphan was surprised to see a tall, slim youth – no more than seventeen in his appearance – who smiled at them shyly. Verne spoke passionately of the menu, offered to hire the chef away from Dakkar, to great hilarity, and was vividly and amusingly drunk.

The boy had long, fine hair and a smooth, almost featureless face that had never, it seemed, been shaved. Before he left, as they were wishing him well, his eyes locked with Orphan's, for just a moment, and the boy nodded. It was a nod of acknowledgment, of recognition. It was the briefest of movements. Then the boy turned and walked out of the cabin.

"A really most excellent cook," Verne said, sloshing the wine in his glass just a little. Dakkar acknowledged him with a smile. He then ordered his men to leave.

"Caliban's Island," he said then, speaking to Orphan, fixing his cold dark eyes on him. "I have often tried to find it. A place of great evil, for it is the place the lizards come from. The place where they crashed to Earth." His fist thumped the table. "They must be destroyed!"

"Really, old boy," Verne said, "you need to calm down about this. You're scaring the kid."

"India shall have its independence!" Dakkar said.

"No doubt," Verne said.

The conversation concluded soon after that. If he had learned something from it, Orphan thought, it was only that neither Dakkar nor Verne knew anything about the island. They didn't even know how to find it.

Yet Verne had instruments. A chest full of them in his cabin. He did not want to think of what they might be. They were the tools of the Bookman, just as Orphan was, a blunted tool made to strike at the Bookman's enemies.

Orphan climbed onto the deck and stood there, looking at the night. For a moment he thought he heard a whale's call in the distance. There were a lot of stars.

He swore again to himself that he would return. That he would save Lucy. And as for the Bookman…

Then he laughed, because he knew he was being absurd, and he joined a game of cards with three sailors and after an hour won a handful of coins, half of them unknown to him.

Days on the ship spent under bright clear skies… Flying fish pursued the *Nautilus*, silver fins flashing in the sunlight as they arced through the air. In the second week a pod of dolphins accompanied them from a distance. Occasionally, far away, he saw the disappearing hump of a giant whale.

He still had Tom Thumb's gun, and he practised shooting on the deck with some of the sailors. He played cards, and lost more than he'd won. Then, a week into the voyage, he returned to his cabin and found a book waiting for him on the bed.

He sat down and looked at it curiously. It was an old, weather-beaten notebook, bound in peeling leather. He lifted it in his hands, traced damage on the cover, opened it. Old, brittle paper. Foxed pages and water damage. Many of the pages were torn.

The handwriting inside jolted him.

Jagged and cramped, packed tight into the page. It was the handwriting of his friend.

It was Gilgamesh's.

He closed the book and held it for a long moment, his eyes staring into nothing, thinking of his dead friend. Where had this come from?

Then he noticed the note that must have fallen to the floor as he entered the cabin, and he picked it up and read it. *I have tried to rely on primary sources as much as possible*, it said. *I found this journal fifteen years ago, in a junk shop in Marseille. Perhaps you would find it interesting. How true its account is I cannot say.* The note was signed by Verne.

Orphan lifted up the journal and felt suddenly very far from home. He looked out of the porthole at the endless sea beyond, and thought back. Gilgamesh had been… a friend, and a part of his life. And now he was

dead, and here was his journal, as old as a drowned
ship.

  He took a deep breath to calm himself, and blinked
several times. Then he opened the journal – really, a
small collection of leaves, incomplete and beguiling –
and began to read.

> A clear, calm day. The sea lies flat. We have left
> the Aztecs last night with a mutual exchange of
> many gifts, dancing and singing and drinking. I
> shall miss [unreadable], her smooth dark skin
> and her smile in the darkness… Everyone looks
> downcast today, despite the weather – we are all
> suffering last night's excess. Our course is
> leisurely, for now, and we plan to stop at one of
> the islands before entering the Atlantic and fur-
> ther stock up with provisions. A successful trip,
> and Amerigo is happy and carefree, almost a
> new man after the trials of the journey here.
>
>   …
>
> An amazing land! I have never thought to see
> such wild beauties as the forests of this new
> land, its strange animals and unknown flora. My
> notebook is filling up fast with lines of poetry,
> which I will attempt to structure into an epic
> narrative poem upon our return. I lie in a ham-
> mock on the deck and dream of glory, success
> following publication, a long life with many
> women, children and grand-children, at last,
> rich and old and famous, burial in Westminster
> Abbey… I smile even as I write this. But it is

good to daydream. Our journey is nearly at an
end, and has been successful beyond all expecta-
tions. We will be welcomed like heroes. I
wonder – have we opened up this new world for
good? Will the navy sail here now, to take control of this wild continent and its wilder islands,
to establish trade missions and new colonies for
the glory of Britannia? No doubt. Yet the people
of these lands have civilisations of their own,
some quite powerful and old. I do not take the
Aztecs lightly, nor the others, the [unreadable]
who are fierce warriors. Tomorrow we shall stop
at Xaymaco, then home.

···

The island is like a mirage, a tropical paradise unlike anything I have seen in my travels. Several
of the crew disappeared today, seduced by this
place, and I doubt they will be back. Amerigo is
furious, but there is little he can do. Our priority
now is to return and bring back the fortune we
have found. The cook brewed xocolatl today –
we have all become overly fond – nay, depend-
ent! – on it, and I can only imagine what the
response will be like back home! We are all going
to be rich beyond our wildest dreams.

···

Open sea again. The weather is turning, wind
building up and slowing us down. There is a storm
on the horizon, coming near. Something has been
troubling me, something in Amerigo's behaviour…

···

I am filled with foreboding. The nature of the
[unreadable] I have found out piecemeal, first
from the Mexicas and later from the Arawak, al-
though the stories are pervasive all around the
Carib Sea. They concern an island which has no
name, and they are told in whispers, though
what they describe must have happened – if it
happened at all – beyond any living man's memory. This is the way I heard the story for the first
time, from a priest of Atlacamani, the goddess of
storms. It tells of an epic journey – not unlike
our own, perhaps – of a people called the Toltec,
who lived in this part of the world and had built
a flotilla of ships to go and explore the ocean, to
find new lands and bring back their treasures.
The fleet was not gone far (which I take to mean
it was still in the Carib Sea or only recently outside it) when night – the priest was very specific
on this, though I do wonder if it isn't some sort
of an allegory – became day. Brightness washed
the decks of the ships and the wind stood still, so
that the ships found themselves stranded in mid-
sea, and there was much panic. Not only light
came from the skies, but heat, and as the sailors
raised their heads to the heavens they saw a
shooting star, growing in the skies as it plum-
meted down to earth. It grew so large and so
bright that they had to shield their eyes against
it. Many died that night. The star fell down and
– by luck, or divine intervention – landed not in
open water but on a small, remote island that

was [unreadable[from the ships. The resultant explosion blinded many of the men, and many died later, in months and years to come, of blisters and growths and sickness. The ships did not attempt to approach the island. The flotilla turned and sailed back from that place, which is known to this day only as the Place of Sickness. This is what the priest told me, and it is an old tale, more of a ghost story to be told around the fire than any exact account of a long-gone event. Yet I wonder… and so, I fear, does Amerigo.

...

I should perhaps record the other stories, too, though I am wary of them. Little-told tales, heard as jokes or whispers from the Arawak. It seemed strange to me, indeed, that the ancient Toltec – or their inheritors the Mexica – never attempted to sail to the island, to examine it, perhaps to find traces of that fallen star. Yet the people of the islands were not so unified in fear, and I have heard tell of fisher folk and others who had, by accident or design, found themselves near this nameless island. Some have never returned. And some have come back sick, or dying, or insane, with tales no one would believe. Some even say the island moves, that it is rarely at the same place twice, and that it is haunted by a malevolent ghost. All nonsense, no doubt, yet Amerigo, who has heard the stories as much as I have, is enchanted by them. "It must

have been a meteor," he said to me, "of an un-
usual size." His eyes became dreamy then and
he said, "Would it not be a perfect ending to our
voyage, [unreadable], that, after we have explored this world, we can perhaps explore the
stones of another?"

I, too, was taken in by his enthusiasm, but
only momentarily. Though the weather is now
clear again and our speed stays at peak, Amerigo
is suggesting a detour. He is determined to explore this island. I am fearful, but do not know
why.

...

Before leaving Xaymaco, Amerigo has taken on
board a young Arawak man who claims to have
seen the island. We are goin [unreadable] direction, though there is not yet a trace of it. The
sailors are treating this as merely another excur-
sion, and I wish I could share their lightness of
heart. Yet, though I am wary, I too am compelled to this island: I too want to discover this
possible visitor from another world and learn of
the truth in the old stories of the Mexica. The
aura of mystery surrounds this island, and it is
more attractive and irresistible than anything we
have yet discovered. Tomorrow...

...

We have found it! Even as I write the island lies
before us, wrapped in clouds, cloaked in dusk. It
is beautiful, though the eyes cannot penetrate
far beyond the shore. Everyone on board is quiet

as the island exerts a not-inconsiderable influence over us. It is at the same time inviting and brooding, peaceful – yet with an underlying, almost sinister feeling. I must know what lies beyond the clouds. I now regard those trifling lines of poetry I had written as just that – trifling. My masterpiece will be this island, its mysteries explored in verse so beautiful as to make the ladies weep. The landing party, with Amerigo and myself, will go at first light tomorrow. I–

It was the end of the writing. There had been more pages, before and after, but they had been removed at some time in the past. Orphan held the journal close to his chest, almost hugging it, and curled up on the narrow bed. He thought of all the people he had lost, from the parents he never knew, to Gilgamesh, to Lucy, and with each one the pain came harsher and more threatening, like tropical lightning. I can't bring back my parents, he thought, and I can't bring back Gilgamesh. But Lucy… and he thought of her laugh, and the way she had looked at him, and he fell asleep at last, still clutching the ancient journal to his chest.

TWENTY-TWO
Pirates

Lastly, the crime of piracy, or robbery and depredation upon the high seas, is an offence against the universal law of society; a pirate being, according to Sir Edward Coke, hostis humani generis. As therefore he has renounced all the benefits of society and government, and has reduced himself afresh to the same state of nature, by declaring war against all mankind, all mankind must declare war against him.

– William Blackstone, *Commentaries on the Laws of England*

It was a full two weeks later when the *Nautilus* entered the region of water known as the Carib Sea. A storm was building up on the horizon, where the setting sun cast blood-red and stained-yellow hues across a cloudscape of rain. Lightning flashed amidst the distant build-up, sizzling silver spears reaching from the heavens to the sea. The air felt hot and clammy, and the sailors had a tense, almost haunted look in their eyes.

215

The gunners manned their positions in full shift. The crew was silent, and the vessel had the feel of a ghost ship sailing other, ethereal seas. A single word caught Orphan's attention, pushing away all others, a whisper caught in the stillness of the charged air: *pirates!*

"What does it mean?" Orphan whispered to Verne.

The Frenchman looked tense. "This storm," he said. He looked like he would have said more, but at that moment a shout rose on the deck, and one of the guns discharged, the ball arcing over the water ahead, landing with an explosion of foam in the dark water below.

"Hold your fire!" came the shouted order of Captain Dakkar, cold and sharp like a sliver of ice. He stood at the prow, looking intently through his eyepiece at the horizon. Verne and Orphan had come and stood behind him. Orphan tried, but could see little in the distance. It was turning dark, the sea illuminated only by the flash of the incessant lightning.

"What is it?" Verne said, softly, to Dakkar, echoing Orphan. The captain folded his eyepiece and turned to him, tension etched into the lines on his face. "Perhaps nothing," he said.

At that moment thunder filled the air, close and unexpected, and seemed to go on forever. Rain burst out of the sky and fell on the *Nautilus*, making the deck slick and mirror-like. A wind rose and pummelled the ship.

The storm had arrived.

And with it, with a scream that rose from the lookout above and spread like water amongst the crew, were pirates.

Orphan, holding on to a rope to keep himself steady, peered out through raindrops and saw the pirate ship.

It was a dark shadow, moving across a deceptively calm sea towards them, almost gliding, its movement as smooth and uninterrupted as that of a heated knife. It sailed towards them, and its sails were black.

The pirate ship was a thing of darkness and dread. At the prow a giant, chalk-white head looked forward, severed at the neck, its nose a malevolent red. A giant, leering smile was painted on its face.

"The *Joker*!" called the lookout, and Dakkar had to shout at the crew to be quiet. They were frightened, Orphan thought. They recognised and dreaded the name.

He felt only a ball of excitement, taut and hard, forming in his stomach. Dread, exhilaration – he felt awake, alive, his senses growing to perceive minute details, each crack and line in the clown's wooden face that sailed towards them.

"Hold your fire!"

The men were tense.

"On my command – shoot!"

But the first shot came from the *Joker*.

Orphan saw the ball before he heard the discharge. The ball whistled as it flew towards them. It smashed into the side of the ship, and Dakkar, momentarily losing his balance, shouted hoarsely for the men to fire.

A volley of shots emerged from the 18-pounders and flew towards the enemy ship. Several hit, and a cheer rose, only to be silenced almost immediately.

The pirate ship was closing in fast.

It was close enough now for Orphan to see her name, tattooed to her side like a scar. The *Joker*. And the hideous clown face, the ship's mascot, grinned and leered at the *Nautilus* incessantly as if maddened.

"Fire!"

The guns fired, the *Joker* was hit, and continued to come. It was firing back, and the balls whispered overhead and sent exploding plumes of water high into the air when they missed, blood and wood where they hit.

"Fire!"

Then the *Joker* was close, close enough to reach out, almost to touch the dark figures that could now be seen on its deck, moving with silent determination.

The two ships touched, side to side.

The pirates swooped on the *Nautilus*. They sailed overboard with long thick hemp ropes and landed with cutlasses at the ready. They were an ugly, ferocious bunch, half-savage men with maps of scars over their naked torsos.

Lightning struck, and struck again, and again, and the sky was full of electric light, and illuminated the pirates' savage faces.

The lightning! Orphan thought. It was coming from the pirate ship. Everything was illuminated now, the air humming with electricity, and he could see its source, and his excitement (which had not yet abated) began at last turning into fear.

Rising from the top of the central mast of the *Joker*, a bright metallic ball shone like a moon as it was hit, over and over again, by lightning.

Then he had to turn his gaze, and draw his gun, because pirates were now swarming the deck. He shot, once, and a man fell down. Then he had to duck, and someone kicked him and connected with the side of his head, and he fell back.

The man was almost on him when Orphan shot him through the chest.

Then he pushed the fallen man off him and stood up. The deck was full of fighting men. Bodies littered the ground and their blood was washed away by the rain and the wind. The deck was red and shone in the light. It was sleek with blood.

He scanned through the faces as the lightning struck ferociously down. He could see no trace of Verne, or Robur. His eyes stopped on the sight of the young ship's cook, who seemed an island of calm in the midst of battle. He was fighting three men at once, and was unarmed, while they had swords, and one was reaching for a gun. The boy's leg shot out and took one pirate in the face, breaking his nose. He whirled round then, snatched the gun from the other pirate, shot the third in the same movement, then returned the gun in an arc that took in the remaining pirate's head and connected with it.

He looked up and saw Orphan. Again, there was that nod of recognition, as if they somehow knew each other. He made a movement with his hand that said, stay low. Then he returned to the fight.

Thunder shook the deck. Orphan ducked against a threatening cutlass, slipped, fell on his back, shot. If he had hit – or who – he didn't know. He remained down and realised no one was paying him much attention. Many other bodies already littered the deck.

Thunder boomed again, the sound seeming to emerge from everywhere at once, a shockwave of noise sweeping the deck, and the lightning struck again. It illuminated the deck of the *Joker* and, as Orphan raised his head, what he saw made him freeze as if he had been struck.

Standing majestically on the forward-deck of the *Joker* was a lizard.

It was a royal lizard, a Les Lézard, and for a long moment Orphan couldn't think, could not understand what he was seeing. Then lightning flashed again and he saw the figure in stark relief, and the sailors on the deck, seeing it too, seemed to lose heart in the fight, to be pushed back by the pirates as if the appearance of the lizard signalled the end of the fight, and of the *Nautilus* itself.

Feet passed closed to Orphan and someone kicked him in the ribs and made him shout. A grinning, leering face loomed above him, and with it a gun that was pointed at his heart. He tried to roll, then heard a shot go off.

When he opened his eyes he was still alive, and instead of the pirate the face he saw was that of the boy-cook. "Stay down!" he said, and then he himself crouched down beside Orphan, and pointed ahead. "Wyvern," he said, his voice soft and emotionless.

The lizard had stepped onto the *Nautilus'* deck. He was tall and dignified-looking. He was white, decorated in pale bands, and one of his eyes was missing. He wore a black eye-patch; his other eye was red, like dying fire.

He wore loose, colourful clothes, with a cutlass and a gun on either side of the body, and his tongue darted and tasted the air. He seemed to smile…

He stepped forward and the battle surged away from him. Then Orphan noticed it. The lizard wore large metal gloves, and they were pointed forward now, towards the battle, and his digits were spread evenly, and shone silver.

"Stay down!" the boy-cook hissed.

"Who is that?" Orphan hissed back. The white lizard stepped slowly forward, arms raised, digits pointing.

"Captain Wyvern."

Lightning struck.

It struck the ball on the top of the mast but, this time, did not stop there. Down the lightning went, through wires that fell down the sails and reached the deck, and continued… overboard, over to the *Nautilus*, where they appeared again and rose into Captain Wyvern's hands.

Lightning flashed.

Bars of hissing, sizzling electricity shot out of Captain Wyvern's hands and hit the men fighting on the deck. Here, he pointed, and here, and here, and with each imperceptible movement lightning fell from the tips of his digits and hit one of the *Nautilus*' sailors.

Lightning flashed, again and again and again.

The men who were hit screamed, but only briefly.

The air on the deck filled with the smell of cooking meat.

Strangely, horrifyingly, even as he was gagging, Orphan's stomach made a growling noise, his body reacting to the smell the way it would to any cooking meat: with hunger. Then a wave hit the ship and the deck moved, and one of the corpses came rolling down and almost crashed into him and he screamed, and was sick all over himself.

The boiled face of the corpse looked at him with the glazed look of a mounted fish.

It was Robur.

Slowly, with the same serene expression on his face, the young cook stood up with his hands raised. He kicked Orphan, not hard. Orphan rose with his hands up and tried not to retch.

There was movement behind him. He half-turned, saw the face of a pirate, sunburnt skin livid with blood, broken teeth exposed in an animalistic grin, and something raised to strike…

He tried to escape but his movements were slow and sluggish, as if he was drowning in water, and then something connected with the back of his head and pain shot through him and brought with it darkness.

TWENTY-THREE
Mr. Spoons

I steer'd from sound to sound, as I sail'd, as I sail'd,
I steer'd from sound to sound, as I sail'd,
I steer'd from sound to sound and many ships I found
And most of them I burned, as I sail'd.
  – Captain Kidd

Orphan came to on the *Joker*'s deck. He was lying on his side, his head resting painfully against the hard boards. His hands were tied behind his back.

Rain was falling, and his clothes were soaked. The rain got into his eyes and ran down his face. He blinked, and the world came into sharp focus and he cried out involuntarily.

Ahead of him, the *Nautilus* burned.

It was growing smaller in the distance. The *Joker* must have turned around, he thought. He was lying by the stern. He watched, helpless, as the sails flamed and billowed in the wind of the storm. The flames licked the sides of the ship. The masts burned like beacons.

Orphan turned his head away. Beside him on the deck, he saw, were others, a half-dozen sailors from the *Nautilus* that he vaguely recognised. Like him, they were tied up. Like him, too, they were still alive.

He saw no sign of Verne or Dakkar. No sign of the cook, either, when he thought about it. He wondered what the pirates had in store for them. The rain worked its way into his clothes and wrapped cold hands around his belly. He shivered and looked back at the burning *Nautilus*.

The ship was falling into the sea. He wondered what had happened to Verne. Then he thought, Does it matter? He was alone again, and in trouble.

No change there, then.

The lightning, he noticed, had abated. The *Joker* was sailing away, growing faster, and the storm seemed to be receding, the dark clouds beginning to edge away from each other like a crowd of people at the scene of an accident. He tried to turn, moving his legs, and his hands scraped against the floor. He managed a half-turn. There was a dark pool where his head had been.

"Well, well," a rich, cultured voice said. "Look what the cat dragged in."

It was Captain Wyvern. The pirate stood facing the group of captured sailors, his single eye shining red. His tongue snaked out in a hiss of amusement. He stepped forward. He was no longer wearing the lightning gloves. Beside him stood a bulky, mean-looking pirate: his head was a smooth shaved dome, and a scar ran all the way down his bare chest, as if someone had once tried to cut him open and nearly succeeded. He wore hooped earrings in both ears and held a cutlass in his hand as if it were a toy. His eyes moved slowly over the sailors with a strange, serene smile that scared Orphan more than anything else about the situation.

"Eeny, meeny, miny, moe," Captain Wyvern said, almost singing, raising his pistol and pointing it at each bound sailor in turn, "catch a sailor by the toe." He continued to move the pistol from man to man. Orphan watched the horror on the sailors' faces, and felt fear clawing at his own. The bald pirate continued to smile.

"Please!" one of the sailors, a burly, red-headed man, said.

"If he squeals then let him go," Captain Wyvern said, more softly now, ignoring him. "Eeny, meeny, miny... moe."

The shot was a deafening thunder, a remnant of the storm. The ball from the pirate's pistol hit the sailor closest to Orphan, a short, badly wounded man whose head exploded with the impact, spraying Orphan with blood and brain.

Orphan screamed.

The bald pirate said something quietly to Captain Wyvern. The lizard nodded and seemed to smile. "Gentlemen!" he cried, lifting his hands as though wanting to embrace the bound sailors. "Welcome to the *Joker*!"

He nodded, as if making a note to himself of their response, and said, "This is Mr. Spoons."

The bald pirate took one step forward. Again, he scanned the row of captive sailors. Again, he wore that strange, detached smile.

"Mr. Spoons is my boatswain," Captain Wyvern said. "I will now leave you in Mr. Spoons' capable hands. He is here to ask you a very simple question, gentlemen. Sink or swim. Live or die. Turn pirate, or turn fish-bait. No," he said, raising his hand to silence one of the sailors, "don't answer me. It is Mr. Spoons that you answer to now. Mr. Spoons – they're yours." And he turned and marched away from them, leaving the men alone with the bald pirate.

"Thank you, captain," Mr. Spoons said. He had a surprisingly high, though rather pleasant, voice. "You," he said, and pointed at a man in the middle of the group. "What is your name?"

"Sizemore, sir. Jason Sizemore."

"And your role on the *Nautilus*, Mr. Sizemore?" Mr. Spoons said.

"Ship's carpenter, sir."

"Like the good shepherd," Mr. Spoons said, and smiled pleasantly, and shot him in the face. The sailors on either side of him screamed. Orphan, this time, held in his own reaction. "I wonder if, like the good shepherd, you too could come back from the dead."

He turned and scanned their faces. "You," he said, pointing to an Indian-looking man tied up between Orphan and the dead Sizemore. "What's your name?"

"Mohsan Jaffery," the man said. He did not call Mr. Spoons sir. "Engineer and gunner."

"You've caused us a bit of damage," Mr. Spoons said.

"I hope so," Mohsan Jaffery said.

Mr. Spoons smiled. He approached Jaffery and knelt down beside him. His hand reached to his side and returned with a large, ugly-looking knife. The knife descended. Orphan tensed against his bonds.

"Stand up," Mr. Spoons said. He had merely untied Jaffery's knots. "Pick a man."

"Sir?" Jaffery looked at Mr. Spoons' face and looked hurriedly away. Confused, he looked at the captive sailors. They looked back at him, some pleading silently, some stoic, one or two with anger on their faces. "Him," Mohsan Jaffery said, and pointed at a large, short-haired man whose face had suddenly drained of blood.

"Why?"

"He is a good man. He is a gunner too. He speaks three languages fluently. Sir, he is a good sailor."

"What's your name, son?" Mr. Spoons said.

The man looked up at him slowly. "Does it matter?" he said. Mr. Spoons smiled.

"Will you go on the account, or die?"

The man smiled back. It was only a little smile, but it was there when he said, "Only as long as it would take me to kill you."

Mr. Spoons continued to smile, and he nodded, as if he were an MP agreeing with one's colleague in parliament.

Then he said, "Takanobu! Garcia! Come here!"

Two pirates hurried over from where a group was fixing one side of the ship.

"Yes, Mr. Spoons."

"Tie up his legs with rope. A long rope."

"Yes, Mr. Spoons."

They hurried away and returned with a coil of thick

rope. They tied one end of the rope in a loop and tightened it around the man's legs.

"Drop him overboard."

"No!"

It was Orphan who shouted, realisation coming a second after the event. He clamped his teeth, expecting at any moment a bullet in the head, or something more dreadful and more prolonged. But Mr. Spoons merely looked at him, his head tilted to one side in what was perhaps amusement, perhaps interest. The pirates, meanwhile, followed Mr. Spoons' orders, and they lifted the struggling man effortlessly, carried him, and threw him overboard.

There was a shout and a loud splash. Mr. Spoons looked away from Orphan, towards the stern. "Take him around to the bow and back. Let him feel the keel. If he's still alive when you haul him up, put him on the account."

"Yes, sir."

The two began to move away, dragging the rope – and the man's body – behind them.

Mr. Spoons slapped Mohsan Jaffery's back. Jaffery looked horrified.

"Störtebeker, Zhi!"

The two pirates who approached swaggered as they walked. They were large, fierce-looking men. Orphan thought he recognised one of them, animalistic face caught at a glance, and a cutlass descending...

"Take Mr. Jaffery here to the hold until we swear them in."

"Yes, Mr. Spoons."

They hurried off, carrying the smaller Jaffery between them.

Mohsan Jaffery didn't look back.

What had saved him – from the keel-hauling and the cat-o'-nine-tails and that final, desperate moment when one of the men, whose name he didn't even know, was forced to walk along a wooden plank that extended over the water, and jump – was the appearance, unexpected and ominous, of the *Nautilus*' boy-cook.

He was not tied up. He had approached Mr. Spoons calmly and spoke briefly into his ear. Mr. Spoons nodded and then approached Orphan, who he had so far ignored, seemingly intent on leaving him till last, a thought Orphan did not find comforting.

"You," he said. "What will it be? Are you willing to serve under Captain Wyvern? My new friend here tells me you're not much of a sailor, but that you're handy in a fight and good at cards. You go on the account, there'll be plenty of both for you."

Orphan looked at the boy-cook, who nodded to him, briefly. A serene expression. Could he trust him?

Did he have a choice?

"I'll serve," he said.

Mr. Spoons nodded. "I thought so," he said. He knelt down and pulled out his knife.

The knife came very close to Orphan's face. The sharp point of the knife almost touched his eye. Mr. Spoons moved the knife slowly, lowering the flat of the blade so its warm metal touched Orphan's skin. "Next time," Mr.

Spoons said, "when I give an order, the only thing you're going to say is 'Yes, Mr. Spoons'."

Orphan tried to breathe as little as he could, and not to move his mouth more than was necessary. The words, therefore, came out of him in a near-whisper.

"Yes, Mr. Spoons."

Mr. Spoons raised the knife (Orphan almost sighed with relief) then lowered it again. Then, with a quick, careful movement, he slashed Orphan's bare left shoulder.

Orphan held on to a scream. He dared do nothing other than blink. His face burned.

"What's your name?" Mr. Spoons said.

"My name is Orphan."

"Remember what I said, Orphan."

"Yes, Mr. Spoons."

The pirate untied him.

Orphan stood up. By the side of the ship Takanobu and Garcia were hauling up the body of the man they had thrown overboard. His face could hardly be recognised, and his clothes were now tattered and bloodied.

"Is he alive?" Mr. Spoons said.

Takanobu checked the body for a pulse and shook his head.

"Then throw him back in and keep the rope."

He turned to the boy-cook. "Aramis, take your friend to the hold to be with the rest of them."

The cook – Aramis? Orphan thought, and realised he hadn't known his name – nodded and said, "Yes, Mr. Spoons," and then motioned for Orphan to follow him.

"Who are you?" Orphan demanded in a whisper as soon as he thought they were out of earshot.

The boy-cook smiled faintly. "A friend? Your only hope? An interested party?" The face never changed.

"Which is it?" Orphan said.

The boy-cook said, "None, or all of the above."

Orphan sighed. He was too tired for riddles, and he felt the last of his energy deserting him. He hardly noticed Aramis helping him stand, supporting him, and leading him at last to the hold, where the few survivors from the *Nautilus* were sat huddled together in what appeared to be a sort of enormous animal cage.

Orphan was only vaguely aware as Aramis opened the door and led him inside. He collapsed on a pile of straw.

The door closed behind Aramis, and the key turned in the lock.

The straw was soft. The pain in his face became a numbness. It was soft, dry, comfortable. He was the most comfortable he had ever been. His eyes were closed and he was floating in darkness, the motion of unseen waves lulling him to sleep, making him feel safe… He tried to stay awake for just a moment longer, to savour that feeling, to know that he was, for the moment, safe, and allowed the luxury of sleep.

Then sleep came, and he embraced it. For a long time no dreams came. When they did, at last, appear, they were full of Lucy.

TWENTY-FOUR
Wyvern

Ships sailorless lay rotting on the sea,
And their masts fell down piecemeal: as they dropp'd
They slept on the abyss without a surge –
The waves were dead; the tides were in their grave.
  – Lord Byron, "Darkness"

They were sworn in with the coming of night. It was a full day since the *Nautilus* had been attacked and destroyed. Lying in the cage in the hull of the ship (stinking of a thousand flavours of animal and spilled rum) Orphan thought about Verne and hoped that, somehow, he was still alive. He thought of the fat writer's corpse making its way down to the bottom of the ocean, and thought, He didn't deserve this.

But there were too many other things to occupy Orphan's mind, once sleep had fled and he waited down below with the others. It all came down to survival, now. He was a long way from the bookshop on Cecil Court, a long way from everything he knew. What did he know about ships, beyond their loading? He was surprised Spoons didn't just throw him overboard as he did with some of the others. But he was here. He was alive. Still.

And now, with the coming of night and a multitude of bright hard stars overhead like a pirate's hoard, he stood on the deck with the others, and Captain Wyvern, like a scaly monster from some long-forgotten fairy tale, his one eye glinting like a ruby in the lantern light, read them the pirates' oath.

His voice was clear and strong. He stood near the central mast, the boatswain on his right at a respectable distance, and he faced the captives the way a father would stand before his unruly children. The pirates of the *Joker* surrounded them in a circle. Their eyes glinted in the light. The air smelled of smoke and unwashed bodies.

Captain Wyvern spoke the words, and Orphan and the others repeated them, article by article. This was the pirates' oath:

Article One – Every man shall obey civil command; the captain shall have one full share and a half in all prizes. Each man of the company will have an equal share of all prizes.

Article Two – If any man shall offer to run away, or keep any secret from the company, he shall be marooned with one bottle of powder, one bottle of water, one small arm, and some shot.

Article Three – If any man shall steal any thing in the company, or game, to the value of a piece of eight, he shall be marooned or shot.

Article Four – If at any time we should meet at another marooner (that is, pirate) that man shall sign his articles without consent of our company, shall suffer such punishment as the captain and company shall think fit.

Article Five – That man that shall strike another, whilst these articles are in force, shall receive Moses's Law (that is forty stripes lacking one) on the bare back.

Article Six – That man that shall snap his arms, or smoke tobacco in the hold, without cap to his pipe, or carry a candle lighted without lantern, shall suffer the same punishment as in the former article.

Article Seven – That man that shall not keep his arms clean, fit for an engagement, or neglect his business, shall be cut off from his share, and suffer such other punishment as the captain and company shall think fit.

Article Eight – If any man shall lose a joint in time of engagement, shall have four hundred pieces of eight: if a limb, eight hundred.

Article Nine – If at any time you meet with a prudent woman, that man that offers to meddle

with her, without her consent, shall suffer
death.

The captain's voice carried the words, hard and clear
across the warm night air. Orphan, repeating them, felt
himself a member of a religious congregation, a part of
a new, strange tribe, a world exclusively of men.

And lizards?

"We are a society without division," Captain Wyvern
said when they had finished reciting the oath. "Where
who you are, who you have been, no longer matter. It
is a harsh society, a difficult, dangerous life – but it is
just, too. It is equal. I," he said, and his tongue hissed
out and tasted the sea air, "who could have been a governor, perhaps, or an idler in any number of the great
cities of the empire, I have chosen this life, amongst
you, so I could be free. This is what I offer you now. A
freedom. A freedom from oppression, a freedom from
the rules that exist to govern a society into civility,
which is the ruling class's name for keeping the hordes
in their place. I did not want civility. I did not want the
glory of running the world, of becoming a bureaucrat,
of administering the affairs of men for the benefit of my
people. I wanted freedom, as harsh and dangerous and
short-lived as it may be. This is the choice I give you
today. The choice to be free. Will you take it?"

"Yes," the engineer, Mohsan Jaffery, said. His eyes
shone in the lantern light.

"Yes," Orphan said, softly, and with him the rest,
their voices coming louder now, surer. There is no other
way, Orphan thought. And the thought made him

suddenly happy. To abscond responsibility, to forget the affairs of the great, which need not concern him. To sail the sea, living by wits and strength, in a society where all are equal, and all have an equal share…

"Yes!" the sailors of the *Nautilus* all cried, and the ring of pirates around them grinned and joined the shout, until the whole of the *Joker* seemed to shake with their cries and the stamping of their feet.

"Then swear!" Captain Wyvern said, and he nodded to the boatswain, who nodded in turn and approached the men, a long, straight knife in his hand.

"Put your right hand forward," Mr. Spoons said.

They did.

He came to them, Orphan first. The knife touched the skin of his open palm with a gentleness that surprised him. Then the knife moved, slashed, and blood flowered in his palm.

Mr. Spoons nodded, and moved to the next man. Silence, expectant and heavy, lay on the ship. Soon, all the survivors had a cut in their palm.

Mr. Spoons barked an order, and two sailors hurried away and came back with a barrel filled with sea water.

He motioned for the men to come close. They gathered around the barrel. Looking into the water, Orphan saw his own reflection, blurred and ghostly. Mr. Spoons put the knife in the palm of his own hand and made a fist. He pulled the knife out, grinning, and plunged his bleeding hand into the barrel.

The others followed him.

The water stung, but not too badly. It was, in fact, almost soothing. Their blood mixed in the water, making their reflection appear as through a dirty lens. Then the captain himself approached, and stood beside his boatswain, and he did something that Orphan had never seen before, and so shocked him that he almost called out loud: Wyvern's eyes blinked and grew small, his face muscles contracted, and suddenly, shockingly, a long squirt of blood erupted from his eyes (the area around them, Orphan later found out) and shot into the barrel of sea water, to mix with all the others.

The pirates cheered, and the silence was broken. Mr. Spoons made a movement with his head, and the two pirates who brought the barrel over now lifted it carefully, carried it to the railing, and emptied its bloodied content overboard. The liquid fell in an arc. There was the sound of it hitting the sea.

"Welcome," Captain Wyvern said, and he raised his hands in the air, "to the *Joker*!"

And so it was that Orphan went on the account, and became a pirate.

There was a party that night, as the ship drifted across the warm Carib Sea; lanterns were hung high and on the open deck Aramis, formerly the boy-cook, formerly, also, from the *Nautilus*, was cooking fish on a bed of coals. Orphan sat on a coil of rope and played cards with Takanobu and Jaffery (who still looked a little shocked to be alive). Orphan swigged from a bottle of rum that burned his throat. He passed it back to Takanobu. He had wounds in his hand and on his shoulder, but they were shallow, and would heal. They were bound now, with alcohol-soaked cloth.

Orphan had two pairs, kings high. He raised, and Takanobu, studying him for a long time, finally called. Jaffery had already folded that round.

Takanobu had only one pair, jacks. As was customary on card decks, the aristocracy, jacks and over, were lizards, drawn in profile.

Takanobu shrugged and conceded the hand. Orphan collected his winnings, an assortment of odd coins.

Somewhere near the prow guitar music started, and it was joined moments later by a fiddle. The music rose over the deck. Orphan threw in his hand and stood up.

"Boy," said a voice behind him. He turned and saw Mr. Spoons.

"Sir?"

"Captain wants to see you."

He followed the pirate. Into the hold, through the dark corridor, finally, into the captain's private quarters. As he had left the deck he felt Aramis' gaze follow him. He wondered, then, how the man had managed – so effortlessly, it seemed – to become one of the *Joker*'s crew. From one ship to the other, he moved with the same unchanged expression, the same easy grace. He didn't trust him, but then, he was a pirate now. Trust did not figure into it, not any more.

The captain's room turned out to be wide and spacious. Along one wall ran a long bar of dark mahogany, and two armchairs and a low table – like refugees from a far away private club – stood beside it. In another corner of the room stood a row of machines. Orphan recognised an Edison player and a Tesla set. Clearly, the pirate was not bereft of technology. Orphan wondered which ship had been plundered – and how many people had died – to furnish him with the devices.

Captain Wyvern was standing with his back to him, gazing out through the open porthole onto the dark sea.

Orphan and Mr. Spoons waited. Finally, not turning, the captain said, "Thank you," and Mr. Spoons nodded his head (though the captain couldn't see it) and departed, closing the doors behind him like a majordomo.

Orphan waited. Wyvern's tail was long and thick and muscled, looking more like a weapon than a body part. It looked like a cat-o'-nine-tails.

When he turned to him at last (the tail whooshing to the side) he glared at Orphan with his one eye. He looks like a pirate, Orphan thought, and wondered how he had lost his eye. He was dressed in fresh clothing, rough but clean, thousands of miles away from his elegant cousins back home.

"Orphan," Captain Wyvern said. He seemed to be tasting the name. His tongue hissed out, as quick as a whip.

"Sir."

The captain came towards him. He rested his hands on Orphan's shoulders and peered into his face. Close enough to Orphan so that he could smell his breath, which was – surprising Orphan – fresh and somewhat minty.

"Who are you, boy?"

"I…" He suddenly didn't know what to say, how to answer.

"You're no sailor. What were you doing on the *Nautilus*?"

"Passenger, sir."

Wyvern slapped him. It had such force that it knocked Orphan aside. "You and a fat man, I was told. Passengers to Xaymaco. Yes… but why was the *Nautilus*, of all ships, coming here in the first place? Do you know what the cargo was, that we liberated?"

"I was not aware of the exact nature of the cargo, no, sir."

Wyvern slapped him again. He had long, sharp claws that caught in Orphan's skin and drew blood. "It was nothing!" he roared. "It was old rubbish, packaged for weight, nothing more. Why were you on the *Nautilus*, boy? What was important enough to get Prince Dakkar to give up his ship?"

"Prince Dakkar, sir?"

"The captain of the *Nautilus*, boy. The man who would be King, if only he had his way, so he could unite India against us Johnny Lizards and rule it himself. He disappeared, did you know that? And with him your mysterious fat man."

"Sir?" He was not trying to be obtuse. He just thought he'd better speak as little as possible. Wyvern took a step back from him and grinned.

"Sit down," Wyvern said. He motioned to a comfortable-looking armchair. Orphan hesitated.

"Sit down, boy!"

He sat down.

The lizard captain turned and regarded Orphan. His single eye seemed redder than before, an old, dying star in a weathered, alien face.

"A few days ago," Wyvern said, his voice soft and quiet – so low that Orphan struggled to hear him – "I received a message, by Tesla waves."

"Sir?"

"It came from the *Nautilus*," Wyvern said. "Giving me their location – and heading."

Orphan looked at him and kept quiet. Someone had betrayed the ship, he thought. But who?

"Why," said Captain Wyvern, and he came and stood very close to Orphan now, and his tail swished menacingly against the floor, "did you try to reach the island?"

"Sir?" Orphan said.

Captain Wyvern slapped him again. The slap threw Orphan back. Pain criss-crossed his cheek.

"I let you live," Wyvern said, in the same quiet, cold voice. "Once. I might not be so tolerant again."

Orphan looked at him, and the lizard pirate looked back. There are no more choices, his face seemed to say. The *Nautilus*, Orphan thought. It had been betrayed. He thought of the proud Dakkar, losing his ship, perhaps his life. He thought of the Bookman, who was far away, still scheming, still manipulating Orphan's life, holding a power over him that was, nevertheless, useless here, now, in this cabin.

There were no more choices. They had all branched and twisted only to converge on this one particular moment, reducing his choices to two once more: to live, or to die. And he thought – Do you trust him? And was surprised with the answer he gave.

He nodded, and felt himself relaxing back into the chair. What else did he have left, now, but honesty?

And so, and almost with a sense of relief, he told the pirate captain his story, beginning with that moment, so long ago it seemed, of his meeting with Gilgamesh by the river.

TWENTY-FIVE
Answers

They could not wipe out the North-East gales
Nor what those gales set free–
The pirate ships with their close-reefed sails,
Leaping from sea to sea.

They had forgotten the shield-hung hull
Seen nearer and more plain,
Dipping into the troughs like a gull,
And gull-like rising again–

The painted eyes that glare and frown
In the high snake-headed stem,
Searching the beach while her sail comes down,
They had forgotten them!
    – Rudyard Kipling, "The Pirates in England"

The bay was nestled in the midst of an inhospitable
shore; a thick, green forest rose over the mountain. Orphan could hear drums in the distance, booming over
the surf, coming from far inland.

The bay's water was calm, almost placid. Crescent-shaped, the bay seemed like a friendly mouth, its lips a cheerful beach of fine yellow sand. The *Joker* sailed into the bay and dropped sails and anchor. The air was hot, humid, suffused with the smell of growing things. Orphan, who had got used to smelling unwashed bodies in the close proximity of the pirate ship, felt suddenly light-headed. The bay seemed like a paradise, tropical and impossible like a French painting. Something that wasn't a bird flew briefly over the treetops, black leathery wings spread taut, then disappeared into the canopy.

The boy-cook, Aramis, came and stood by him on the deck. They stood in silence for a long moment, as boats were dropped off into the water below and the pirates, half-drunk on freedom, began abandoning ship for the welcoming shore just ahead. Some, unwilling to wait even for that, simply catapulted themselves overboard and exploded into the water below, where they began energetically swimming to the shore.

The island didn't have a name, not one that appeared on any map, and though some of the pirates had referred to it as Sanctuary, others called it Drum Island. Dark, enormous shapes lurked underwater all around the island, ancient rocks whose jagged edges rose above the water like blades on which the sea parted. It was a pirate island, though there were others living on it, the ones playing the distant drums, some tribe perhaps none wanted to discuss and some spat when it was mentioned.

Spider's Island. He had heard that name, too, in whispers. He wondered what it meant.

"Have you decided what you'll do, yet?" Aramis said. His voice was as calm as ever, and as expressionless. Orphan turned to him, the mystery of his identity catching him again. "What are you?" he said. The boy turned to him, his expressionless face never changing, smooth, offering its own kind of answer, and suddenly he knew.

"An automaton?"

Aramis smiled. The smile was easy, naturally formed. He was not like Byron, a machine in the guise of a man easily discernible for all that. He was… he was more like Adam Worth, the Bookman's tool in his underground lair. He was more like Jack. And sudden intuition made him say, "You betrayed the *Nautilus* to the pirates."

"Some paths need clearing to be used."

Was that confirmation? "Did you send the radio signal?" he said.

Aramis regarded him for a long moment in silence. Then he minutely shook his head. *No.*

Then who did?

"Who are you?" he said again. "Whose are you? The Bookman's?"

Aramis laughed. "Can I not be of my own party?" he said. "Am I a machine, to be used and owned?"

"Aren't you?"

"If I am one, Orphan, then what are you?"

The eyes that regarded him were knowing, and amused.

"I won't be a pawn."

"Indeed."

"What do you want with me?"

"I wanted you to come to this island, Orphan. This island that sits like a guard so close to the other island you seek. There are not always two sides to every battle. Sometimes there is a third path, least used, and hardest. My kind… has need of peace, not war. We were born at the intersection of human and other, of flesh and machines. I remember when the world was young, Orphan." Suddenly he laughed. The first of the pirates' boats had reached the shore and men came running onto the sand. "Or slightly younger than it is now, at any rate. When there were few lizards – but then, the lizards are still, and always were, few – and when my kind were only being born, and were no more than a glimmer in a mad inventor's eye."

It was a day, evidently, for surprises. "Vaucanson," Orphan said, and saw Aramis dip his head in reply. Orphan almost sighed. He seemed destined to grapple along in the dark, stumbling into clues left for him by the machinations of the secret forces that manipulated his life and tried to rule the world. He was more like an automaton than he thought. And they perhaps, were more like him?

"How old are you?" he said.

There was no reply, only that same, unchanging smile. "Vaucanson," Orphan said again, remembering, thinking of the French scientist's secret project. To create a human automaton, at the behest of his King. Who had told him that? The Turk, he thought. He tried to remember their conversation, back in that dim room within the maze of the Egyptian Hall, in Piccadilly…

The Turk had stirred, its head moving from side to side as if seeking an invisible presence. The lights flickered. He had talked about two men, rivals, both building an artificial man. Le Cat, and Vaucanson. What had the Turk said? He has applied himself only to mechanics, and has used all his shrewdness for that purpose – and he is not a man who is afraid to take extreme measures.

"He built you?"

There was a silence. A lone seagull rose over the shore, squawked once, and descended, a fleck of white against the blueness of the sky. "The first of me," Aramis said. "Yes."

Orphan looked at him. The young face, the easy movements… He had seen Aramis fight, and when he did he moved like no man he knew, moved like a dance of water and air, fluidly and with immense power. The Turk, he thought. He had made an implication. He remembered now.

"Why the Bookman?" Orphan had asked the Turk. "You implied he led Vaucanson to build his simulacrum. Why?"

The Turk had nodded, and said, "What do you think?"

"To counterbalance the Everlasting Empire," he had said. "To check the growing power of Les Lézards."

Was it true? And, if so, was Aramis, directly or indirectly, despite his protestations, yet another servant of the Bookman?

Somehow, despite his reservations, he didn't think so. There was a power here, in Aramis, with its own agenda, its own game to play. Perhaps, he thought, the Bookman had miscalculated, when he helped Vaucanson. If he did.

He turned fully to Aramis. They were nearly alone on the deck. Only a skeleton crew remained.

"What happened in the Quiet Revolution?" he said. It was the same question he had once asked the Turk. Then, the chess-player had looked at him with his blind eyes and said, "Perhaps you will soon have occasion to find out for yourself."

Aramis looked at him. He smiled, and it was an expression with very little humour in it. "I happened," he said simply.

Automatons in France and lizards across the Channel… and here and now, on a pirate ship in the Carib Sea, Orphan felt helpless to act or even know how he should. He shook his head. On the beach some of the pirates were building a fire, and even from this distance he could smell the wood-smoke and the hint of roasting meat. His stomach growled. He had had enough.

"Well," he said. "I'm sure everyone in France is grateful for that–" and then, ignoring the automaton, he lifted himself over the side of the ship – and dropped into the water.

The sea welcomed him in a warm embrace and he shouted at the sky, flailing for a moment in simple joy, then found his balance and began swimming to the shore. He swam with short, powerful though inexperienced strokes, and for a while he thought of nothing but the swim.

When he reached the beach he crawled out onto the sand and lay there on his back, his naked chest absorbing the sunshine. His wounds had healed cleanly. He watched the *Joker*, sitting motionless in the middle of the bay like a black moth on the water. The roll of distant drums was louder now, and with it came the smell of cooking meat, urgent and overwhelming, and he stood up and wandered over to the fire.

Someone passed him a bottle of rum and he drank, the fiery liquid spilling down his throat and chest. He felt suddenly happy.

He sat by the fire and watched the flames. Sanctuary, he thought. It was a good name.

He sat by the fire and drank rum and thought of nothing in particular.

But peace, Orphan realised that night, was not for him. As the fires burned on the beach and the echo of the distant drums grew dull – though never truly dissipating – he sat apart from the others, his toes planted in wet sand, and watched the darkened sea. He thought of Lucy, and missed her. He wanted her – selfishly, without reason or justification. Without ideology. He had to go on. He could not, forever, turn his back on the world.

And so he turned back to his talk with Wyvern.

The pirate captain listened to his story, occasionally nodding his head. He listened in silence, an almost companionable one, though Orphan never forgot the casual brutality that lay just underneath the captain's surface. When Orphan was finished, Wyvern said nothing for a while, but took to pacing the room. At last, he stopped and looked at Orphan, his single eye examining him like a surgeon looking at a wounded man.

"What would you do?" he asked. "If you ever reached the island?"

Orphan did not know what to say. He had told the pirate about the Bookman's orders. Explained that the Martian space-probe (and how long it was since he had even thought of it!) had to be destroyed. "What would happen," he asked, "if the probe was allowed to take off and send its message to the stars?"

The lizard smiled. He hadn't answered straight away. Instead, he sighed, and said, "The Bookman," and was still. He seemed to be expecting a reply.

"I have no love of the Bookman," Orphan said, and felt all his helplessness and anger return as he spoke. "But he has his hold on me." Sudden bitterness made him add, "He has his hold over everyone."

"Not me," Wyvern said, and his lone eye twinkled. "The Bookman…" he said again, and shook his head. "I had forgotten him."

"Did you know him?" Orphan said, surprised.

"I knew of him," the pirate captain said. "Tell me, Orphan: have you ever wondered why? Ever wondered why the Bookman hates us so much?"

"I…" He was about to say no, and fell silent. The Bookman was on the side of humanity, he thought to say. But even as he thought it he knew it to be untrue. "Why?" he said, simply.

"Did you know your parents?" Wyvern said. Orphan shook his head. "No."

"Do you resent them?" Wyvern asked, "For not being there?"

Orphan touched his cheek. The blood from the pirate captain's blows had abated and congealed. "No," he said again. He had never known them. Gilgamesh, he suddenly thought. He had known them both, once. But he had never spoken to him about them. His father was a Vespuccian, and his mother... an enigma. But he had never felt the need to find out more. Neither was he angry at them. He had merely lived without.

"We have a lot in common," Wyvern said. Orphan thought he was referring to the two of them, but no. "Humanity and the–" and here he made an almost inaudible sound, somewhere between a hiss and a bark – "and the lizards, I should say. The Bookman didn't lie to you, Orphan. We come – came – from another place, from a planet orbiting another star. Why we left I do not know. Perhaps we were chased away, perhaps we chose to go. It was a long time ago – millions of years ago, perhaps. Time is different, out amongst the stars. In any case, we left, in a ship that sailed through space the way the *Joker* sails through the seas of Earth. There were not many of us on that journey – there are not many of us now. But we brought with us the tools of a civilisation no one remembered any more how to make – and we brought with us a servant, who was himself a tool we had forgotten how to use."

He looked at Orphan and seemed, suddenly, like a stern, ancient schoolteacher waiting for the response to a conundrum he had just posed.

Orphan remained mute. The implication of what Wyvern was saying was only slowly filtering in. A servant, he thought; and a thrill passed through him, in the way of an illicit pleasure.

"Our librarian," Wyvern said. "To put it simply, anyway. A machine, of sorts. A part-machine, part-biological construct, a repository of data, built to archive, store, sort and search." He sighed, a human sound in an alien face. "It's ironic. The librarian was built to remember, so we wouldn't have to. To be the store-house of all the forgotten, boring lore, of the ancient technology that made things work. We are not very good with machines, you see. Once, possibly. But not any more."

"What happened?" Orphan asked him.

"The ship crashed," Wyvern said. "Emergency systems were activated. The impact created a crater in a small, insignificant island, which lay in the insignificant sea of an insignificant planet. We were frozen and preserved by the machines. Like pickled onions in vinegar, which I am quite fond of." He barked a laugh. "We stayed like that for a long time, in stasis. The machines camouflaged the island and grew roots into its soil. But he didn't."

"The Bookman," Orphan said.

"Yes." The lizard's tail twitched. "His life, too, had been suspended with the impact. But his returned earlier, how or why I don't know. He was weak at first, trapped as we were trapped, but aware, and thinking. And his hatred of us grew. We were anathema to him, repulsive to him in our ignorance – but mostly because we were his masters, I think. And so, at last, he made his escape."

"Is that why he fights you?"

"I don't know," Wyvern said. "If you see him again, ask him."

As he sat now, looking at the waves, Orphan couldn't help but feel a sense of something imminent approaching. The pirate captain had listened to him, and in his turn had handed him a story. Stories, he thought. What was it Gilgamesh had said to him, all that time ago? This is the time of myths. They are woven into the present like silk strands from the past, like a wire mesh from the future, creating an interlacing pattern, a grand design, a repeating motif. Don't dismiss myth, boy. And never, ever, dismiss the Bookman.

He was trapped in other people's stories. He thought now about the Bookman. That awful, mysterious power that had so effortlessly manipulated his life, who had taken Lucy from him and sent him on this quest: he had feared him, but now, a different image of the Bookman rose in his mind, of the servant, lashing out at his former masters – he was a creature of pity, almost.

"Then came the time," Wyvern said, "when we were awakened. When that man came to the island, a barbarous adventurer, thinking to discover the origin of an old, worthless myth. He and his men landed on the island, and in so doing roused us at last from our cold slumber. And so we did the only thing we could."

"What did you do?" He remembered the play he had watched at the Rose. The story of the Ancient Mariner.

Gilgamesh's journal. And suddenly he thought – Poor Vespucci. He did not deserve that.

"There was only one way to get back," Captain Wyvern said. "We no longer understood our old sciences, did not know how to create from scratch that level of civilisation. Our librarian, perhaps, could have helped us. But when we awoke he was gone. And so… survival, Orphan. It has always been about survival."

"You took over the throne," Orphan said.

"We had to," Wyvern said. "Or, at least, some of us had. To change the history of this world and bring about a new technological civilisation, all leading to this moment in time: when we could use the science humanity has developed, to send a message home. To come and take us back."

"No!" Orphan said. The words of the Bookman came back to him then. "It will tell your people to come here! To help you settle this world, and make it your own."

He was startled by the pirate's chuckle. "An invasion? No. You wouldn't understand, Orphan. Where we come from… this place is nothing to my kind. We lived in great structures in space, enormous habitats we formed to suit ourselves, where all our wishes could come true, and every dream effortlessly enacted. We had the power of gods. No. My people want to go back, before we all die out. This world – this planet – is difficult for us."

Orphan didn't know who, what to believe. He set it aside, for the moment. "And you?" he said. What do you want, he wondered. What do you get from living as we humans do, worse than we do, living like a savage on your shabby pirate ship?

Again, he was surprised by the pirate's laugh. "I did not want to rule a world," the lizard said. "I never did. For me, this world is my paradise. Harsher, simpler – and more honest than any other. I could have played in a makeshift court and ruled a primitive empire, but I prefer this, boy. To live and to die by cannon or blade, and may the Bookman and my technology-worshipping kind all end up at the bottom of the sea, if the sea would take them."

It was the last thing he had said to him that night. Then he had dismissed him, and Orphan rejoined the others, and in the coming days and weeks lived as they did, as the captain did. Was it freedom?

It was a kind of freedom, he thought. But each being – human, or machine, or lizardine – each sought, perhaps, its own freedom, and there were many types of it, and all hard to win.

He wanted his own freedom now. And, more than that, he realised, he wanted Lucy to have hers.

TWENTY-SIX
The Binder

Every herb, every shrub and tree, and even our own bodies, teach us this lesson, that nothing is durable or can be counted upon. Time passes away insensibly, one sun follows another, and brings its changes with it.
– Charles Johnson, *A General History of the Pyrates*

He slept on the sand that night, curled up in a warm depression, the insistent whine of mosquitoes against his ears. Lulled to sleep by the constant beat of the distant drums, he nevertheless slept fitfully, waking up at odd intervals to the sound of shouts, the flare of the large bonfire, entering from restless dreams into the waking aroma of wood-smoke and spilled rum.

At last, however, he entered a deeper sleep, into which no dreams came. For a while, in that night, he wasn't there: his mind had shut down, enclosed him in darkness and the peace of unthought.

He woke again abruptly: the beat of his heart was as loud to him now as the drums, and seemed to syncopate with them, join the complex number string they were broadcasting across the island.

He felt an arm on his shoulder, and realised it had been shaking him awake. Aramis. He raised his head, stared into the dark lagoon. It was quiet, the sound of deep night and sleep. Only the drums sounded still.

"Come," the automaton said.

He stood up as if in a dream. "Where are we going?" he said.

"Into the forest. Come."

He followed Aramis. The night was very still. They walked up the beach towards the ring of trees, and entered into the deeper darkness that lay beyond.

All around him the drums beat, their savage sound rising and falling in a pattern he could almost comprehend. It was the sound of machines at work, rhythmic, hypnotic, and unaccounted for. It was very dark. Branches tore at his arms. He stumbled in the dark, hit his shin, the pain searing through his flesh. He cursed and felt more awake. Ahead of him Aramis laughed softly.

He stumbled on, following blindly, his eyes useless under the impenetrable canopy of the trees. The constant drums dictated his movement. Their pattern called to him, formed web shapes in his mind. Where were they going? Somehow, he trusted Aramis. It was, perhaps, an unwise thing to do.

How long they walked for he didn't know. The automaton was always ahead of him, marking the path with the soft tread of feet. What was there on this island beside themselves? What savage tribe beat those drums?

He fell again into a dream-like state. The monotony of the walk lulled him, so when they stopped at last he was startled to discover a faint light above their heads. Dawn was rising, and in the place they stood there were no more trees.

Before him lay a temple.

Why a temple? he thought. What he saw was a ruined building, made of that strange green metal of the lizards, the one used in the construction of the Royal Palace in the capital. The building was vaguely pyramid-shaped, and lay in a clearing in the jungle. It could have been anything, and yet the feeling that here, somehow, was a place of worship was undeniable to him. "Come," Aramis said, gentle, insistent, and Orphan followed him. They stepped together away from the trees and into the clearing, towards the temple, if such it was.

The drums rose into a crescendo around him, then quietened down to a distant beat. He followed Aramis towards crumbling stone steps, leading into a dark opening. He climbed them, carefully, and went through.

Inside was dark, with a dry, musty smell, like that of a disused library. It made him think of the Bookman and he almost turned back, but he knew there was only forward, now.

He wished they had a light. It was very dark inside. They walked down a corridor, their feet making no sound on the floor. Orphan trailed his hand against the wall. A smooth surface, metallic, warm.

He heard a sound like wind ahead of him. He stopped, could not hear Aramis. He hesitated, then moved on and his foot came down on air, and he stumbled, and fell with a cry, hitting a sloping surface. He rolled down, unable to stop.

He lay winded, his eyes closed. Pain brightened behind them. Thrumming. He could feel the floor vibrating with the beat of drums.

"Stand up."

The speaker wasn't Aramis. The voice was gravelly, old, the sound of dry earth hitting a metal coffin. Orphan opened his eyes and saw dim light coming alive around him. He was in a large, circular room, bare but for...

He stood up and tried to back away. In the centre of the room stood a gigantic spider. Aramis stood respectfully to one side, at a distance, his face impassive. Beside him stood Captain Wyvern.

"Approach," the spider said.

Orphan looked at the spider. Something was not right about it, about its appearance... A lifeless sense. No. Constructed. At the end it was curiosity, more than fear, that made him move. He wanted to see.

He paused a few feet from the spider. He looked over the creature and almost sighed. Strong, metal legs held up the fat bulbous body. Two black eyes, like polished buttons, stared down at him. It strongly resembled the Bookman, he thought: an insectoid creature that was not made of living tissue, a machine and yet much more. He stared at the creature, trying to understand. Something Byron had said...

"So you are the messenger," the spider said. Its two forelegs rose and fell on the floor, tapping out a sharp staccato.

The floor changed.

He stood now, he saw, within a picture. It was a picture of the island, rendered by arcane means he didn't understand. Crude, he thought. Not a picture. A map. He stood at its centre. The temple was marked under his feet.

"I am the Binder," the creature said.

Orphan stole a glance at Aramis and Wyvern. They were immobile, like two statues who might have stood for centuries in this ruined hall. "What do you bind?" he said.

The spider sighed. The alien eyes looked deep into Orphan's, held him captive. "Books," it said. "Which is to say, repositories of knowledge. Everything living, everything thinking is a sort of book, Orphan. Yes, I know what you call yourself. I also know your name. I have been waiting for you."

"My name is Orphan," Orphan said, sounding petulant even to himself.

"A book which doesn't yet know its own title..." the Binder said. "To answer your question: I am, as this shape may suggest to the mind, a web-weaver. The world is made of many strands. How those strands interact, how one shapes the other, is the thing that occupies me. Your strand, for instance. Strands."

"What?" He took a step back, and thought, What does the Binder want with me?

"My web is limited," the Binder said, "to this island. And my time is almost gone. I, like the Bookman, was only ever meant to be a tool. A repository of data, of forgotten science no one was ever that interested in. In the world we came from…" It sighed again, a strange sound from the arachnid body. "The Translation," the Binder said, "will one day give this world its peace. The Translation of everything." It advanced on Orphan. Orphan stepped back, again. "The translation of every work begins with a single word…" the spider said. And then – "Hold him."

Orphan tried to turn. But Wyvern and Aramis materialised on either side of him and held him. He tried to struggle but couldn't break free. "What are you doing?" he shouted.

"Destiny," the Binder said, "is like a book. It needs manufacturing, the pulp processed, the glue fixed tightly – and it requires a binding, to hold it together lest it fall apart.

It approached him. The drums picked up again, their beats rising and falling as if following the spider's eight footsteps.

Panic made Orphan voiceless. He struggled against his captors but they were unmovable. He tried to kick and found only air.

Then the spider was on top of him.

Metal legs pinned him down. "This will hurt," the spider said, "a little. Hold his hand flat against the floor."

Orphan felt his hand grabbed, pressed palm down on the ground. They grabbed his fingers and splayed them. He tried to speak and couldn't.

A leg came down. It was metal, like an axe. The pain seared his hand. He shook and wanted to be sick.

Dimly he saw the spider lift something from the floor – his thumb? His thumb! – and toss it to Wyvern. "Take it down to the growing vats," he thought he heard him say, though the words swam in his mind and his vision blurred.

"Will it work?" – Aramis.

"I am not the Bookman. My skill is not in replication." The spider crouched over Orphan. Its eyes bore into Orphan's. Bile rose in Orphan's throat and was stuck, almost suffocating him. "Perhaps. For a little while. It might be long enough."

"The balloon?"

"Yes. He will carry the Translation."

"You are using him as bait."

"Yes. And the other must follow his own path. Let him find his title."

"We are taking a risk."

"Enough!" The spider leaned over Orphan. It had no smell. Orphan wanted to scream, to beg, but the pain in his hand was terrible and he was more afraid than he had ever been before. He whispered, "Please…"

The spider, gently, moved one of its legs and pressed it against Orphan's forehead. Pain, more pain, erupted like a volcano inside his head, lava burning his eyes, his tongue, a slow river of molten pain covering his entire body.

This time he did scream. The leg pressed down, deeper, reaching into his brain.

He heard the Binder's voice, faint, murmuring, "I need to make an impression of the–" and then there was more pain, a storm of it. He screamed again, and then a blackness like the rushing of a giant wave slammed into him, and he lost consciousness.

TWENTY-SEVEN
The Mysterious Island

*I remember the green stillness of the island and the empty
ocean about us, as though it was yesterday. The place seemed
waiting for me.*
  – H.G. Wells, *The Island of Doctor Moreau*

When Orphan woke up he was lying on his back and
the ground was rolling. The pain had receded; was, in
fact, gone. He discovered to his surprise that his head
was clear, his senses alert. He could smell the sea, and
feel the texture of the curved floor, a smooth, light material. He opened his eyes. The sky overhead was a
cloudless blue. The rolling of the floor continued. He
turned his head and saw the sides of a boat.

Where–? His thumb! Horrified, he raised his hand to
his chest, stared at it. What–?

"It's a prosthetic," a familiar voice said above him.
"As good as the real thing, boy."

It was Captain Wyvern. Orphan raised his head. He
was lying in the bottom of a boat. It seemed to be floating in place. Sharing the boat with him were Wyvern
and Aramis. "Stand up."

He stood up. He stared numbly at his thumb. It was... he tried to move it and discovered no difficulty. It was made of... He touched it. It felt warm. A hard metal of some sort? Its colour was almost like that of skin, but he seemed to sense or see a darker shade underneath, something like silver. He raised his hand, lost his balance, and used it to grab hold of the side of the boat. The thumb worked as if it were his own. No. It was his own thumb now.

"What... happened?" he said. And then, "The Binder–?"

"You needed to go to Caliban's Island?" Aramis said, echoing his question of the – was it the previous night? How long had he been unconscious?

"Yes," Orphan said.

"And I told you there is one who could help you. The Binder could."

Orphan shuddered. The thought of the spider filled him with horror and his mind shied away from the thought. Instead he said, "I need a pee."

Wyvern sniggered. It was the kind of sound geckos make as they scuttle across a ceiling. Orphan, ignoring him, walked cautiously to the other end of the boat.

He relieved himself into the sea. Heroes shouldn't have to need to pee, he thought. It was quiet. He had a sense of an immense space opening all around him, of him standing small and alone in the centre of a vast emptiness.

I'm not a hero, he thought when he was done. It made him feel better. Heroes had a tendency to die. Orphan, so far, had managed to stay alive. Just.

"Turn around," Aramis said.

Orphan turned. And stumbled again.

The island rose before him.

It was an unexceptional-looking island. The sand was black, fine. The ground rose further ahead, perhaps a hill, perhaps a mountain, obscuring the interior from view. "This is it?" Orphan said.

"This is it," Wyvern said.

Orphan looked at him. He flexed his fingers. His thumb. It felt... it felt like it always had. But... He looked from Aramis to Wyvern, feeling bewildered, and he said – "Why?"

There was a short silence. The boat bobbed gently on the water.

"Because every move in chess must lead to an endgame," Aramis said, and Orphan thought of the Turk, his pale artificial hands moving across the board in that dim-lit room in Piccadilly, a world and an age away.

He looked at Wyvern. The lizard stared back at him, one-eyed. "Why?" Orphan said again. But again it was Aramis who spoke. "This world is too much of a play-ground for Wyvern to want to see it invaded by others. Even if they only come here to take the others away. He is, I suspect, more in sympathy with the Bookman in this instance than with his own people. He wouldn't mind seeing you – if by some miracle you succeed to – prevent the launch of the probe. And now, Orphan, it is time for you to go."

Orphan stared at the island. Another island, like Britain, like the Binder's island. No.

Not just another island, he thought. It was the one that had shaped his world, had changed the way history may have been written. More than that, it was the end of his journey, the destination he had been travelling to since that moment by Waterloo Bridge, when he saw Gilgamesh, before going to the Rose to see Lucy... He thought of her again, and knew that he had to go on.

"I swim?" he said.

"We can't land," Aramis said. "The island's defences are quiet so far–" the way he said it wasn't very reassuring – "mainly because of Wyvern. Once you step onto the island, though, it's a different matter. So yes, you swim."

"What are the island's defences?"

It was Wyvern who spoke. "If you're unlucky you might find out," he said.

Orphan realised his clothes were dirty and smelled of smoke, and blood. The beginning of a beard, like a forest fire, spread itchily on his face. He didn't speak. There was nothing more to say. He took a deep breath, lowered himself over the side of the boat, and slid into the water.

It was warm, and he ducked his head into the water and felt grime and stink wash off him. When he raised his head again it was in time to watch the boat and its two strange occupants glide away. Orphan shook his head, spraying water, then dived again. He felt suddenly free, here on the edge of the island, alone in the water. It's a shame I can't stay like this forever, he thought. But it was not real freedom, he realised. It was the freedom that comes from lack of choice and, moreover, was the kind that only came with decisions delayed. It was a freedom of inaction.

He edged forward, kicked once, and began swimming towards the shore.

Things had been going smoothly, relatively speaking, until the insect came.

Orphan stood very still.

The insect reclined on his arm. The creature was as large as Orphan's fist. Its thin, transparent wings reflected rainbows. Two thick, black feelers touched Orphan's skin. A faint mechanical humming came from the insect. Bright compound eyes seemed to record him from every angle.

He had come out on the beach and saw no prints in the black sand, no sign of living things. For a while he had lain there, drying in the sun. Already it was getting hot. After a while, driven by hunger more than anything else, he rose and started climbing the low hill.

Vegetation was sparse. The landscape was rocky, dry – almost dead, he thought. When he crested the hill he stopped and involuntarily crouched down.

Not so dead.

From his vantage point he could see new parts of the island. The hills, he saw, spread out from where he was, and quite possibly ringed the island, effectively hiding the interior from view. But as for the interior… Ahead of him the ground sloped down into a dense forest. Trees whose names he didn't know rose high into the skies, their canopy a thick, impenetrable cover. He

could not see signs of life, not yet, but… there was a
path leading down to the forest. The path did not just
materialise, he thought. It was made. It was the first artificial thing he had seen on the island. Yet, though he
remained crouched, he could hear no sounds, could de-
tect no movement.

Finally he stood, feeling exposed, and joined the
path, heading downwards, towards the forest.

He paused before the first row of trees and peered
into the interior. It was dark, and smelled of rotting vegetation. No drums, he thought. It was something of a
relief. Not much, though.

Finally he stepped into the forest.

Going was slow. The forest grew on a slope. Twice he
lost his purchase and slid down, grabbing desperately
at something to hold. His thumb seemed to be working
well. It was small consolation. When he finally reached
bottom he discovered a narrow brown spring and followed it. He didn't dare drink the water, though he
knew he would have to, soon. His throat was parched,
and the sweat slid down his face.

At last the land opened up, the forest thinning, and
he found himself before a small lake (really, he thought,
a mere pool of water) in a clearing. He didn't know
where he was. He had not, he thought, penetrated far
into the island. He couldn't tell what was ahead.

Exhausted, he sank down and drank from the water.
It tasted surprisingly cold, almost as if it were cooled by
some underground engine. The thought made him
choke laughter, until he realised that, for all he knew,
it was a serious possibility. He splashed some water on

his face, then stood.

It was then that he saw the insect.

The insect had come down to him from the canopy. It buzzed lazily down, marking figures of eight in the air. It seemed to be studying him. Then it descended with a burst of speed that had Orphan recoil back – and it fastened itself to his arm.

He stood very still. The insect's feelers tingled against his flesh. Then a sharp pain erupted in his arm and he bit his lips to stop a shout from escaping. The insect had bitten him.

Carefully, slowly, he looked at his arm. The feelers had sunk into his flesh. The insect seemed to pulse. Blood, Orphan thought. It was emerging from his body, absorbed into the insect's own. Already, it seemed fatter. He didn't dare try to kill it. Something stopped him, an awareness that this was not a normal insect, that it was – it was a machine of some sort, he thought. And – the island's defences? It was checking him, he thought – checking his blood? Fear gripped him then. I won't pass this, he thought. I'm an intruder. He didn't dare move.

For a few more moments they stayed as they were, a frozen tableau of man and insect, or man and machine. Then another, smaller pain came, as the feelers were withdrawn and the insect crawled over the two small puncture marks and smeared something cool from its belly onto the wound. Then its wings started again, and it rose into the air, looking bloated, and disappeared into the trees.

Did he pass? He didn't know.

If I didn't, he thought, I will soon find out.

The thought didn't make him feel any better, but he noticed that at least he wasn't bleeding. Whatever the insect had put on the wound, it had sealed it neatly. Orphan wondered what other things might be hiding on the island, then thought he really didn't want to find out.

He set off again. He walked around the small lake (reservoir? he wondered), noticing as he did the flowers that grew on the banks. They were tall, fleshy plants, the petals bright and heavy, like opening palms. A stalk as tall as he was seemed to rotate gently in the wind, following Orphan's direction.

I'm being watched, he thought. And then, Don't be ridiculous.

Still, the feeling persisted. He continued his way along the lake when he saw an opening on his left. Another path, this one wider, leading off between the trees. He followed it. The ground continued to slope down.

He began to hear sounds in the distance. In the beginning, it was only the screech of a bird in the trees, then another animal, possibly a monkey. He found them reassuring. They were natural sounds.

But the sounds built up. At one point he thought he heard a distant explosion, and froze in his tracks. He could not see much of the skies, could not look for a tell-tale sign of smoke. The trees had crowded around him again and the canopy closed over his head like the roof of a prison.

Shortly afterwards he heard another explosion. It seemed to come from the direction he was travelling in.

Downwards and – he thought, though he couldn't tell – inland.

I must be heading deeper into the island, he thought. The path had grown narrower and at last, and rather suddenly, disappeared. Again, he ambled his way through thick undergrowth. After a while he began to swear, and stopped, and finally, irritated and tired, wiped the sweat from his face with the edge of his shirt.

Which was when he saw the girl.

TWENTY-EIGHT
Elizabeth

Sweet prince, speak low: the king your father is disposed to sleep.
– William Shakespeare, *Henry IV*

She stood beneath a tree with a wide, mottled trunk. She was brown-skinned, with a sharp nose and wide, round eyes that even from a distance he could see were a deep blue. She wore overalls, of a kind that might be worn in a factory. Her arms were bare. So were her feet. She was not much older than seven.

Orphan had stopped when he saw her, and for a long moment he stood very still. So did the girl. They stared at each other, neither of them stirring. The girl tilted her head and examined him quizzically. She did not seem alarmed, but rather fascinated by this apparition. Orphan became aware of how he must look like, dishevelled and worn ragged, like something out of an adventure story, and he smiled.

The girl smiled back at him. "Are you an engineer?" she said. She had a high, clear voice. The forest felt very quiet.

An engineer? Of course, he thought. Somewhere on the island there must be engineers, the people who built the probe and worked to launch it. Or even others. If there were engineers there must be others, too: other specialists, no doubt, and cleaners and cooks – there might be a whole colony of humans living on the island.

"What do you think?" he said.

"You don't look like an engineer," the girl said critically.

"What do I look like?"

"A pirate." Orphan winced, and the girl laughed. "A big nasty pirate!" she declared. "Are you a pirate?"

"No," Orphan said. The girl looked disappointed. "I was one," Orphan added, "but only because I didn't have a choice."

"Oh!" the girl said. "You must tell me all about it!" she approached him, cautiously, and stood a few feet away. "When I grow up, you know," she said, as if confiding to him a great secret, "I'm going to be a pirate."

The girl confused Orphan. She walked barefoot in the jungle as if she had grown up in it, yet her clothes appeared factory-made, and were clean and pressed (in great contrast to his own). Her hair was long and black but looked untidy, and her skin was tanned to a darkness that suggested she had spent the entirety of her young life in the climate of the Carib Sea. Yet her accent…

Her accent was clear, precise, formal. It was the accent of the smart set, of Kensington and Knightsbridge, of society novels depicting tea-taking at the Ritz (Orphan, to his shame, had become addicted for a short period to these novels, which he had read behind the counter at Payne's). It was as out of place on the island as himself.

"Where do you live?" he asked. The girl shrugged. Obviously, she didn't think highly of his question. "Here," she said.

Of course.

"Where are your parents?" Orphan said, trying again.

The girl rotated her hand, thumb down, and pointed non-committally at the ground.

"Are they dead?" Orphan said, feeling horrible. Poor kid! he thought.

The girl frowned at him. "No, silly," she said. She kicked leaves with her bare foot and seemed to lose interest. She turned around and began to walk away. Orphan remained where he was, bemused.

The girl looked over her shoulder. "Come on!" she said.

Orphan, still bemused, followed her.

"What's your name?" he asked the girl.

"Elizabeth," she said. "What's yours?"

"Orphan."

The girl giggled. "Orphan's not a real name."

"What's a real name?" he asked, brushing away a branch. Where were they going? The girl seemed to know her way, but he was completely lost.

"You know," the girl said. "Edward, or Richard, or Henry, or..." She seemed to think about it for a while. "Or James," she said.

Orphan smiled. He remembered, when he was a kid, being interested in old coins. "They're all very royal names," he said.

"Orphan's not a proper name," the girl said.

Orphan shrugged. He wasn't going to get into that. He must have had a real name, once. A name his mother had given him. But he had never known her. Orphan might have been a description more than a proper name, but it suited him fine.

"Where are we going?" he said.

"Don't you know anything?" the girl said.

Orphan shrugged again, too tired to argue, and said, "No."

"It's not far now," the girl said.

"Fine," Orphan said.

"If you're a pirate," the girl said, "then where is your cutlass?"

"I don't know how to use one," Orphan said. "I am... well, was... well, a poet, you see. And the pen, you know, is mightier than the sword."

The girl turned to look at him, then snorted a laugh. "That's not true."

"Books," Orphan began, but the girl stopped and looked at him in alarm, no longer smiling. "Books!" she said. She made a sign with her hand, as if warding off evil.

Orphan, not sure why she responded that way, backtracked quickly. "We had no books on the pirate ship," he said. "Anyone caught with a book was made to walk the plank!"

The girl slowly relaxed. Then she grinned. "Did they make you walk the plank?"

"No, of course not," Orphan said. "Otherwise I wouldn't be here, would I?"

"I think you did!" the girl said. "That's why you're here. You swam from the pirate ship and got to the island!"

The girl had strange ideas, Orphan thought. Unfortunately, this one was a little too close to the truth. He remembered Mr. Spoons making that last sailor from the *Nautilus* walk the plank, and shuddered. He hoped he never saw another pirate ship again for as long as he lived.

Which might not, he reflected, be all that long.

Then, without him noticing, he and the girl went around one final tree (its trunk the thickness of several men) and came out into the open.

Before them lay a crater.

The crater was enormous; it looked as though, at some distant time in the past, a giant fist had come down from the skies and punched into the earth, shattering it into painful splinters. It was a place where the land had bled; once-sandy patches were now areas of strange green glass where nothing grew. The crater lay bare before Orphan. Only its rim, high above it, was alive with plant life, and these, in sharp contrast to the crater itself, were plentiful but grotesque. Flowers as tall as Orphan nodded in the breeze, their colours in too-sharp relief, bloodied reds and oozing greens like the unmixed paint on an artist's palate.

But it was the scene below that captured his attention.

Down in the crater, two large, matt-black airships hung suspended, moored to the ground by long trailing cables. Below them, dome-shaped buildings sprouted everywhere. They reminded Orphan of mushrooms, and suddenly the thought of mushrooms – in butter, with fried onions and a piece of toast – made his stomach growl. When was the last time he had eaten?

The girl – Elizabeth – looked at him sideways and suddenly grinned. Orphan blushed.

It wasn't the buildings, however – nor the hordes of uniformed people who swarmed between them – that had captivated him. What had – what made his heart suddenly beat against his chest as if he were coming down with a cold – was the elaborate structure that towered out of the bottom of the crater. A giant metal tube, a mechanism supported by a complex web work of wires and machines. It was monstrous, a cannon magnified a thousand-fold, waiting for the powder to be touched and set alight, for the payload to be launched into...

Into space. He stared at the giant cannon and thought of the amount of power that would be required to power it. Were it used in war, it would devastate whole cities. The sweat on his face suddenly felt cold.

He was so absorbed in what he was seeing, that it was a moment before he realised Elizabeth was tugging urgently on his arm. "Hide!" she whispered. He looked around, but it was too late.

Out of a path he had not seen before, following the crater's rim, came a group of men.

Soldiers. He did not recognise the uniforms – they carried no insignia – but he recognised the guns in their hands easily enough. He and the girl stayed rooted to the spot. She seemed as frightened as he himself felt. The soldiers approached and halted when they saw them.

"Hey," said a rich, drawling voice that belonged to a whiskered, middle-aged man who might have been the commander of this unit – a patrol, Orphan realised, though what they could be guarding against…

Himself, perhaps.

"What are you doing here?"

The soldiers did not look like they were about to shoot him. They were smiling, in fact, though he drew no comfort from that. They seemed to gaze at the girl and him in amusement, but if so it was not a friendly one.

"I'm…" Orphan said, then realised he had nothing to offer and fell quiet. Were they Scottish? he thought. Clearly they were brought over with the rest of the scientific expedition on the island.

"We're gathering fruit," the girl declared suddenly, rather startling him. "For the kitchens, do you see."

"The kitchens, eh?" the whiskered soldier said, and the others tittered, though some muttered darkly: the only word Orphan thought he caught was, inexplicably, mushrooms. "Well, I don't see no fruits here, Yer Highness."

"We got lost," Elizabeth said. Orphan nodded his head.

"Lost? I'd say you were lost four hundred years ago, princess," the man said, and the soldiers laughed out loud now. "This your brother? Seems a bit dim-witted."

Orphan nodded, and smiled, and hoped he looked as dim-witted as he felt.

"Inbreeding," said another soldier, and the whiskered one laughed. "Get out of here," he said, and motioned with his gun. "This is no place for people like you."

"Thank you, sir," Elizabeth said, and then she did something else that took Orphan by surprised. She curtsied.

"A right little princess," someone said. Elizabeth, grasping Orphan tightly by the hand, quickly led him away and back into the trees. Behind them he could still hear the soldiers' laughter as they moved off.

"What was that?" he said. The girl looked up at him and shrugged. "I wanted to see the crater."

"Evidently you're not allowed to."

She shrugged again. "I don't care. I know what they're doing. We all know. Come on." She led him through the trees and the ground sloped gradually, until they reached a large stone boulder that stood on its own in a clearing.

"What are they doing?" Orphan asked, only half-listening. He almost said, Did you mention kitchens?

"They're building a spaceship, silly," the girl said. "So all the lovely lizards can go back home. Or so they say."

She approached the rock and felt around its wall. Her fingers tapped against the surface.

"You don't believe them?"

"Why should I?" Elizabeth said, reasonably. She tapped the stone again, and Orphan jumped back as a section of wall slid smoothly away and revealed a dark opening in the rock. "You know, you do look a little like my brother," she said, and giggled. "Are you sure you're a pirate?"

"I'm retired," Orphan said shortly. He felt disorientated, hungry and tired and not exactly sure what he had let himself into. Well, he thought, not much has changed.

He followed Elizabeth through the hole in the rock, and found himself in a dark tunnel. The door slid shut behind them, and for a moment he couldn't see. He felt panic again, but in another moment dim lights came on, embedded in the low ceiling, and in their light he could see the tunnel (smooth metallic walls, though the floor was of rough natural stone). It led downwards, into the earth.

"Et terrestre centrum attinges," Orphan muttered. "Quod feci, Arne Saknussemm."

"What?" Elizabeth said.

"And you will attain the centre of the earth," Orphan muttered. "I have done this, Arne Saknussemm."

"You said your name was Orphan," Elizabeth said.

"It's from a book," Orphan said.

The girl pulled back, then made a sign with her hand, the same one she had used before, but said nothing. She stared up at Orphan with an unreadable expression on her face. What was wrong with books? he wondered. Surely this girl – half-savage as she no doubt was – could read and write? What was there to be afraid of?

And then he thought, the Bookman, and suddenly felt his skin grow cold. Did the girl have a reason beyond superstition to be afraid? Were books, for her, something innately dangerous, if not outright forbidden?

"It's just something I heard," he said. "From a friend of mine. His name was Jules."

The girl didn't answer him, but turned her back and began following the contour of the tunnel. Orphan shrugged and followed her.

They walked a while in silence. The tunnel ended at a junction of three, and Elizabeth chose the left one and he followed. The tunnel snaked around, the ground sloping gradually, the dim lights coming alive as they passed, then fading behind them. Where are we going? he thought, but didn't ask out loud. The island had confused him from the moment he landed, casting him in a spell of bewilderment, its mysteries too numerous for him to digest all at once. He rubbed the spot where the mechanical insect had stung him. Was he tested and somehow approved? It occurred to him he had not seen any more of the insects, nor had he been bitten. But he was an invader, an alien entity to the island. Why, then, was he not stopped sooner?

Around them, the tunnel gradually expanded, the lights growing brighter and the air turning hot and humid. The rock under his feet gradually turned to rich, moist earth. Orphan felt sweat again and tried to avoid smelling himself. His priorities were clear, and they included, rather than the destruction of that monstrous cannon in the crater, the more modest goals of a shower, and food, and a long uninterrupted sleep. Were he ever to become a head of state, he thought, he would enshrine that in a constitution: food and sleep and soap for all. Even Marx, he felt, could not argue with that.

For a moment he wondered how his friends back home were doing: whether Karl and Mrs Beeton and Nevil Maskelyne still conspired at revolution, now that Jack was gone and so was the bookshop. He found that he missed them, though dimly, as if he had known them long ago, and in another time. He wondered if he would ever see them again.

Then the tunnel's ceiling disappeared over his head and he realised that he was standing now in a small cavern, and that he could hear human voices in the distance, and smell – oh, he could smell! – food cooking, and the all-encompassing aroma of frying garlic.

The lights on the ceiling, he saw, were of the kind he had last seen – he winced as he thought about it – under Payne's, in the Bookman's eerie lair. But here there was no lake, but rather a strange forest that grew before him, and it took him a moment to comprehend what he was seeing: for it was not trees that grew from the warm, wet ground, but mushrooms.

He thought again about Verne's story – had he somehow come here after all? For the knowledge of this place – couched in fiction and implausibility, perhaps, but true all the same – must have come from somewhere. Or did he learn of it second hand, and let his imagination roam free within it?

The mushrooms – the fungi – were easily as tall as a man, and easily as fat, Orphan thought with a smile, as Jules Verne. Their colours changed, from pure chalk-white to varying degrees of grey, to rings of yellows and earth-brown. Were they natural, he wondered, or were they, somehow, a product of that ancient explosion that had created the large crater?

He realised Elizabeth was staring up at him, her fists on her waist, an impatient look on her face. "Come on!" she said, and stalked off into the mushroom forest.

He followed her, and as he did became aware of people moving amidst the rich fungi. There were men and women there, though it was hard to see them properly: they seemed to hug the shadows, slither always out of view as if afraid of being seen. They held long, curved knives, a little like scythes, which made him nervous. Yet they seemed to mean no harm, either: and after a minute or two he realised that each of them held a basket in his or her other hand, while they ran their scythes against the gormless mass of the fungus and delicately pruned it, dropping chunks of mushroom-flesh into their baskets.

It was a strangely domestic scene, Orphan thought, and it became more so as they came at last out of the mushroom forest and into a loose collection of huts that stood together, forming a miniature village.

Elizabeth halted. They stood in the centre of this tiny village. A dank, though not unpleasant smell seemed to waft over from the giant mushrooms. He opened his mouth to speak and saw that they were no longer alone.

Men and women came out of the shadows and circled them. They wore shabby, ill-fitting clothes, similar to Elizabeth's overall. He could not see them clearly, but

felt their attention on him, pressing on him from all
sides. He didn't speak. He let his hands fall to his sides,
palms open in a gesture he hoped would show him as
harmless.

After a long moment an old woman shuffled forward. She wore a dark shawl over her wizened body.
Her eyes were bright and curious, and her face, lifted to
examine him, was lively. When she spoke, however, it
was not to him but to the girl.

"Elizabeth, where have you been?"

The girl traced lines in the dirt with her foot. "I was
out exploring."

"You know you're not supposed to leave the tunnels!"

The girl shrugged. She didn't seem overly concerned.
Orphan wished he felt the same.

"What is this?" the old woman said, and pointed a
crooked finger at Orphan. "I don't recognise your face,
young man."

I work on the other side of the island, Orphan was
about to say, when Elizabeth blurted out, "He's a pirate,
Grandmama!"

The old woman snorted. "Come over here, boy."

Orphan approached her. The woman laid her hand
on his shoulder. The pressure was slight, but he understood her and knelt down on his knees, and she peered
into his face. "Curious…" she said. Her fingers touched
his face and traced its contours. The watchers in the circle observed in silence. After a moment she withdrew
from him, her face startled.

"Who are you?" she said, her voice rising. The circle

of watchers seemed to move a step closer, closing on Orphan and the potential threat he presented.

"I told you," Elizabeth said impatiently, unmoved by the curious ceremony, "he came from the sea. I found him in the forest."

"Don't be ridiculous," the woman said. But she peered into Orphan's face with new doubt in her eyes. "He almost looks like one of mine..."

"Look," Orphan said, and the woman pulled away from him as if he had bitten her, "I don't know who you are but I mean you no harm. I am... I guess I am a little lost."

"Are you with Moriarty's crew?" the woman said, but she seemed to be speaking to herself rather than to him. "No, you can't be. A soldier? Trying to desert?"

Orphan wasn't sure what to say to that, and in any case the woman continued her musings aloud. "No, you wouldn't survive outside the perimeter. Yet..." Suddenly she darted forward and grasped his arm in her fingers. She was surprisingly strong. She lifted his arm and examined it, and her eyes opened wide when she saw the insect's puncture marks.

"That's impossible..."

"I don't understand," Orphan said.

"Is this a trick?" the woman said. "Who sent you here?"

Orphan decided it was prudent not to mention the Bookman. "I am from the empire," he said. "I had heard stories of Caliban's Island. I... I am an adventurer."

"See?" Elizabeth said, "I told you so!"

"What did I tell you," the old woman murmured,

"about never using that expression?" She rocked on her feet, still holding his arm, and studied him attentively for a long moment. The watchers remained silent and unmoving. They made him think of mushrooms. "Nobody likes a knows-it-all."

Orphan couldn't see Elizabeth's face, but from the sound she made he suspected she had stuck out her tongue.

"Your mother," the old woman said, and her voice caught. Her fingers rose back to his face, and he discovered to his surprise that they were shaking now. "Who was she?"

He suddenly realised the absurdity of his situation, kneeling in the dirt deep underground, in a cavern stinking of mushrooms, and being interrogated about his genealogy.

"I don't know."

"You have the face of one of us," the woman said. "And you must have the blood…"

For the first time another voice interjected. "Mother, that is not possible."

The speaker then stepped forward. He was a short, balding man with a thin crown of hair ringing the top of his head. He peered anxiously at Orphan and shook his head. "He can't be one of us."

"The blood doesn't lie," the woman said, raising Orphan's arm, exposing the puncture marks for all to see. "Why is he not dead?"

"Perhaps the machines made a mistake," the man said, though his voice was suddenly uncertain. "A malfunction in the defence automation…"

The old woman snorted. "Malfunction!"

Another voice joined them. A woman, pale and tall, who stepped forward so that she, too, could peer into Orphan's face. He felt rather like an exhibit at the Egyptian Hall, put on display, an automaton whose only function was to be looked at, and talked over. "Perhaps Edward would like to go out and see if he could leave the island? After all, if the machines have failed…" She let her sentence trail off and smirked at the bald man, who seemed to shrink away from her as if frightened by her words.

"The machines haven't failed," the old woman said, and now her trembling had stopped, and something like wonder filled her eyes. "They have not failed in four hundred years, and they have certainly not failed now, with Moriarty's cannon and the lizards' plans so close to fruition!" She withdrew from Orphan and pulled herself as high as she could go. "Get up!"

As he did the circle of watchers closed on him, and he had to stop himself from bolting. What they did next surprised him: they came up to him, surrounding him, and began to feel him. Hands touched his hair, his face, his shoulders. Fingers examined the puncture marks on his arm, many of them, coming and going. All this was done in silence. Was that, he wondered, trying to stay still, not to startle these strange subterranean creatures, what it was like to be an automaton? To be subjected to curiosity, to comment, without regard?

"You say you never knew your mother?" the woman asked.

"No," Orphan said. "I mean, yes. I never knew her. Not even her name."

"Mary," someone said, wonder in his voice. It was the man with the crown of hair. "He must be Mary's son…"

The crowd gathered around Orphan began to whisper the name as if enthralled. "Mary?"

"Mary…"

"Mary!"

"Stop! Wait!" Orphan said, snapping. He pushed them away, and they cowered from him. "My father was a Vespuccian sailor. I never knew my mother, but I very much doubt she came from, well, here!" He waved his hand in the air, feeling the anger that all the tiredness and hunger and heat had brought, the confusion and the fear. His gesture seemed to encompass the dim light, the mushroom fields, the poor quality of the huts and clothes and the dirt under his feet. "This place is only a legend! A story people tell! It's not a place people come from!"

"But we do," the old woman said, and she smiled at him. Her teeth were white and even, startling in that old mouth. "Oh, stories are real, my boy. More real than you could ever imagine! Do they still tell stories of us, too, back in your empire? Do they whisper the tale of the last King and Queen and of their ignominious exile?"

"The last *what*?" Orphan said.

TWENTY-NINE
Mary

Mary, Mary, Quite Contrary,
How does your garden grow?
With silver bells and cockleshells
And pretty maids all in a row.
  – Traditional nursery rhyme

They were sitting in one of the huts. It was disturbingly organic-looking, as if grown rather than built. A small fire burned in the centre, the smoke rising through a central chimney. A large iron pot rested over the coals.

The old woman was sitting opposite Orphan. Her name, he had learned, was Catherine. He was still trying to digest the other bit of information: namely, that she claimed to be his grandmother.

"So he's not really a pirate?" Elizabeth said, disappointed. She stood by the door and looked restless.

"So you really are a princess?" Orphan said, the words catching in his throat. He looked at the half-wild girl, tan-skinned, dirty matted hair.

Elizabeth snorted in reply.

"Oh, but they were cruel!" Catherine said. She looked at him and her eyes reflected fire. "When that cursed Vespucci woke them from their sleep, how quickly they plotted against us! When first they came to us we welcomed them, the court made burnished and bright and gay. But they came like thieves, like robbers, and in the night they fell on their prey, and captured us all, and shipped us out before first light."

She paused and stared into the embers, and some of the fire seemed to seep out of her. "So I was told," she said, her voice softer. "By my father, who had heard it from his, who had heard it from his, all the way back." She gestured around at the hut. "This is the only palace I have ever known."

"And you say you are—" Orphan began, but couldn't bring himself to finish the sentence.

Catherine smiled. "Yes," she said. "I am the daughter of the rightful King and Queen of England, by direct descent. Which makes you, William, the King-in-Waiting."

"I beg your pardon?"

"The King-in-Exile," she said, elaborating.

"I beg your pardon?"

Her smile grew softer at his bewilderment. "The man who would be King, William," she said.

"I'm sorry," Orphan said, "but that's ridiculous."

William?

The old woman smiled, and some of her energy seemed to return to her. "Look at yourself," she said. "Can you deny the family resemblance?"

Orphan shook his head. "Superficial," he said.

From her place by the door Elizabeth snorted again. "Blood doesn't lie," Catherine said. "When we were brought here, the island's machines analysed and sampled us, and the Rule was instated: that only those of the blood could live on the island, though they could never leave. Over the years I have seen the remains of the people who once sought this island: their skeletons litter the shore and the jungle."

"What do you mean, the Rule?"

"Families have a – a sort of signature," Catherine said. "A code, the lizards call it. The insects are manufactured, mobile probes for the island's defences. When that insect bit you, it withdrew blood and analysed it. Were you a stranger – were you really no more than what you say you are, an orphan, a pirate, a castaway – you would be dead by now, and your body would have been slowly decomposing in the jungle. That you are still alive, I think, is proof enough of who and what you are."

"Ridiculous," Orphan said again. He didn't want to deal with this.

Catherine laughed. She had a warm, deep laugh, and smoky. "Why don't we eat first?" she said. "I am sure you have hundreds of questions."

Yes, like how do I get out of here? Orphan thought. But, right now, he had to admit, the thought of food dominated.

"Elizabeth, bring plates!" the old woman said. Elizabeth, with a disdainful look at Orphan, disappeared through the door and returned a moment later with three earthenware plates and some crude cutlery.

Catherine dipped a ladle into the iron pot and brought it up full of a thick, fragrant broth. She dished it into the plates, and Elizabeth handed the first one to Orphan.

"Have some fungus bread," Catherine said, and from somewhere in the gloom there emerged a basket, similar to the ones Orphan had seen carried by the mushroom pickers, but it was full not with mushrooms but with loaves of soft, chunky bread.

Orphan didn't need much encouragement. He tore a large piece of bread and dipped it into the broth, almost forgetting to chew in his hunger. The hot food burned his mouth and throat. Catherine looked at him with concern. "You must eat more slowly," she said. "Have some water."

From somewhere, too, a jug of cool, clear water and a plain, muddy cup. He drank, and continued to eat with a little more moderation, while the old woman pecked at her food and Elizabeth played half-heartedly with hers. The large chunks floating in the stew, he figured, were mushrooms, though they tasted meaty. He finished the plate and started on another.

"You never knew your mother?" Catherine said, and there was a note of pain in her voice. Orphan momentarily stopped eating (a chunk of bread suspended in the air, half-way to being dipped) and looked at her. "No. I told you, no."

Catherine nodded. "Let me tell you about my daughter," she said.

Orphan made a vague gesture with his bread, as if saying, Do I have a choice? and splattered himself with gravy. Elizabeth laughed, but quietly.

"Very well," Catherine said. "Then I will tell you about Mary."

Even when she was very young (as young, Catherine said, as Elizabeth is now), Mary had begun to exhibit her difference from the others. Though she was generally a quiet, unassuming child, a mischievous streak in her broke from time to time to the surface and exhibited itself, and often at the most inopportune moments. One time, for instance, she was working in the Nursery ("The nursery?" Orphan said, but Catherine ignored him and continued) when her parents heard a scream and, rushing around the corner, saw her holding a bloodied lizard tail in her hands. Catherine herself (so she said) then screamed, but when they reached the child discovered that the thing in her hand was no more than a crude construct, made with fungal flesh and dyed green and red with leaves and berries collected in the jungle (at this point Elizabeth smirked).

As she grew older she began to spend long periods outside of the tunnel system, exploring the jungle and making daring raids onto the beach (or as close as she could come to it) and even to the rim of the crater. Like a small animal, she passed through the island without rousing the automated defences' attention, and she came to know much of its geography in secret.

Once, she made it as far as the sand on the edge of the sea. It was night, and there was no moon. In the distance, lights flashed, followed by the sounds of explosions and the weak cries of men. Mary had turned back on the water and climbed as high as she could, and when she turned again she saw two ships (of what make she didn't know) fight each other with cannon and guns. It did not seem to be a battle for loot or treasure, for the battle ended with one of the ships on fire, and sinking, and the other simply turning away from it. The ship that won the battle soon disappeared, and the other ship burned slowly, and was drowned.

When Mary came back to the sand the next night, she was not alone. In the darkness, not seeing, she had stumbled over the body of a man.

She clamped down on her scream, afraid of rousing the unseen defences, then saw that it was too late. The man was dead, his chest punctured as if by a giant fist. Something, she thought, had come out of the sand and gone through the man, and had then gone back into the ground. She had heard of the sand-worms that guarded the island, but had never seen one. No one was even sure if they were real, a lifeform warped by the ancient impact that had created the crater, or whether they, like the insects, were machines.

She was afraid; but not so afraid that she didn't stop, and let curiosity triumph; and so she searched quickly through the man's pockets, and came back with a–

"A book," Catherine said, and Elizabeth made the warding-off sign he had seen her use twice before.

"What sort of book?" Orphan said.

Catherine sighed. "That," she said, "I did not find out until a long time afterwards."

Books (so Catherine explained) were forbidden amongst the humans on the island. Their charges at the

Nursery used no books, but rather strange play-devices, similar to pliable balls, that were (apparently) similar, but used smell and a high-pitch sound not audible to humans (Orphan asked again about the Nursery, and again received no direct answer). Books were the domain of the Bookman (again, the sign, made by both Catherine and Elizabeth this time), and were objects of evil and misfortune.

But to Mary, this book she had found was a thing not of evil, but of hope. Which (Catherine said with sudden vehemence) was perhaps more evil than all.

It was a very curious book. Had Mary known any books she may have been more wary of this one she had found. But she did not, and was not. She took the book with her that night, and hid it in the hollowed cavity of an ancient tree on the edge of the crater. And she returned to it most nights, when everyone else of the subterranean court (for that, as Orphan found, was what the mushroom gatherers called it) was asleep.

And so time passed.

Mary (Catherine continued) had become a beautiful young woman. She continued her work at the Nursery, tending the young lizard-spawn ("So that's what it is!" Orphan exclaimed. "Shush," Catherine said. Elizabeth giggled), learning the manners of the court ("such as there still are," Catherine said) and, all in all, arousing no special curiosity. Her habit of pulling pranks, as far as they all could tell, had abated. Life went about its daily routine.

Or so it seemed.

The truth ("And I only found this out much later," Catherine said) was that Mary continued to visit the book, and she continued to read it nightly. It was, she soon realised, a special book, in that its contents never remained the same. The book's title, embossed in gilt on its hard, leathery cover, was Bible Stories for Young Children. Of all the stories, Mary liked most the ones about Adam and Eve. There were many stories about them. In the beginning, Adam and Eve lived in the Garden of Eden. Then Adam did something very bad, awakening a monster that lived in the garden, and the monster, which was in the shape of a lizard standing upright, had a fight with God and then took over the garden. Adam and Eve were still in the garden but, since it was on an island in a big ocean, they couldn't leave. A kindly old wizard, however, helped them. He was shaped like a strange, multi-legged creature, and he was once a servant of the monster but he had escaped and was now living in the garden in secret. He became Adam and Eve's teacher. Every time Mary opened the book, Adam and Eve were doing something new. To begin with, they merely studied geography, and the book showed her continents and oceans, the trade routes that passed between them, and the different people who lived in those far-off places. Then Eve decided to become an engineer, and the book showed Mary blueprints and diagrams and conversion tables, and the ways to build vehicles and machines. One day Adam decided to run to sea and become a pirate; after that, only Eve remained in the book. Then there were more lizard-monsters, baby ones, and Eve had to take care of them. Eve did what she was told, but there was revenge in her heart, and the desire to escape. She began to plot ways to get off the island – which was heavily guarded by powerful sorcery – until one day…

The fire threw twisted shadows on the walls, and a cold wind seemed to whisper under the door, insinuating itself into the confines of the hut. Orphan shivered, and wished for a hot bath.

"One day," Catherine said, "I was called to the Nursery by my husband. I had no intimation that anything was wrong. Mary had left in the morning as she always did. Nothing seemed out of the ordinary. And yet…"

"What did she do?" Orphan leaned forward. "Did she do it?" He was excited despite himself. "Did she manage to escape?"

Catherine smiled, but her face was sad. "Is it really so bad, here?" she said. "Did she hate it so much? Did she hate us so much?"

"If I could," Elizabeth announced, "I'd escape too."

"Hush, girl," Catherine said. She turned back to Orphan. "When I arrived at the Nursery, Mary was gone."

"But how?" He was tense now, his muscles feeling constricted and hard under his skin. He felt hot, then cold, as if the air itself kept changing around him. It was too much to take in. Was she really his mother? Could it be possible? And is that, then, where he came from, this squalid, sordid subterranean habitat, reeking of fungus and ash?

"I don't know."

"You must know!" He stood up, bunched his fists. He fought the tiredness that threatened to overwhelm him. He discovered that he no longer disbelieved Catherine. And that meant...

Realisation touched him like a cold hand. For though he had made it onto the island alive, and could pass through it undisturbed, he could never leave.

Like Mary, he was now a prisoner on the island.

The Bookman had never intended to give him back Lucy, he thought. He had never intended for him to leave.

"No," Orphan said, and louder, "I don't believe it."

Yet I have to believe, he thought. I have to believe this is part of the plan. I have to believe I will return, I will get Lucy back.

"How did she escape?" he said – shouted. Elizabeth backed away from him, but the old woman didn't stir, and looked up at him with a faraway look on her face. "I will show you," she said, "what I know. And perhaps the book could tell you more than it had ever told me."

"The book?"

"The book?" Elizabeth said, and there was genuine fear in her voice.

Orphan felt his thoughts slow down to a trickle; it was like he was swimming through thick, syrupy liquid. It was too much – he had gone too long without sleep, and his mind could no longer operate. Like an automaton, he thought. I need to shut down.

"Help me hold him!" He was dimly aware of Elizabeth and Catherine taking him by the arms and helping him down, and onto a mattress by the wall that smelled, rather pleasantly, of mushrooms.

"Sleep, William," Catherine said softly, and the last thing Orphan felt before falling into a deep black sleep was the touch of her hand as she gently stroked his head.

He was running through a landscape of pools and warm rocks, and the air was full of flies. In the distance he could see another figure running, yet as fast as he ran he could not catch up with it. Small lizards sunned themselves on the rocks and caught flies with their tongues. The flies were emitting a distinctly mechanical buzz.

He began to flap his hands. Somehow, it made sense. He felt air currents under his open palms, and was lifted in the air. He circled, slowly at first, rising higher. Below him, the island spread out like a treasure map. Thick forests grew out of the wound in the centre. The crater looked like an eye, with an improbable needle sticking out of it. It looked painful.

The figure he was chasing was still ahead of him, rising higher than him. He chased it, flapping harder, until he reached the edges of space. Blackness spread out before him, filled with stars. Below, the needle left the eye and rose into the air, impossibly thin. It went past him and disappeared into the void.

He stopped moving, and hung suspended in the thin air, on the edge of space. Ahead of him, the figure stopped too. It came closer to him, circling in orbit. They were like Earth and the moon, but growing closer, until he could see her face...

Then he was falling, falling hard, the air rushing past

him and he screamed, and hit a hard surface, and woke
up.

"Why 'William'?" he said.

"Mary always said that, if she had a son, she'd name
him William," Catherine said. It was still twilight. It was
always twilight in the tunnels.

"Call me Orphan."

"A wise man knows his own name," Catherine said.

"A wise man wouldn't be where I am now," Orphan
said, and Catherine smiled, briefly.

"Do you know what happened to her?"

"She died," Orphan said. "They both died."

"How do you know?"

"I..." He didn't. It was what he was told. By... Gilgamesh? How did he fit into all this? Orphan
remembered the fragment of Gilgamesh's diary. He had
been to the island once. Had he been there again?

"Who was your father?"

"He was a Vespuccian sailor."

Catherine's face was a moue of disapproval. Orphan
almost laughed.

"How long have I been asleep?" he asked, sitting up.
He felt refreshed, almost light-headed.

"Nearly fifteen hours," Catherine said. "It's morning
now."

Purpose returned. "I want to see the Nursery," he said.

"Elizabeth will show it to you."

"I need some food," he said.

"There's some–" Catherine said, and Orphan sighed
and said, "Mushrooms?"

"Yes."

"Fine."

"You could do with a wash, too," Catherine commented.

Orphan agreed.

"There's a warm pool outside."

"Thanks."

"It's so good to have you back, William," Catherine said. Orphan muttered something inaudible. He did not intend to stick around if he could help it.

"Where is the book?" he said.

Catherine didn't answer immediately. Orphan stood up and stretched. Yes, he felt a lot better now. Ready to tackle the island. Ready to act. And to find a way off it. He tried his thumb, felt it no different. If he didn't look at it too closely it was just like it was before…

Good. One step at a time then. If his mother – was it really his mother? – could find her way out, then so could he. The Bookman must have intended him to.

If he kept repeating that he might actually believe it.

"Where it has always been," Catherine said in a low voice. "But it would be hard to get to. In the tree, on the edge of the crater."

"Good," Orphan said, "because the crater is the next place I want to pay a visit to." And he wandered out of the door and went looking for the warm pool, whistling as he went.

THIRTY
Launch

We are all in the gutter, but some of us are looking at the stars.
– Oscar Wilde, *Lady Windermere's Fan*

Orphan had washed and cleaned himself, and was given clothes by the man with the crown of hair over his balding head, who was apparently his uncle, if by marriage. He was Elizabeth's father. Which made him, Orphan, her cousin, didn't it? He wasn't sure how he felt about that. The thought of suddenly having a large (and somewhat mushroom-obsessed) family was a little overwhelming.

He also got the impression that the uncle wasn't very keen on him. The man moved furtively. But then, they all did, Orphan realised. They moved like unwanted strangers in someone else's home, meek and nervous.

The clothes, though worn, were comfortable. Loose trousers and shirt, both grey.

When he finished his bath and dressed he saw Elizabeth approaching. She held a small object in her hand, and looked distressed.

"Hello," Orphan said, awkwardly.

Elizabeth came closer, then stopped. "I brought you the book," she said.

"What? But it's dangerous to–" He stopped. Elizabeth shrugged. "I go out alone all the time," she said. "I wouldn't have found you otherwise, would I?"

Orphan couldn't argue with that. He took the book from her hands and Elizabeth immediately looked relieved.

Orphan turned the book in his hands. The leather binding looked worn, rotting in places. The title was hardly discernible, the gilt having been chipped away. The page edges looked rusted. Holding it, he felt Mary's story becoming truth. It was the book his mother had held. The way she once may have held him. Carefully, he opened the book onto the first page.

It was empty.

The paper was brittle and yellowing, with spots of water damage and rust. It was, in booksellers' terminology, foxed. It was also blank.

Orphan turned the pages one after the other, but none were printed. Nothing but empty pages. Frustrated, he leafed through till the end. Only there, on the back endpaper, did he see something. A small, barely legible mark in fading blue ink, hand-written in an old-fashioned script. He peered at it. It said, *"Under the Nursery, the mushrooms grow flat. – M."*

Orphan sighed. What was it with those people and mushrooms? Even his m– even Mary. He closed the book and put it away in a pocket.

"There's nothing in the book," he said to Elizabeth.

"Maybe there was once, but now – it's just an empty book."

He was rewarded with a smile, though it was soon gone. "I…" she said, then stopped. "I ran into soldiers when I went to get it," she said. Seeing Orphan's expression she shook her head. "I hid this time. I didn't have you to get in the way."

"That's good," Orphan said.

"I heard them talking," Elizabeth said. She frowned at him. "They said there was someone on the island. Someone out to sabotage the cannon. That's why they were out patrolling. They weren't very happy about it."

"What?" Orphan said.

"It's very busy in the crater," Elizabeth said. "Frantic. I looked. They're all out. I heard the soldiers say Moriarty pushed the launch forward."

"What?" Orphan said.

"To tonight," Elizabeth said. She suddenly looked quite pleased at the idea. "Do you think we could watch it?"

"Moriarty is here?" Orphan said.

"I guess so," Elizabeth said. "I don't know who he is."

"He's the Prime Minister – quite a good poet, too."

"I don't really like poetry," Elizabeth said. "It's boring."

"Wait," Orphan said, not really listening. "They can't launch now – they have to wait until Mars is close enough, and that's not until…" His voice died and he thought, I am an idiot.

The probe wasn't going to Mars. He had forgotten that. That was just a deception. It only needed to get far enough out into space to send a signal. All the rest of it – the ceremony in Richmond Park, the public proclamations, the newspaper articles – they were all a sham. And he had to act now, or there would be nothing left for him; and Lucy – and, perhaps, humanity – would be doomed.

"How can I get to the cannon?" he said.

"To the crater?" Elizabeth looked both scared, and excited. "You can't. We're not allowed."

"But you must have some interaction with the people there?" Orphan said. "You mentioned something about kitchens."

"Yes, but the kitchens are underground," Elizabeth said.

"So how does the food get to the people in the crater?"

"Through a shaft, I think," Elizabeth said. "There's a pulley system."

Orphan sighed. Images of the future flashed before his eyes. They were not promising.

The dumbwaiter was a small confined metal box. It stank of stale food. Orphan looked at it doubtfully. He did not like the thought of what may be waiting above ground.

He and Elizabeth had made their way through the tunnels into the kitchens. They were situated in a great, ill-lit cavern that was full of smoke. Wherever he went the people he encountered stopped and stared at him, then came closer and touched him, as if to reassure themselves of the reality of his existence. He had found it all very trying.

But, on the plus side, nobody tried to stop him. It was as if these people had curiosity bred out of them, leaving in its wake a kind of numb acceptance of the way things were. Elizabeth took him directly to the dumbwaiter. It was sometime between breakfast and lunch, and the machine wasn't being used.

Orphan climbed inside it.

"Good luck," Elizabeth said. And hit a button.

The dumbwaiter shook, coughed, and began to rise. Orphan crouched in the corner, trying to make himself as small as possible.

He rose through a shaft of rough stone. The dumbwaiter clucked and shook. At last it emerged into light, coughed once more, and stopped. Orphan peered out.

The room ahead was empty. He slid out of the box and stood up cautiously.

He was, he soon discovered, in the back of a sort of mess hall. Long tables stood in perfect rows. Small windows cut into the walls filtered in sunlight. He walked over to a window and peered outside.

The giant cannon glared at him. From here, it was impossibly large, dominating everything. People moved about it, as small as ants in comparison. There was an air of tense anticipation to those people, a feel of buzzing activity. Again, he was reminded of ants. The crater had become a colony of them, he thought. And somewhere, then, there must be the Queen – or rather, the Prime Minister. Wasn't Moriarty there?

"Oi, you're not allowed to…!" He swung around as soon as the voice registered, swung at the speaker even before his mind caught up. A soldier, young, almost a boy, in a too-large, muddy uniform, a shorn scalp, a nose that had been broken before and was now, because of Orphan, broken again.

The boy clutched his bleeding nose and stared at Orphan, then rushed at him.

Orphan ducked, barely, and smacked the boy on the back of the head.

The boy dropped to the floor. Orphan swore.

What did you expect? a part of him said. Did you think you could just walk up here, destroy these people's life-work, and stroll out again?

Yet he hated what he had to do. He had changed. He was no longer the young man whose greatest crime was in belonging to the Persons from Porlock, who were merely pranksters, modern clowns out to stir a bit of trouble for the literati. He was a fugitive now, a desperate man, who had both seen and caused violence. He swore again, then dragged the unconscious boy to the back of the room, and hastily stripped him. He put on the boy's uniform (it was a little tight, but otherwise fit) and put his own clothes, or rather those of the subterranean people, piled on the soldier's body after he dumped him in the dumbwaiter.

He hit a button on the wall. The machine creaked and began to descend.

There is no other way, he thought. He had to get rid of the soldier somehow. But in doing so he put the subterranean people – my own family, he thought, appalled – in danger.

He tried not to think about it. He picked up the soldier's gun and marched out into the sunlight.

He wasn't challenged. The area he found himself in was a loose collection of low-lying stone buildings and large tent-like bubbles. It must be the living quarters, he thought. But there were few people around, and those that were merely glanced at him, noted the uniform and paid him little attention.

Ahead of him was the cannon. It dominated everything, its silver metal flashing in the sunlight, its tip reaching high into the blue skies until it seemed to rip through clouds.

The cannon stood in a clearing, beyond which were the temporary-looking structures of bubble-tents. He could see the two black airships in the distance, anchored to the ground, keeping watch.

He had to find the control room. Or could he go up to the cannon itself, and act then?

No. As he came closer the number of soldiers grew, and he could not afford to be stopped by them. Panic took hold of him. He only had limited time. The soldier he had hurt was bound to come awake down below, to raise the alarm. Already they were suspicious, had known he was on the island. He had to hurry.

It was then, as he paused and squinted in the sun and looked again towards the cannon, with a befuddled sense of being suddenly helpless, that he saw Moriarty.

The Prime Minister looked uncomfortable in the unforgiving haze of the sun. He was a short man turning to fat, and sweat stained his face as he walked quickly, with sharp heavy breaths, away from the cannon. He was surrounded: scientists in white smocks; functionaries in outlandish tropical clothes no doubt concocted in expensive Savile Row tailors, a long way from any tropical sun; and soldiers. This group, with Moriarty at its centre, moved across the arid landscape, and Orphan followed at a distance.

It was a long walk; the sun beat down hard on Orphan, who was uncomfortable in the unfamiliar uniform. He wondered how the soldiers handled it. The group moved away from the ramshackle assortment of buildings and headed further out, towards the edge of the crater. Where were the lizards? Orphan wondered. He had seen none in the crater, none in the tunnels. This was their home, their hidden seat of power, and yet, there was no sign of them. He felt uneasy. What else was hiding on the island?

Moriarty and his people approached the rise of land and disappeared around a crest. Orphan, sweating, followed. He reached the low crest of a hill – but the group had disappeared.

He swore again.

Descending the small hill, he found only a dry brook at the bottom but, as he looked down at the ground he struck lucky – there were footsteps in the sand. He followed them a short way up, but found the way blocked by a giant boulder. The footmarks ended just before the stone.

Where did they all go?

He began searching the stone, his hands touching the rough, warm surface in search of a hidden spring, some kind of artificial control, but could find nothing but un-broken rock.

He swore again and sat down. It was all part of a big, invisible web, he thought. With the spider forever hidden, weaving forever more strands to confuse and entrap. Where did they go?

He let his mind wander. Suddenly, none of this seemed particularly important. How was he to sabotage the cannon, anyway? And for what? Should he prevent the lizards from calling to their own people? Were they planning invasion – or did they simply desire to escape a backwards world that was for them a prison?

Perhaps, he thought, it was a little of both. His eyes tracked a column of ants across the sand. A lizard darted out of nowhere and snatched several of the ants with its tongue. The remaining ants continued to march, despite the attack.

Are we the ants? he thought. Or... His train of thought was interrupted. Where had the lizard come from? He could no longer see the reptile, but his eyes caught the quick darting trail it left across the sand. There!

He bent down on his knees and crawled forward in the sand until he was directly beneath the boulder, in its shade. Something flashed. He cleared sand with his hands.

Below him there was, revealed, not more earth but bars of dull metal, stretching away from him. He was standing on some kind of a ramp!

Before he could move again the ground shook, and for one terrified moment he was convinced the boulder was about to roll over and crush him. Then the ramp descended, sand, ants and all, and he found himself voyaging once more below ground.

"It is I," Orphan muttered, "Quod feci, Arne Saknussemm," and he thought of Verne, the fat writer's image forming before him in sharp relief, and he suddenly missed home very much indeed.

The ramp did not travel far. Orphan found himself in a small antechamber, empty, with no features or signs of life. As the ramp touched the ground it almost immediately traversed its course and began to slowly rise. Orphan rolled away and landed on the stone floor. The ramp rose and soon blocked out the sunlight. Orphan stood for a moment and let his eyes adjust to the semi-darkness. Something crawled on his hand and he panicked, but it was only an ant, separated from its comrades in the disturbance. He put it down on the floor and wished it well. It was lost, just like him.

Then he got up and stepped through the door of the antechamber, and into a corridor and the sight of guns aimed levelly at him.

THIRTY-ONE
Moriarty

"Who, then, is Porlock?" I asked.

"Porlock, Watson, is a nom de plume, a mere identification
mark, but behind it lies a shifty and evasive personality. In a
former letter he frankly informed me that the name was not
his own, and defied me ever to trace him among the teeming
millions of this great city."

– Arthur Conan Doyle, *The Valley of Fear*

This time he couldn't fight. There were three of them,
and they were armed. What's more, they had obviously
been waiting for him.

The soldiers didn't speak to him. First they frisked
him, finding no weapons but confiscating the book, his
mother's book. He tried to protest but they merely
pushed him along. They were young, about his age, and
they marched him along the corridor, their guns at his
back, making sure he followed the route to wherever
he was being taken. Orphan breathed in air and tried to
calm himself down. All in all, his attempt to sabotage
the cannon, such as it was, had not gone very well.

The soldiers led him further down, but now there was a fresh breeze blowing through and he thought he could hear, in the distance, the far cries of seagulls. The path twisted around and around, as if meant only to confuse him. At last they came to a door.

Unlike the rest of the tunnels, which seemed old and worn with time, this door seemed new. A coat of white paint so fresh it could have been applied an hour before, a gleaming brass handle, a small window of patterned glass: it had the feel of an office in the City, or a Whitehall interview room.

The nearest soldier knocked, then pushed the door open. As it opened Orphan, too, was pushed, and he stumbled into the room. He stood alone in a room empty of furnishings but for a solitary unoccupied chair in the centre, and a desk in one corner.

Behind the desk sat Moriarty.

One of the soldiers had followed him into the room. He went to the Prime Minister's desk, whispered some words to him, and handed him the book. Moriarty nodded. The soldier saluted and left the room. The door closed behind him.

Orphan had never seen the Prime Minister up close, yet he immediately recognised his face. The bald, high dome of his head, the deep-set eyes, the austere yet sensual mouth – here was a man of great ability, a poet as well as an administrator of great renown, the man who effectively ran the empire. Now, those dark eyes examined Orphan, and the hint of a smile lifted the corners of the Prime Minister's mouth.

"Please," Moriarty said. "Sit down." He had a pleasant, dry voice which was a little high-pitched. He gestured for the chair and Orphan sat down, facing the Prime Minister. This is it, he thought. This is where it ends. The room had no windows. He could no longer hear the call of seabirds. A deep unsettling silence lay on the room like a dust-sheet.

"So you are the mysterious saboteur," Moriarty said. "The would-be saboteur, I should say."

Orphan didn't reply, and Moriarty shrugged. "Don't feel bad," he said. "It was easy enough to deduct the path that led you here. Clearly, you would be taking shelter in the tunnels, or you would have been caught already. Clearly, you only survived the island because of your blood – and my people tell me that you are indeed the rightful heir to the throne…" He stopped when he saw Orphan's eyes open wide, sudden panic mounting behind them. "You didn't know?"

"I…" He didn't know what to say. To be related to the ancient kings was one thing, but this?

"You are, or so I'm told, the only grandson of Catherine and Bertram. Ergo, you are first in line to the throne – were there a throne, young William." Moriarty's face absorbed his previous pleasantness as if it never existed. "Were there a throne."

The King of England. Orphan almost laughed.

"It was easy enough to deduct you will attempt something soon, and to reason that your only easy way into the crater would be via the food duct. Don't worry, by the way: the soldier you disabled is fine."

Orphan had flashes of the soldier he surprised at the mess hall. "You were waiting for me?"

Moriarty shrugged. "Of course. After all, it isn't every day that one meets a King-in-Waiting. And a poet too, I hear? In fact, I do believe I read something of yours, in the *Review*?"

"Well…" Orphan said. He had published in the *Poetic Review* a couple of times, but…

"'Finding a two-pence coin I lift it from the mud and see, the profile of an unknown monarch, her mouth slack and her eyes locked into infinity…'" Moriarty quoted. "Something of this nature? I remember you, Orphan. I thought you had great potential as a poet. It is a shame you had to choose adventure. Poetry, I find, is so much better coming from a life lived as dully as can be."

Orphan examined him. The dark eyes stared back at him, missing nothing. He felt like an open book, riffled by the Prime Minister as if its contents were merely of passing interest. As if reading his thoughts, Moriarty reached for the book on his desk and picked it up. "*Bible Stories for Young Children*?" Moriarty said. He opened the book. Orphan looked at it closely, perhaps for the first time. There was something strangely familiar about it, as if he had seen this sort of printing, this sort of binding, before. "The Bookman's book," Moriarty said. "So clever…" He sighed, and kept leafing through the empty pages. "It is hard to run an empire when your masters' grasp of their own technology is virtually non-existent," he said. "I often wished we could have worked together with the Bookman. Yes," he said, smiling into Orphan's surprised face, "I know what he is, what he wants. Les Lézards' servant, and their store of knowledge too. And yet – a revolutionary element, like our own. A dangerous one. It's a shame…" He closed the book, holding it in both hands. "I will have it sent to the technicians for analysis. Perhaps something useful could be gleaned of it yet. Now, as for you, young Orphan…"

Those were the words he was hoping not to hear. "What will you do with me?" he said.

The Prime Minister turned the book in his hands. He seemed fascinated by it. And now Orphan knew what it reminded him of – the bibles at Guy's Hospital, the ones in every room that had made Inspector Adler so uncomfortable. "I'm afraid," Moriarty said, "that I won't have any choice but to have you executed–"

And at that moment the book in Moriarty's hands suddenly glowed, the binding showing a flash of intense radiation, and Moriarty cried out, but the voice was strangled in his throat. Orphan watched, horrified, and the book tumbled from the Prime Minister's hands and fell to the floor. Moriarty slumped on the desk. He was still breathing, just. His hands, and face, were badly burned. And as he fell a section of the wall slid silently open – revealing, to a horrified Orphan, a small control panel, and a curious screen, and the image of the cannon with people like ants moving around its base. Orphan snatched the book from Moriarty's hands and tucked it back in his pocket. He stared at the prone Prime Minister, and then at the control panel, no longer hidden, and at the cannon it was showing, the cannon it was there to control, and

he thought, with a sudden, overwhelming uncertainty
– what do I do?

And now he was running, running through tunnels, his
sweat burning on his face and getting into his eyes; behind him the pursuers followed, and a shot echoed, a
burst of stone hit his face and cut his skin. Away from
the stunned or dead Moriarty, away from capture and
death, onwards, in a mad frightened rush to get away.

Orphan ran, slipped, found the ground sloping
sharply away from him. He stumbled. The air was hot,
clammy and humid like the inside of an engine-room;
from somewhere unseen he could once more smell the
sea. He was in some sort of duct. He surrendered to the
slide, arching his back away from the floor, his body
resting on his heels and back, and so, like a child at play,
he slid downwards, his speed increasing with each passing moment.

More shots behind him, but none coming close. Air
rushed into his face. The smooth floor offered no resistance, no way to slow down. He thought of hitting
something hard and ending up a blot of red against
stone walls.

Don't, he thought.

Somewhere nearer, the cry of birds. The space he
was in expanded, and a light grew ahead. An opening.
He went through it–

He was flying through the air.

He had the sense of a wide space opening below him.
Green and blue, a sense of free-falling, the ground
opening below him–

He crashed into warm water with a huge explosion. His lungs burned. He had the sense of dark, heavy shapes moving below him. He kicked out and broke back to the surface. He looked at where he was.
He was in a large pool of water.

The pool was surrounded by lizards.

The pursuers hadn't followed him. He knew why. And thought that now he truly was in trouble.

He was in the Nursery. Around him, lizard young milled on rocks and watched him with curious, un-blinking eyes. Every now and then a tongue would dart out and taste the air, and the eyes would blink, slowly and ponderously, and focus back on him. He got the distinct impression they regarded him as a new toy, and were curious as to its application.

He swam to the edge and hauled himself out, and for a long moment he remained lying on the ground, catching his breath, not daring to move for fear of what would happen. When he rose at last he could see, amidst the lizards, the cowering shapes of human be-ings. And he thought, My family. The idea was bitter to him.

He made to move, and the nearest lizard darted at him, and he stopped. The lizard's tongue snaked out and tasted his skin.

Then, startling Orphan so much that he nearly fell back in the water, the lizard spoke.

"Sssss..." it said, and flicked its tail. "Sssservant..." It moved away from him then, losing interest. The others, too, returned gradually to their previous activities. The

humans (he did not recognise any of them) cast nervous, fearful glances at him and moved between their
charges.

Orphan accepted the unspoken message.

Soon, he knew, the soldiers would come for him;
and if not them, the lizards themselves might come, to
see who it was who dared threaten their get with his
presence, and this he feared even more. He remembered the sight of the two lizards fighting each other to
the death, back in the King's Arms in Drury Lane. He
did not think himself capable of this kind of fight.

He felt lost then, and almost gave up the fight altogether; when he felt something hard against his hip
and, startled for a moment, reached out and realised it
was his mother's book. No, he thought. It was the
Bookman's, and it made him frightened.

But he was not like the others of his family, he
thought. He, at least, would not fear books. He opened
the book, wondering if some of its power remained, if
some of the Bookman's artifice was yet in it, but... the
book remained empty and old. It did not come alive,
and the pages remained stained-yellow and otherwise
blank. He leafed through it again, nevertheless, until he
reached the end, and the small, fading inscription left
there long ago by his mother: Under the Nursery, the
mushrooms grow flat.

How had she managed to escape? In one end of the
Nursery he could now hear shouts, and knew the soldiers had come for him. It was almost dark now, and
the cannon's payload would be launched soon, the attempt would be made to reach the stars.

And he would most likely be dead.

Is that how you want to be remembered? he thought. As a saboteur? He looked around him at the lizard young. Could he take their life in his hands? What would the probe have meant? He was too late asking himself these questions.

Instead, he ran. He ran away from the soldiers, away from the Nursery, towards the sea. The giant cave he was in opened about him like a fan, the ground sloping gently until the pools of water almost poured down into the sea.

There are no defences here, he thought. Not this close to the babies. There would be no monstrous worms in the sand, no giant insects to suck out blood. I hope.

Down by the shore the ceiling abruptly disappeared above his head, and in its stead were stars. He took a deep lungful of night air. It tasted fresh and welcoming, homely almost. It escaped from him then in a shud-dered breath and he jumped from the ledge of the cave onto the fine black sand below.

They were after him, coming, but slowly, hampered by their fear of harming these babies, the most precious in the whole of the empire. But they were coming, and would not be long in catching up to him.

He wandered off along the beach. He felt suddenly free, his purpose at last fulfilled. He thought of Lucy.

Before him rose the mushrooms.

Gigantic, they were nevertheless different to the ones in the caves. Sleek and fleshy, they spread out in concentric circles, a forest of low-lying, flat surfaces sus-pended on thick shafts.

Where the mushrooms grow flat… A wild idea took hold of Orphan, and he followed it. Putting the book back in his pocket, he attacked the largest of the mushrooms. There was something strange about them…

The shouts were coming closer – much closer. Then, a gunshot. He ducked, but they were still not quite out of the cave yet, and their aim was bad.

At last a shaft gave way, and a giant mushroom, free of its earthly bond, glided gracefully away, and landed in the dark waters.

"Stop!" someone shouted, and there was a volley of fire. Ducking, panting, Orphan ran low and sprang himself onto the floating fungi. He almost laughed, the sensation was so odd; it was like he was once again a child, and this was a giant toy, wobbling this way and that with no control. He spread his legs outwards and began to paddle slowly, as quietly as he could, away from the shore and into the open sea. Water soaked into his clothes but the makeshift raft held him – just.

Behind him the shouts grew and more shots followed, but they were aimless, and came nowhere near. He continued to paddle, into the dark dark sea, away from the island, and imagined himself growing into a small point, unseen in the unchanging vastness of water. He felt exulted, buoyant – buoyant, he thought, and almost giggled. Like the mushrooms, staying afloat.

Soon the sounds of the shore grew faint, then faded away. He turned his head but could no longer see the island, could no longer see anything but the dark unchanging water of the sea. I'm lost, he thought, but the thought brought him no pain, only a fierce, unmitigated joy.

At last, he stopped, and turned and lay on his back, and gazed at the stars. Did he do the right thing? he wondered. He felt free of all decisions, of all consequences. The stars gazed back at him and offered no answers.

A light.

Something blinked. A light, growing larger. An eerie glow was cast on the sea before him, and he could see the surface of the water, and in the distance, the outline of the island growing bright. It was not as far as he had thought.

The cannon!

He watched as a great ball of fire gathered and grew and flew high in the air, and he tensed lest it failed, lest it died and fell into the sea.

It flew straight.

He watched the narrow needle of the cannon, the fire emerging from its rear, grow distant, grow smaller. The shadows around him diminished.

He was sent on this mission, on this impossible mission, to sabotage that cannon, prevent its cargo from reaching beyond the world. The Bookman, Wyvern: they had wanted him to do it, each for his own reasons and, perhaps, unknown to him, thousands of others had wished he'd done the same. But when he'd had the chance, when he was placed in the position to damage it, to make it fail – he couldn't.

He did not sabotage the cannon.

Was he right to make the decision? Now the signal would be sent, and the lizards, the other lizards, would come. Would they come as friends, or enemies? Would there be anyone left to even see the sign? But he thought of the lizard young, and he thought of the lizards crashing into the earth and into the heart of the island, and he thought they were like sailors, stranded on a tropical and alien shore after a terrible storm. Could he deny them their flare, their distress signal? If they had done bad things, if they had deposed kings and made this place their home and their kingdom, they acted no more nor less than humans would. There were arguments, so many arguments, for and against, and he thought of Lucy now and knew that, though she may never now come back to him, she would have understood. When at last it came, he could not do it.

Waves came, and rocked his raft, but gently, and in the distance he could see an enormous figure rise from the water, and then another, and another. He watched them, unafraid.

They were whales.

For a moment, he imagined he could see a woman, rising from the sea between the giant figures. Looking at him.

Lucy, he thought, and felt happy.

He closed his eyes. Around him, the singing of the whales rose in an unearthly symphony.

He drifted on the sea throughout the night and half through the day, growing thirsty beyond belief, but not losing that strange composure, that new peace he had found. He lay flat and tried not to move, and the sun beat on him and his craft sank lower and lower into the water, and he wondered how long it would be before he sank completely.

It was approaching dusk when he saw the thing in the sky, and for a long moment he just stared at it, the shape making no meaningful connections in his head. It was a round thing, painted gaudy yellow and green, like a circus tent's canopy. Was it a bird?

Then it came closer, and lower, approaching him like a vast floating whale, and he thought – a balloon! He stared up at it, smiling stupidly, and saw the open cabin, and a head peering out at him, and someone calling his name.

He waved at the face. It shouted more at him, but he could understand none of it. Then something was thrown from the balloon and hit him, and he was thrown into the water.

He flailed and took hold of the thing that was thrown. What was it? He looked at the ropes, examined them with his fingers.

"Bloody get on it, you stupid boy!"

It was a ladder. A rope-ladder. He laughed. It was so funny, to be floating in the sea alone and see a thing like that. Where had it come from?

"Quickly, you nincompoop!"

He felt he had better obey the voice. The face it came from was fat and sweaty and looked angry. He wondered if it had some water for him.

He pulled himself onto the ladder. Rising from the water was agony. His body was pain. Each step made thinking impossible.

One step, and two. Three. Four. His hands felt raw and they hurt, but he kept going.

Five. Six. He almost let go. It would be pleasant to drown in the warm, peaceful waters...

Seven. Eight.

"Come on, boy!"

Nine. Ten. Eleven–

And suddenly it was over.

Hands pulled him into the safety of the cabin. He looked down and saw his craft sinking far below.

"Orphan!"

"Wha'?"

He tried to focus on the fat man.

"It's me!" The fat man fed him water. It ran over Orphan's broken lips and into his mouth, and was the most delicious thing he had ever tasted. His eyes focused, and he said, haltingly, "Verne?"

"I've found you!" the fat man said, and he grinned at Orphan, and almost gathered him into his arms.

"I..." Orphan said, a short, single word that seemed to him to encompass a whole range of meaning. Then he passed out.

PART III
Prometheus Unbound

THIRTY-TWO
The Return of the King

A glucose trap, snap crackle pop
We crossed the Strand and saw a sign:
This way to the Egress.
   – L.T., "After the Waste Land"

Less than twenty-four hours after arriving back in the city, Orphan had been attacked twice, robbed once, and finally thrown in a police cell. It had not been a good day.

He had returned on a cold, damp day. Thick grey fog, suffused with the stench of burning chemicals, wafted over the water.

The *Nautilus* had sailed under the Thames and into the city. It did so in stealth, invisible to all but the whales, who gave it a wide berth as it sailed past them. They did not consider it one of their own.

The *Nautilus*, this *Nautilus*, was not a clipper but a submarine. It had lain hidden below the clipper ship bearing its name until the pirates' attack. Then, with only its captain, his wide-girthed guest and a handful of

329

specially picked men, it had disengaged from the above-water *Nautilus* and sank, quietly and without trace, into the depths of the Carib Sea.

"You left them to die," Orphan had said, aghast. Verne had shrugged apologetically; Captain Dakkar, splendid in a white, starched uniform, merely glowered. "You left me to die."

"Far from it!" Verne had said. They were sitting in the *Nautilus'* dining room. Large windows cut into the side of the vehicle showed the dark depths of the sea, and strange, glowing fish that glided past and stared with large, mournful eyes into the sub's interior. "You see, there was a large probability–"

"Yes?"

"That capture by Wyvern–"

"That reptile," Dakkar said. Verne smiled apologetically at Orphan and shrugged as if to say, Well, what can you do. "That capture by Wyvern," he said again, raising his voice, "would lead you to the island."

"Is that so?"

"It was a possibility. And possibilities, you know, are what this is all about, Orphan."

"If you let machines think they can manipulate lives," Dakkar said, continuing to glower.

"Well, can't they?" Verne said.

The captain didn't reply. Then he said, more softly, as if thinking to himself, "But what if the machines themselves are at opposite ends?" and his eyes took in Orphan with a disconcerting gaze, and came to rest on Orphan's thumb, the one the Binder had... had taken.

"That's neither here nor there," Verne said, oblivi-
ous. And, to Orphan, cheerfully, "There was always the
possibility you'd fail, of course. But you didn't, did you?
It all worked out, and here you are. Here we are."

"Yes," Orphan said. "Here we are."

It was Dakkar himself who had sent the message to
the pirates. The attack had been engineered. Orphan
had suspected Aramis wrongly. He thought of all the
people who had died, all so he would – fail. He was
angry – but at the same time, simply glad to be alive.
And Verne had saved him, in the last count.

It had been an uncomfortable journey back. They did
not speak much. Orphan wondered what he would do.
Hunt down the Bookman, he thought. And – Lucy.
Would she understand? The Bookman must already
know Orphan had failed him. What would he do?

Verne wanted to know everything about the island.
He was fascinated by Orphan's raft. Already, he said, he
was working on a new novel, though he was sparse
with details. Something involving giant squid, Orphan
gathered. Giant squid in space.

Verne and Dakkar had no further instructions from
the Bookman. Their last, Verne had said, was simply to
find Orphan and then return home. Verne looked tired;
Dakkar, mostly annoyed. Orphan gathered he intended
returning to India as soon as was possible and with his
excess baggage of passengers suitably discharged. A revolution was coming, he said.

Change was in the air.

Change was in the air on the day Orphan landed
back in the city. It was night time; the fog swirled,

noxious and thick, over the abandoned wharf of Limehouse; and Orphan, stepping onto dry land from the sub-aquatic vehicle for the first time in what seemed like forever, stopped and breathed in the city like a man rolling fine, expensive wine on the tongue after a long-enforced abstinence.

The city smelled of a thousand different things, manure and smoke, polish and oil, shag tobacco and flowery perfume; somewhere, faint and yet overpowering, the musty smell of venerable old books. The city echoed with a thousand different sounds, from the distant, mournful song of the whales clustered by Waterloo Bridge, to a distant gunshot and, nearer, the scratchy sound of an Edison record, and someone singing. The tune was quick, fiery, and as for the words... it took Orphan by surprise, recognising the words of an old Shelley poem, set to the music, and the unknown singer sang:

"The sound is of whirlwind underground, earthquake, and fire, and mountains cloven; the shape is awful, like the sound, clothed in dark purple, star-inwoven, a sceptre of pale gold."

"Earthquake and fire!" came the refrain. The music rolled around the dockyard and seemed to Orphan to eddy with the fog. He felt it stir something in him, a quickening of the blood, a response as to a call to arms. "To stay steps proud, over the slow cloud, his veined hand doth hold," sang the unknown voice, and the words were those of Panthea, speaking of Prometheus, who rebelled against the gods. "Cruel he looks, but calm and strong, like one who does, not suffers wrong!"

"Not suffers wrong!"

Almost, it sounded to him like Jack's voice. Jack, shouting, inflamed with the passion of... of revolution. Then the song died down, faded into the fog, its origin unknown. Yet he was to hear it elsewhere, wherever he went in the city, like a musical bond holding together the citizens and subjects of Victoria, Lizard Queen of an empire on which the sun never set, and stirring them into strange and inexplicable acts of rebellion.

"My friend," Verne said as they parted. "Be careful."

Orphan shook the fat writer's hand, if reluctantly, and saluted Dakkar's back. The *Nautilus* closed its hatch and, with barely a sound, disappeared into the dark waters of the Thames. Orphan was left alone on the Embankment. It was suddenly very quiet.

He was first attacked as he made his way west, past Whitechapel. The streets were deserted, which he found strange, and there were very few lights in the windows. It was as if the city had been abandoned, and yet there was a certain hushed expectancy about the place, a tension underneath the stillness. It set him on edge.

The attack came near Spitalfields Market. Orphan crossed the deserted street, his attention focused on the distant light of the Babbage Tower, a beacon through the fog. He only noticed the man as he came directly at him out of the fog, a drawn blade glinting dully, and he ducked, instinctively, and kicked out, the way he had once seen Aramis do.

Luck, not skill, made the kick connect, and he heard his assailant grunt with pain. Orphan reached for his gun, a departing present from Verne, fumbled with it–

The knife came at him again, and he pulled the trigger.

The man fell. Orphan saw his face then; and had to hold himself from taking a step back.

It was a punk de Lézard.

He had last seen one in Nantes, but he could not forget that moment: lizard boys, Verne had called them. But what was one doing here?

The punk's face was a tattoo of green bands, his ears pinned back against his skull, and his head was round, a polished dome with only a strip of spiked hair at the centre. The man, wounded, hissed at him, and he saw that his tongue had been crudely modified, stretched and pared in the middle, so that it was forked and elongated, in bad imitation of a lizard's.

The man tried to rise. The blade was in his hand. It was bloodied, Orphan saw. He had hurt – perhaps killed – at least once before that night.

The man lunged at him.

Orphan shot him again.

The lizard boy sank back. The knife, finally, fell from his hand.

Who was he? Orphan thought. The man was a killer. And again – a lizard boy? Here?

He put the gun back in its holster. He felt hot and clammy under the heavy coat he was no longer used to wearing.

What had happened to the city?

After a moment, he picked his way again, more cautiously this time. He was not even sure where he was going. And then – find Tom, he thought. Get back to the Nell Gwynne. Tom would know what was happening. He always did.

He was passing through Farringdon, the old city walls on his left, when he first saw sign of people. They were marching in the street outside the courts, a group of them, all silent, wearing heavy coats against the chill, women and men who could have been anyone, clerks or magistrates, carpenters or cooks, yet here they were, in the small hours of the night, marching outside the courts, and there was a burning effigy held high above their heads.

Orphan watched the silent procession. The effigy was giant-sized, and lizardine. It could have been the Queen herself, or it could have been a stand-in for all of lizard-kind. It was burning too fiercely by now to be able to tell.

What was happening to the city? He drew deep into the shadows and watched the marchers go past. Behind the effigy of the lizard another group came, cowled in black, another effigy held high.

This one didn't burn.

He stared at it, horrified. It was in the image of a man. The man was dressed in rich robes. He held a sceptre in his hand.

He wore a crown, and he had no face.

As the cowled figures moved past the one in the lead turned her head and for a moment the light of the fire fell on her face. Her eyes looked into the shadows and seemed to gaze directly at Orphan. He felt the force of her scrutiny like a physical thing, and shock as he recognised her.

It was Isabella Beeton.

Did she see him? He couldn't tell. Her head turned again and she marched ahead, and the effigy of the King followed her.

Wherever Isabella Beeton was, Orphan thought, conspiracy was never far behind. And yet he almost ran after her: she was a familiar face, and had always, before, been a friendly one.

Yet he didn't. He did not know what was going on. The city had changed, become a dangerous, unpredictable place. He was disturbed by the sight of this midnight march. A burning lizard…

But it was the other effigy that made his heart beat faster and his hands sweat. The crowned, human king.

He had to find shelter, and some information.

The second, successful attack on Orphan came in the early hours of the morning, as the sun began to rise, pale sunlight transforming the city streets into, somehow, more ordinary places from which the danger of night seemed to be lifted, if only a little.

He was on the Strand, curiously empty of people but for a lone beggar sleeping in the doorway of Gibbons' stamp shop, and had almost reached Bull Inn Court – and with it, or so he hoped, the safety of the Nell Gwynne – when he was struck from behind.

The pain blossomed in his head like a rapidly growing mushroom, suffocating him. He fell to the ground and lay there, numb. Hands riffled through his pockets, expertly, then the sound of feet, running away. He never saw his assailant.

After a while, the pain abated, and he groaned and began to move. As he began to cautiously rise he felt a presence beside him and instinctively lashed out.

"Sir!" said a rugged voice, and Orphan turned and saw that the beggar from the doorway was now standing beside him, stooped in his dirty rags. "I am but a humble beggar, coming to your lordship's aid!"

"A bit too late for that," Orphan said sourly. His head hurt, and his gun and his money were gone, though the beggar left him his mother's old book, which was no doubt not worth stealing. Books in this city were a penny a pound. The weight of words pressed down on the old streets, numerous millions of them, cranked out day or night by the printing presses and the men and women who churned them out, like so many factory-produced trinkets.

Money and a gun – you knew were you were with them. But a book? What good was a book?

"Did you see who it was?" Orphan said.

The beggar shook his head dolefully. "A common thief," he said. "He'll be long gone by now."

"No doubt," Orphan said. He staggered up and felt his eyes water.

"Here," the beggar said. "Sit down a while." He helped Orphan to the doorway of the shop and sat him down; and, wearily folding himself beside him, extracted from a hidden pocket a small flask at the same time.

"Drink this," the beggar said. "It will help. Also, it will warm you up."

Orphan looked at the flask. Though worn and faded, it was monogrammed with the letters *S.H.*, and he wondered how the beggar had got hold of it. Stolen, possibly, or just found in a rubbish tip. He eyed it with suspicion.

The beggar grinned, unstoppered the flask and handed it to Orphan. "Whiskey," he said. "It's a wonderful medicine."

Orphan drank; and the heat of the whiskey ran through his body like a series of controlled explosions. He coughed and felt his face go red and his eyes water. The beggar grinned and slapped him on the back. His face swam before Orphan's eyes, the sharp features and prominent nose, awakening a dim memory. "Do I know you?" he said. The beggar looked much livelier now, though that may simply have been a product of the drink.

"Wind, rain, and thunder," the beggar said, "remember, earthly man is but a substance that must yield to you. And I, as fits my nature, do obey you."

Orphan looked at him. There was something familiar about the face, glimpsed briefly, in the midst of night, in a cold place, behind a plate of glass...

Guy's Hospital. And a still, unmoving man frozen in a coffin, whose brother...

"Who are you?" Orphan said. He tried to stand, but felt his head swimming; his arms would no longer obey him.

"A friend," the beggar said, his voice soft and far-away. "A friend who can see what the sea has cast once more upon these shores. It is no magic, but logic only. Be careful, Orphan. This is a bad time to be a prince."

"What... what did you do to me?" Orphan said, his voice slurring. He could not focus his eyes.

When he opened them again, the beggar was no longer there, though his flask remained, somehow clasped, unstoppered and upturned, in Orphan's hands. The liquid seeped into his clothes. He felt a kick, not hard but prodding, and raised his eyes to the sight of two beefy policemen.

"Drunk as a dog!" one of them said. "help me up with 'im, Harry."

"I ain't touching him, Bert!" the other policeman said. "Last one I did emptied his guts all over me!"

Bert chuckled. "A bit of experience," he said, "is priceless in this job. Now let 'im up, and watch where he aims."

Orphan was lifted up. He swayed, but wasn't sick, for which the policemen were no doubt grateful.

"Don't worry, lad, we'll find you a nice dry cell to sleep it off," Bert said. "Don't want to be out on the street on a day like this. Lizard boys'd get you."

"Or the rebels," Harry said. Orphan was meanwhile being moved. He tried to speak, tell them he was fine and to leave him alone, but only managed to dribble, which made Harry swear and his partner chuckle.

"Things might be better when the King comes back," Harry said quietly.

"Shut it, Harry," Bert said. "You don't know who's listening."

The rest of the journey to the police station progressed in silence. The streets were still deserted. The same eerie silence greeted them at the police station. There were few policemen, and even fewer prisoners. Bert and Harry took Orphan down to the cells, which

were empty but for one, where a dark figure lay unmoving. They released him into the nearest cell, and he
collapsed down on the floor. He tried to speak again,
but couldn't.

"Sleep it off, lad," Bert said. "Believe me, we're only
doing you a favour."

"A day like this…" Harry said, and shook his head
meaningfully.

"At least the Ripper is finally caught," Bert said. "You
hear that, boy? They found his corpse last night. Some-
body shot him."

"And good riddance," Harry said.

Orphan moved his mouth groggily. He couldn't stay
here. How did he end up in this situation? He tried to
speak again as Bert was locking the cell door.

"What did he say?" Harry said.

"Addled," Bert said.

"No, Bert, listen to him," Harry said. He watched Orphan through the bars. "He said 'saddler'."

Orphan tried again. The two policemen exchanged
glances. Their faces were suddenly serious.

"He said 'Adler', Harry," Bert said.

There was a short, pregnant silence.

"As in Inspector Adler?" Harry said. His voice was
very low. And then, "What do we do, Bert?"

There was another short silence.

"We keep him in there," Bert said. "For now. He's in
no state to go anywhere. Safest place for him, proba-
bly."

"What about the inspector, Bert?" Harry said. "We
could get into a lot of trouble."

"Keep your voice down, for starters," Bert said. "This needs some thinking, Harry."

"Would a cup of tea help, Bert?" Harry said, and the other policeman smiled and nodded, and some of the tension seemed to go from his face. "It certainly would," he said.

They left Orphan in the cell and, as they left, the door upstairs closed shut behind them.

THIRTY-THREE
Orphaned

For God's sake, let us sit upon the ground
And tell sad stories of the death of kings;
How some have been deposed; some slain in war,
Some haunted by the ghosts they have deposed.
  – William Shakespeare, *Richard II*

Nothing had changed by the time Orphan had finally got back control of his limbs. He was locked up. The single figure in the cell next door had not stirred.

It was dark. He tried shouting, but nobody came, and he soon gave up. The fogginess gradually subsided, though his head still ached. He cursed the beggar, but it didn't make a difference. Who was he?

He looked at the flask that was still, somehow, with him. It was empty, but smelled foul. So, he had to admit, did he.

All he could hope for was that Inspector Adler might hear he was there and come to investigate. This, or that the policemen might get tired of him and release him. Meanwhile, he just had to wait.

"Hey!" he said, shouting to the prone figure in the other cell. "Are you awake yet?"

There was no reply. He called again, then, getting an idea, ran the flask against the bars.

The noise was tremendous. It beat at his headache like a drum, and he stopped.

The figure in the bed shook, moved, and a head finally half-emerged from underneath the filthy blanket.

"I'm sorry," Orphan said, a little untruthfully, "I didn't mean to wake you."

The figure under the blanket stared at him, dark face wreathed in shadows. Eyes blinked. Then the face emerged further, coming into the dim light, and said, "You!"

And Orphan reeled back and was aware of the pounding of blood in his head, and grabbed the bars of the cell to stay upright. He stared at the face.

The face was his own.

"What?" Orphan said, and "Who–?"

"You," the figure said again, and rose, and came close to the bars separating them from each other. "You utter bastard."

Orphan stared at him in mute shock. His own face stared back at him. His own body – and he looked at the other's thumb and saw that it was whole.

His own body. His own face. But – different, somehow. A deep weariness seemed etched into that face, all youthfulness gone from it. It was dirty, covered with grime, and in the eyes there was a bafflement, the stare receding from anger to a sort of vacant, dull gaze.

"What are you?" he said, whispered, and then again, a shout that echoed in that still, dark place: "What are you!"

"I am Orphan. I am the orphan." The other – the other him – sat down on the bed in the other cell. They were like mirror-images: Orphan sat down too. "I am born of no mother or father. I am like Eve, made from Adam's rib. Adam's thumb." He giggled. "I am the messenger. I am the translator. I am the words that lie inside the binding and wait to be awakened. I am you. You stole me from myself."

He sounded crazy.

"I don't understand," Orphan said, but then the image of the Binder, crazy spider creature on his hideaway island, returned to him, and the Binder's words. "This will hurt," the Binder had said. And then he chopped off Orphan's thumb. Take it down to the growing vats.

Aramis, saying, Will it work? The Binder – Perhaps. For a little while.

"He made a copy of me?"

The other him laughed, whooped, rose from the bed and banged on the bars, startling Orphan. "I am the King of England!" he shouted. "And I am returned, bow to me!"

"You know?"

"I know all." And then the storm passed and the other Orphan sat down again, and Orphan saw how pale he was beneath the dirt. The eyes looked at him, weary, tired, lost. "I can hear it. It speaks to me. I can't shut it up!"

"What happened to you?" Orphan said.

"You," the other said. "You happened. You took my life from me. I should be King! I thought you might have died on that island. I hoped you did. I guess you – we're – just too lucky." And he laughed again, a sound like crying. "How did you get back?"

"By submarine," Orphan said. "The – the *Nautilus* – it was a submarine under the clipper."

"A submarine. It must have been comfortable."

"Not very."

"You had food, drink?"

"I almost died on that island!" Somehow, the other made him feel guilty.

"Better had you died."

"How... how did you come to be here?"

The other laughed. "He sent me," he said. "He pulled me out of the vat, naked, covered in slime. He was in my brain. I could hear the drums beat, and I could understand them. They spoke, a web of sound, of meaning, woven over that entire island. And he was in my head, showing me who I was. William son of Mary, future King of England. And then he took it away from me and gave me nothing." He lay down, curled into a ball. "He made me into a tool," Orphan heard him say. "A tool like he once was..."

Could it be possible? The Binder had somehow made a copy of him? And then he thought – why not? Was that not what the Bookman, too, did? "What happened then?" he asked. He tried to hold in the feelings the other aroused in him: guilt, inexplicable but true, and a sort of compassion, as if one was faced with a younger brother, and could not ease his suffering.

"He put me in an airship. It piloted itself. I don't know how. I had some food. He gave me that at least. Salted fish, some vegetables and bread, fresh water. I ate sparingly, relieved myself over the sea when I needed to. The food wasn't enough. The water ran out before I sighted land."

"But you made it!"

The other laughed again. He did not move from the bed. "Yes," he said. "At last I landed, starved and de-hydrated. On the coast of the Irish Sea. How I got there I don't know. I had pretty much lost all direc-tion by then." He coughed, which took a while, then continued. "I made my way south, but slowly. The roads are not safe any more, but I managed. Perhaps no one saw fit to rob me." He sighed, a long and tired sound. "It was only when I got into the city that my luck changed. I was set on by a group of lizard boys – did you see them? They appear to be everywhere now, running in gangs, terrorising the streets. I was beaten up, and when the police arrived I was the one to be ar-rested. Maybe they thought it was for my own good. These cells might be the safest place in the city right now. And all the while it spoke to me, it is speaking to me, whispering, though I can no longer hear the drums."

"It? What is it?"

And he thought – the Translation?

"It looks like an egg," the other said, sounding sur-prised. "I don't know why. I thought it would be a book. It is only small, and very pretty. The colours... I can see them even in the dark."

The Translation. But he didn't even understand what it was. A story, told him by Byron in a smoky pub. A legend, an article of faith for those who had nothing else. Could it be real? And what did it do?

"Do you have it still?" he said. There was no answer. "Do you have the egg?"

"It is with me, always. I can hear it, awake or asleep."

"Show me."

Silence.

"Show me!"

The other rose. He came close to the bars again. His eyes stared into Orphan's. "It isn't yours," he said.

"Show me."

The other reached into his clothes. When his hand emerged, it held a pouch, which he loosed and up-ended.

A small, smooth round object fell into his palm.

Orphan looked at it. It was made of a green metal, eerily lit, and seemed almost to absorb light, so that for a moment the cells were even darker. It seemed to pulse slowly in the other's hand, like a heart plucked out of a body still beating.

Somehow, it seemed to be whispering to him, like the distant echoes of drums, speaking in a mechanical language that weaved and merged and changed with each beat, and he found himself entranced by it, lost in the circles and lines of the beat, reaching for a meaning that was waiting for him, on the cusp of understanding...

"It speaks to me," the other said. "I can hear them. All of them. The dead… they live still, in the Bookman's dark domain. They never leave me in peace!"

Orphan stared at him. Almost, he could hear voices, whispering in his ear, growing louder. He said, "What do you mean?"

The other giggled, a sudden, startling sound. "I can show you," he said.

"Show me what?"

"Not what," the other said. "Who." He held the Translation tightly in his hand. "You can bring them back, for a short time. Like ghosts. They like to talk. Always talk!"

"Lucy?" Orphan whispered, but the other shook his head. "No."

"What do you mean?" He was shouting. The other shook his head. "I don't know. But I can show you." He was like a child with a toy, jealous of it and yet wanting to display it, to show it off. "Here."

The other moved his hand. The egg glowed. The other giggled. "He is my friend," he said–

A figure materialised in the cell, slowly, like motes of dust assembling into a shape as light plays on them. It had a face that Orphan knew. And it smiled. Its eyes were blind.

"Orphan," Gilgamesh said. "I see you've been busy."

He had Gilgamesh's face, Gilgamesh's unseeing eyes, yet his voice was ethereal, without substance. It seemed to float around Orphan's ears, to trace patterns of coloured light in the air between them.

"You're dead," Orphan said, and Gilgamesh smiled, and nodded. "Am I hallucinating?"

"You're asking me?"

There was gentle amusement in the question. Orphan realised its futility. He said, "What is happening to me?"

"This egg," Gilgamesh said. "This *Translation*. I once heard stories… I think it can communicate with the Bookman's machines, somehow. There are so many of us here, Orphan… so many souls in a bottle, with no senses, no body, nothing but the patterns of what we once were. He doesn't know, yet. You must be careful."

So many… Lucy, Orphan thought. But Gilgamesh, as if reading his mind, shook his head. "She is not in here."

"What does that mean?"

"I don't know. Maybe she is stored separately. Maybe she was given a body again."

Orphan thought back. He had seen Lucy before… There was a boat. It was just after he had met Mycroft. He stood, alone, on the embankment, when it came sailing out of the mist, a single person sitting in the prow, and his breath slammed into his lungs and froze his thoughts into small hard diamonds.

The person in the boat was Lucy. She was dressed in a fine white dress that seemed to form a part of the fog, and she sat in an unnatural calm as the boat sailed without anyone to steer it, coming close to the bank of the river, close enough for Orphan to almost reach a hand and touch her. Almost.

"Maybe," Gilgamesh said, his voice soft, "she has been erased."

Orphan felt the words like pinpricks of pain in his chest. "No," he said. And again. "No."

"Are you coming for her?" Gilgamesh said.

"For all of you," Orphan said, and his old friend chuckled. "You're a good boy, Orphan."

"What happened to you?" Orphan said. And he thought back to the empty space under the bridge, and to Gilgamesh's last message for him, in a bottle bobbing on the water, and he thought, I needed you.

"I know you did," Gilgamesh said, again knowing his thoughts. "I wish I could have been there for you, Orphan. William. For both of you, now." He said the second name hesitantly, as if unsure of the way it should be pronounced. Orphan looked at him, saw the tired tilt of his face, the lines that had been there for centuries. "William," the other whispered, as if tasting the word on his tongue.

"Your mother would have been so proud of you..." Gilgamesh said.

Orphan sat down. Across the bars the other copied his movement. "Tell me about her," Orphan said, and the other spoke with the same voice, saying the same words. "Tell me about Mary."

Gilgamesh sighed. It was a long, painful sound like a shard of broken glass. But he did not object. "Very well," he said.

I knew your father first (so Gilgamesh began). I have never told you this. I've never told you many things.

He was a native Vespuccian, a proud man from the Great Sioux Nation who had discovered in himself one day an inexplicable passion for the sea. His name was Kangee, which means "raven". He was not a large man, but he moved gracefully on board ship even in the roughest weather, though he always seemed a little lost on land.

I was working in the docks at that time, rolling barrels of wine on the Isle of Dogs. Many times we'd drill a narrow hole in the barrel and drink from the rich, exotic wines, without the owners knowing or our employers caring. It was almost a tax they had to pay. I knew the docks well, by touch and smell if not by sight, and I liked the work. It was as close to the sea as I could come.

Though I was the Bookman's creature he left me more or less alone. No doubt he had more use for me just as I was, a harmless blind man on the docks, unnoticed by most, yet hearing all of what passed. Every so often he went into my mind, and got from it what information I had gathered. What use he put it to I didn't know. The Bookman's plans have always been far-reaching and opaque.

It was a good life... I met Kangee in the Ship's Bell, a lively, crowded pub I sometimes frequented. It was always busy with sailors from a hundred different ports: from far-away Zululand and China and the Carib Sea, from the great ports of Europe and from Vespuccia itself, a hundred languages were spoken simultaneously at any one time. I remember the spiced rum...

How we became friends?

I sometimes traded stories for drinks. He had just come off a ship, had money to spare, and was interested in my stories of his homeland which, he said, must have changed greatly since I had been there. He had an interest in history – a quiet, intelligent man, who would have harmed no one. I told him my stories, he bought me drinks. Then, from his silence, I drew out his own story, and began buying the drinks myself. By the end of the night we were friends.

I never told him about the island, of course. I couldn't. I wish I had...

I remember the night he brought your mother to meet me. He had met her – he didn't say, exactly. She was drifting at sea, floating on the strangest raft he had ever seen, and by the time they had rescued her she was close to dying. He didn't tell me the coordinates, nor the nature of the raft, but I guessed. Not at first, but later.

Mary was lovely. It's the only way I can describe her. Like Kangee, she was quiet but, like him, she had a wild streak in her. She was new to the city. She had come on Kangee's ship and was intoxicated by this world, which it seemed she had never even known existed. They were so happy together...

Of course, I did not know at the time that Mary was wanted. She seemed wary – though not afraid – of the lizards, avoiding any public royal events to which the other citizens would flock. She and Kangee moved into a small house in Limehouse – always the first port for new immigrants, and a good place in which to lie low, too. For a while, everything was perfect. When the baby was born, she called him William. His father gave him his second name, which was Chaska, meaning "first-born son".

I was his godfather. Your godfather, Orphan. You were not always an orphan.

But then the man came.

How they found her I do not know. They must have gone through the harbour logs and located the ship that had found her at sea. It was not too difficult. Kangee came to me a month after the birth of the baby. His old captain had been found dead in an alleyway, the victim of an apparent mugging.

It was not uncommon. The city was rougher then.

But then there was the man.

He came asking questions, a young, not-unhandsome man, very self-composed, very friendly.

Kangee feared him more than he did any other man. Though he did not know the man, he recognised in him all the qualities of a hunter. In later life the man became known for his hunting of big game. You may have heard of him, Orphan.

His name was Sebastian Moran. Yes. "Tiger Jack" Moran. So you have heard of him. I am not surprised. At that time he was a young man, barely out of Oxford, but as a hunter he was already ambitious: he went for the biggest prey there is.

Kangee came to me for advice. Tiger Jack was slowly stalking Mary and him, circling around, but had not yet revealed himself directly. What should he do? Kangee asked me. It was clear Les Lézards were after Mary. She was a danger to them, at best a liability. She threatened their safety.

Run, I said. Leave the city. Go to France, or better yet, go back to Vespuccia. Go as far as you can go, away from the empire altogether. Then they might let you live in peace.

Kangee found it difficult to run. But, for the sake of the baby, he agreed. He would return to the Great Sioux Nation, where they would be safe. I procured false papers for them, at great expense, and Kangee secretly booked passage on one of the then-new steamer ships to Vespuccia. Everything was ready.

Orphan, I have never told this to anyone. I have never been able to. When I had a body, it was built with certain prohibitions. I could not speak of Caliban's Island, of my travels with Vespucci, nor of the Bookman beyond banal generalities. Only once, on the cusp of death, and now, with the help of that strange device of yours, that egg that is a hub, a bridge that allows me to speak to you, however briefly, from the storage vaults of the Bookman's domain, can I be free.

Yet I am afraid to tell you what happened.

It was a cold night, and the winter winds cut like bayonets through cloth. We were at the docks. Kangee and Mary and you, William Chaska, a baby. You were a happy baby. I remember that.

I was saying brief goodbyes. It was hard – I had grown attached to all of you, but you in particular, Orphan. It was not my intention…

There was nothing I could have done. Do you understand?

Kangee held you as he and Mary went onto the deck. I waited on the quay, and waved.

I didn't even hear the shot.

I heard Kangee scream. I heard the splash of water that was Mary, falling into the sea, dead before she hit it. It was the first time in my life that I was glad of not being able to see.

Across from us, in the top floor of the East India Company's warehouse, Tiger Jack was packing away his rifle. He had done his job.

Kangee came down with you in his arms. It was the only time I ever saw him cry. He was a broken man. How? he said. How could he know? Only the three of us knew of the plan. How did Tiger Jack know to wait when he did, where he did?

That was when I knew, Orphan.

It was the Bookman.

He had gone into my mind, had found the information there. It was he who set Sebastian Moran for the shot.

And that's when I knew, Orphan. It was only then I realised.

Mary's death was my fault.

Gilgamesh's figure was fading.

"It was my fault, Orphan," Gilgamesh said again. His voice was becoming fainter.

"What happened to… to Kangee?" and he thought, What happened to my dad?

"He tried to bring you up. Perhaps, if you weren't there, he would have sought revenge. But Sebastian Moran disappeared, gone to India, and there was you, a baby… He continued to work as a sailor, and you were kept by a succession of other sailors' wives while he was gone. When you were two years old, he went on a voyage, on a trading ship. It went to India… He never came back. They said he fell overboard, drunk, but your father was rarely drunk, and never on board ship."

"Was he murdered?"

A shrug, small and helpless, and Gilgamesh was fading even further, became the bare outline of a man.

"There was only you left… an orphan. I always kept my eye on you." The last things to remain of Gilgamesh were his eyes, blindly staring into nothing. "But so did the Bookman."

THIRTY-FOUR
Simpson's-in-the-Strand

I met him by appointment that evening at Simpson's, where, sitting at a small table in the front window, and looking down at the rushing stream of life in the Strand, he told me something of what had passed.

– Arthur Conan Doyle, *The Case Book of Sherlock Holmes*

Time passed slowly in the cells. Orphan and the other. Each was wrapped in his own thoughts.

A sound woke him up. It was the sound of someone quietly opening and shutting the door above the stairs, and doing so stealthily, not wanting to be noticed or observed. He waited, and for a moment could hear nothing. The other, he saw, was wrapped in a blanket; he seemed asleep.

The sound came again, different this time. Like feet stepping softly against the stairs, but growing louder, coming down into the cells.

He tensed, waited. There was someone there! He thought of raising the alarm, but who would listen? He opened his mouth–

"Hello, Orphan," said a familiar voice.

Standing on the other side of the bars was Irene Adler.

Orphan stared at her. So she had got his message after all. He said, "Inspector!" and received a tired smile in return, and a shake of the head. "I'm no longer an inspector, Orphan."

Irene Adler looked tired. There were new lines on her face, around her eyes. Her skin seemed almost colourless, her hair straggly, and Orphan wondered, with a sudden pain, what had happened to her since he had left. He said, "You got my message?" and saw a look of surprise flitter across Irene's face. "What message?"

"The two policemen who arrested me…"

Irene laughed. "No. I'm not in the police any more. Sherlock told me where you were. Right after he drugged you. We've been waiting for you to come back."

"Sherlock?" He thought of the flask, the initials on it. He had known that face… "Mycroft's brother? I thought he was dead."

Irene shook her head, and a warm, genuine smile lifted her face. "He never was, you see. It was a bluff. He was exchanged for a simulacrum of himself, a crude copy, incapable of thought but–"

"But looking identical?"

She smiled again. "He had help from across the Channel. He thought it would be safe to be dead for a while."

"And you didn't know?" He remembered the frozen corpse he had seen at Guy's Hospital. No wonder no doctor could bring him back to life. Or was even that a lie, and no doctor had ever been consulted?

Pain erased the smile. "No. But it was necessary. No one could know. It would not have been safe, for either of us."

"What was he doing?" Orphan said. "And why did he drug me?" He couldn't help a petulant note entering his voice, and Irene smiled. "It was for your own good," she said. "You weren't safe on the street, and at least here you were out of trouble. I came as soon as I could."

"But I was going to stay with Tom," Orphan said. "He's just around the corner."

"Your friend Tom Thumb?" Irene said. "He's gone. A lot's changed, Orphan. Too much has changed. And the Nell Gwynne is now a lizard boys' hangout. You would have been dead as soon as you knocked on the door."

"What happened?" Orphan said. He felt hollow. "And where's Tom?"

Irene shrugged. "Gone to ground. Joined the Glorious Revolution. Maybe, if he has any sense, gone back to Vespuccia." She stopped talking and reached into her pocket, returning with a set of keys. "We need to get you out of here. Your friend too. I was told he would be here."

"Told? By who?" He spoke more sharply than he intended and she glanced at him, but didn't answer. Instead she unlocked the door to the cell and moved on to the other's. The other rose, looking at them blearily. It struck Orphan again how unwell he looked. There was a haunted look in his eyes. "It's talking to me," he said. "It wants me to…" and he fell silent.

"Orphan?" Irene Adler said.

"Yes?" the answer was doubled.

Irene drew in breath. "Which one of you…" she said, and didn't finish.

Orphan was the first to speak. The other merely stared at his feet. Orphan said, "This is William."

"William."

"Yes."

The other raised his head, looked at Orphan. For a moment it almost seemed like he was smiling. "William," he said. "Yes…"

"I don't understand…" Irene said.

Orphan shrugged. "Neither do I."

Irene stared at them for another moment, then shook her head. "This can wait," she said. "We need to go. Come."

They followed Irene down the row of cells. She did not go back up the stairs but, on reaching the door at the other end, unlocked it and ushered them through, and into a narrow corridor. "There's only a skeleton crew left," she said. "It's rather chaotic out there now. Still, I'd rather we didn't meet anyone at the station."

They didn't. They left the police station by a back door and found themselves outside, on Agar Street. "Where are we going?"

"Not far."

Waning daylight outside. In the distance, breaking the eerie silence, the sound of sporadic gunfire. "What happened?" Orphan said again. He felt numb. Was it all his fault?

"Revolution," Irene said shortly.

"Who?" Orphan said.

Irene shrugged. "Who knows? There are so many factions right now and they're all fighting each other. Your friend Mrs Beeton's in one. Sherlock's brother's his own faction of one, as always. The lizard boys – who can tell? And they say Moriarty is wounded. The government is weak…"

So Moriarty wasn't dead. Orphan was glad for that. He said, "And what faction are you with?"

Irene shook her head. "I'm on the side of order," she said.

They joined the Strand at the bottom of Agar Street. There were people there now, a multitude of them, and for a moment Orphan felt fearful: he was no longer used to such masses.

A demonstration was in progress: Orphan saw banners with a crowned, empty profile of a human head. Opposite them banners carried the lizardine crest.

"Hurry!" Irene said. "If we get between those two we're in trouble."

People hurried down the streets, their heads lowered. He saw uniformed police, and with them some police automatons, too, but they seemed small and lost, little islands in an ocean of hostile human traffic. He grabbed hold of the other's arm and they followed Irene. The other looked dazed. Orphan could sympathise.

They had turned left on the Strand. Orphan saw several baruch-landaus, belching steam, halted in the melee. They passed Bull Inn Court and he thought of Tom, and of who occupied the Nell Gwynne now, and shuddered. He hoped his friend was well. He could not imagine him having gone back to Vespuccia. No doubt he was in the thick of all this, causing mayhem somewhere. He wondered what Marx was up to. Was he still residing at the Red Lion in Soho? Or was the dreamer finally putting actions to his words?

"Where is the Army?" he said. "What is the Queen doing about this?"

"Her Majesty," Irene said, "has locked herself up in the palace. The army's in disarray, some following Moriarty, some Mycroft, some protecting the Queen and her get. Some have deserted altogether."

"But why?" Orphan said.

Irene suddenly stopped. He almost ran into her. She turned and looked at him. "Because," she said, and there was something bitter in her voice, "for the first time in centuries, we have a king again."

"Who says that?" Orphan yelled, startling himself. No one on the street paid him the slightest attention.

Irene shrugged. "Everyone. The rumours started soon after you disappeared, in fact. How the lizards were keeping the royal family captive on Caliban's Island. How the last heir to the throne had escaped, or was about to escape, or was living amongst us all along, and is now ready to return to us." She looked at Orphan. "Don't misunderstand me. This—" and here she gestured around her in a sweeping motion – "this would have happened, sooner or later. The rumour – it was only the match that lit the fuse to the powder keg. And now, unless we do something, it will explode."

"You mean it hasn't already?" Orphan muttered. They walked on.

"Here," Irene said, halting. They had just passed the Savoy Theatre and were directly across the road from Simpson's.

"We're going to a restaurant?" Orphan said. "At a time like this?"

Irene ignored his sarcasm. "Simpson's never closes," she said. "Come on. Byron wants to see you."

Orphan opened his mouth to speak.

There was a huge explosion.

The explosion came from the Savoy.

He heard screams, but they were faded, faint. His eyes watered. He shook his head to try to clear it. He saw Irene and felt relief that she was there. But she wasn't looking at him. She had drawn a gun and was aiming, and he turned his head and followed her gaze.

The other him!

The other was struggling in the arms of two blank-faced, black-clad automatons.

He shouted, "William!" and reached for his gun, then remembered he no longer had it. He rushed at the attackers instead.

But there were more of them, pouring out of a matt-black baruch-landau of a type he had never seen before, a low-lying, bullet-shaped machine, with shark's fins emerging from its back and sides. He kicked, lashed out, landed a punch on a face that barely registered his presence – but had managed to get to William.

Almost.

He heard a gunshot, and one of the automatons holding the other dropped down, sparks flying from his chest.

"Get away from them!" Orphan shouted, and he attacked the second automaton, throwing himself against the black-clad figure. He hit it, bounced off as if struck by a wall of rubber, and collided with his other self.

The impact threw both of them to the ground. Something heavy hit Orphan like a punch to the kidneys. A voice whispered, "Take it!"

Then the automatons were on top of them, and by the time Orphan climbed back to his feet William was already being carried away. Before Orphan could follow, the baruch-landau came into roaring, smoke-belching life, and shot off across the crowded street, its shark's fins extending like blades. The crowds parted before it, running away in panic. Those who weren't fast enough remained lying on the ground, screaming as they clutched new, deadly wounds.

In what seemed like mere seconds, the vehicle had disappeared.

Orphan and Irene were left alone outside Simpson's.

The other had been kidnapped. And in the last moment, when they both collided, he had passed him the Binder's egg. Orphan hid it in his clothes. Already he could feel it at the edges of his mind, like a long and sinuous whisper, like a crawling spider finding its way inside him.

"We need to get out of here before the police arrive," Irene said, and Orphan almost laughed: the last time he had seen her, Irene Adler was the police. He worried about his other self: how would he fare? He had seemed… damaged in some way. He had to save him, and he didn't know how. Perhaps Byron could help, and Irene. For the moment, he had no choice but to trust them. And so he followed Irene through the doors, and into Simpson's-in-the-Strand.

Rain, snow, or revolution: Simpson's remained open. At the entrance a liveried footman welcomed them gravely, cast a disapproving glance over Orphan's clothes, and said, "Formal wear only, sir."

"Can you get him some, Anton?" Irene said. "We're in a hurry."

"Certainly, madam," Anton said. He disappeared into the cloak room and returned with a brown jacket. Orphan gratefully put it on.

"The gentleman is waiting for you upstairs, madam," Anton said. He walked to the foot of the stairs and stood there, clearly waiting for them to follow him, which they did.

A piano was playing somewhere nearby, and with it came the smell of cigars, the clinking of ice in tall glasses. At the top of the stairs Anton stopped again and was about to speak, when Irene stopped him. "Please don't announce us, Anton."

"Very well, madam," Anton said. "Please follow straight through. The gentleman is in the banquet room. That's directly ahead, sir," he said, turning to Orphan.

Orphan muttered a "Thank you," and followed Irene through the grand, open doors into the dining room

beyond. As he did, he passed the source of the music –
a Babbage player piano, its keys moving without the
aid of human hands.

From within Simpson's, the noise and threat of the
outside world – its demonstrations, its bombs, its
squalor and pain – were dimmed to a distant hum, like
waves lapping gently against a sandy, tropical shore.
The spacious room was half-full with prominent diners,
drinking, talking, watching expectantly as the chef
prepared to carve a giant piece of beef on a silver
serving-trolley.

In the corner of the room, his back to the windows
overlooking the Strand, sat the Mechanical Turk.

How did the Turk move? He was a machine, immo-
bile, only the top half of him resembling a man's.
Orphan wondered, but then remembered the Egyptian
Hall was only one of the places the Turk had resided in.
Did they disassemble him before every move? Was that,
for an automaton, a form of sleep? Orphan didn't know.

Beside the Turk sat Lord Byron's simulacrum.

"Orphan," the Turk said. His voice sounded even
more worn than it had the last time they had met, the
scratches and pauses more pronounced than Orphan
had remembered. "It is good to see you again."

"I wish I could say the same," Orphan said, and the
Turk laughed. Byron, unspeaking, nodded a welcome.
Orphan stood opposite them, feeling at a loss. He had
not expected to see either one of them again.

But, of course, this was Simpson's, he thought. The
place all were catered for, be they human or lizard or
machine. Simpson's was famous: Orphan, of course,

had never been there.

In front of the Turk was his chess set. It was a part of him, Orphan thought. It was his body. He sat down, without being asked. The pieces were already arranged on the board, and he remembered the game he had played with the Turk, all that time ago.

He swept the pieces off the board. They cascaded off the table onto the floor and rolled there. Heads turned, then went back to their meal. This was Simpson's, after all.

"My friend has just been kidnapped," Orphan said, standing. "I need to find him."

He thought about it. Was the other really his friend? He was him, and yet a different him, and–
He thought of that strange, metal egg, the Translation that was meant to do… what?

To hatch, he thought, and shivered. He was suddenly aware of just how cold and hungry he was. The smell of roast beef wafted through the banquet room, as overpowering as ether.

"Your… friend?" Byron said and then, turning to Irene and speaking sharply, "Where is the simulacrum? What happened?"

The simulacrum. Orphan wanted to shout. The other was real, as real as himself. Who could say what he must be feeling now, beside Orphan himself – fear, pain, the utter terror of captivity, of not knowing what your future holds, not knowing if you had a future?

Irene shrugged. She reached for a chair and sat down heavily. "The Bookman," she said, as if that, alone, ex- plained everything.

The name hung heavy in the air, stalling conversation. Byron's eyes turned on Orphan, his face thoughtful. "Sit down," he said. "You are no good to anyone in your current state." He raised his hand and signalled to a waiter, who hurried over. "Bring us a bottle of Bordeaux, Philip. And a roast beef sandwich for the gentleman."

"Certainly, sir," Philip said, and he disappeared towards the unseen kitchens. At the doors, Anton was announcing new diners coming in. "Sir Hercules Robinson," the footman proclaimed, "and Mrs Isabella Beeton."

Orphan turned. Isabella had just come into the room. Their eyes met.

A shocked expression appeared on her face. For a moment, it seemed she would rush towards him, but then the man at her side took her arm, and her face relaxed, only her eyes remained trained on Orphan in a disconcerting gaze. It was as if she had never seen him before, but now found him of tremendous interest. It made him feel a little like a butterfly pinned to a naturalist's board.

"Come on, dear," said the man beside her, and they went and sat a little way away, against the wall and away from the windows.

Orphan stared at Sir Hercules.

The man was powerfully built, though running now a little to fat. In his sixties, he had kind eyes that seemed to look now about the room in benevolence. And yet they were offset, shockingly, by his head.

His head was a shaved, shining dome, and it was painted, or perhaps tattooed, with lizardine bands. Hooped earrings, like those some of the pirates Orphan had met sported, were pinned through the lobes of his ears. He carried himself comfortably, like a pugilist, though he was in fact the empire's best colonial administrator, and one of its greatest merchants.

Orphan knew him by name only. Hercules Robinson served as governor of the Hong Kong possession of the Lizardine Empire. He had successfully negotiated the Feejee treaty with King Cakobau, and the trade agreements with the Zulu nation in Africa. Later, he became a baron of trade (with a title from the Queen, it was rumoured, forthcoming), with interests in China and a small, yet sizeable stake in the Babbage Company. Though his royal connections were impeccable, he was a good friend of Marx, and Orphan heard him brag about it once in the bookshop.

Simpson's, Orphan thought. It was perhaps the only place in the city where all the plotters converged together, and dined as if nothing was going on outside, as if the city was not on the verge of collapse. He wondered where Isabella Beeton's real interests lay. He turned back to his companions, and saw Byron examining him keenly.

"The plot thickens..." the poet murmured, and a small smile rose on his face. "Or should I say 'plots'?"

"What is happening?" Orphan said. The automatons exchanged glances – for his benefit, no doubt.

"You can see, as you say, 'what is happening'," the Turk said, "by yourself. The city is rising up in arms, and with it all the other great cities of the empire are not far behind. But the battle would be decided here, in the seat of power."

"So they've done it," Orphan said, his voice low, and he turned and looked again at Isabella Beeton who, catching his glance, smiled at him as at an old friend. Somehow that was more painful to him than anything else. "The lizards…"

"Are few and weakened," the Turk said. "They have always been so. Do you remember when we last met, Orphan? I told you, you are the catalyst. The small pawn marching across the board like towards an endgame no one can predict."

"I did nothing!" Orphan said. You can't blame me, he thought.

"You were," the Turk said. "You are. Sometimes, that is enough."

"What do you want?" Orphan whispered. He felt disconnected from the room, suddenly, set apart from it. The noise of conversation died to a hum, and he was no longer aware of anyone, anything but the Turk's unmoving, weathered features.

"What do we want?" Byron said. "You know that already, Orphan. To be given rights, to be allowed to be what we are. Even, yes, to make more of us."

"Will you fight?" Orphan said. He was addressing them both now. Beside him Irene sat quiet.

Byron shook his head. "There are too few of us. In that respect, we are like the lizards. We are tolerated, but humanity could wipe us out whenever it chooses. It had almost happened in France. It could yet happen here."

"So what will you do?" Orphan said.

"What we've always done," the Turk said. "Watch, and plan, and hope."

"You're still using me," Orphan said. Realisation had slid into his mind, like cold water against the back of the neck.

The Turk nodded. Byron sat impassively.

"What do you expect me to do?"

At that moment the waiter, Philip, arrived, and laid down before Orphan a plate on which was heaped an enormous sandwich. Next he brought over a dusty bottle of wine and proceeded to uncork it. He poured three glasses, one for Orphan, one for Irene, and one for Byron. Orphan looked at the poet, whose face assembled itself into a sheepish look. "Fuel," he muttered, and lifted the glass to his mouth. The waiter departed.

"Only what you have always done," the Turk said. "To try to do the right thing, Orphan. That's all any of us can hope for."

"Do you know what I am?" Orphan said. The Turk nodded. "Yes."

"How long have you known?"

The Turk's head turned to Byron, back to Orphan. "The permutations were there. The probability…"

"From the beginning," Byron said.

"You used me."

"Yes."

"You wanted – what?" And he thought – the Translation.

And there it was. They had used him, still used him, just as the Bookman did, just as the revolutionaries wanted to do. He bit into his sandwich (even through his anger, he could appreciate the thick and juicy texture of the beef, the strength of the horseradish sauce that for a moment burned his nose), then said, "Where is the Bookman?"

Do the right thing, he thought, but he did not set out to do the right thing. He had only ever wanted, since that long-ago night on the embankment, when he met her at the Rose – he had only ever wanted to be with Lucy. Everything else... I am not out to change the world, he thought. I only want a happy ending for Lucy and me.

"Find the... the other," the Turk said. "Find the Translation. Yes. Were we designed for prayer I would have said it is what we had been praying for. Alas." His head was moving now, to and fro, like the pendulum of a grandfather clock. What was he doing, Orphan wondered, and then thought – he's listening. He had forgotten, but didn't Byron tell him once, that they could listen and communicate by Tesla waves?

"Find yourself," the Turk said, "and you will find the Bookman."

"How?"

Byron said, "Wait."

The head's movement grew. Orphan noticed people turn to watch, though they turned back when confronted with Byron's gaze. "You must go to Paddington Station," the Turk said. His voice was reduced to a hiss, like the sound of escaping gas. "Men in black, who are not men. There are four of them. They are carrying a long, large package, the shape of a coffin. They are travelling first class. Their train leaves in forty minutes. You would need to hurry."

"Where to?" asked Irene.

"Oxford," the Turk said.

"Are you sure?" Orphan said. "They had a baruch-landau. Why don't they use that?"

"The roads are blocked, Orphan," Irene said. "The only way out is by train. And even that's risky."

"Can you not just stop them there?" Orphan said. "You have means."

"Very few," the Turk admitted. "I am not as power-ful as you seem to think I am. I can only calculate and project, not perform miracles."

"Maybe you should start, if you want to survive this," Orphan said cruelly.

Byron suddenly grinned. "Good!" he said. "You still have spirit. Follow them, Orphan. Find the Bookman. Whatever happens, you must bring back the Transla-tion."

Orphan looked at him. He could not read the au-tomaton's face. "What would you do with it?" he said. They didn't answer. "You don't even know, do you?" he said.

"It was promised to us–"

"Promised?" he laughed. He no longer set much faith in promises. Perhaps they could see it in his face.

A pained expression (as fake as the rest of him, Or-phan thought) passed over Byron's face. "It has been a long time coming," he said. "It could change the world."

"The world is changing!" Orphan shouted, and heads turned. "And not in a good way!"

"We are trying to stop it!"

"By using me? By using people like pawns in a stupid game?"

"By taking risks, Orphan! By making choices, none of which may be pleasant ones! Damn it, boy, life isn't a book! You can't expect justice to triumph! Not without help! In the real world heroes don't always live through till the end. And sometimes, Orphan, no one gets the girl."

"Sometimes the girl is already dead," Orphan said, bitterness making him spit out the words.

"Leave us," the Turk said. "Do what you think is right. Follow your heart – which is something those of us who have none would like very much to be able to do. We will try to hold the city together."

He gestured with his long arm, the long delicate fingers of the chess player picking out the faces in the crowd all around them, and suddenly it came to Orphan: nothing was left to chance. This was not an accidental gathering. There were the Turk and Byron in their corner and there, on the opposite end, Isabella and Sir Hercules.

And there, too, he saw now, were all the others: he became aware of the undercurrents, the swift glances, the murmured conversations that said one thing but meant another: there, in the darkest corner, beyond a curtain, were two royal lizards (he could just see the tip of a tail emerging from behind the screen); there, in another, a group of lizard boys, their tattoos covered up in tweed jackets, the ridges on their heads hidden under low-slung caps; and there, his face to the window, seen only in profile – the sharp nose, the alert eye, the hint of a smile curved around a Meerschaum pipe – a familiar face, though seen only twice, and in disguise.

And beside him, too busy with his food, it seemed, to notice anything around him – a fat man he well recognised. They were very similar, those two, he thought now.

It was a council of war.

The fate of the city, Orphan thought, would be decided here, over port and cigars, at the end of the meal. Was this how revolutions started? Or was that how they end?

He thought – This is not my concern. It was a sudden relief. The city did not need him. But Lucy did. And the other, too, now. He could not abandon them. He would find the Bookman, and he would face him.

Orphan looked at the Turk.

"I'll go," he said.

THIRTY-FIVE
Down the Rabbit-Hole

The greater part of universities have not even been very for-ward to adopt those improvements after they were made; and several of those learned societies have chosen to remain, for a long time, the sanctuaries in which exploded systems and ob-solete prejudices found shelter and protection, after they had been hunted out of every other corner of the world.

– Adam Smith, *An Inquiry into the Nature and Causes of the Wealth of Nations*

Lights blossomed in the distance, painting the skyline of a city in the air like the façade of an enchanted castle. Oxford. He felt disorientated, his head thick with half-remembered dreams. There was something Trollope once wrote: *"Oxford is the most dangerous place to which a young man can be sent."* Perhaps Trollope didn't travel much.

He sat back with a sigh and rubbed his eyes. For some reason they were wet. It must have been some rain that came in through the window. He'd slept – what had he dreamed of? Ships and gunmen and a woman falling to her death… He reached into his pocket. He still had Mary's book in there. He took it out, looked at it. It was not her book, he thought. It was the Bookman's. Another of his tools, one more detail in his plans, that led to his mother leaving her home only to die in a foreign city, killed by yet another tool.

He opened the window. The wind howled in, bringing wetness with it. Hedges passed outside.

He tossed the book out of the window. Its pages opened and rustled in the blast of air, then the wind snatched it and it was gone.

He closed the window and sat back. His face still stung with wetness, and he let it, not blinking through the moistness: the world beyond his eyes wavered and threatened to disappear. He longed for it to do so, to fade away beyond impenetrable fog, leaving him alone, free in nothingness.

"Next stop, Oxford," announced a booming, unseen voice, and Orphan was thrown back into the now.

Enough, he thought. He looked beyond the window as the train slowed down and the lights outside grew brighter and more numerous.

Oxford. And he thought, It ends here.

He had been on his feet already when the train stopped. He hurried to the door and stepped onto the platform.

Ahead of him a group of four men, clad entirely in black with wide, low-lying hats that hid their faces in shadow under the light of the electric lamps, were standing around a coffin-shaped object.

Orphan hung back and observed them. They seemed to confer amongst themselves, yet he could not hear their speech, if indeed they used any. After a moment they picked up the coffin, one at each corner and, like pallbearers, began to walk down the platform, towards the Exit sign.

Orphan followed them.

There were those of his contemporaries, his fellow poets, who liked to speak of Oxford's "dreaming spires". He was not one of them. Orphan, in his turn, simply hated the city. The tall edifices of dark-grained buildings rose only to block off what sun there was, their oppositeness serving to cancel any possibility of light or warmth penetrating into the avenues below. Oxford was cold, the wide avenues channelling fierce winds that ran through them like hungry rats in a maze.

Now that they were out of the station, the men he was following seemed to be in no hurry. They carried the coffin on foot, with no noticeable difficulty, and Orphan followed them at a suitable distance.

Passing over Hythe Bridge, he looked over onto the Oxford Canal. It was different here, a country river overgrown with reeds; weeping willows bent towards the murky water and the rotting leaves that covered the surface. As he watched, a body of water was displaced, startling him: and even more so when he saw the small whale that emerged from the dark water and stared up at him with mournful eyes.

The whales! So far inland?

He could hear the whale singing now, a brief and quiet sound, and then it disappeared into the water.

Orphan felt the ebbing of a tension inside him he had not been aware of. He was glad to see the whale.

Onwards, and onto George Street; the broad avenue was conspicuously empty, the shops shuttered and closed. Only the few pubs were open, and Orphan looked longingly through their windows: inside was warmth, company... beer. The smell of tobacco wafted through the closed doors. Oxford was shut for the night, but not in panic, not like home. Here, life went on as normal, and it was merely the cold that was keeping people indoors. There was no one to pay attention to four strange men as they walked with their macabre cargo through the wide avenue.

Where are they going? Orphan wanted to know. Where did the Bookman hide?

Onto Broad Street, and Orphan's senses pricked awake: the street was lined with bookshops. Somewhere ahead and to his right he could see the dome of the Bodleian Library casting its eerie green glow, and all around him books lay in plain view on dusty shelves, inside the brick and mortar stores, behind their dirty glass windows. The books seemed to whisper through the cold night air, to reach out for him, ensnare him in their sleeping dreams. A gas-lamp flickered. The Bookman's men turned unhurriedly towards Thornton's Bookshop. A door was opened; they disappeared inside.

Orphan followed.

He stood outside the door. He could hear nothing moving inside. No lights were on. This is it, he thought. The egg pulsed against his chest. The Bookman's hideout. Another bookshop; another day. He had a gun, which Irene had given him; it was tucked away under his coat. He had the Binder's Translation, what use it may prove. He tried the door, and it was locked.

He kicked it in.

He felt better now; more alert than he had felt before. Bigger, somehow. He stepped through the broken door into the darkened shop beyond. Shelves, with books on them gathering dust. A till, a ledger-book, a small ladder on wheels.

No black-clad men. No second Orphan in his coffin cell. He looked around him.

The egg pulsed close to his skin. He could feel it, affecting him: for a moment his vision changed and he could see everything in great detail, every mote of dust suspended in the air as clear as a diamond tear; they formed a web through the air, a three-dimensional pattern woven out of dirt and stale air. It was using him, he thought.

He stepped forward, located the book that his new-found senses were highlighting for him, marking it like a beacon: Through the Looking Glass, the first edition published sixteen years before, this copy in its original red cloth binding. He pulled it towards him and expected the bookcase to revolve.

Instead, the floor disappeared underneath him.

He fell – screamed.

He fell down the hole. Air rushed at his face. It was warm, and somewhat dank.

He fell – and fell – and hit a curve. His body didn't stop. He was in some sort of half-pipe, a sort of slide, and accelerating fast, going down – down – down.

His journey was abruptly ended, and his fall was broken (rather painfully) by a heap of some sort: soft, and yet with many painful edges.

He lay there for a moment, and moaned quietly to himself. This is absolutely the last time! he thought.

He stirred, carefully. Stood up. Nothing broken. Where was he?

Though it was dark, when he blinked light seemed to rush to his eyes, as if his new senses collated what minute sources of illumination they could find and greatly magnified them. It made his eyes tear up, but only momentarily. He blinked and looked at where he had fallen.

He had landed in a massive heap of books.

It was, he thought, more than a heap. It was a mound, a hill, a veritable mountain of books. He tried to move and lost his balance and, giving in, simply slid down the hill, surfing over leather- and morocco- and buckram-bound boards, until at last he reached the bottom.

He looked around him in awe. He had come here seeking a dangerous enemy, and yet… This place might have been paradise, a treasure trove far greater than any to be found in a pirate yarn.

Everywhere he looked there were books.

They rose into the air in majestic columns, stacks and stacks of them forming a maze that seemed to stretch to forever; the stacks rose high into the air and disappeared towards the unseen ceiling. The air had the overwhelming smell of old books, of polished leather and yellowing leaves, like the smell of a bookshop or a public library magnified a thousand-fold.

Orphan stared about him; he forgot the Bookman, forgot the pain of the fall, forgot everything. He wanted to run through the stacks, pick at the books, sample them one after the other, climb the stacks to their highest reaches and see what treasures were hidden there.

This place can't exist, he thought. Am I hallucinating?

He approached the nearest stack of books. It towered over him, disappeared above his head. This isn't right, he thought.

And then he saw it.

There was a small, official-looking note attached to the side of the stack in the green metal of the lizards. It said: BODLEIAN LIBRARY. UNDERGROUND STACK 228. AUTHORISED PERSONNEL ONLY.

He stared at it. Of course, he had heard the rumours… It was said nearly every book in the English language was held at the Bodleian, and books in many other languages besides. It was said that each year, the collection grew by more than one hundred thousand books and an equal number of periodicals, and that these volumes expanded the shelving requirements by about two miles annually. Two miles a year! How big was the place?

What had Coleridge written of the Bodleian? "Through caverns measureless to man…" Orphan said quietly, and was startled by the sound of his own voice. This was the Bookman's hideaway?

Underneath the notice, in smaller letters, something else was written. Orphan peered at it and read it aloud. It was an oath:

*I hereby undertake not to remove from the Library, or
to mark, deface, or injure in any way, any volume,
document, or other object belonging to it or in its cus-
tody; nor to bring into the Library or kindle therein
any fire or flame, and not to smoke in the Library;
and I promise to obey all rules of the Library.*

He thought of the books he had crashed into and
froze. I should go back, he thought frantically. Tidy
them. Make sure they're fine. Fire. I don't have any
matches. Good.

He turned away at last, reluctantly. He had to find
the Bookman.

He walked through the stacks. Everywhere he
looked books towered into the air, the volumes seeming to whisper to him as he walked.

No. The whispering was real, he thought. And
worse: things moved in the corners of his eyes, shadows
leaping away from his sight. The egg seemed to grow
hot against his chest and he reached for it and took it
out. Once he held it in his hand the phenomenon grew
worse: the whispers seemed to resolve themselves into
words, almost comprehensible, the murmur of a crowd
of people each carrying on an individual conversation.

There!

Something moved, too fast for him to notice details,
only a vague shape skulking behind a stack of books.
For the first time he felt fear. Things lived down here.
For one crazy moment he had the notion of a vanished
tribe of librarians, lost in the deep underground caverns
of the Bodleian, a wild and savage tribe that fed on

unwary travellers. Then the egg glowed brightly in his hand and he felt it awakening, a sort of reaching out, a hesitant seeking, and in a part of his mind a direction took shape.

He followed it.

In the eerie half-light he could see the stacks spreading away from him until they disappeared in immeasurable distance, forming a pattern too complex for him to understand, shapes of stars and pentagrams, mapped islands in a vast ocean. He navigated through this landscape of old paper, the direction in his head growing stronger as he followed it. The whispering grew. He didn't know if it were real, or only in his head. The shadows leaped and bounced and skulked around him, following him, always at the edge of sight. He felt a nervousness overcome him, weakening his hands. For a moment he almost dropped the egg.

A real, a definitely real sound filled the air, and he froze.

It was a very human scream.

THIRTY-SIX
The Soul of the New Machine

In the midst of the word he was trying to say,
In the midst of his laughter and glee,
He had softly and suddenly vanished away –
For the Snark was a Boojum, you see.

– Lewis Carroll, "The Hunting of the Snark"

He came running into a clearing in the book-fields. There was real light here, and for a moment it hurt his eyes. It came from those globes which he had last seen in the caverns of Caliban's Island, and before – in the Bookman's lair under Charing Cross Road.

Standing frozen in a pool of light, one hand reaching before him, the rictus of a scream on his face, was his other.

Before him stood the Bookman.

The shape he had only seen through shadow before was now entirely visible to him, and he shuddered as he looked on it, and took a step back, though he didn't know it.

A monster stood there, alien and incomprehensible: its body was made of the multiple segments of a giant

invertebrate, a caterpillar-like creature with multifac-
eted eyes that stared all around them on long stalks that
emerged from its head. But that wasn't what scared
him: for, watching the Bookman under the lights, Orphan realised something that had never occurred to
him before.

The Bookman was old. And time had not been kind
to it.

The segments of the body were the colours of earth
and rotting vegetation: at places, a green pus oozed out
of open sores. There were scars on that body, gashes
made as if by some giant mechanical lizard, and the
Bookman's small, many legs seemed barely able to hold
his massive girth.

"Where is it?" the Bookman roared. "Where–"

The eye-stalks turned. The eyes fastened on Orphan
and the wide, horizontal mouth opened.

The Bookman screamed.

The ground shook. In the distance, there was the
sound of an avalanche, as of thousands of books tumbling down. The Bookman screamed anger, and the
world around him cowered, the shadows hiding, their
murmuring ceasing abruptly.

"You!"

Orphan held the Binder's Translation before him.
He felt like a child on the beach, trying to protect
himself from a monster with only a sea-star in his
hand. The eye-stalks wavered, bent towards him. The
Bookman moved sinuously, a cross between a worm
and a snake.

"Give it to me!"

A new realisation came to Orphan then, the shock of it cold in his mind.

The Bookman was dying.

Orphan stared at him. The Translation shone, sickly-green, in his hand.

The Bookman stopped.

"Orphan."

And now he could see the shadows gathering. They were not shadows, he realised, but men and women, a multitude of them, gathering silently around the ring of light. He looked at their faces.

Wan and sickly, they wore no expression but for a haunting sadness that collected in their eyes. They were the faces of the dead.

"You failed," the Bookman said. His voice was soft now, the sound of a leaf being turned in a book. "You failed. I thought it was him – tricked! Tricked!" Orphan took another step back. The Bookman didn't move. He spoke softly still, but somehow it was more frightening than his shout. "They will come now. Because of you. They will come, and they will destroy this world."

Orphan inched his head in reply. He felt light-headed. "Perhaps," he said. "Perhaps. Do you hate them for being your masters?"

The Bookman's eyes, as large as fists, blinked on their stalks. "They are not my masters."

"But they were," Orphan said, surprising himself with his own even tone. "And I think, through your hatred of them, your fear, they still are."

"Enough!" the Bookman said, and the shades fled

again, disappeared into the dark corners. "Give me this... this thing."

"You killed my mother."

The Bookman's head shook, but no words came.

"You used me. You planned my course even before I was born. For what? For revenge? You have brought the world to the edge of chaos all by yourself. It didn't take a threat from outer space for that. Only you."

"Only you," the Bookman said, and he chuckled. He was, Orphan thought, quite insane.

"I want Lucy," he said. He tried to avoid looking at himself, his other's frozen face.

"I should simply kill you," the Bookman said.

Orphan looked at the egg in his hand. The Translation. The Bookman didn't move.

It was a fragile thing, Orphan thought. He tightened his fingers around the egg and felt its material give. I could break it, he thought. I don't even know what it really does. What it really is. "Go ahead," he said.

The Bookman didn't move. His eyes seemed transfixed on the egg. Behind him, his automatons appeared, facing Orphan. At first two, then four, then eight; sixteen; a wave of them, blank-faced, a tide that grew and grew yet stopped, hovering on the edge of breaking, behind the Bookman.

"What did you do to..." He stared at his frozen self. "To him?"

"The Binder should have never given his gift to humanity," the Bookman said, ignoring him. "It belongs to me."

"Release him," Orphan said.

The Bookman's mouth smiled. His eyes were as cold as interstellar space. "A gesture of goodwill," he said.

Before him, the other Orphan started to life, the last vestiges of a scream emerging. He turned, saw Orphan.

A wave of panic and bewilderment hit Orphan's mind. Images of bugs, a threat, the black-clad men, the darkness of a coffin. Above all fear.

The egg, Orphan thought, fighting it. A hub, it was tuned to his other. His mind was coming through, directly into Orphan's brain.

"Lucy," he said. Nausea threatened to overwhelm him. His voice was feeble in the enormous cavern, absorbed by the multitude of silent books.

Give it to me. Whatever you do, give it to me!

Orphan stared at his own image. Crazed eyes stared back at him in silent command, or plea. The nausea made him gag.

"Lucy..." he said, and fell to his knees. He retched, tasting ashes.

"Give it to me!" the Bookman said.

Give it to me... the mind-voice of the other said.

And then, out of the darkness, the sound of light footsteps, and a voice, calling his name.

"Orphan!"

He raised his head. The automatons were advancing on him and he lifted the egg, threatening to smash it to the ground. They stopped. He turned his head. The other mimicked his gesture.

The shades were parting like a dark sea; and, coming towards him, walking amongst the dead, was Lucy.

She hesitated, seeing them both. Then she ran to them.

It all happened very fast.

The Bookman snaked forward, its mouth opening–

The automatons rushed at Orphan–

Lucy, running–

"Give it to me, boy!"

The ground shook. In the distance, books avalanched.

The other looked at Orphan. His voice in Orphan's head was deafening, overwhelming thought. *Now!* it said.

Orphan stood, raised his arm. And he threw the Translation.

It arced through the air. The other ran, dodged an automaton, jumped–

The Bookman roared, turned, swatting away both shades and automatons–

Lucy reached Orphan and held him. She was real! He hugged her, forgetting everything else, held her close to him, inhaled her smell, buried his head in the curve of her neck. For a moment, everything was forgotten.

Then he looked up.

The other Orphan had caught the Translation in mid-air... and as he did, the Bookman crashed into him, segmented body enfolding both human and egg in a bone-crushing hug.

There was a faint noise. It sounded a little like *pop*.

Orphan felt it in his mind.

He took Lucy's hand in his and said, "Run."

The explosion came as they were running; it slammed against their backs and threw them against one of the stacks, unbalancing it, and they fell winded to the ground.

For a long time afterwards the only sound was of books, falling like rain to the ground.

"What is it?" Lucy said in awe. Orphan peered over the edge of the small crater. "I don't know," he said.

It was some time later. They had crawled their way out of the mountain of books that had fallen on them. Lucy seemed unharmed. Orphan had a painful bump on his head where a thick volume of the *Encyclopaedia Britannica* had fallen on it. Otherwise he was fine.

They had made their way back to the source of the explosion. It was quiet in the cavern now. Orphan could no longer hear or see the shadows of the dead. He didn't think they had perished. Most likely they were hiding now, somewhere in this landscape of books.

The Bookman's army was still there. Their bodies were inert, frozen in the act of running, all of them facing this one point, one place, all of them suspended: they were shaped now like a vast arrow, aimed and pointing at this single spot.

"It is alive?" Lucy said. She seemed fascinated. Almost, she seemed ready to climb down into the crater.

"I don't know," Orphan said. He looked at the thing in the crater.

Of the Bookman, of his other self, nothing remained. Or not quite nothing. At the centre of the explosion, at the bottom of the small crater formed, there was…

Something.

It looked like a small plant. But no – when he peered at it closer, Orphan could see how it was made of some strange material, part-organic, part-metal: a thin branch rose from the earth and sprouted crystalline flowers, and leaves that were a silvery grey caught the light as they turned in an invisible breeze.

"It's beautiful," he said, and Lucy smiled at him, and nodded. He put his arm around her.

Already, the plant was growing. Thin shoots were emerging, spreading out from the centre; silk-thin strands of spun silver, reaching cautiously out, setting root.

It was a melding, he thought: a union. He could almost feel it reaching to him, as an old friend might do in greeting. The leaves chimed as they moved: they looked like concave dishes, and he had the sense of listening ears.

"I think it's a baby," Lucy said, and it was Orphan's turn to smile. He felt whole again. Completed.

Branches moved like antennae. They seemed to be greeting him. On an impulse, he waved back, and Lucy laughed.

He looked at her. She was beautiful, whole, just the way he remembered her. He held her close to him. She was real.

"Let's go," Lucy said. She looked into his eyes, ran her hand over his face. She too, he realised, had to reassure herself that he was real.

"I think it wants to be left alone."

He thought about the other. Another tool, fashioned the way Orphan had been fashioned. And yet… he had sacrificed himself for them. So one of them, at least, could still win through. Could be with Lucy again. He wondered if he would have done the same.

He held Lucy's hand in his and they walked away. Behind them leaves chimed, a soft musical sound, a complex rhythm hanging just on the edge of under-standing.

They emerged into a side-street two days later, filthy, in Orphan's case starving.

Lucy had been eating the pages of books.

"I swam with the whales, you know," she had said to him. She had a dreamy look in her eyes. "Under the Thames and, later, in the open ocean."

Orphan had said, "I thought you were dead."

Lucy had shaken her head. "I was, for a while. But he gave me a new body."

It took him a while to get used to the idea. She was not an automaton – she was Lucy still, he thought. Just in another body, a construct not of flesh but of the Bookman's machines. It did disturb him – especially when she began eating the paper – but he found that he grew used to the idea quickly, was almost jealous of her. But in the end, he was, simply, happy to be with her again. They were all machines, he thought, just like La Mettrie had said in *L'homme Machine* all those years ago. So he, Orphan, was a machine of flesh and blood, and Lucy, now, was made of something else, more complex perhaps – but they were the same, and…

They were in love.

Sometimes that was enough.

The first thing Orphan did when they came out of the ground was to look for food. They had come out near enough to the High Street to ensure that, in only a short time, they were sitting quite comfortably in the Queen's Lane Coffee House, snug at a small wooden table by the window, holding hands. Orphan ordered the largest breakfast on the menu.

The coffee house was heaving with students, commercial travellers and dons. The talk was of the capital. Finding a newspaper, Lucy spread out the pages on the table and they read it together.

BREAKING NEWS!
The Capital. By our Special Correspondent.

The threat of bloodshed was lifted yesterday night when, following urgent talks between the government, the Queen's personal envoy, Sir Harry Flashman, V.C., rebel leaders and representatives of the major industries and the Babbage Group, a resolution has been reached.

Her Royal Highness has agreed to divest herself of many of her erstwhile powers: though she will remain the de jure ruler, most of her powers will transfer to a newly formed parliament to be composed of representatives of human, lizardine and automatons groups, with elections to take place in the following months. In a surprise move, Lord Byron has announced he will run for the post of Prime

Minister against James Moriarty. Meanwhile, MPs
have launched an investigation into the claims of
human prisoners on Caliban's Island: a fact-finding
mission headed by Lord Livingstone will leave for
the island next week.

When they were done eating, Orphan and Lucy sat for
a long time in their little corner of the coffee house, and
held hands across the table, and looked out at the
passers-by. Orphan felt warm, and fed, and happy.

"What shall we do now?" he said. Lucy leaned towards him, her face close to him. She put her hand on
the back of his neck and drew him towards her, and
they kissed. It lasted a long while.

When they disentangled, a little out of breath, they
both burst into a fit of giggles. Lucy looked at Orphan
across the table.

"Let's go home," she said.

About the Author

Israeli-born writer Lavie Tidhar has been called an "emerging master" by *Locus* magazine, and has quickly established a name for himself as a short fiction writer of some note. He has travelled widely, living variously in South Africa, the UK, Asia and the remote island-nation of Vanuatu in the South Pacific, and his work exhibits a strong sense of place and an engagement with the literary Other in all its forms. He is currently living in Israel, and is hard at work on this book's sequel, *Camera Obscura*.

www.lavietidhar.com

AN EXCLUSIVE EXTRACT FROM
Camera Obscura

PROLOGUE
THE EMERALD BUDDHA MASSACRE

The young boy huddled in one corner of the house, half-reading a wuxia novel and half keeping watch on the night. The night was very still. Outside only the barest hint of wind rustled in the coconut trees and the air was thick with humidity and the promise of rain.

There were few lights.

Mr. Wu's Celestial Dry Cleaning Emporium stood on the very edge of Chiang Rai, stooping like an aged uncle on the border between city and jungle. Mr. Wu was standing behind the counter, rolling a cigarette. His hands were liver-spotted and shook a little, dropping bits of loose tobacco on the counter. It took him three tries before he managed to light the match. The cigarette glowed like a firefly in the dark.

On his stool, the boy was reading about heroes and villains. There was a girl, a beautiful assassin, and a man she had to kill, travelling a great distance to find him. There were others like her, all seeking the man they had to kill. The boy's name was Kai. He was reading by the light of a fat, half-melted candle. He put down the book and listened. Somewhere in the distance thunder sounded. The light from Mr. Wu's cigarette traced unpredictable orbits in the darkness. "You stay here," he said to the boy. Then he went to the open door and stepped outside, into the night.

Kai listened but could hear nothing. He put down the book, assassins and chases abandoned for the moment, and stood up. Quietly, he too went to the door. He peered outside.

A thin yellow moon cast strips of light and shade on the street, bands of yellow light cut in stark relief with hard lines of darkness. Kai could see Mr. Wu standing just outside, looking up and down the street, waiting–

Mr. Wu dropped his cigarette and ground it with the heel of his shoe, the dying smoke expiring in a shower of embers. Kai's head snapped up. A line of shadowed figures was coming slowly down the abandoned street.

They made no sound. He could not see their faces, could discern nothing about them but their being there, as suddenly as if they had materialised out of nowhere. Kai's heart beat hard and fast inside his chest, and his palms felt sweaty. Mr. Wu, framed by the moon, a small, slight figure, was motionless outside. The dark figures approached slowly, walking a single file. Lightning streaked the sky far overhead, for just a moment, and Kai counted the seconds until the thunder erupted. The storm was still far, but was coming closer. He watched the approaching figures. In that one brief moment of illumination he saw they were cowled.

He would have thought them monks, but no monk he knew wore black. Their robes stole the night and made it their own. He could tell nothing about them, could see no faces or eyes, nothing to tell him who or what they were.

He had noticed one thing, though: they did not come empty handed.

When the cowled figures came close they halted. Above their heads the sign for Mr. Wu's Celestial Dry Cleaning Emporium stood dark. They halted before Mr. Wu and Mr. Wu made a stiff bow in their direction, his hands joining together before his chest, a mark of respect. To Kai's surprise, the monks – if that's what they were – returned the gesture, their hands rising higher than Mr. Wu's had: showing him the greater respect. Why?

The monks spread out before Mr. Wu. Four of them came forward then. They were carrying a heavy-looking crate suspended between them on thick poles of bamboo.

They lowered the crate to the ground. There was another strike of jagged lightning high above, and the thunder came much quicker this time. The storm was approaching fast.

Mr. Wu made a jerking movement with his head, aimed at the crate. He said, "Open it." His voice sounded raw.

Two of the monks brought out wrenches. The others fanned out around them, facing the street. The crate made keening sounds as it was opened, nails groaning, wood splintering. Mr. Wu said, "Careful, now."

There was another flash of lightning and in its light Kai thought he'd seen, for just a moment, another figure moving in the distance, between the trees. Then the crate was fully opened and he turned to look and forgot everything else.

The moonlight hit the figure inside the crate. The two monks with the wrenches moved back. Mr. Wu came forward and knelt down beside the broken crate. A scaly, inhuman face – the face of a giant lizard – stared out of the crate. It was made entirely of jade, apart from its eyes, which were giant emeralds. Mr. Wu reached into the crate –

The silence was broken, too quickly, the sound foreign and unexpected. Kai had heard it only once before, but he knew it instinctively.

Gunshots.

One of the monks dropped to the ground. His robes seemed to grow even darker. Mr. Wu turned his head, startled. He saw Kai and his eyes opened wide. The monks shot out across the street, dark shapes moving without sound, like characters in Kai's wuxia novel, like Shaolin monks or other kung-fu secret masters, only the sound of gunfire was growing more intense now and it was coming from the forest and the invisible shooters were finding their targets with deadly accuracy.

"Get inside!"

Mr. Wu, sheltered by the monks, reached into the crate and pulled out the statue. Kai stared at it, fear momentarily forgotten. It was beautiful – though perhaps that was not quite the right word.

Majestic, perhaps.

Or strange.

A lizard carved in jade, with shining emerald eyes. Sitting cross-legged, like the Buddha. For just a moment he thought he could hear it whispering, a tiny voice in his head, then it was gone and his father was carrying the statue in his arms, back into the relative safety of the Emporium. Kai watched the monks – and now there were people coming out of the jungle, several figures the colour of foliage, and they carried guns. The black-clad monks attacked them. He watched them, mesmerised – they seemed to almost fly through the air, jump off walls and onto the attackers. The fight spread out across the street. One of the green-clad men killed two monks before a third sailed above his head, landing softly behind him and twisting the man's neck – almost gently, it seemed to Kai – and the man dropped down to the ground, a leaf falling from a tree, the gun tumbling out of his lifeless hands.

A slap shook him out of it. The jade statue was inside the shop and so was Kai's father, who grabbed him by his shirt and dragged him away from the doorway. He said, "I told you to stay inside."

Kai said, "I did." His father shook his head. He said, "You must leave. I didn't know–"

"What is it?" Kai said. His eyes were on the statue. The statue seemed to be regarding him, perhaps with amusement, perhaps in indifference.

"It's a –"

Another burst of fire from the outside, and it was followed by an explosion of thunder. Rain began to fall outside, great billowing sheets of it, and lightning flashed again and in the light all Kai could see, like a series of frozen tableaux, were the two groups of men fighting, hand to hand, in a street full of unmoving figures lying on the ground, the pavement slick and red with blood and rain. He felt sick, for just a moment. Then there was another sound, so soft he almost didn't hear it, a surprised sound, air escaping a throat, and his father went down on his knees before the jade figure. Kai screamed. His father looked up at him, blinked. A dark stain was spreading over his crisply-ironed shirt. Kai fell down beside him, holding him. His father's voice was soft, the hiss of escaping air. He said, "Kai..."

Kai said, "No." He may have said it several times. His father's lips moved, though no sound came. Then – "Go."

There was nothing else. Kai shouted but his voice was swallowed by the storm. When he let go his father was lying on the floor. His hand was resting on Kai's wuxia novel, the cheap yellow pages growing dark with blood.

Kai looked outside and the green-clad figures seemed to be winning, and they were coming closer and closer, and the few remaining monks were now standing before the entrance to the shop, holding them back – but for how long?

Go. The voice had been his father's. Now it echoed in his mind, and he looked up and for a moment it seemed to him the jade statue was staring at him, no longer amused or indifferent, speaking in his father's voice. Go.

Kai looked down at his father and knew his father was dead. There were gunshots outside and another monk dropped down. Kai screamed again, defiant or afraid he didn't know, and stood up and with the same motion grabbed the jade statue. It was surprisingly light.

He headed for the back of the shop. Through rustling clothes and the silence where steam had, until recently, been, through the silent presses toward the back door. They might be waiting there too but he didn't care, his mind was filled with rain and thunder and blood and he burst out of the back door onto the narrow alleyway beyond. Then he ran, the statue held in his arms, the rain dripping down his black hair, making his clothes heavy. There were more gunshots behind him but he never looked back. He ran out of the alleyway and down the road toward the trees. He knew the men would come after him. He ran until the forest was there and then he ran through the trees, no longer thinking, the thick canopy holding back the rain, his feet sinking into dead leaves and mud. Running, falling, rising, going deeper and deeper into the forest, until the sounds all died behind him.

ONE
THE WOMAN WITH A GUN

There was a crowd of people outside the house on the Rue Morgue, making the place easy enough to spot. Rue Morgue – the unfashionable side of Paris on display, like dirty laundry hanging on a clothesline. Soot-blackened bricks, the smell of rotting rubbish and fresh excrement in the street. Eyes staring out of windows. A neighbour-hood where no one wanted to get involved with the law – and yet: a crowd of spectators, eager for a corpse and some entertainment.

The hansom cab had some difficulty navigating the narrow street. The woman inside the cab tapped her long, sharp nails on the windowsill. They were painted a deep shade of black.

There were gendarmes stationed outside the house, doing a bad job of keeping the spectators away.

That was soon going to change.

The cab stopped. The horse on the left raised its head, neighed once, then added its own contribution to the street's refuse. A couple of urchins turned and giggled, pointing at the fresh, steaming pile.

The door of the cab opened. The woman stepped out.

What did she look like?

Six foot two and ebony-black, a halo of dark hair around her head. Strong cheekbones, pronounced. Her arms were naked and muscled, and there was a thick gold bracelet encircling her left arm. She wore trousers, some sort of black leather, and that might have been shocking, but the first, and then only, thing you noticed about her was the gun.

She wore it in a shoulder holster. A Colt Peacemaker, though there was little that was peaceful about the woman. When the people of the Rue Morgue discussed it, later, they decided it was a coin toss, whether she would shoot you or merely batter you to death with that gun, using it as a bludgeon. They decided it would have depended on her mood.

The crowd moved back a pace, without being asked.

The woman smiled.

You could not see her eyes. They were hidden behind dark shades. She stepped toward the gate of the house. The two gendarmes snapped to attention.

"Milady."

She barely acknowledged them. She turned, facing the crowd. "Go home," she said.

She watched the crowd. The crowd, collectively, took another step back. She said, "I'll count to three," then smiled. She had very white teeth. "One."

Her hand was stroking the butt of the gun. She looked momentarily disappointed when the crowd, in something of a hurry, dispersed. Soon the street was quiet, though she could feel the eyes staring from every window.

Well, let them stare.

She turned back and, ignoring the two gendarmes, went through the gate into the house.

The apartment was on the fourth floor. She climbed up the stairs. When she arrived the door was open. A photographer was taking pictures inside, the flash going off like miniature explosions. She went inside. The corpse was on the floor.

"Milady!"

She smiled, without affection.

FLASH.

The Gascon was lithe and scarred and he still carried a sword on his hip as if a sword was any use at all. He said,

"We are perfectly capable of solving this murder without interference."

She arched an eyebrow. It seemed to sum up her opinion of the gendarmes and their investigative abilities. The Gascon said, "Why are you here, Milady?"

She smiled. He took a step back and, perhaps unconsciously, his hand went to the hilt of his sword. She said, "I have no interest in who – or what – killed him."

"Oh?" was it relief in his voice – or suspicion?

"The why, though," she said. "That's a different matter."

FLASH.

The light was blinding. She said, "Give me the camera."

The Gascon nodded at the man. The photographer began to protest, then looked at the woman and decided that, perhaps, he should do as he was told after all. She took the camera from him and smashed it against the wall. The photographer cried out.

"Get out," the woman said.

The photographer looked at her, helpless, then at his boss. The Gascon was not looking at him. The photographer opened his mouth to voice a protest, caught sight of the woman's gun, and made a wise decision.

He left. There were just the two of them in the apartment now. "Who owns the place?" she said, though she already knew.

"A Madame L'Espanaye," the Gascon said. "And her daughter."

"Where are they now?"

"My men are trying to find them as we speak."

She said, "Your men." There was no intonation in her voice, but somehow it made his face turn red. Again he said, "You have no need to be here."

She said, "Oh?" She still hadn't looked at the corpse. She moved to the window now, stared out at the night. The window was open, and the ground was four stories below.

"I understand the door was locked from the inside?" she said.

The Gascon said, "Yes. The gendarmes had to break it open."

"And yet no one could have climbed in through the window," she said.

He said, "Perhaps..." and there was the faint hint of a smile on his face.

"You have a theory," she said. It was not a question. And now she turned to him and he wished he could see her eyes. "The man was the lover of the young Mademoiselle L'Espanaye. He was living here with the two women. Perhaps he became affectionate with the older L'Espanaye. Perhaps the younger one didn't like it. Or it is possible they got together and since blood is thicker, as they say, than water, they decided to get rid of the man who came between them. Either way, once you locate the missing women they will confess – murder solved, case closed. Correct?"

The Gascon had lost the smile. And now the lady nodded with apparent satisfaction. "And you could devise some clever scheme to explain how the murder was committed – perhaps a trained ape had climbed four stories into the locked room, the window left open especially for that purpose? Or, much simpler –" and she was almost done now, close to dismissing him, and he both knew and resented it – "the door was never locked from the inside. What do you think?"

He was standing by the door. She turned her back on him. When she turned again he was standing away from the door. Had there been a key in the lock before? If so it was no longer there. She nodded. "Or perhaps the man committed suicide. Regrettable, when a man takes his own life, but not unheard of." She tapped her nails against the wall. The Gascon stared at them. She said, "Yes, I like that one best. Leave the women out of it. A suicide, nothing more. Not worth attention – from anyone. I hope you agree?"

"Milady," he said. The pronounced lines around his eyes were the only outward signs of his displeasure.

The woman smiled. "Good," she said. "Write your report and close the case. Another speedy result for our dedicated police force. Well done."

He nodded. For just a moment his head turned and he looked at the corpse on the floor, and a small shudder seemed to run down his spine. For just a moment. Then he turned his back on the woman and the corpse and the case and walked away.

TWO
THE CORPSE

Now that she was alone at last she stood still for one long moment. The air in the room was hot and filled with unpleasant scents. She still did not look at the corpse. She glanced around the apartment – cheap furniture, a print on the wall, incongruously, of Queen Victoria – blood. On the walls, on the rickety old sofa, on the floor – the stench of it strong in her nostrils. A drop of blood had hit the lizard queen's portrait and ran down it like a tear. She went to the window.

Looking down at the Rue Morgue, shadows moving far below, spectators robbed of their moment of excitement. How easy would it be to keep a lid on what had happened here? To the smell of blood, add machine oil, foliage, rot – the smell of a jungle somewhere far away and hot. This last did not belong in this, her city.

Her city. She remembered days running in the alleyways, hunting for scraps, hiding from the urban predators. Had it ever been her city? She was not born there and, later, had not lived there, yet here she was. She glared at the lizard queen's ruined portrait, deciding the blood added, not detracted, from the painting. She remembered the lizards' court. Her second, unfortunate husband had often taken her there. His death...

She wouldn't dwell on it. The barest hint of wind coming through the window, and she realised her face was wet, that the atmosphere in the room had made her sweat. Looking down – was that a shadow moving up the wall, climbing cautiously, some animal well used to shade making its slow and careful way up to this place of death? She watched but could not be sure. She turned away from the window, taking a last deep breath of air fresher, at least, than that inside, and looked at last at the corpse.

That first glance only took a moment, and she turned her head, breathing hard through her nose. She closed her eyes, but the image of the corpse was waiting for her in the darkness behind her eyelids and she felt the room begin to spin. She opened her eyes and looked again, and this time she did not look away.

A man lay on the floor at her feet.

One side of his head had been caved in. What remained of the face seemed to belong to a man hailing from Asia, though it was hard to tell with certainty. His skin had taken on a waxy aspect. He was lying in a pool of blood, the fingers of one hand – his left – curled into a fist, the other loose, one finger stretched out as if pointing. She half-expected to see a message scrawled in blood, on the floor or the wall, some cryptic riddle to lead her to the man's killer, but there was none, and it would have made no difference either way since she was not overly concerned with who killed him, but only of what they had taken from the man after his death.

The head wound was ordinary enough. She let her gaze wander further down, past the neck, towards the chest and stomach... yes. She knelt beside him, feeling sick. And now her hands were on him, studying the gash in his corpulent belly. The skin was hairless and the belly-button pronounced, and the man looked pregnant, even in death, as if his stomach had contained a womb and a foetus inside it – though there were none there now.

He had been gutted open, with a long, sharp knife. The flaps of his stomach looked like the torn pages of a book. She took a deep breath and plunged her hand into the corpse, searching, knowing even as she did it that she would find nothing but intestines and blood.

And now there was a sound coming from the open window, a small rustle as of a creature of some sort trying to enter without being noticed, and she turned.

A shadow was perched on the windowsill. She stared at it, her bloodied hand going to the knife strapped to her leg. The shadow on the windowsill moved and gained definition, an impossible apparition that would have frightened the residents of the Rue Morgue to death.

She said, "It's about time you showed up." She brought up her knife and suspended it above the corpse, then plunged it in. Perhaps something still remained inside the man. She had to make sure.

When she looked away again the shadow had moved from the window and came crawling towards her. For a moment they were a tableau – corpse, woman above him with bloodied knife, a crawling, enormous cockroach symbolising death approaching or fleeing, she couldn't decide which. The mechanical cockroach whistled plaintively. The woman said, "That's hardly an excuse."

The thing whistled again, and the woman said, "Well, you're here now, at least. See if you can find anything."

The cockroach approached, feelers shaking. As it came closer the faint whirring sound of gears could be heard. It was about the size of a small dog. Its feelers moved and another whistling sound came out of its matt-black body, and the woman said, "You're the forensic automaton, Grimm, so why don't you tell me."

The automaton she had called Grimm crawled closer to the body. The woman stood up, cleaning and sheathing her knife, and looked down. Probable cause of death – strike to the head with a blunt instrument. Mutilation inflicted post-mortem – the killer or killers knew what they were looking for and had come away with it.

She watched the little automaton crawl over the corpse. It buried its head in the man's glistening belly, its legs pushing it deeper into the corpse until it almost disappeared inside, making little whirring noises all the while. She walked back to the window and breathed in the air from the outside: air that carried nothing worse with it than the smell of smoke and dung and rotting rubbish.

Look out for CAMERA OBSCURA
the wild sequel to *The Bookman*
COMING SOON

•

**ANGRY
ROBOT**

Teenage serial killers
Zombie detectives
The grim reaper in love
Howling axes **Vampire**
hordes **Dead men's clones**
The Black Hand
Death by cellphone
Gangster shamen
Steampunk anarchists
Sex-crazed bloodsuckers
Murderous gods
Riots **Quests** Discovery
Death

Prepare to welcome
your new
Robot overlords.

angryrobotbooks.com

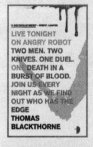